TWISTED LIES

ROBIN PATCHEN

JDO PUBLISHING

To Lexi, my precious daughter.
My arms don't spread wide enough
to show you how much I love you.

ACKNOWLEDGMENTS

There are so many people involved in writing and publishing a book. Without these people in my life, this story and all my stories would be nothing more than files on my laptop.

Thank you, Quid Pro Quills—Kara Hunt, Jericha Kingston, Candice Sue Patterson, and Pegg Thomas. Also, thanks to Normandie Fischer, Sharon Srock, and Terri Weldon. Your critiques make me a better writer, and I'm proud to call each of you friend.

Thank you, Ray Rhamey, for your insightful edits.

Thank you, Lacy Williams, for your marketing brilliance.

Thank you to my family, who puts up with me and all my imaginary friends.

And, of course, thank you, my Lord and Savior, Jesus Christ, for the grace that makes living possible.

ONE

NATHAN WALTER BOYLE had come to New York City with a
handful of dreams. He was leaving with a truck full of
nightmares.

Well, not a truck, exactly. He stopped at the bay window
and looked out front. There in his driveway sat the weird
container his father'd had delivered. The Pod was as big as a
Dumpster, only shiny and white.

Nate had called his father before the delivery truck pulled
away. "A U-Haul would have been fine, Dad."

"This will give you time to sort it all out."

Nate had a lot more to sort out than just the paraphernalia
he'd accumulated in the fourteen years he'd lived in the city. If
only he could figure out how to pack the nightmares away along
with the detritus of his life.

He grabbed a packed box from the kitchen table and headed
for the front door. He stepped onto the front porch, where he
took a deep breath and blew it out slowly, like he did a thousand
times a day. All was well. The guys who'd taken him were dead.
He was safe.

Tell his pounding heart that.

It was sunny and chilly, mild for late March in New York. Spring had always been his favorite season in the city. The once slushy streets were clear. Trees budded along the sidewalks. Flowers bloomed. Even the people seemed to reawaken after their long grouchy winters. As the weather warmed more, kids would soon skateboard along the sidewalks, cords dangling from their ears. In city parks, the thump-thump of dribbling basketballs would serve as the rhythm for the season, while little children's laughter would supply the melody.

For just a moment, Nate wished he could stay.

He looked up the street. Cars were lined in both directions in front of the 1920s-era houses so similar to his own. His neighbor pushed her double stroller on the sidewalk, heading away from him, out for her daily walk. A couple of houses down in the other direction, a woman walked toward him. Frizzy brown hair hung over her tan raincoat. A big black purse dangled from her shoulder.

He ignored his racing pulse and maneuvered down the porch steps toward the storage container. At least he was out here, doing this, all by himself. A small victory, but he'd take it. There'd been a time just stepping outside the door was a battle he could barely win.

In the Pod, he deposited the box on a pile of others.

Outside, the roll of tires crunched on loose gravel. The car slowed and stopped.

He was stepping out of the Pod when he heard a scream.

The frumpy woman was on the sidewalk in front of the house next door to Nate's. A man was trying to wrest her bag from her shoulder, but she held on tight. A silver sedan, its door standing open, idled beside them. The man was easily eight inches taller than the woman, and muscular. He had a crew cut and wore a goatee. Though the woman had screamed, now they were both quiet as they tugged on the bag. The man landed a punch to the woman's shoulder, but she didn't let go.

Every instinct told Note to run into his house and lock the door, but that wasn't who he was, no matter how loudly fear pulsed in his ears. He forced his mouth to open. Forced a shout.

"Hey!"

The man spotted him, gave one last yank on the bag.

The woman, arms hooked in the straps, stumbled forward and landed on the sidewalk. Her head hit the cement with a thud.

The man gave up on the purse, jumped in his car, and squealed away.

Nate looked at the car as he ran to the woman's side. Newish Chevy, silver. No plate.

He reached the woman and helped her sit. Blood trickled from a wound on her forehead.

"Are you okay?"

She winced and squinted. "I...I think so."

He recognized the signs of a pounding head. He crouched beside her. "Don't try to move yet. Just take a deep breath. I'll call 9-1-1."

"Did you get a plate number?"

"There wasn't one."

"Don't bother. They won't care." While she calmed herself, he looked for other wounds. A little blood had dripped into her eyebrow. She had plain brown eyes and a pale complexion. Aside from the bleeding head wound, she seemed all right.

"You sure you don't want me to call the police?"

"They'll never find the guy."

She wasn't wrong. "Does anything else hurt? Your shoulder? Looked like he hit you."

She rubbed the shoulder. "Just bruised, I think."

"Can you stand?"

She started to nod, stopped herself with a wince, and said, "Yeah."

He helped her to her feet. "Do you live far?"

"Kind of."

He looked at his front door, then back at the woman. She seemed harmless, and she was injured. He had nothing to fear. "Why don't you come inside, and I'll help you clean up that cut."

He expected her to protest. What intelligent woman goes into a house with a man she's never met?

"Thanks."

Okay, then. A risk taker. He walked beside her to his door. "I've already packed a lot of my furniture."

She stepped inside and looked at the nearly empty living room. "I see that."

"There's a chair in the kitchen."

He led her into the kitchen and indicated the single chair, then pulled a paper towel off the roll and handed it to her. "You're bleeding."

She pressed it over the wound.

"Be right back."

In the bathroom, he located bandages and antibacterial gel, thankful he hadn't packed these things yet. Back in the kitchen, the woman was looking around at the cluttered space.

"Where you moving?" she asked.

"Home. New Hampshire."

"How come?"

"Time for a change. How's your head feel?"

She took the paper towel off and looked at the blood that had soaked it. Her skin paled even more. "I'm not good with blood."

"You're doing fine." He urged her hand back to the wound. "Let's get the bleeding stopped before we bandage it. You want me to get you a Tylenol or something."

"It doesn't hurt that bad." She smiled. "Thanks for not letting me bleed to death on the street."

He chuckled at her attempt at humor and leaned against the countertop. "Were you on your way somewhere? Is there someone I can call?"

Her pale skin turned slightly pink. "Actually, I was on my way to visit you."

He pushed away from the counter. Glanced toward the door and forced his gaze back at the woman. He was being paranoid, but he couldn't help it. Nor could he help the demanding tone in his voice when he said, "Why?"

"You're Walter Boyle, right?"

He crossed his arms, clenched his fists. Made himself take a deep breath. "It's Nate, but yeah. Walter's my middle name."

"But in the *Times*—"

"I'm Walter Boyle. Who are you?"

She smiled, but he didn't return it. "We've never met. A few years ago, you worked on a story with my sister. Marisa Vega. Do you remember?"

The name had him steadying himself against his counter again. Remember her? She'd sat beside him on the bus, given him the story of a lifetime, and then, after a few weeks in hiding and with a little help from him, she'd disappeared.

Marisa. Her name rose like a crocus blooming after a long cold winter, changing the gray tones of his world into a bright hopeful spring.

Sheesh. He sounded like a bad poet.

She'd been twenty, five years younger than he. About five feet, five inches, shiny brown hair cut to shoulder length, deep brown eyes he'd not allowed himself to dive into. She'd looked like a cross between a younger Eva Longoria and an angel with wings unsullied and eyes unspoiled.

Not that he'd noticed. It was all about the job. At least that's what he told himself as he'd listened to her story, trying desperately to focus on her words and not on her pink lips forming the sounds. He'd been planning their future when she'd dropped the bomb.

The word *fiancé* had caused his pencil to stall. The word *murder* had him dropping it on his lap. Her story had launched his career. And ended life as she'd known it. Over the course of the next few weeks, Marisa had told Nate the facts as she understood them in an effort to bring down the people responsible for her fiancé's death. And in doing so, she'd placed herself in the crosshairs of some very dangerous men. Then she'd escaped.

Marisa's image faded. The woman at the table was staring at him as she dabbed at the wound on her forehead. "I take it you remember her."

He hated to think what emotions had crossed his features during that sprint down memory lane.

"How could I forget her? Thanks to her, I got a job at the *Times*." He couldn't imagine that the Marisa in his memory and this woman were related. "Marisa is your sister?"

"Half-sister. She's seven years younger than me. We have the same mother." The woman's lopsided expression didn't do anything for her plain features. "Marisa looks like her father."

Had his thoughts been that obvious? "So what can I do for you, uh...?"

"Leslie. Leslie Johnson."

He stepped forward and held out his hand. "Nice to meet you."

She shook it, held on tight. "I have to find her."

He pulled out of her grasp. "I wish I could help."

"She left a clue with you."

He shook his head. "The feds combed through my files after she disappeared. She left nothing."

"Trust me, she left a clue with you, and I have to find it."

"There's nothing—"

"Not to be cliché," she said, "but it's a matter of life and death."

"Is that so? Whose life is on the line?"

She sat taller, swallowed hard. "Mine."

Nate studied the woman. "How so?"

Leslie took a shaky breath. "Last night, somebody broke into my house." Her voice trembled. "It was late, and I was in bed. There were two of them, a man and a woman. I'd been asleep. I woke up when the man grabbed my hair." She stopped and set the bloody paper towel on the table.

Nate handed her a fresh one. "Go on."

"He held a knife to my throat and told me not to move. He said that I had seven days to return the money that my sister had stolen or I would die. I told him she didn't steal it." She wiped tears with her trembling fingers. "He laughed and said I'd better get the money or find out exactly what happened to it."

Leslie's tears fell faster now, and she lowered her gaze. She used the fresh paper towel to wipe her cheeks. "I don't know what else to do. I could hide, but my life is here. And anyway, I'm afraid they'll find me. But if I find Marisa, what if I put her in danger?"

Unfortunately, Nate knew exactly how Leslie felt. "Do you think you could identify them?"

She shook her head, winced, and rubbed her temples. "They wore masks."

"So how do you know the other person was a woman?"

Leslie blinked. "Her voice. She told the guy to hurry up. That's when they left."

He nodded slowly, thinking fast. "That guy who just tried to grab your purse. You think he was connected—?"

"No. No, that was just... I don't think that had anything to do with it. Just bad luck. I'm a magnet for bad luck."

"Why don't you think they're connected?"

"Why would they try to snatch my purse? They could have stolen that when they broke into my house."

A good point. "Did you call the police last night?"

"No! They told me not to, or they'd kill me."

But they wouldn't kill her, because Leslie was their only link to Marisa. And for some reason, Leslie believed Nate knew where her sister was.

If he wasn't careful, he'd get pulled into this.

Marisa's image filled his mind's eye. He shook it off. The last thing he needed was another drama. After what he'd been through, he knew he was meant to be on the sidelines of life, not in the thick of it. The reporter telling the world about the good and bad deeds of others. Always the byline, never the hero. That was his fate.

"They think Marisa stole the money?"

"They were sure of it."

That's what everyone had thought. Everyone but Nate.

"I'm sorry, Leslie, but I have no idea where your sister is."

"She left a clue with you. She told me she would."

"When?" His skepticism must've been obvious in his voice, because her eyebrows lifted. He had secured Marisa a hotel room until he got the whole story, but she wasn't supposed to have contacted anybody. Maybe she'd risked contacting her sister.

"Through your stories," Leslie said. "Remember the false name you used for her?"

He thought back. The name had been important to her. "Piper, right?"

"I had a doll when we were growing up. We played a game with her—like hide-and-seek. One of us would hide the doll, and the other would try to find it. It was a silly game, but our apartment was too small to play real hide-and-seek, so this was our variation. The doll was named Piper. So the game was called Peek-A-Piper."

Nate couldn't help but smile.

"Maybe it sounds stupid to you, but she could've used a thousand names. She insisted you use Piper, right?"

She had.

"It was her way of telling me you'd be the way to find her."

"All of which sounds so sweet and nostalgic, but how do I know any of it's true? You don't exactly look like her."

Leslie pulled a little photo album out of her purse and handed it to him. "I carry this with me everywhere, just to remember..."

Her words trailed off while he flipped through the photos. There was a young Marisa, beautiful even as a child. And beside her in picture after picture, this woman.

"Okay, so you're sisters. Doesn't change anything. Like I said, the FBI—"

"They would have missed it. Did she give you anything? A painting or a drawing, a letter? Anything like that?"

She'd given him a little drawing. It was a pencil sketch of a cabin by a lake, created after he'd shared with her that if he had to run, he'd like to find a place like that. From his description, Marisa had drawn a work of art. She'd made him promise to keep it forever, a keepsake. And he had.

"A sketch."

She dropped the paper towel on the table. "Can I see it?"

"I think it's in the Pod."

Her pale brown eyes brightened, and she stood. "Let's go."

"Wait." He waited until Leslie sat again. What he wanted to tell her was that no, he wasn't going to help her find Marisa. No, he wasn't getting involved. And no, he didn't think it was a good idea to pull Marisa into whatever drama was unfolding in New York. But he couldn't miss the hope in Leslie's eyes, the fear just behind it. He knew what it felt like to be threatened, and he knew how he'd feel if it were someone he loved in danger, someone he loved who needed his help. He'd do anything for his brother. It wasn't his place to decide for Marisa what should be done.

"Let me bandage that wound."

Her foot tapped while he squeezed out the antibacterial gel. As he pressed the bandage to Leslie's forehead, he said. "I don't want her to get hurt."

"They threatened to kill me."

"I know. I'm not... It's not okay if you get hurt, either. But pulling your sister in puts you both in danger. How do you know they won't kill both of you? And besides, Marisa doesn't have the money."

"How can you be so sure?"

"She told me—"

"Stealing that money was a federal offense. You really think she'd confess to a reporter?"

"I protect my sources."

"How could she have known for sure?"

"She trusted me with her whereabouts. With her life."

Leslie stood. "I know. And I never thought she took it either. But this guy—he seemed really sure. And Marisa knew every-thing. She knew—"

"I know the story, Leslie. I wrote it, remember? I'm just saying, I never thought she stole the money."

"Maybe I want her to have it because if she doesn't, I'm dead." She lowered her gaze and covered her face with her hands. He barely heard her next words. "I don't know what else to do."

"And you want to find your sister."

She looked up. "I need to know she's okay."

He imagined his little brother. Also a half-sibling, also much younger than he. Nate had never lived with Finn, but he loved him just the same.

"Okay." He snatched a box cutter from off the counter. "Let's see if we can find it."

They searched the Pod until they found the box marked photos, then dug inside. The item they uncovered was a color sketch on cream-colored paper. He'd had it professionally mounted in a thick gilded frame. The drawing depicted a little log cabin surrounded by tall trees and nestled against a sparkling blue lake. In the bottom corner, Marisa had written her initials in tiny letters.

The artwork was simple. And it wasn't. With her talent and a box of colored pencils, Marisa had made the scene come alive. Nate could almost smell the flowers she'd drawn in the dainty window boxes, hear the lapping of ripples on the serene lake.

"May I?"

He handed Leslie the picture. "Your sister is immensely talented."

"I know." Her tone was flat. "She's good at everything."

Was that jealousy? Probably, but who could blame Leslie? Her little sister wasn't just talented, she was beautiful. The kind of beautiful a man couldn't forget. Not that Nate hadn't tried over the years, knowing he'd never see her again.

Leslie stepped out of the Pod, and Nate followed, closed the door, and locked it behind him.

Back in the kitchen, Leslie opened her purse and pulled out a magnifying glass.

Nate stared at the top of her frizzy head while she studied the picture. He couldn't imagine she'd find anything. That picture had hung over his bureau for years. He'd looked at it a thousand times, and he'd never seen anything out of the ordinary.

"Got it." Leslie didn't look up. "Can you write this down for me?"

Just like that? So much for his powers of observation. He snatched a Sharpie and an old newspaper from his pile of packing supplies. "Go."

She recited an email address, and he wrote it down, a random scattering of numbers and letters at a Yahoo account.

She looked up, triumphant. "We got her."

He wasn't so sure. "May I see?"

She handed him the magnifying glass and pointed to a spot on one of the logs that made up the cabin. He looked at the spot with his naked eye and saw nothing. But through the magnifying glass...

He looked up. "How did you know it would be there?"

She shrugged. "She's my sister."

He handed her the magnifying glass and ripped away the edge of the newspaper where he'd written the email address. He held it out. "Here you go."

She looked at it, looked at him. "I think you should email her."

He took a step back. "Why me?"

"They might be monitoring my email."

"But if I email her, then when she emails back, I'll have to contact you. Won't that be just as dangerous?"

"I'll wait."

He stepped back, lifted his hands. "Whoa. Look, I was happy to help, but now I'm out."

"Marisa trusts you."

"She trusts you, too." He pointed to the drawing. "Or she wouldn't have left you that message."

"She left it with you, Nate."

"It doesn't matter. I can't—"

"I'm scared to go home, okay?" She paused, swallowed, as if

the admission had cost her. "I just...can I please just stay here? I'll help you pack. I'll be quiet, I promise, and...Marisa trusts you. So I trust you."

He glared. He didn't need this woman here, cluttering up his life. He'd planned to finish packing the next day and and move for good. The house was already under contract. With no job in Manhattan, no former coworkers who cared to keep in touch, no friends here in Queens, there was no reason to hang around. Certainly not to help this woman with whatever wild goose chase she was on. Even if she was in danger.

Even if Marisa was in danger.

The thought made his pulse race, and he pulled in a deep breath, then another until he thought he could talk again.

As Leslie watched, her eyes filled with fear and pleading. "I'm a good packer. And I own a cleaning company. When you're through, I can have my crew clean the house for you, no charge."

Was she crazy? Did she think he'd risk his life to avoid cleaning his own house?

Okay, he was being melodramatic, and her offer was tempting. He could use the extra set of hands. And the woman needed his help.

And to communicate with Marisa again...

He could practically hear his counselor's voice. "To not risk is to not live. The world isn't that dangerous."

It was, though. Danger lurked around every corner. And perhaps right here, right now.

But Leslie was in danger. God knew, he wanted to send the woman away. But no matter how much the thought of helping her terrified him, he couldn't live with the alternative.

"Fine. Let me get my computer."

TWO

When Marisa Vega was a little girl, dreaming of her future, this life had never crossed her mind. Who knew it could be so good? She'd escaped New York eight years earlier and thought her life was over. Without Vinnie, without her sister, without her parents, what did she have to live for?

She brushed her teeth, showered, and braided her hair before she tiptoed back into her bedroom and looked at the sleeping form on the far side of the bed. Curly dark brown hair peeked above the blanket. Marisa had memorized the beautiful face hidden beneath, those dark chocolate eyes. She'd fallen in love the first moment she'd seen the child as a newborn, still pink from birth, silent as if she'd given up on the world. Aside from when she slept, that may have been the last time Ana was quiet.

"*Despertarse.*" She rubbed her hand over the messy hair. "Wake up, *pajarita.*"

Ana slowly turned over and opened her eyes. "Mama, why do you call me little bird?"

Marisa smiled at her daughter and supplied the same

answer she gave every morning. "Because you're always chirping."

Ana sat up, wrapped her slender arms around Marisa's neck, and kissed her on the cheek, her lips rose-petal soft. *"Buenos dias."*

"Good morning." Marisa responded in English. "Hurry and get your clothes on. Are you hungry?"

"Si."

Marisa laughed. "That's the other reason I call you little bird. You eat like a bird—three times your weight every day."

Five minutes later, they stepped into the sunshine. The early morning humidity would only get worse, and by afternoon, the air would be stifling. Marisa held Ana's hand, and they walked across the narrow gravel road to the orphanage that had been Marisa's place of employment since she'd arrived in town years earlier. The scent of coffee from the shop on the corner had her mouth watering. Sometimes on Saturdays, she would let Ana play with a neighbor and go to the coffee shop to enjoy one perfect cup. She'd take her sketchbook and pencils and draw what she saw—or what she remembered. Sometimes, the front of the old mission that had become the orphanage. Sometimes, the street she grew up on back in Queens. Sometimes, the face of her fiancé, dead eight years now. Often, she'd sketch Ana.

There'd be no sketching today, but maybe later, during siesta, she could set up her paints in the mission courtyard. An hour, no more, to satisfy the urge to create while her daughter and the rest of the town slept.

They entered the orphanage, passed the office, and headed down the long hallway to the cafeteria, their feet tapping on the faded red Spanish tiles. Marisa paused at the entrance. "Behave yourself and—"

"I know. Eat my eggs."

"They have protein. You want to grow healthy and strong."

Ana was halfway to her chair by the time Marisa finished the sentence. She waited until Ana had taken her seat beside her best friend at one of the long tables. The two tables each sat twenty kids on long benches. There seemed to be more than the room could accommodate this morning.

In the kitchen, Marisa served herself two *huevos rancheros* from a platter and poured a cup of coffee. She carried her breakfast to the office.

"Did we get more kids?" she asked when she stepped inside.

"Sí." Carlita looked up and rubbed her eyes. Her hair seemed grayer this morning, her skin paler. "A single mother dropped off three last night. She said her husband had disappeared, and she couldn't feed them."

Disappeared. Happened too often in this part of Mexico, and most of the time, the people never turned up except in the form of dried bones in the desert.

"So were you up all night?"

Carlita shrugged.

"We have room for the new kids?"

"Barely."

Marisa set her breakfast on the table in the corner of the small room, a good spot to feel the morning breeze, which fluttered the gauzy curtains and carried the scents of dust and the manure piles the mules deposited daily. Marisa gazed at the picture on the wall across from her. The village at sunset, children playing in the foreground, the mission a silhouette behind. Marisa had painted that one and all the pictures that hung in the orphanage and in her small house. And a few at the coffee shop. There were pictures she'd painted or sketched all over town, gifts Marisa had given the people who'd taken her in, made her feel at home.

Marisa prepared her lessons for the day while she ate. She'd been teaching English at the school attached to the orphanage for years, so preparation didn't take that long. Thirty minutes later, she made her way to the first classroom.

The children greeted her with smiles and waves when she walked in. The small room had one window and four rectangular tables long enough to comfortably fit two students each. Four sat at each today, kindergartners through second grade—and little Ana, whom Marisa had insisted be included with the kindergarten class. Theirs was the only school in town, so the kids came from all over the village. Most were barely subsisting with their meager income, but a few came from families whose fathers were involved in the drug trade. They were the only ones with money to spare.

Marisa moved on to teach the next grades up when the youngest class filed out. Carlita was determined that no matter what, no student would leave the orphanage without speaking and writing English well. That alone would set them apart from kids in nearby schools, where the teachers rarely knew much more than the kids and the curriculum was often not just outdated, but sometimes, outright wrong.

Marisa returned to the office after her last class of the morning and looked longingly at Carlita's computer. She'd hoped to order painting supplies, the only luxury she allowed herself. Carlita looked up from her paperwork and lifted her eyebrows.

"Would you mind if I—?"

"I'll grab some lunch. And maybe a nap." The older woman stretched and stood.

After Carlita left, Marisa slid into the cracked leather seat in front of the new desktop, her portal to civilization, and typed. The computer had been a gift from the church in Oklahoma that supported the orphanage. Marisa tried to get on the computer once a day, mostly to remind herself there was a world outside of her little village. She loved to read the news and check Facebook. Her sister's posts were rare, but any time Marisa was able to see Leslie's face, even if the photograph was old, it made her heart sing—and yearn for home. Most of the time, their Internet was too spotty to waste time. She navigated to the paint supplier's website and ordered the things she needed. Since Carlita wasn't back yet, Marisa clicked over to her email, though she knew it was pointless. She checked almost daily. She hadn't received an email in eight years.

But today, there was a message in her inbox. The sender's address gave no indication who it was.

Her hands shook, though from excitement or fear, she wasn't sure.

She clicked on the message and read the text.

It's Nate Boyle. I'm here with your sister. She needs to get in touch with you. It's an emergency.

Marisa stared at the words, almost afraid to move. Afraid they'd disappear, a mirage in the Mexican heat. Her heart pounded as if she'd been running. She swiped her moist hands on her shorts.

Her feelings were a knotted ball of multicolored threads, and she wasn't sure which color to untangle first. She was excited to hear from them, of course. Excited, but another thread had her heart thumping wildly, because if Leslie had gone to the trouble to find her, something must be very wrong.

Marisa looked up from the screen to see if anybody was watching. Old habits and all that, but she was alone and the space was quiet, if you didn't count the sounds of the children playing in the courtyard and the rumble of carts and clunker cars on the gravel out front. And she didn't—those sounds had become as common to her as the rattle of the radiator and the blast of car horns had been in New York.

She stared at the words. Nate Boyle. She'd first known him

as Walter Boyle, no more than a byline in the local paper back in Queens. She wouldn't have known what he looked like if not for the times he'd filled in for the regular columnist and had his photograph printed above the column. She wouldn't have cared if she hadn't recognized him as the guy she saw almost daily on the bus on her way to class. And she wouldn't have noticed him at all if he hadn't been so attractive.

The memories rolled through her like armed trucks through the village. She thought of that fateful time, of Vinnie's admission, his terror, his murder. And of her decision not to let it go.

She had flashes of cowering in the hotel, dyeing her hair, followed by bus rides and trains, by leaving everything behind.

She pulled in a deep breath and looked around. She was safe here. She'd made a life here, and if she sometimes longed for America, she pushed those desires away with thoughts of her beautiful daughter, of the home they had.

Ana.

Marisa could handle anything as long as she had her daughter. She was safe. They were safe.

Marisa looked back at the message.

Just an email. No one would be able to track her, would they?

Slowly, she typed, words she'd longed to say to her sister about her life, her daughter, her job, and her village. She added how much she missed Leslie. She'd missed Nate, she realized. Yes, she'd thought of him over the years. If, when she'd met him, she hadn't just lost her fiancé and had to flee the country, perhaps something could have come of that relationship. But Marisa had learned years before that *if* was about as valuable as excrement and could foul up your life just as fast.

Good thing word pictures didn't come with scratch-and-sniff.

She was losing her mind.

She deleted everything and started over.

Hello, Nate. Is Leslie OK?

She stared at the line. The two sentences were arrows drawn, full of potential, itching to be released. Seemed harmless enough, but those two sentences could change everything.

She swallowed, took a deep breath, and hit *Send*.

Marisa stood, paced to the door, paced to the window. She crossed her arms, folded her hands together, and then crossed her arms again. She should do something else. Go for a walk. Go see the children. It would probably be a while before she heard back, but how could she close the program and go back to work as if nothing had changed?

She alternated between praying silently in Spanish and rehearsing her fears in English.

What could have happened that would cause Leslie to contact her? Maybe the police had found the real thief, and maybe Charles had decided he didn't want revenge. Maybe Marisa was finally safe.

A little bud of hope formed in her heart.

She imagined packing their meager things and moving back to New York. Would Ana like the city? Going to a normal school, one not filled with orphans and children parents couldn't afford or didn't want. Would she enjoy the cold weather, the snowfall? Marisa could picture her daughter making snow angels in fresh powder. Flashes filled Marisa's artist's eye—Ana with snowflakes on her long eyelashes, Ana posed beside a lopsided snowman, Ana snuggled between her aunt Leslie's legs, sledding down the hill at the park, their hair poking out from their knit caps and fluttering in the cold wind.

Would Nate be around? She could still conjure his image. Still thought of him often. Too often, considering they'd never had anything but a business relationship. Well, business plus a lot of meals together. The fact that he'd helped her stay alive probably went beyond the typical reporter-source relationship.

Marisa was telling herself for the millionth time not to think about Nate Boyle—a futile command if she'd ever heard one—when the email program dinged.

She stalked to the computer and looked.

Leslie is safe for now, but she needs to see you.

She stood straight again. Odd that Nate was emailing instead of Leslie.

Okay, not completely odd. She'd made it so they would need to contact each other in order to contact her. Her pathetic little fail-safe. Nate had held onto the drawing while Leslie had always had the ability to find the information it held. So neither could just contact her on a whim, and they'd both have to agree. Nate probably hadn't even known he could. So yes, it made sense they were together. But once Leslie had gotten the email address, why keep Nate involved?

Marisa trusted Nate. Of course she trusted her sister, too, but Nate had proved over and over he was not only trustworthy, but able to protect her. Maybe Leslie understood that Nate's presence would make Marisa more comfortable.

On the other hand, what if she was being duped? What if these people weren't Nate and Leslie at all? What if Nate had second thoughts about protecting her? What if he'd discovered the email address and given it to that FBI agent?

Worse yet, it could be one of Charles Gray's men. Charles was still in prison, but he'd had enough friends on the outside to force Marisa to run for her life. What if one of them had gotten ahold of the email address?

Maybe one of them was forcing Leslie to email her right now.

Marisa had to know.

She sat and clicked reply. *Leslie is with you right now?*

He answered immediately. *Right beside me.*

Ask her... Marisa paused. She thought for a moment, then typed, *Where was the doll's favorite hiding place?*

A moment passed. Marisa stared at the screen. If it took too long, she would know. But what would she do about it? If it was Charles's men, Marisa couldn't let Leslie be hurt, tortured even, to save herself.

She thought of little Ana. If she had to choose between her sister and her daughter...

The inbox dinged. Thank God.

Hi, sis. She liked to hide on the shelf beside the macaroni.

It was an old argument. Marisa thought the doll preferred the floor of Mom's closet, beside the pretty shoes. Leslie argued that the poor doll needed to eat sometimes. Another message came in.

She was easy to find there, though.

But at least she wasn't hungry, Marisa replied.

Tears filled her eyes. It was truly her sister. Her only relative, her best friend. She couldn't help but add, *How I've missed you! Are you all right?*

Long story. I need to see you.

Marisa sat back and blinked. See her? *Impossible!* she typed. *I'll come to you. Pick a safe place. Wherever you want.*

No way Marisa could risk that. Another message came in.

It's a matter of life and death.

She swallowed hard. Marisa had put her sister at risk when she'd told Nate the story and escaped New York, but nobody, including Marisa, believed Leslie knew anything about the money or the business. Nobody had ever suspected Leslie. After eight years, what could possibly have happened? Was it serious enough to risk Marisa's life?

Nate is still there? Marisa asked.

Yes.

What if it wasn't Nate, though?

She stood and paced. What would only Nate know? What would nobody have cared to ask him, in all the years?

She sat back down and typed.

What's my favorite sandwich shop?

Nate probably wouldn't have forgotten. He'd brought her dinner nearly every night for weeks.

A message dinged in.

You call that a sandwich? It was a salad shoved in pita bread. It's not technically a sandwich if it has no meat.

She smiled. He'd said that every time she ordered it.

The message dinged again. *And no, feta cheese doesn't count.*

She replied, *I wanted to be as thin and beautiful as Aphrodite.*

You were always that and more.

She paused at the compliment. Yes, she remembered that, too. He was one of the kindest men she'd ever met. She let the words drench her the way she used to drench that sandwich in dressing.

But you haven't told me the name of the restaurant, she typed.

Change the subject—an old trick. You're blushing, aren't you?

She touched her warm cheeks. Nate hadn't known her for long, but he'd known her very well.

Before she could respond, he said, *And it's Aristotle's. We always laughed because we had assumed it was named after Mr. Onasis until I met the owner. Good old Ari. I still eat there, and he's still fat as Jabba the Hutt and just as handsome.*

So it truly was Leslie and Nate, the only two people in America she would consider trusting. Still, to meet them?

What do you mean, a matter of life and death?

A pause, and then, *It's Leslie again. I'll tell you when I see you.*

Marisa had to think it through. Could she risk exposing herself?

Marisa, they're going to kill me.

Cold fear dripped down Marisa's spine, and she shivered in the heat. A death threat. She'd experienced the feeling of knowing there were human beings, not so different from herself, people with minds and bodies and hearts, people who wanted to destroy her. Marisa had faced two choices—stay and risk it or run. She'd chosen to run. Chosen this life, however meager, over a violent death.

Marisa had been gone from New York for years before she'd let herself get comfortable again. Let herself believe she might actually get to live a long, healthy life. Maybe not what she'd planned, because living in an impoverished Mexican village had never made her list of goals when she'd been a child in Queens. But to live beyond twenty years old, to make it to twenty-two, twenty-five, now twenty-eight. She'd allowed herself to believe the danger was all behind her.

But she'd been wrong. So wrong. Because they were catching up with her now, those human beings who wanted her dead. Because Leslie's life was in danger, and it was Marisa's fault. Could she turn her back on her sister? No, of course not. So what choice did she have? She had to find a way to meet them without exposing the only home she had. She couldn't go on the run again. She had Ana to think of.

Their home and Ana needed to be protected.

What to do?

She had to meet them, but not here.

She returned to the computer and typed, *How soon could you get to Acapulco?*

Mexico?

Marisa didn't respond to the stupid question. Finally, her sister typed again.

Hold on. We're checking.

While Marisa waited, she clicked to a travel site herself and checked the bus schedule from Chilpancingo to Acapulco. The website said the buses ran hourly. She rarely found anything in Mexico to be so organized or consistent. But at least she could get to Acapulco eventually, assuming she could hitch a ride to Chilpancingo.

The inbox dinged.

I can be there tomorrow morning.

Leslie alone, not with Nate? Her fingers rested on the keyboard, and she closed her eyes. What should she do?

The answer was obvious, but they weren't going to like it.

I want Nate to come, too.

Why?

Marisa struggled to formulate an answer that made sense.

The next message arrived.

It's Nate. I'm sorry, but I can't.

She'd checked his column in the *Times* enough to know he was no longer with them. *You got a new job?*

Long story.

You can tell me when I see you, she typed.

You don't need me, Marisa.

She wanted to argue, because she did need him. Even now, whenever she felt the slightest bit of danger, she longed for Nate. *We may need your help.*

But would getting him involved put him in danger? There she went again, weighing other people's lives against her own. But it wasn't just her life on the line now. It was Leslie's life. It was Ana's life.

Nate typed, *I'm sorry. I can't.*

Marisa sat back and surveyed the small office. Nothing had changed. Her little corner of her little village seemed exactly the same. The people here were at peace, while for Marisa, a storm raged.

Nate had kept her safe before. She wasn't willing to expose herself without knowing he'd be there to keep her safe again. It wasn't just for herself, either. It was for Leslie, too. And Ana. Marisa squeezed her eyes shut and prayed again. When she opened them, she typed, *Then I can't meet you, Leslie. I'm sorry.*

THREE

NATE FORCED his gaze from Marisa's message to face Leslie.

She hugged herself as if she were trying to keep from flying to pieces, though from fear or something else, he wasn't sure. Her entire body seemed to tremble.

He stood and let her sit in his chair.

"Why does she want me?" he asked.

Leslie sniffed, though he saw no tears in her eyes. "I don't know."

He filtered back through his memory to his conversations with Marisa. She'd only had good things to say about her sister. "What am I missing?"

"I can only guess here, but I assume she thinks you can keep her safe. You did it before."

The laptop dinged with a new message. *You guys still there?*

He snatched his computer off the table and set it on the kitchen counter. *Give me a minute, please.*

I know it's a lot to ask, her next message said. *I'm scared.*

He stared at those last two words before he turned the laptop away, as if that would keep Marisa's words from swaying him. He met Leslie's eyes. "Does she not trust you?

"I don't think it's about trust. You kept her safe before. She didn't believe I could protect her."

"But if you don't tell anybody where you're going—"

"I wouldn't, obviously. But the trick is convincing Marisa she doesn't need you."

He turned to the computer, then to the kitchen counter, strewn with stuff he still needed to pack. True to her word, while they were waiting to hear back from Marisa, Leslie had packed five or six boxes of Nate's books and other items from his office, which was now nearly empty. He was almost ready to leave, to escape to New Hampshire.

Go where he would be safe.

"Nate, what are you thinking?"

"I can't go."

The computer dinged.

I only have about five more minutes on the computer, Marisa said. *I won't be able to get back on until tomorrow, if then.*

Five minutes to make a decision that could cost him his life. Okay, fine. So he was being a little melodramatic. He hoped. Still.

Leslie looked over his shoulder. "She says—"

"I can read." He hadn't meant to snap.

"What should I tell her?"

He angled the computer away from Leslie and typed, *You're asking too much.*

I know.

Gee, as long as she knew.

He paced back into the living room and surveyed the remains of his life in New York. He'd had enough excitement for one lifetime just six months earlier, and no amount of therapy had helped. He needed to get out of the city, away from all the people, and recover. He needed to stay out of danger. To never play the hero again. And that's exactly what Marisa was asking—that he step into the role of hero, as if he had any idea how to protect her.

His one attempt at heroism had nearly gotten a lot of people he loved killed. Thank God the bad guy and the cop had been there to fix the mess he'd made. No way could he do that again.

No way.

Leslie touched his arm, and he ducked away.

"I can afford the plane tickets," she said. "I'll finance the whole trip."

"It's not about the money. It's about..."

After a few seconds, she asked, "Your job?"

He didn't have a job. He'd figure that out after he moved home. Until then, he could live off his savings and his father's generosity. And Rae and Brady's, probably, since they'd offered him whatever he needed. Nothing like being the charity case everybody else had to support.

Leslie tried again. "Why don't you tell me what the problem is?"

How could he tell her he was afraid? Could still feel the ropes binding him to the chair, the pain ricocheting through to his face, his head, his ribs, with every blow. The agony that had lasted for months, long after the wounds had healed. The fear that still gripped him.

"If I don't get to my sister and figure out who took the money, they'll kill me."

He turned to Leslie, who stood tall, shoulders back. "I'll go anyway, because I have no choice. I'll search for her. I guess I'll lose my house, my business. But what other choice do I have?"

Guilt trip. Nice tactic. "You haven't given me one, either."

"Marisa did that, not me." She glanced at her watch. "We're down to two minutes. Then it's tomorrow, if she even responds.

Maybe she'll be gone for good. Maybe this is my only chance to find her."

He turned and stared out the back window at the small weed-infested yard. He'd had such plans for this house. For his work. For his life. Now all he wanted was to run home.

"There's a guy," Leslie said. "A good man who loves me. He wants to marry me. He's saving up for a ring, but he already proposed."

"Congratulations." His tone was flat.

"Can you imagine, some guy wanting me? But he does, and..." She paused. "I want to marry him, too. Is that selfish, knowing what Marisa's doing, how she's had to hide all these years? I just want her home and everything to be normal again. I want my sister back." The last words were carried on a sob. "By the time you make up your mind—"

"I know, okay?"

He whipped around to see Leslie's shoulders slumped. What was he doing, considering sending this woman away? What kind of man was he?

He stalked back into the kitchen and pulled the laptop toward him.

He typed the sentence and paused before sending it. Was he insane? Why did he feel like this trip would change everything?

And did he really want everything to stay just like it was right now? Barely surviving? Cowering whenever a car back-fired? No.

And he wouldn't leave these women to fend for themselves.

And none of it had anything to do with the fact that he'd never been able to get Marisa out of his mind.

He hit Send and reread the line he'd sent. *Fine. Where shall we meet?*

You're coming, Nate?

You haven't given me a choice.

I know. I'm sorry. A pause. *What time do you land?*

If we can get the flight we looked at, 9:30 *a.m.*

Meet me at the Chapel of Peace tomorrow afternoon.

Chapel of Peace? Somehow, he doubted there'd be much peace in this adventure.

How HAD Nate gone from packing his kitchen to meeting an international fugitive?

He slid into the backseat beside Leslie, into the same taxi that had brought them from the airport to the hotel. The driver, Luis, had been kind enough to return after they'd checked in and freshened up. Leslie had arranged transportation while they'd laid over in Mexico City. Nate's insistence that they reserve hotel rooms had led to their first argument. Leslie had decided they'd stay with Marisa when they arrived in Acapulco and couldn't imagine why that would make him uncomfortable.

"We have no idea where she lives," he'd said during the flight. "No idea if she wants us there or has room for us."

"She'll make room. I'm her sister."

"I'm not."

"But she insisted you come."

"Reserve a hotel room—one for each of us—or I'm flying straight back to Kennedy."

Leslie had growled at him, but she'd done it. For all her mousy hair and sad looks, she could be stubborn. Well, she'd sucked him into this drama, so he got some say, too.

Leslie'd found two rooms at a very cheap *resort* among what looked to be the oldest stretch of hotels in the city. It'd probably been old when the *Love Boat* had docked nearby. And no, it wasn't impressive that the only reference he had for Acapulco came from a TV show popular before he was born. His mom had enjoyed the reruns while she was going through chemotherapy. "Dreaming of all the places I'm going to go someday." Turned out the only exotic place she got to see after her diagnosis was the inside of the hospital.

And heaven, if there was one.

Unlike Nate, who was now on his way to La Capilla de la Paz with a woman who'd been a total stranger barely more than twenty-four hours before.

Luis drove them through the Technicolor world of resorts and fauna alongside the bluest ocean Nate had ever seen. They headed out of town amid the sounds of traffic and the local music playing on the radio.

The Chapel of Peace was located, according to Google, at the highest point above the city. A few times, Nate had already spied the giant cross that stood beside it, which was supposedly visible from everywhere in the city. He didn't doubt it.

Was this where Marisa had lived for the past eight years? Not a bad place, he supposed, and with her Puerto Rican coloring, she'd certainly fit in. Though Mexico had become increasingly dangerous through the years, the resort towns were generally considered safe. He would have chosen someplace less touristy. And he certainly wouldn't have chosen this oppressive heat. The only place he'd ever been that was hotter than this was Tunis. The African city had been just as hot but dry. Not comfortable, but at least his sweat had evaporated before it soaked his short hair.

He wiped his moist forehead and frowned. The fact that the Tunis trip, a necessity for a story he was following, had been the impetus that had led to his kidnapping and torture a few months earlier did not sit well. He boxed up that thought and stored it in a container labeled *don't open 'til pigs fly in a frozen hell.*

Leslie shifted beside him, and he glanced at her. A frown

creased her face. When she noticed him looking, she smiled. "This seems like a decent place. I've wondered over the years what kind of life Marisa was living. Most of my guesses have made me think of... I don't know, slums I guess, but this doesn't seem so bad, right? I mean, sure, it's not New York."

Spoken like a true New Yorker. Most city dwellers seemed to believe living anyplace outside of the five boroughs was akin to choosing among different degrees of third-world nations. He braced himself for the inevitable next line—something about culture or diversity or education. But Leslie only turned back to the window.

Five minutes later, she said, "Must cost a lot of money to live here."

"I doubt it. I'm sure there are cheaper places to live in Mexico, but I don't think there's any place as expensive as Queens, much less Manhattan."

"Good point. I wonder how she's supporting herself. I mean, assuming..."

Her words trailed off. "Assuming what?"

"You know." She lowered her voice, so the driver wouldn't hear. "That she didn't steal the money."

"You think she did?"

Leslie shrugged. "I never did before, but now"—she indicated the luxurious hotels surrounding them—"it's hard to say."

"The people who work in Acapulco live near here, too, and not in hotels." He nodded to the taxi driver, who certainly wasn't living the high life on his income. "Doesn't mean anything."

"You're right, of course."

Of course, but the intruders who'd threatened Leslie certainly thought Marisa had the money.

Refusing to come on this trip had seemed like too cowardly a thing to do, even for him. But now he wondered if coming here was a mistake. Would his interference help lure Marisa into some trap that she'd avoided for eight years?

There was no time for second-guessing now. If it all crumbled like a Jenga tower, he'd have plenty of time for regrets later. Hadn't the last six months proved that?

Nate peered out the window as the taxi snaked up the side of a small mountain on a too-narrow road. The jarring of the little VW Beetle turned his stomach. He'd never been a good backseat rider. Every few moments, he was rewarded for his willingness to endure with a glimpse of Acapulco Bay and its deep blue water.

Luis veered to the right and came to a sudden stop. "Stay here, si?"

He stepped out of the car and had a rapid conversation in Spanish with a man standing nearby—a gatekeeper of some sort, perhaps? There seemed to be some disagreement, but a moment later, Luis climbed back in the car. "They wanted your identification, but I vouched for you."

"They wanted to see them?" Leslie asked. "Like for security?"

"They like to hold onto them, but I say no, you're okay."

Nate reached over the seat and clasped the man's shoulder. "Thank you, Luis. You're right—that would have made me uncomfortable."

Luis nodded, and Nate took his hand back.

"He say the chapel is closed until four," Luis continued, "but is okay. The gardens are *muy* beautiful. You will enjoy. Or you want to go and come back later?"

"We'll stay," Leslie said.

"I should wait for you?"

"Um..." Leslie looked at Nate, a question in her eyes.

"Can't hurt," he said. As long as she was footing the bill.

She turned back to the driver. "Yes, please wait."

Luis pulled forward on the small drive and parked. "I wait here. Many photos from *Las Manos de la Hermandad.*"

"Um, okay." Leslie looked at him and shrugged. "Thanks."

They meandered up the walkway and peered in the windows of the chapel. "Mid-century modern," Leslie said. "Not my favorite style. And for a church?"

"It has its charm." Nate led the way toward the gardens, where they followed the path for a few minutes, both of them scanning the area for Marisa, before they discovered what Luis had been talking about.

Las Manos de la Hermandad was a giant sculpture of two hands, fingertips touching as if in prayer. The sculpture stood near the foot of the giant cross Nate had seen from town. Nate read the sign, printed in both English and Spanish. "The Hands of Brotherhood."

Leslie nodded and studied the intriguing sculpture. "Or sisterhood," she said.

"Of course."

They moved on. The chapel was open in the mornings and again in the evenings, but closed between one and four. Siesta. And what intelligent person would choose to be outside right now? He wiped the dripping sweat from his temples, as if that would help, and continued looking for Marisa. Was she here yet? Had something kept her from making it today, or perhaps, had she changed her mind?

They strolled through the gardens and all manner of flora—palms and flowers and spindly plants that had grown high on each side in this particular part of the garden, so Nate and Leslie could hardly see ahead more than a few feet at a time. The effect made him claustrophobic. He focused on the beauty, the scent of the flowers and the twitter of exotic birds, and tried to push the growing fear away.

Suddenly, a little girl dashed around a bend toward them,

giggling and looking over her shoulder. She had brown skin and shiny black curls. Nate would have guessed she was Mexican until she turned and called over her shoulder, "You can't catch me, Mama," in perfect English.

No more than four, she froze when she saw them. Her baby-toothed smile faded as she looked up into Nate's eyes.

"Hi, there," he said.

Leslie smiled at the girl.

"*Hola*," the girl said. "I'm Ana."

"Nice to meet you. Where's your Mama?"

As he said it, a woman rushed around the corner. "Ana, don't run off like that. You scared me!"

Leslie gasped. Nate's reaction was quieter but no less shocked. So focused on the little girl, the woman hadn't looked at them. Her hair was longer, and her braid had fallen over her shoulder and nearly reached her waist. Her build was slender, her face a little more mature, though not at all wrinkled. If anything, Marisa had only grown more beautiful in the years since he'd seen her.

Leslie seemed to pull herself together. "Marisa."

Marisa looked up from the little girl, and he caught the first glimpse of her eyes. Oh, he'd forgotten those eyes. Big, innocent eyes like... What was that princess's name from his little brother's favorite Disney movie? Jasmine—yes, that's who she'd always reminded him of.

Her jaw dropped, and then she smiled. "Leslie." The large canvas bag she'd held fell to the path, and Marisa stepped forward into her sister's embrace. They held each other and rocked and cried.

Nate looked at Ana and smiled. "I guess they know each other."

The little girl nodded. "Si. Mama said we might meet my aunt today."

Might. Like she'd doubted they'd show. Well, he'd doubted Marisa would, hadn't he? But now that she was here, all those doubts slid off him like the latest beads of sweat. Somehow it seemed as if this reunion had been destined since the first moment he'd laid eyes on Marisa more than eight years earlier.

A ridiculous thought, but there you go.

Marisa stepped out of the embrace and turned to him. She looked as if she might want to step in for a hug, but she held back. "Thank you for coming."

He nodded, itching to embrace her and feeling sort of shy himself. And foolish. Very foolish. "You knew I would."

She nodded. "I sort of did, yeah."

Leslie bent toward Ana. "And who's this little girl?"

"I'm Ana."

She held out her hand, but Leslie pulled her into a hug. "It's lovely to meet you, Ana. I'm Leslie."

"Aunt Leslie." The girl pulled back and looked at Marisa. "Right, Mama?"

"Right."

Leslie stood straight and looked at her sister. "We need to talk. Can we go back to your place?"

Marisa turned to her sister. "Can't we just talk here?"

The smile the older sister had worn faded. "You're in such a rush to be away from us?"

"Worried. You said your life was in danger."

"Right. I'd rather talk about it someplace private. Is your house far from here?"

"I don't live in Acapulco. We just arrived in the city today."

"Oh." Leslie seemed confused. "Where do you live?"

"It's a little village a few hours from here." She glanced at Nate, then back at Leslie, and bit her lip. "I should have told you that. I hope you have a place to stay."

Nate couldn't help the smug expression he felt on his face,

though Leslie was careful not to look. "We do. Do you have a car, or—?"

"Nope. We took the bus."

Leslie wrapped her hand around her sister's. "All right. I'm glad we had our taxi wait for us. Let's go."

FOUR

MARISA DIDN'T HAVE to coax Ana into the Volkswagen Beetle that served as Leslie and Nate's taxi. The little girl so rarely rode in cars, she was thrilled at the opportunity—though Beetles were almost as common as cockroaches around here. Ana's initial shyness had faded away, and now she chattered constantly as they made their way back to the city. Marisa let her, content to study her sister, who sat on the other side of Ana, and Nate, who sat in front.

Leslie was turned to Ana, though she seemed to struggle to focus on her words. Well, who could blame her? She and Nate had spent all night on a plane before they'd driven up here to the chapel. Marisa should have suggested a place nearer to town, but she'd never been to Acapulco, and the chapel was the only place she knew to meet.

"Mama, are they coming home with us? Where will they sleep? On the floor? Or I can sleep on the floor, and they can sleep in your bed. But maybe not him." She tugged on Nate's shirt, and he turned back to face her. "You'll have to sleep on the floor with me. Did you bring a sleeping bag?"

"Uh..."

"It's okay," Ana said. "We can borrow blankets. Do you mind sleeping on tile? Abby says it's uncomfortable, but I don't mind. It's cool."

"Pajarita." Marisa chanced a glance at Nate, whose eyes were wide. She tried not to giggle. "They are not coming home with us. We're going to visit with them here."

"But I'd love to see where you live," Nate said. "I bet your house is very pretty."

"It is. Mama's paintings are on the walls, and she brings in flowers sometimes and puts them on the table. I like yellow flowers. Do you like yellow?"

"Of course," Nate said. "Is yellow your favorite color?"

"No." Ana shook her head solemnly, as if Nate had asked a very serious question. "My favorite color is blue."

"No way!" Nate said. "Me, too."

"Mama, did you hear that? His favorite color is blue! Can we drive in this car all the way home? Oh, wouldn't Abby be jealous."

Marisa smoothed her daughter's hair. "That's not a very kind thing to say."

Ana frowned and nodded. "You're right." She brightened immediately. "But we could give her a ride, couldn't we? Oh, can we, Mama? Abby's never even been on a bus before!"

"Not this time, pajarita. We are going to visit with Aunt Leslie and Nate for a little while before we take the bus back."

Ana's disappointment lasted long enough for her to take a breath. Then she started chattering again like a little bird.

More than once, Leslie looked between Marisa and Ana, eyes squinted as if she were trying to work out a difficult problem. Leslie looked older, of course, but aside from a few wrinkles, she seemed just like the big sister she'd been eight years earlier. Brusque, impatient, but kind and protective. Marisa's heart swelled as she took in her sister's presence. How Marisa had missed her.

"She's adopted," Marisa said. "Or almost. It's a really long process in Mexico."

"Oh." Leslie's glance went to Marisa's left hand. "Are you married?"

"Nope."

She waited for Leslie's next question, but Ana's sweet voice started up again.

Marisa listened to her daughter while she studied Nate in the front. He'd aged, too, of course, but the few wrinkles she could see when he smiled only made him look better. His hair was a bit shorter. His eyes wiser, kinder, maybe. Nate had improved in the eight years since she'd seen him.

Had he always been so handsome? Perhaps she'd just missed it, wracked as she'd been by grief and fear all those years ago. She wasn't missing it now.

The taxi driver pulled up outside of what had to be one of the oldest hotels in Acapulco, if the design were any indication. This three-story structure was the ugly step-sister to the top-quality high-rise resorts that lined the beach. Still grand luxury compared with what Marisa was accustomed to.

Leslie paid the taxi driver in American dollars, which made him smile wide and insist on giving them his cell phone number in case they needed him again. He waved wildly as he pulled away. Though he'd probably overcharged them, compared with a taxi in Manhattan, it was a bargain price. And Marisa didn't blame the guy. The twenties Leslie handed him could probably feed his family for a week.

"We can go to my room," Leslie said, leading the way inside.

Ana was silent as she took in the fancy lobby. Marisa followed her gaze to the tile floor and the gleaming chrome of the bar on the far side.

Marisa couldn't help gaping herself. Old, yes, but still, it was air conditioned and freshly painted. Bright pink and aqua contemporary sofas and chairs dotted the lobby like confetti, flanked by shiny white tables. A bowl of candy sat on one table as if these people had money to burn. A man sat in one of the chairs, focused on his cell phone. Two women behind the tall desk smiled when they walked in.

Leslie and Nate were headed toward the elevators when Ana pulled on Marisa's hand. "Hold on," Marisa said.

They paused and turned.

Ana, suddenly shy again, wouldn't speak until Marisa crouched down beside her.

She spoke in Spanish, an extra measure of security for the four-year-old. "Mama, do you see?" She pointed out the rear door to the sparkling blue water of the swimming pool. "Can we, Mama? Please?"

Leslie and Nate had stopped to wait. Nate wore a pleasant smile, though his eyes looked tired. Leslie's gaze flicked from the elevator to the child.

"Could we talk outside?" Marisa stood and faced her sister. "She's never seen a pool before, and we've been traveling since dawn."

Leslie's jaw dropped. "Never seen a pool? What do you mean?"

"There are no swimming pools in our village, Leslie." She turned to Nate. "I know how hot it is, but maybe there are fans running somewhere, and we can watch her from the shade."

Nate shrugged. "It's fine with me."

After a nod from her mother, Ana raced ahead of them all, pushed open the door, and bolted to the pool.

Marisa was glad she'd borrowed a swimsuit for her daughter, which Ana wore under her clothes. She'd promised a dip in the ocean, but right now, the pool would do nicely. Marisa found a life jacket and put it on her daughter. She gave her strict instructions about where she could play in the water.

"If you disobey, you will get out. *Comprendes?*"

"Si." Her head bobbed, and she raced to the wide steps of the kiddie pool. Marisa watched a moment. Joy bubbled at her daughter's happiness, followed quickly by sadness. What American four-year-old had never been swimming? She shook off the thought and joined Leslie and Nate at a table beneath the thatched roof of the tiki bar. The area was deserted except for the waitress and bartender, who seemed deep in thought at the bar behind them.

"I hope this is okay," Nate said. "It seems like the best vantage point. And I do need the shade."

"Thank you. I promised her we'd walk to the beach, too, before we go back. She's never seen the ocean."

"Why not?" Leslie asked.

"We live pretty far inland."

Nate leaned forward, eyes narrowed. "Where exactly?"

Marisa opened her mouth. She'd kept the secret so long, she couldn't bring herself to say the name of her village. "You've never heard of it. We live in a little village about thirty kilometers from Chilpancingo."

He scowled. For the first time since she'd met up with them, the kindness disappeared from Nate's gaze. Now, it was hard and demanding. "Why in the world would you choose to live there? Do you have any idea how dangerous Mexico is?"

"Um, yeah, Nate. I live here."

"You escaped New York to save your life only to move to one of the most dangerous places on earth? I mean, if you lived near here—"

"It's a long story."

Leslie looked between them. "Is Mexico that dangerous?"

Nate ignored her. "Weren't those students from around

there?"

She was impressed by his knowledge about Mexican issues. Not that the kidnapping and murder of forty-three college students hadn't made the international news. "That was years ago, and it took place in Ayotzinapa, about two hours east of Chilpancingo. We don't live—"

"It was in Guerrero, though."

"Wait," Leslie said. "What's that?"

Marisa turned to her sister. "That's the state we're in." To Nate she said, "Yes, it's dangerous, if you speak out. If you make waves or cause trouble. I don't do that. I teach English and help at the orphanage. I am well-liked, and I fit in."

"I didn't help you risk your life to tell your story so you could..." Nate seemed to falter, struggle with his words. Fatigue couldn't help, and he was getting pretty riled up. "Could risk your life..."

Marisa lifted her eyebrows. "Wasting my time?"

"Well, no, but—"

"Because little Mexican kids' lives aren't as important as my own?"

"I didn't say that."

Leslie jumped in. "Just relax, both of you." She turned to Marisa. "I think he's just worried about you, that's all." She turned to Nate and said, "Right?"

He sat back in his chair. "I just wish you'd chosen somewhere less dangerous."

She started to defend herself and her choices, then stopped. She didn't have to justify herself to Nate or Leslie. She could understand his worry. If anybody had asked her nine years ago where she thought she'd be now, she certainly wouldn't have guessed this. But despite Nate's fears, Marisa felt she lived right where she was supposed to. She wasn't sure what she believed about God or destiny or whatever, but Ana was meant to be her daughter. And if all the craziness after Vinnie's murder eight years before was the price to find her precious girl, Marisa would gladly pay it again.

She watched Ana run after a bird into the pretty gardens surrounding the pool, waited until she returned poolside, and turned to Leslie.

"Tell me what happened."

Leslie shared a horrifying tale. Someone had broken into her house in the middle of the night and threatened her. Marisa felt the details deep in her soul. Marisa had never been threatened in that way exactly, but hadn't she lived with the fear of it for years? Hadn't she worried that any minute, some gun-wielding crazy person would find her, threaten her, hurt her? The fear of it had been bad enough.

Leslie had lived it.

Marisa had to do what she could to help her sister, as long as she could also keep Ana safe.

Ana. She jolted upright in her seat. How much time had passed? She'd been so caught up in her sister's story, she'd forgotten about Ana. Her daughter wasn't in the pool, wasn't beside it. Where was she?

Nate reached across the table and patted her hand. She looked at him, then followed his pointed finger. "She found a playmate. See?"

Indeed, Ana and another little girl ran from the gardens. They jumped onto the top step and into the shallow pool. Their laughter filled the space.

"Thank you."

He nodded, and Marisa turned back to Leslie. "So they think you have the money?"

"No. They think you have it, and they thought I could get it from you."

"But I don't have it. I don't know who does."

Leslie took Marisa's hand. "Listen, I never thought you stole it, not back then. But they seemed convinced. If you did, if you come clean now, we can figure out what to do."

"Come clean?" Marisa yanked her hand away. "Come clean! You think I stole it? After everything—"

"Don't be angry," Leslie said, all big-sister-like. "I'm just saying that maybe—"

"You flew all the way to Mexico to call me a thief and a liar?" Marisa looked at Nate, whose jaw had lowered.

"Do you believe her? That I stole the money?"

"I never doubted you, and I still don't." He stood and stretched. "Why don't I give you two some privacy? I'll keep an eye on Ana while you talk." He walked toward the pool and sat on a lounge chair to remove his sandals.

With his shorts, he could get wet to the knees, and at least he was away from the squabbling sisters. Smart man.

Marisa turned back to Leslie. "I didn't take the money."

Leslie's eyes filled with tears. "But you have to have it! If you don't, I'm dead."

MARISA SHIFTED in the most comfortable bed she'd slept in since New York. Part of her had wanted to stay awake to enjoy the luxury—soft sheets, a real mattress that wasn't fifty years old, and air conditioning. It was like heaven.

Instead of enjoying it, she worried. Who could have threatened Leslie, and what could Marisa do to help from her home in Mexico? Though she'd known just enough about the illegal real estate deals Vinnie and his boss had been involved in to put Nate on the case, he knew a lot more than she did about what went down the night the money was stolen.

Marisa couldn't tell Leslie or the people who'd threatened

her anything that Nate and the FBI didn't already know. But if somebody thought Marisa had the money, then whether she had it or not didn't matter. Leslie was in danger.

And there was nothing Marisa could do to help her. She'd been over what she knew a thousand times, hoping for some way to prove who'd taken the money, because if she couldn't figure it out, she'd never be able to go home again, not while Charles believed she'd done it. Charles had resorted to murder once. She had no doubt he'd do it again to get his money back, even from prison. So she was stuck, unable to help without more information, and how could she get more information without exposing herself?

She turned over, twirled one of her daughter's curls in her finger. A tangible reminder that there was more at stake than her own safety and Leslie's.

Her thoughts spun until they nearly made her dizzy. But she still had no new ideas about who'd threatened Leslie.

Meanwhile, Leslie had fallen asleep almost immediately in the other bed. Of course, she'd traveled all night, so exhaustion must have helped.

Finally, little Ana's gentle breathing beside Marisa lulled her to sleep.

SHE WOKE EARLY to discover Leslie had slipped out of the room. Ana was awake and bouncing on Leslie's bed.

"Look at me, Mama!" She jumped high, pulled her legs up, and landed on her bottom.

Marisa smiled but shook her head. "We don't jump on beds."

"Why not?"

"You'll break the springs."

Ana tilted her head to the side, a twinkle in her eye. "But I'm just a little bird, right?"

"A hungry bird, I bet."

Ana nodded, and the two dressed and headed to the restaurant. Marisa's meager funds wouldn't keep them here for long, and she needed to hold onto enough money to get back to Chilpancingo, where they'd hitch a ride with some folks from her village who worked in a factory there. And Marisa should offer to cover some of the cost of gasoline. Money was always tight for the folks in her village.

Nate looked up from his seat in the small restaurant when they walked in. He waved them over. "They have a delicious buffet. You two hungry?"

Ana had already spied the long, colorful table covered in chafing dishes and glass trays filled with goodies. She gaped at it with awe. "Mama, can we? Look at all that food! Look, the fruit. And eggs! And... What are those?" She pointed to a tray of pastries.

"Cinnamon rolls." She turned to Nate. "But the buffet must be expensive, and we can't really—"

"We'll take care of it."

Marisa looked around. "Is Leslie here?"

"She was when I got here, but she just went back to the room."

"Oh. We must have missed each other on the elevators." Marisa remembered what he'd said. *We*, meaning him and Leslie. "Are you and my sister together?"

Nate laughed, caught himself, and shifted into a neutral expression. "No. I just meant that, between the two of us, we can manage your meals."

Marisa pretended her relief had everything to do with the ability to eat and nothing to do with the handsome man. "Have you eaten?"

"I was waiting for you."

Marisa and Ana filled their plates while Nate followed,

making suggestions and explaining the different items to Ana, who took at least one of everything on the long table.

The three of them enjoyed their breakfast feasts, and Marisa didn't even make her daughter eat the eggs. Good thing, too, because Ana filled up on cinnamon rolls, sausage, and bacon— all delicacies she'd never had—a fact that left Nate speechless.

When Ana's plate held nothing but uneaten eggs, she stood to get more.

"No more, pajarita. You'll make yourself sick."

"Please? One more cinnamon roll? I might not ever have them again."

The thought made Marisa want to cry, but she smiled instead. "One more."

The girl skipped back to the buffet table, and Nate chuckled. "She's adorable."

"I am very blessed."

Nate seemed about to say something, then reached for a grape off his plate instead.

"Be careful with the fruit."

He tilted his head. "Fine time to tell me that, now that I've finished off the cantaloupe and mangoes."

"You've been eating cut fruit. It's washed on the outside, but it's peeled, and the outsides are tossed away. You eat the outside of grapes."

"And...?"

"They wash it in local water, and the water will make you sick. Some say it's a myth, but I believe it. It took me a long time to become accustomed. At the hotel"—she shrugged—"perhaps it's filtered, but I wouldn't count on it."

He dropped the grape. "That makes sense. Speaking of which, your sister didn't look very good this morning."

"Is she sick?"

"She didn't say so, but she didn't even finish a cup of coffee before she took off."

"Uh-oh. Maybe I'd better go check on her."

Nate glanced at Ana, who was making her way back from the buffet table. "If you're finished with your breakfast, go ahead. I'll stay with Ana."

"You sure?"

"We'll take a walk in the garden. You'll find us there. Okay?"

Marisa agreed, and five minutes later, let herself into their hotel room.

She could tell by the nauseous odor snaking beneath the bathroom door that Leslie was not okay.

Marisa knocked softly on the door. "Can I do anything for you?"

A moment passed. The toilet flushed, the water ran in the tap, and the door opened. "It's probably just from traveling. You know how I am."

Leslie didn't even like to go upstate. "This seems like more than that, though."

"We didn't sleep at all the night before last," Leslie said, "and the night before that..."

Marisa remembered the story, the intruders, the threats. "Right. You've had a rough couple of days."

"And traveling doesn't agree with me—never has." She hobbled to her bed, bent with her arms wrapped around her stomach. It seemed an effort to climb in.

Marisa pulled the covers over her sister and tucked them in, remembering their few vacations as children. Leslie had always gotten sick at least once.

She brushed hair away from Leslie's forehead. "Try to get some sleep."

"But we need to talk about this. Figure out—"

"When you're better, sis. Right now, sleep."

Leslie's eyes closed. "Okay. I'll try."

FIVE

Nate walked alongside Ana, who stopped to admire every pretty flower in the hotel's garden. There were lots, even a few blue ones Nate and Ana agreed were the prettiest. He snapped photos of the girl, but as soon as she spied his iPhone, she lost interest in the flora. "Can I see?"

She studied his smartphone with something like awe.

"Have you ever seen one before?"

"There are men in town who have phones like this, but they are"—she lowered her voice and looked around—"bad people. Mama says to stay out of their way."

Why would Marisa live in a place like that? Had the woman no sense? Especially with a vulnerable little girl.

Ana was watching him closely. "You'd better do what your mother says. You want to take a picture?"

She nodded, so he showed her how. After that, she took photos of every flower they came across.

It was still fairly early, so the gardens were quiet. Nate spotted a man up ahead of them, but the guy must've gotten a phone call, because he pressed his cell phone's screen and turned in the other direction. Nate stared after the guy. With his long jeans, he didn't seem to belong here. Nate's PTSD kicked his heartbeat into overdrive, but surely it had been nothing.

Ana tugged on his hand, her soft grip pulling him away from his dark thoughts. He turned and smiled.

"Let's sit down." She pointed to a park bench. He discovered that if he stood on top of the bench in just the right spot and looked between two hotels across the street, he could see Acapulco Bay. He lifted her so she could see, too, and she snapped a few more photos.

They sat next to each other, and she filled him in on her life, her and Marisa's small house, the orphanage, and her school-work. Marisa had told him Ana was four, but the girl seemed so mature for her age. Not that he would know much about that.

"Let's take a selfie," he said.

"A what?"

He explained it while he rotated the view of the camera. They spent the next few minutes taking silly photos of them-selves. Her innocent giggles seemed to melt a long-frozen place in his heart, and he had a sudden urge to wrap his arms around her and hold her tight. To protect her from all the evil in the world.

He'd probably scare the kid away.

"There you are!"

He looked up to see Marisa walking toward them.

Nate stood. "How's Leslie?"

"You were right. She's resting."

"Stinks to get sick when you're traveling."

"Typical for—"

"Mama!" Ana tugged on her hand. "Uncle Nate and me took pictures. Wanna see?"

"And I." Marisa's eyebrows lifted, and she looked at him. "Uncle Nate?"

He shrugged. He hadn't given Ana the idea, but he liked the title.

Marisa sat beside her daughter on the bench. Nate sat on the far side, and together, they scrolled through the photographs while Marisa oohed and aahed. Finally, she laughed. "My goodness, how long was I gone? I think you've taken a thousand pictures."

"Can I take them home with me, Uncle Nate? Abby has a picture in her room because sometimes she misses her mama and papa. I want to show her where we were. Oh, and can we take a picture of the pool?" She looked at Marisa. "We saw the beach"—the little girl pointed—"through there. Can we take pictures of the beach? Are we still going to the beach? Can we, Mama?"

Marisa tweaked the girl's nose. "I promised, didn't I? But maybe not yet." She looked at Nate. "It's nice right now. I thought we might explore, go shopping or something, and go to the beach later when it gets hot."

He wiped his brow and chucked. "*When* it gets hot?"

"It'll get hotter still, trust me."

He remembered the day before well enough. "Sure. Shopping sounds great. Maybe we can find a place to get those pictures printed. And you can show me around."

"This is my first time to Acapulco."

"Right." He'd forgotten.

The concierge directed them to a shopping plaza designed with American tourists in mind. It was within walking distance. Nate had hoped it would be inside and air conditioned, but no. It was an open-air market. At least the stores were cool, and the shopping wasn't bad. The company, though—that couldn't be beat.

He walked alongside Marisa while Ana led the way, talking nonstop and pointing in awe about every two minutes.

"You'd think she'd never been shopping before," Nate said.

Marisa watched with a smile. "There's a market in town, of course. It sells mostly local food. But other than that, she hasn't." She glanced at him, then away. "There are no malls in my village."

"Where do you buy your clothes and stuff?"

She watched Ana, who'd stopped at a fountain and was dipping her fingers in the water. "The orphanage gets donations. Most of them come from this church in Oklahoma that supports us. They send all sorts of stuff. Most of her clothes come from there."

"What about yours?"

Her cheeks pinked. "That's where I get most of mine, too. I order some things online. Like... Well, stuff you wouldn't want to wear hand-me-down."

He could imagine.

"It's amazing how little we need. I used to spend more money on makeup and lotions than I spend on food now."

"Wow," he said. "A woman who doesn't shop."

Marisa looked into his eyes. "I gave up everything, Nate. Everything." She turned back and stared at her daughter. "But I gained even more."

He watched the sweet little girl play in the fountain. He'd seen that kind of sacrificial love last fall when his friend had been prepared to die to save her son. He didn't understand it—not personally. But he could appreciate it. In fact, on Marisa's face it seemed the most beautiful thing he'd ever seen.

She turned and caught him staring. Rather than look away, she met his eyes and held his gaze.

He itched to grab her hand. But would she recoil? Maybe not now, but if she understood what he'd done, how he'd almost gotten his friends killed, she certainly wouldn't want him to touch her. To be near her at all.

"Mama, Uncle Nate, come on!"

The moment shattered as Marisa turned to her daughter. "We're coming, pajarita."

"What does that mean, pa-ha-ree-ta?"

"Little bird."

"Ah. It fits."

They failed to find a place that could print the pictures, but Ana had forgotten about them already. Maybe if he could coax Marisa's address out of her, he could mail the photographs to Ana after he returned to the States.

Ana and Marisa admired pretty things in every store, and Nate wished he could buy all of them for the two beautiful ladies. He couldn't buy them all, but he did take a yellow sundress for Marisa and a blue one for little Ana to the counter in one store, despite Marisa's protests.

But he had an ace in the hole, having seen the small bag Marisa had brought to town. "You have a suitable dress for dinner?"

She blushed and shook her head. "I thought we'd do something casual for dinner. We don't have a lot of money. And our clothes are fine. We washed yesterday's out last night, and we'll wash these tonight."

"You travel light, huh?"

She lifted the ugly brown canvas bag. "This is the only luggage I own."

He thought of the Pod at home stuffed with all his worldly goods. His life seemed suddenly bathed in riches. "But surely you left New York with a suitcase or something."

"My duffel bag was in rags by the time I settled."

He pulled a bag of candy Ana was staring at off the rack and snatched a pretty beach bag he'd seen Marisa admire and set them on the counter. "These, too," he said to the shopgirl. He turned to Marisa. "Now you have dresses for dinner and slightly nicer luggage."

"You really shouldn't."

He handed the girl across the counter his credit card. "I really should. And it's rude to refuse a gift."

The girl behind the counter nodded as she ran his credit card. "He's right, you know." Her accent was thick, her smile wide.

Marisa seemed to consider it before she smiled. "Okay. I guess I can't argue with your logic."

"Can we put them on now, Mama? Please?"

"After the beach, okay?"

At the reminder of the beach, the girl couldn't get there fast enough. After a quick stop at the hotel, the three of them splashed and played and rode the waves—small as they were in the bay—until Nate and Marisa were exhausted. The girl had energy reserves Nate lacked.

After giving her daughter strict instruction, Marisa fell into the lounge chair beside his with a sigh. "She'll be okay, right?"

"Between the life jacket and the lifeguard"—he pointed to the attentive man who seemed to have his eyes everywhere at once—"and you and me watching, I think so."

"She loves it."

"What's not to love? It's wonderful."

Marisa sat back and sighed, her smile fading. "We haven't talked about the threat all day."

"I know."

"Who do you think they were? Leslie said it was a man and a woman. I've been racking my brain trying to figure it out, but I have no idea. Charles is still in prison, right?"

"Unless he busted out."

Her eyes widened.

"Just kidding. He didn't. He's still safe and sound at Sing Sing."

"Sheesh. Scare me, why don't you?"

"Sorry."

"We should ask Leslie how old she thought they were."

"I did," Nate said. "On the plane. She said she didn't know, but she'd guess middle-aged. She also said she thought the man was tall, over six feet, and built. The woman was shorter but not short, according to your sister, and thin. It was dark, and they wore ski masks, so she didn't get eye or hair color. They both wore black."

"Thorough description. I can imagine you asking all the right questions to get that much out of her."

He shrugged.

"I remember that. You're good at getting people to remember things they didn't even know they knew."

"It's what I do." *Did*, but he didn't mention that.

A big wave created by the wake of a speedboat headed toward Ana. Marisa started to stand, but Nate touched her hand. "She's okay."

He itched to keep his hand there, to take hers.

Marisa looked at Nate's outstretched fingers. He pulled them back.

Ana jumped over the wave and looked at her mom, who clapped. "Very good!" Marisa leaned back again. "What are we going to do?"

An excellent question, one he'd been mulling since they'd found Marisa the day before. "You can't really do anything. Nothing has changed for you. You need to stay hidden, and you seem to have a life here. Though if you want, I could certainly help you find a safer place to live, maybe get you a job—"

"I have a job. If I can't go back to the States, I'll stay where I am."

"Ana said something about dangerous men in your village. Maybe you should consider—"

"Don't."

He shut his mouth, reluctantly.

"Besides," she said, "Ana's adoption isn't final. We have to stay where we are until it is."

"You can't move to a safer town?"

"Ours is pretty safe."

"When will the adoption be final?"

She shrugged. "This is Mexico. There's no telling. It's already been four years."

Ridiculous, but she was right. Mexico was not a paragon of efficiency and justice in the world.

Marisa pulled a bottle of sunscreen out of her old, ugly bag. She'd refused to bring the new one to the beach, lest it get dirty. She squeezed lotion onto her hand and rubbed it over one long, brown leg. Apparently, she didn't own a swimsuit, so she'd been swimming in gray shorts and a loose pink tank top. She could have worn sweatpants, and he'd still find her beautiful. Maybe she should have worn sweats, because he couldn't stop staring at her legs as she flipped her long braid over her shoulder and got to work on the other one.

She seemed unaware as she watched her daughter. "Which brings us back to the question—what should Leslie do?"

He forced his gaze back to Ana, who had met up with the girl from the pool the day before. They were building a sand castle. "I've been thinking about it, and Leslie has no choice. She needs to go to the police."

"But the people said they'd kill her if she did."

"They said they'd kill her if she didn't give them the money, too. And she doesn't have it."

Marisa finished her legs and worked lotion into her arm. The scent of coconut surrounded them and reminded Nate of vacations with his parents when he was a small boy, before cancer had stolen his mother away.

"But that's not really what they said," Marisa said. "They said they wanted her to give them the money or find out who stole it."

"Well, but..." He paused. She was right. That's what Leslie had said. "Why would they care, as long as they get the money?"

She held out the sunscreen, and he took it.

A second application, and he'd probably still burn to a crisp, thanks to his Irish genes. He'd bought himself a baseball cap in town, so at least his face wouldn't char.

"Maybe it's about justice, too," she said.

"If that's the case, that should help us narrow down who it could be."

"Meanwhile, though, my sister's life is in danger. We have to figure out how to protect her."

"And keep you and Ana safe."

"But if I keep us safe, Leslie will be in more danger." She looked at her daughter. "It's an impossible choice, Nate. How do I protect them both?"

He knew exactly how she felt.

AFTER A SHOWER AND SHAVE, Nate went to the small lobby— the only place in the hotel with reliable WiFi. The old walls had been repainted bright white. The pink and aqua furnishings had faded to bland. The lobby was cool, and the faint scent of flowers wafted from the fresh centerpiece on the amoeba-shaped coffee table in front of him. A few women in sundresses and men in Bermuda shorts sat in the bar on the far side of the lobby, where a hand-written sign advertised happy hour specials. In the seating areas scattered around the lobby, more people sat, teens and children and adults alike, all looking at their electronic devices. So much for family vacations.

While Nate waited for the ladies to join him for dinner, he used his iPhone to pull up the news stories he'd written that had been prompted by Marisa's information. Nearly eight years had passed since he'd penned the words. After re-reading the articles, Nate navigated to his cloud account and scrolled through the research he'd collected back then, which he'd thought to upload before they left New York.

The door that led to the pool opened, and Leslie walked in, bringing the humid evening air with her. She spotted Nate, beelined toward him, and sat on the sofa catty-corner to him. "You look busy."

Nate reluctantly lowered his phone. "I figured you were upstairs with Marisa and Ana."

"I needed some fresh air after being cooped up in the room all day."

She had a little color back in her cheeks, so in that respect she looked better. The humid air had done a number on her already frizzy hair, though. "Feeling better?"

"Much. Thanks. What are you doing?"

"Trying to see if I missed anything, trying to figure out who threatened you the other day."

She leaned forward. "Any luck?"

"Not yet, but hope springs eternal."

"In my experience, it's trouble that's eternal. Hope is fleeting."

No good answer to that.

"I've never really understood what it was all about," Leslie said. "Charles and those guys were doing something, and Vinnie was involved somehow. He was no Boy Scout. So why did he get murdered? I mean, I sort of understand, but what did they do that was so bad that it was worth killing over? Charles went to prison for the murder, not the rest of it."

"He was convicted of mortgage fraud, too. He'd have gone to prison for that, but the state's murder charges trumped the others. The stuff he and his cronies did led to a lot of people losing a lot of money, and not just when the housing bubble burst."

"I remember that. My house lost like a quarter of its value."

"Charles and his friends capitalized on the hopes and dreams of thousands of America's working class, sucking them into mortgages they couldn't afford, then turning around and tricking them out of the little equity they had in their homes when the people couldn't pay their mortgages."

"That's just cruel."

"It was more than that. When people were turned down for mortgages, G&K found a fresh way to pad their pocketbooks. They colluded with loan processors who were willing to overlook forged payment stubs and tax returns. They bribed property assessors to inflate the property values of homes. In doing so, they were able to secure inflated mortgages for borrowers—who had no idea what was going on, by the way—to put money in their own pockets. Over the course of about a decade, they took in hundreds of millions of dollars."

Leslie shook her head slowly. "And you're saying Vinnie was involved in that?"

"He was a small cog in a very big machine. He found and befriended a lot of the buyers. He earned their trust, then worked with the assessors and processors to get the deals done. From my research, it seemed that Jeremy Kinnison was the mastermind."

"He wasn't even there, though. I remember cleaning the office after his going-away party."

Nate had forgotten how well Leslie knew these people.

She'd cleaned their building, and she'd hired Marisa to help her. That's how Marisa and Vinnie had met in the first place. "Right. Kinnison was smart and cashed out before Vinnie started working there. But Charles Gray carried on his practices and even expanded on them. The whole scheme was a series of felony on top of felony on top of felony that screwed thousands of buyers out of millions of dollars."

"Wow. Charles seemed like such a nice guy. Vinnie, though, I was never sure."

"Vinnie was going to do the right thing."

"Or go to prison. I wouldn't call that noble."

"Better than warning Charles. Or running. But your sister said he'd become disillusioned. One of the borrowers had tracked him down and threatened him. Told him how he'd lost his house, lost everything, because of what Vinnie had done."

"So Vinnie grew a conscience," Leslie said. "That's good, I guess. Except probably why Charles had him killed. And at the end of the day, when it all hit the fan, the money was gone."

"Apparently, at some point after Charles was arrested for Vinnie's murder, but before the feds searched the building, the money in both Charles's personal account and in the business's operating account was funneled out. Millions of dollars, and the feds never found it."

"Why do they think Marisa took it?"

He nodded to her. "Because of your business, of course. The money was stolen at night, and she had access because she cleaned the building."

"But all the employees had access."

"But as far as anyone knows," Nate said, "only Marisa knew the feds were coming."

"How do they think she got access to it, though? She's not some super computer hacker."

"That's a good question. I don't know."

Leslie sat back and crossed her arms. "It doesn't make sense. I never believed she took it. Even now...I don't know what to think."

"Obviously, somebody else knew what was going on. Because Marisa didn't take it."

Leslie sighed, looked away. "The people who threatened me seemed pretty sure."

"They are wrong, Leslie. Your sister wouldn't—"

"Of course *you* believe her." Leslie laughed, but he wasn't sure of the joke.

"Meaning what?"

"Oh, come on." Her smile seemed forced. "You think I don't see how you look at her? How every man in the whole world looks at her?" Leslie looked away a moment. When she looked back, her expression had softened. "Did you know that when she was in high school, some modeling agency offered to represent her? I thought it was probably a scam and did some research."

"That was nice—"

"No, it wasn't." She shook her head. "I think I was jealous. Okay, I know I was jealous. I wanted it to be a scam, because things always came easy for her. She acted like I was this awesome big sister, but really...I was always jealous."

Nate wasn't sure how to respond, so he said nothing.

"Anyway, the modeling agency was totally legitimate. A swanky upscale place in Manhattan. I got there, found it filled with tall, skinny girls, just like Marisa. She could have done it."

Nate wasn't surprised, though maybe it wasn't nice to say so. "Why didn't she?"

"She thought about it. And Mom was all for it—which is probably why she didn't do it. She was in a rebellious stage. That and her father didn't want her to."

The way Leslie said *father* made Nate ask, "You didn't like her father?"

Leslie looked at her hands. "He was my father for a few years, too. He and Mom married when I was about a year old. He was the only father I'd ever known. And he loved me, treated me really good. I knew they were trying to have a kid, and I was happy about it. I wanted a little brother or sister to play with. Marisa was born when I was seven, and it was like Daddy forgot I existed. They divorced a few years later, and to me, Daddy became Carlos, Marisa's father."

"What about your own father?"

She shrugged. "Never knew him. Mom never told me anything about him."

"Your mother passed away, right?"

"Yeah, I'm an orphan. Like Ana." Her smile was sad. "At least me and my niece have something in common."

"Marisa, too, right? Didn't her father die?"

"He was killed in a motorcycle accident a year before Mom died. But at least she had a dad all those years."

He tried for a gentle tone. "None of that was your sister's fault, you know."

"I know. I love Marisa. I'd do anything for her. But...well, everyone thinks she has the money. Except you. I'm just saying, just 'cause she looks like an angel doesn't mean she is one."

Hadn't he had that very thought? "Point taken. But if she had millions of dollars, why would she be living in a tiny Mexican village?"

"Well, we don't actually know where she lives." Her gaze scanned the lobby a moment before she turned back to him and smiled. "But I know you're right. Of course she didn't steal it. She was always so good. Not perfect, of course. I used to be so jealous of her, but now... Well, it's not like her life's been all roses and cream, right? The last few years with her gone, I've

realized how much she means to me. I just want my sister back."
Leslie blew out a long breath. "But I have to find that money, or
they're going to kill me."

"We're not going to let that happen, Leslie." His words
carried a confidence he didn't feel. "We'll figure it out."

SIX

Marisa was used to men looking at her and usually paid no attention to it. It wasn't as if she had anything to do with the way she looked. A gift of genes and luck. She hadn't done much to enhance her appearance in years. But tonight, she blew her hair dry with the dryer the hotel provided and left it down. She couldn't remember the last time she hadn't worn it in a braid. She even borrowed some of Leslie's makeup—not that her sister wore much. And with the new dress, she was pleased with the results.

When she and Ana stepped off the elevator, the awe in Nate's expression woke up places Marisa had let lie fallow for years. She tried not to smile, failed, and gave in as she followed Ana across the tile floor to where Nate and Leslie were seated. They stood as Marisa and Ana neared.

Nate stared at her until her cheeks warmed. Finally, he shifted his gaze to Ana. "You look so pretty."

"Thank you for the dress, Uncle Nate. It's a little long, but Mama says I'll grow into it, and when I grow out of it, I can give it to anyone I want at the whole orphanage." She turned and looked at Marisa. "As long as it's someone littler than me, right, Mama? Like I can't give it to Abby, 'cause she's my size. Right?"

"Right. Maybe little Julianna, though."

"*Si! Bueno!* I'll give it to her." She held out the skirt and twirled, face to the ceiling. "I'm the prettiest girl in the room." She stopped. "Right, Uncle Nate?"

He nodded solemnly. "Absolutely."

Marisa had to agree. Ana had never looked so pretty. If they were in the States, Marisa would buy her daughter new clothes all the time. And take her to the zoo and the park, where she could run and play and feed the ducks and pigeons.

She pushed away the thoughts. Their lives were fine. Better than Ana would have had if Marisa hadn't found her. Better than Marisa could have dreamed when she escaped New York. She couldn't focus on what they didn't have. With Nate so close, that was harder than usual.

He met her eyes. "Wow. You look... Man, I don't even..."

A moment passed. Finally, Marisa winked at Leslie. "He's a writer, you know."

Leslie laughed, and Nate joined her. He banged on the side of his head as if trying to shake something loose and started over. "You look very nice, Marisa. Shall we go?"

She took Ana's hand. "Where are we headed?"

Leslie led the way to the glass doors. "I'd like to hit that shopping plaza you guys went to earlier, if you don't mind."

Marisa shrugged. "Fine with me. There were a bunch of restaurants there. As long as we can go someplace where I can get a good old American hamburger."

They walked along the sidewalk toward the plaza, Ana stopping to look at every flower and lizard and bird along the way.

Nate walked slightly behind the girls on the narrow sidewalk. "Marisa," he said about halfway there. "Tell us how you ended up in this town you keep talking about."

She turned to look at him. "It's a long story."

"I'd like to hear it," Leslie said.

Marisa sighed. "Okay. Well, I'd moved to Mexico City."

"Why there?" Leslie asked.

"That's another long story. Which one do you want to hear?"

She shrugged, and Marisa continued. "I was teaching English at a private school. It was fine, but Mexico City isn't New York, and I was wishing I could go someplace less... I don't know. Less dangerous. Less ugly, maybe. Anyway, one day this man approached me and told me his sister's kids were in my class and learning a lot from me—a lot more than they'd learned before. He wanted to know if I'd consider moving to teach English elsewhere, so his own kids could learn. He promised me a clean house and a steady job and a decent salary.

"Of course I asked for more information, and he told me where the place was. I'd hoped it was in the north where it's a little cooler." She smiled and wiped her brow. "No deal. But the pay was good, better than I was making, and with the promise of a house, I would have all the money I needed. Which is very little around here, you know?"

Marisa looked back to Nate, who smiled, though it seemed forced.

Leslie nodded. "So tell us about this guy."

"I had no idea what he did for a living, but he seemed nice." She paused, knowing they wouldn't like it. "He's a drug lord. The biggest one in town. I traveled with him and his family back to our village, and they moved me into the house across the street from the orphanage. The orphanage runs the school in town. All the kids go there."

"Did you have something going on with this guy?" Leslie asked. "I mean, surely he liked you for more than just your stellar English skills."

"He was married. He wanted me to teach his kids."

"It's not like it would be the first time a guy got a little some-thing on the side."

"I'd like to think you know me better than that, Leslie. He was a married drug lord. You really think I'd mess around with a guy like that?"

Leslie shrugged. "Well, Vinnie wasn't exactly squeaky clean."

"I didn't know about that. And he wasn't married. And Vinnie was a good guy. He was going to do the right thing."

"Just seems like that drug dealer wouldn't give you a great job and a house for nothing."

"What is wrong with you?" Marisa hissed the words so Ana wouldn't hear. "I'm a good English teacher, and I'm good with the kids, and he knew that. I can't believe you think—"

"I don't think anything. I'm just trying to figure out how you ended up here."

Nate physically stepped between them, so the three were shoulder-to-shoulder on the narrow sidewalk. "I'm sure you didn't do anything wrong, Marisa." He looked at Leslie, and Marisa imagined the look he might have given her.

"Of course." Leslie sighed. "I didn't mean anything by it."

Nate turned to Marisa. "Are you and this drug lord still on good terms?"

"I quit taking his money when I realized where it came from, but the orphanage pays me just fine. He understood, and nobody gives me a hard time. Everybody knows that Ramón is my...friend, I guess. At first people were a little scared of me. I think they thought what Leslie thought—that something was going on between us. But after a while, people accepted me. I have friends there." She looked past Nate to Leslie. "Friends who believe in me."

"I never said I didn't."

"Whatever."

They walked in silence a few minutes. Nate broke it with, "Is that why you feel safe there?"

"Nobody messes with me."

"Good. That's good. Not that it's healthy to be friends with drug dealers, but if he can protect you..."

"He appreciates how well his kids are learning English. He's hoping to send them to the States for college."

"Oh, good," Leslie said. "Just what America needs, up-and-coming drug lords." She softened the jab with a wink. Typical Leslie. Incapable of saying anything encouraging.

Marisa glared at her sister. "I'm hoping the kids choose a different profession than their father did."

Nate chuckled. "You two are hilarious. Did you fight like this when you were kids?"

Marisa said, "She started it."

"Did not!"

Their laughter filled the sidewalk as they continued to walk.

THE RESTAURANT they chose was located near the center of the market overlooking the fountain. Like many places, it was open to the outside, just separated from the passersby by well-spaced pillars and oversized pots of flowers. Local music was piped through speakers, barely heard over the conversations of the diners and the clattering of dishes.

As soon as they sat, a server placed a large bowl of tortilla chips in the center of the table and small bowls of salsa and queso in front of each of them—perfect for little Ana, who dug right in. Marisa ordered a cheeseburger and fries and tried not to notice Nate's stare as she conversed with the waiter in Spanish.

Most of the meal was spent laughing, catching up, and

shooting pictures with their phones. Nate promised to get the photos printed for her, especially the ones of Leslie and Ana, if she could share her address.

If only they could've been a real family. At least her sister'd had the opportunity to meet her daughter. It would have to be enough.

Dinner was enjoyable, but beyond the laughter and stories, the seriousness of their visit hung over them like steam from the fajitas the servers carried by. They smelled so good, Marisa almost wanted to order some of those, too. When they got home, she would miss the variety of delicious food she'd sampled on her visit to Acapulco. It had taken her a long time to get accustomed to the local diet. Now she'd have to do it all over again. Totally worth it, she thought, as she bit into her cheeseburger. She ate every bite.

Ana scarfed down her french fries. "These are yummy, Mama! We should make them every day!"

"You know Carlita doesn't like to fry foods. It's not healthy."

"Maybe we can make them at home. Miss Carlita won't even know!"

Marisa giggled. "We'll see, pajarita."

Ana pointed to the fountain. "Can I go play, please?"

Marisa looked around and saw mostly families, tourists, wandering by. The fountain was only a few feet away, just beyond the half-wall between the restaurant and the market. And Ana was very well behaved. "Promise to stay where I can see you, okay?"

"Sí, Mama."

"Remember, if you can't see me—"

"Then you can't see me. I know, I know."

Sometimes, her daughter seemed four going on fourteen.

"Okay. Be good."

Ana skipped away, and Marisa turned back to Leslie, who was pulling out her credit card.

The waitress cleared the table. "You want anything else?"

"No, thanks," Leslie said.

Nate had twisted in his seat to watch Ana, who'd climbed on the edge of the fountain and was walking around it as if it were an oversize balance beam.

"Nate?"

He turned to her. "You really think she's okay?"

Marisa's seat faced her daughter, so she could keep her in view. "She's fine. Have you talked to Leslie about what you think she should do?"

Leslie looked at Nate. "What?"

He leaned forward and blew out a short breath. "You're not going to like it, but you don't have any choice. You're going to need to go to the police."

Leslie pushed back in her chair, scraping it loudly against the tile. "No. No way. They said they'd kill me."

Marisa leaned toward her. "But what choice do you have? The police can protect you."

"Says the girl living in Mexico."

Marisa sat back, kept her eyes on Ana. She hadn't trusted the police to protect her, true. "But they thought I stole the money, too. I was afraid they'd throw me in prison. Or, even if they did believe me, by the time I convinced them, Charles and his guys would have killed me."

"I know. I understood at the time, anyway. But running made you look guilty. Maybe you should've stayed, proved—"

"How could I prove it?" She glanced at Nate. "I had no alibi for that night. I hadn't left my hotel room."

"You could have tried," Leslie said. "Instead, you ran away. And left me holding the bag."

"What bag? How did it affect you at all?"

"It's affecting me now!" Leslie's shout had heads turning from the surrounding tables.

Nate leaned forward, between them. "Let's calm down. Arguing isn't going to help."

Leslie crossed her arms. Marisa kept her focus on Ana, who was teetering as if about to fall into the water. Marisa started to get up, but Ana straightened and continued her stroll along the edge of the fountain. One wrong move and she'd go over. Marisa prayed she'd land softly in the water and not against the brick pavers on the other side.

All she wanted was for her daughter to be safe. She looked back at Leslie's scowl. She wanted her sister to be safe, too.

Marisa sighed. "I never meant for you to get hurt."

"But here we are."

"I don't know how to help you. I have no idea who took the money."

"You must have some guesses," Leslie said. "You need to come back with us—"

"Absolutely not." Marisa pushed back from the table, then made herself stay seated. "I can't."

Nate faced Leslie. "How would that help?"

"Maybe Marisa knows something she hasn't even thought of yet."

"She and I went over all of it. Many times. I don't think—"

"God forbid something happens to Marisa." She turned to her sister. "What? Are you afraid they'll find you, after all these years?"

"I am, obviously, or I wouldn't still live here." She leaned toward her sister and held out her hand. "But I don't want anything to happen to you, either."

Leslie slipped her hand into Marisa's and squeezed. Leslie had never been the touchy-feely type, and the gesture meant a lot to Marisa. "I'm sorry I'm being such a jerk," Leslie said. "I never understood before how you felt when you ran away. Now, I think I do, at least a little. It's hard believing people want to hurt you. And look at all you've done here. I so admire you for making a life like you have. And I miss you so much." She looked at the table, took a deep breath, and looked back up. "You know how I get when things are out of my control. I'm not mad at you. I'm just... I'm scared. Will you forgive me?"

"Of course. Always." She checked on Ana, saw Nate was watching her daughter, and focused on Leslie. "I want to help. I just don't know how."

"Help me figure out who stole the money."

"They're not going to hurt you." Nate turned his attention to Leslie, so Marisa watched Ana.

"You're the only chance they have at getting their money," Nate said. "As long as they think you can get them the money, you're safe. You have to go to the police before they realize you can't help them."

Leslie pulled her hand out of Marisa's. "No way!"

Marisa blew out an exasperated breath. Her sister was still stubborn as a jackass. Daddy had always said that, and now that Marisa had seen enough jackasses in Mexico to last a lifetime, she had to agree.

"Please, Marisa." Leslie leaned across the table and took her hand again. Marisa could feel her sister shaking. "Please help me."

Marisa squeezed. "If not for Ana, I would risk anything to protect you. Truly. But I can't take her out of the country. She's not legally my daughter." Marisa considered the situation. "Why don't you stay here with us?"

Leslie yanked her hand back. "Right. And do what?"

"I don't know. I could get you a job at the orphanage, or somewhere in Chilpancingo." Marisa loved this idea—to have her sister close by! "You could live with me until—"

"I'm not moving to Mexico. Are you nuts? What about my business?"

Marisa sat back. "I'm sorry. I'm just—"

"Why can't you leave Ana at that orphanage you keep talking about?"

"I'm not going to leave her. What kind of a mother—?"

"You're not even her mother yet. And we're not talking about leaving her forever. Just until we figure this out."

"It's been eight years, Leslie. After all this time, what do you think I can tell you that you don't already know? That Nate and the authorities don't already know?"

Tears filled Leslie's eyes. "I don't know. It's just my life, but hey, don't worry about it. Your daughter's more important than your sister."

"I never said that, just—"

"Forget it." Leslie pushed her chair back and stormed around the corner toward the restrooms.

Marisa sat back and sighed. "What am I supposed to do?"

Nate's eyes softened. "It's an impossible choice."

"If I thought I could help, I would. I'd try, anyway. But I have no idea who stole the money. Never did. Doesn't she think that if I knew, I would have told the FBI? I mean, I'm here because everyone thinks I took it."

"I know. Your sister knows, too. She's just scared."

Ana had stepped back onto the ground and was leaning over the edge of the fountain, her fingers dipping inside. She was probably trying to figure out how to get to the pennies below. Marisa looked back at Nate, who'd shifted his gaze to watch Ana, too.

There was nothing else Marisa could do. They needed to return to Chilpancingo tomorrow and catch a ride home with the guys from her village. At least she and Ana would be safe. If Leslie didn't want to join her, that was her choice.

Leslie returned from the restroom and approached Ana, and the two of them sat on the side of the fountain and talked.

"I'm glad they got to meet," Marisa said. "I've talked about Leslie a lot, tried to tell her about the rest of our family."

Now that Ana was safe with Leslie, Marisa could focus on Nate. His warm brown eyes held hers, and he reached out and took her hand. "You're a wonderful mother. I'm proud of what you're doing here in Mexico. Your sister would be, too, if she weren't so scared."

Poor Leslie. Marisa knew exactly how it felt to be targeted, threatened, given impossible choices. Leslie had been her rock after their mother died. They were both orphans then, since Daddy'd already been gone a year at that point. But Leslie'd been older, established. Aside from her father's family in Puerto Rico, whom Marisa had never met, Leslie was Marisa's only relative.

She'd do anything to help her sister, except abandon her daughter. Tears stung her eyes.

"Hey," Nate said. "It's going to be okay."

Marisa wiped them away with her free hand, the other still gripped in Nate's. She felt safe when he was with her, always had. Hadn't he kept her safe in New York all those years ago? Maybe he could do the same for Leslie. "How is it going to be okay?"

His gaze dipped to the table. "I don't know."

"You'll help her, though?"

He looked up with a sad expression she couldn't identify. "A lot of stuff has happened. I don't know how much help I could be, honestly. She needs to go to the police."

Marisa was about to ask about that stuff when she spotted Leslie and Ana walking toward her, holding hands.

"We're going for a walk," Leslie said. "She wants to show me a toy store she saw yesterday."

Marisa stood. "Okay. Sounds good."

"We thought we'd go alone, if that's all right with you."

"I'd rather stay with her."

"Don't you trust me?"

"It's not that, Leslie." She stifled the irritation. "I just don't usually leave her."

"I'm her aunt." Leslie squeezed Ana's hand. "We'll be fine. We want to get to know each other a little."

Marisa looked from one to the other. "Okay. I guess. We'll meet you back here in... How long?"

"An hour. Okay?"

Marisa nodded and sat back down and watched them leave. As soon as they were out of sight, she stood. "Let's go."

"We could stay. You want to get a drink?"

"I don't drink."

"Still?"

"I need to stay on my toes. Always. Alcohol makes you vulnerable." She took in Nate's tall, strong frame. "Well, maybe not you, but it makes me vulnerable."

Nate gave her a look she couldn't quite decipher. "I understand being vulnerable." He stood, and they walked to the entrance of the restaurant. "Where are we going?"

"I never leave Ana anywhere alone but the neighbor's and the orphanage, and even then, I'm always close by."

"You left her with me yesterday."

She had, hadn't she? "Well, that was different. There are too many people around here. I'm just being paranoid, I know, but we're going to follow them."

"Let's go."

THE SHOPPING PLAZA had filled with tourists while they'd been at dinner. Now, with the evening coming, tiny lights lit up the trees and bushes that dotted the outdoor market. American music Marisa didn't recognize was piped through hidden speakers, just loud enough to make the atmosphere festive. Laughter filtered from the many restaurants they passed, as did the scent of every kind of food imaginable. Marisa was full, but if she spotted an ice cream place, she might have to force down a scoop. She couldn't remember the last time she'd had ice cream.

Marisa and Nate followed Leslie and Ana, who held hands and window-shopped. After about ten minutes, they ducked into the toy store. Marisa leaned against a large planter a couple of stores down to wait.

Nate perched beside her. "If your sister knew you were following her, would she be annoyed?"

Marisa shrugged. "She wouldn't understand. If she were annoyed, I'd probably deserve it. Leslie was a good big sister. I'm sure she'll be a fine aunt."

"But you're worried."

"Not about Leslie's ability to watch her. It's just... There are people who want me dead. That's not a fear you get over."

Nate stared toward the store's front door and nodded. "I know what you mean."

Seemed he did, too. Interesting.

"It's been a while," Marisa said. "Maybe we should go in and check on them."

Nate checked his watch. "It's been three minutes."

"Oh." She tapped her foot. "It feels longer."

Nate nodded. "So tell me what your life is like."

"We get up, dress, and walk to the orphanage for breakfast. We stay there until late afternoon, after siesta. Most everybody rests."

"Not you?"

"I never got into the habit. I read or prepare lesson plans. It's a quiet time in our village. My least favorite time of the day. My thoughts sometimes drift to New York and what the streets would look like. To how many people would be out at that time." She forced a smile. "But there's no place I'd rather be than with Ana."

"You really miss New York."

"Yes. And no. I miss America. I miss warm showers and soft sheets and all the luxuries that seem like necessities. I miss tall trees and snow and warm boots and..." She watched the store front. Even this place seemed a million miles from her little village. "I'm not sure I could go back to the city now that I've become accustomed to rural life. Even here in Acapulco, all the noises and all the people—strange faces I don't recognize. It makes me nervous."

"You could probably get used to it again."

She could get used to this. To Nate, to the feeling of safety she had when she was with him. To those warm brown eyes peering at her so intently. She'd missed those eyes. Even when she was still grieving Vinnie, she'd known Nate was special. He'd changed since then. She suddenly really wanted to know why. "What about you? I saw you quit—"

"There they are." Nate nodded to the store's entrance, where Leslie and Ana stepped out, hand-in-hand. Ana swung a plastic bag in her other hand and filled the air with her chatter. They turned in the opposite direction from where Nate and Marisa sat and continued their stroll. "They still have forty-five minutes."

"I wonder if Leslie will get tired of her?"

"How could she?" Nate asked. "Ana's delightful. I'm more worried about Ana getting tired of Leslie."

Marisa batted his arm. "Stop. That's not nice."

"Sorry." His smile said he wasn't, but she didn't push it. Leslie hadn't been herself on this trip. She'd been argumentative and short-tempered, unusual for Marisa's big sister. But after what she'd gone through, it was understandable.

They passed a jewelry store, and Nate paused. Marisa peered over his shoulder to see the display of watches. "Nice. You going to get one?"

"Those are Rolexes." He pointed to a gold one. "That's probably fifteen, maybe twenty grand."

She stuck her nose in the air. "Cheap junk. I much prefer a Timex."

As he chuckled, a local came out of the store and approached. "You would like to look, maybe for the lady?"

She giggled. "Go ahead. I'm going to keep following."

"Um..."

She walked away before he could say anything else. She didn't want to lose Leslie and Ana, but Nate didn't have to share her paranoia. If he couldn't find her, they'd all just meet at the restaurant. Though she'd prefer to spend the hour with Nate, maybe she'd be better off walking away. Everything about him was magnetic. She couldn't get pulled in.

And she didn't need him to walk with her. She could do this alone. The thought had her checking over her shoulders. Shoppers, tourists, employees. She was safe here.

She peered ahead, through the throng of people who suddenly seemed to be moving at the speed of cold honey. Leslie and Ana had to be just ahead. After a minute, Marisa still didn't see them. "*¡Perdóneme!* Excuse me," she muttered as she pressed through the crowd. Her stomach filled with panic. Foolish. Her daughter was with her sister. And Leslie would take good care of Ana.

Tell that to Marisa's racing heart.

She reached the stairs that led to the road at the entrance to the shopping plaza and looked down. There they were, crossing the street toward the bay. The traffic had stopped for the light, but one car whizzed from far down the street in the empty right lane, gunning straight toward them. Marisa opened her mouth to shout a warning, but there was no way Leslie could hear her. The car approached faster, and Marisa had a flash of insight, what life would be like without the two people she loved most in the world. The thought stole her hope.

At the last second, the car screeched on its brakes and slid toward them.

Leslie yanked Ana forward, and the two bolted to the far side. They'd barely touched the sidewalk when the car sped by.

Marisa leaned against the stair rail, breathing as if she'd just run a marathon, and watched as Leslie and Ana made their way to the water, untouched.

Marisa sat on the top step away from the crowds and watched them walk in the gentle waves. Ana was diligent to keep her dress lifted high, so it didn't get wet. She was careful with her things, the few she had. Her daughter had learned to appreciate possessions like most American kids never would. Not that Marisa wanted that for her. She wished she could spoil Ana like Daddy had spoiled her.

If only Ana had a father like that.

Any father at all.

Marisa checked her watch—not even the quality of a Timex. It was nearly time to meet back at the restaurant. Marisa had assumed Nate would eventually find her—she wished he had— but when he didn't show, she figured she'd wait for Leslie and Ana and head back with them.

The two were walking back toward the road now, shoes and shopping bag hanging from Leslie's hand. Ana kept stopping to pick up shells. The two made a beautiful picture against the fading light of the setting sun. If only Marisa and Ana could return to the States. They could all be a family.

And there was Nate, on the sidewalk on this side of the

street, right below her. He must have left from a different entrance and been circling. He spotted Marisa, and she waved and pointed at Ana and Leslie just as they reached the crosswalk.

Though the light hadn't turned red, a van stopped suddenly on the street in front of Leslie and Ana. Another car's horn blasted, and the car barely avoided crashing into the back of the van.

Nate had turned back to Marisa. She pointed at the van. He glanced at it, then back. His eyes widened, and he opened his mouth to yell.

Someone grabbed Marisa from behind. She turned to look, but a man pulled her close, wrapped his arms around her, and covered her head with a heavy coat. He yanked her toward him, and she lost her footing and crashed against his chest. Her nose filled with the scent of body odor and raw power.

She fought to get away, but his arms squeezed her like a vice. He pulled her with him, and she stumbled along, trying to fight, unable to do anything.

She screamed. The sound was muffled inside his heavy coat. They'd gone just a few feet when she heard Nate's voice. "Let her go!"

The man did, yanking his heavy coat with him.

Marisa gasped in fresh air, stumbled, and banged her shoulder into the stone face of the market. She turned just as Nate reached her.

The pounding of the man's footsteps faded as he rounded a corner in the market and disappeared.

Nate gripped her arms and looked into her eyes. "Are you okay?"

Marisa nodded and turned to check if Ana had seen. She hoped she hadn't. How it would scare her to watch her mother accosted.

But her daughter wasn't there.

"Leslie and Ana." Marisa peered down the stairs. She peered at the crosswalk. She peered at the sidewalk. Her sister and her daughter had been there just a moment before. They should have been staring back up at her, waving, smiling.

But the place they'd stood was empty.

SEVEN

NATE SCANNED THE AREA. Leslie and Ana had to be close by. They had to be.

Only seconds had passed since he'd seen them.

His heart still raced after seeing that man grab Marisa. What had his endgame been? If his plan had been to kidnap her, it had been flawed, considering that without going down the many stairs to the street, he wasn't going to get far with her. Maybe he'd planned to drag her into a dark room. Nate didn't want to think about what might have happened next.

He glanced at Marisa, whose gaze was still darting around. "Where are they?" The pitch of her voice rose to near-panic mode.

He stepped closer and placed a hand on her shoulder, trying to calm her down. "They have to be here somewhere. Maybe they..." He tried to come up with a plausible explanation. But beyond the street was just the sand, and beyond the sand was just the water. He studied the beach in the fading light, but none of the silhouettes looked like them.

"What?" Marisa stepped away and turned to him. "Maybe they what? Where could they be?"

"Maybe they forgot something on the beach."

She started walking down the steps. "We should go over there."

He took her elbow. "We have a great vantage point right here."

She climbed back to the top of the steps and looked like she was going to walk back down. In the yellow lights of the plaza, he could see her face pale. "The van. Where did it go?"

He looked back to the street. The van was gone.

"Someone took them!"

"Why would somebody—?"

"Oh, my God. We have to call the police. Do you have a phone?" She looked around frantically, as if a cop might materialize.

A phone rang. She looked at him, but the ring wasn't familiar.

"That's not my phone," Nate said. "It must be yours."

"I don't have a phone." She looked around, but there were no people within ten yards of them.

His heart sunk into a deep crevice that felt frighteningly familiar. "Look in your bag."

She shook her head. "I don't have a phone, and we don't have time..."

It rang again. The sound was clearly coming from her new colorful bag.

"Maybe that guy dropped it," she said.

A stone formed in Nate's stomach, twisting and expanding as the seconds passed. "Please answer it, Marisa."

She dug through her bag and pulled out a cheap phone. He looked, saw the number was blocked. She pressed the button. "Si."

She listened for a moment. "Yes." Her expression confirmed his fear.

He leaned in.

"By now..." The man's voice was marked by a heavy New York accent. "You must realize we have your sister and your daughter."

Marisa crumpled. He wrapped his arm around her and helped her sit on the stairs.

"Marisa," the man said. "You need to answer me. You understand I have them, right?"

"Yes."

"Do you want to see them again?"

"Please, whatever you want me to do. Just... Please, let's do a trade. You can take me and let them go."

"If I wanted to take you, I would have you. You understand?"

She looked at Nate, eyes imploring. He nodded, and she said, "Yes."

"That man who's with you, Nate. Is he listening?"

Nate nodded again, and Marisa said, "Yes."

"Okay, good. You two need to get the money that was stolen from Charles Gray's account. Two million. You have one week. We'll make the trade in the States."

"Wait, but—"

"Keep that phone with you, and I'll call with the details."

"But I don't know where the money is."

"I would prefer small bills."

"I'm not lying. Please, I'll do anything to get my daughter back—"

"Get me the money or show me who has it. That's the deal."

"Who are you?"

"Money or proof. Do you understand? Yes or no."

She opened her mouth, but Nate shook his head. He put his hand over hers on the phone and leaned it toward him. "We need to talk to Leslie and Ana, make sure they're all right."

A moment passed, and Nate feared the man had hung up. But then Leslie's voice said, "Marisa?"

"Oh, thank God." Marisa angled the phone toward her. "Are you okay? Is Ana okay?"

"We're fine. Please just do as he says."

"Can I talk to Ana?"

A second passed before Ana said, "Mama?"

"Baby, are you all right?"

She didn't answer into the phone, but they could hear her crying over the man's voice when he spoke again.

"One week. Get me the money or proof, and don't go to the police. You understand?"

"I understand."

The line went dead.

NATE GUIDED Marisa to rest on the step and sat beside her. He wrapped his arm around her back, whispering words of encouragement that he didn't believe. Because how in the world were they going to come up with two million dollars in seven days?

The phone still gripped in Marisa's hand, she crossed her arms, laid them on her legs, and dropped her head on top. Her shoulders shook from her sobs.

"Shh. It's going to be okay."

"What if they hurt them? What if they...?"

"Don't think about it. It won't help you to think about it. We just have to focus on doing the next thing."

She looked up. "How can you say that? How can I not worry?"

"I know you can't stop, Marisa. But I also know worry and fear aren't going to get your daughter back. We have to go."

"But..." The word floated on the humid air while Nate

watched her process the information she had. He knew when she got there by the determination he saw in her eyes. "I have to go back. I have to go back to New York."

"To the States, yes. We can't do this from here."

She pushed herself away from him. "Do what?" she demanded. "What are we supposed to do?"

"We have to figure out who took the money."

"I have no idea. I never knew. Oh, my God, he's going to kill them. He's going to—"

"Marisa, stop."

She blinked and nodded.

"Let's go back to the hotel."

"But how—?"

The words of his therapist fell off his tongue. "We're going to do the next thing. We're not going to worry about what comes three or twenty-three steps down the road. Right now, we're going to go to the hotel. Can we just do that, please?"

She stood. Silently, they went down the steps to the street. She was in no shape to walk, so Nate hailed a taxi.

He held Marisa's hand while his own fear settled on him heavier than the scent of body odor and tobacco in the old car. Could Marisa hear his heart pounding? It was all well and good to tell her to focus on the next thing, but how could she do that? How could he? He couldn't stop thinking about what Leslie and Ana were going through. The memories all came back—the ropes chafing his wrist, the blood dripping from his head. The fear, the overarching, debilitating fear.

And this wasn't one of those false trigger moments, either. Somehow, he'd landed smack dab in the middle of another life-or-death situation. He squeezed his eyes closed, hoped against reason that he'd manage this one better than he had the last.

He just had to get through this minute. The next, he'd handle in sixty seconds. Marisa needed him. Leslie and Ana needed him. He would do this. It might destroy him, but he'd do it.

At the hotel, Nate led the way to her room. "Get all of your sister's things. I'll wait."

"Why?"

"Just do that, okay?"

She walked inside slowly, like she might collapse from the weight on her shoulders. He held the door open and waited while she did as he'd told her. She gathered her own, too, shoving them in the ugly canvas bag. Tears dripped from her eyes as she lifted Ana's clothes and held them to her face. She pushed them in the bag, too, and stepped into the bathroom.

He'd seen Marisa like this before, after Vinnie died. The way she'd shut down sometimes, when the fear overwhelmed her—he'd feared for her safety. Not that she might commit suicide, but that, in her grief, she might do something to expose herself to Gray's men. There was only so much a mind could take.

Didn't he know it.

She emerged from the bathroom carrying the clothes she and Ana had worn the first day, dry now. She stuck them in the bag. "I'm ready. Now what?"

He stepped in the room, lifted the bags, and led her to his room. He got her settled in the desk chair, where she stared, still crying, at the wall.

"You want to turn on the TV?"

She shook her head.

"A drink? Anything?"

She didn't say anything.

He searched Leslie's things. Sure enough, he found a folded piece of paper bearing the confirmation code for their return tickets. Their flight was scheduled to leave at eight o'clock, two mornings later. He dug some more and came up with her passport.

He grabbed the phone, started to dial, and stopped. The pit in his stomach hadn't moved since that phone had rung at the shopping plaza. Right now, it expanded. "Marisa?"

She blinked and looked at him.

"Do you have your passport?"

Her eyes narrowed and she shook her head. "Yes, but no, not here. I have it hidden at home."

"How far do you live from here?"

"The bus is an hour and a half, and then we hitch a ride—"

"If I rent a car, how far is it?"

She shrugged. "I've never... Probably two hours or so."

"Okay." He used the hotel phone to call the airline. It took some finagling, but he managed to switch his flight and make a reservation for Marisa for the next morning. He checked his watch—about twelve hours from now. Well, it wasn't like they'd get any sleep, anyway.

Marisa watched him. When he hung up, she said, "What are we doing?"

"Why don't you use my computer to figure out how to get to your home? We can send the directions to my phone after, okay?"

"Your phone works here?"

"I have an international plan. I used to travel a lot."

"Okay." She crossed the room to his laptop.

He dialed the concierge and asked for a rental car. The concierge apologized profusely but said they were hard to come by. "Maybe tomorrow?"

Nate hung up. No cars. This was a problem.

"What's going on?"

"Nothing." He could hire a taxi or buy a car. Or maybe... He called Luis. After explaining who he was, he said, "I'll give you five hundred dollars if you let me borrow your car overnight."

"I drive you," the taxi driver said. "Where you want to go?"

Nate didn't want to explain the situation to Luis, and he didn't want to tell the man where they were going. No need to expose Marisa's home, in case she was ever able to return there.

"You remember the pretty lady we met at the chapel?"

"*Muy hermoso*. Very beautiful."

"Well, I sort of have a romantic evening planned, but I can't seem to get a rental car."

More finagling, but Luis finally agreed when Nate promised to have it back to him by seven in the morning. He didn't mention that he'd probably be leaving it at the airport. For five hundred dollars, Luis could manage a little inconvenience.

When he hung up, Marisa said, "Are you going to tell me what the plan is?"

"We're going to get your passport. We're on a flight tomorrow morning." He paused, closed his eyes, and said, "Is your passport still valid?"

"*Sí*. I renewed it before it expired."

He blew out a long breath. "Thank God."

"You believe in God?"

He went into the bathroom and filled his shaving kit. He returned and threw it in the suitcase.

"Do you?" she asked.

"I don't know. Right now, I..." He looked around. Was he missing anything?

His phone charger. He unplugged it and stared at it. His phone was almost dead, but they didn't have time to charge it. He'd have to buy a car charger in the store in the lobby—if they had one.

"Your phone won't work."

He looked up. "What?"

"Once we get out of Acapulco, it probably won't work. The service is spotty. Maybe we can print these directions."

Seemed he wouldn't need a charger after all.

"Figure out how to print them. Call the concierge if you need to." Not that he couldn't do it in half the time the way she was moving, but he needed to keep her busy.

"Okay." She made the call, and he finished packing. When she hung up, she told him where the printers were located.

Fifteen minutes later, he left Marisa in the hotel room with all their bags—one didn't need luggage for a romantic date—and went to the lobby. He printed the directions to Marisa's village and met Luis in front of the hotel. Nate had withdrawn enough money from his savings account to make up the five hundred. Luis pocketed the money with tears in his eyes. "This will help us. You don't know."

Nate clasped him on the shoulder. "I promise to take good care of your car. I'll call you when it's back, okay?"

"Sí." He winked. "Have a good time."

When Luis was out of sight, Nate ran up the stairs and got Marisa and all their stuff. They left without checking out.

IT WAS NEARLY eleven and too dark to see much by the time they pulled into Marisa's village. The village seemed to be a couple of streets of one-story, flat-roofed buildings. The main street was gravel, but the rest looked like packed dirt. On the right was an old Spanish mission with an arched facade, an ancient door, and what looked like a belfry on top.

"That's the orphanage," Marisa said.

"It's beautiful."

"It's old. They've remodeled it over the years, but the chapel is still intact. The rest is offices, a cafeteria. They've built dormitories on the back."

He drove slowly past and wished he could see it in the daylight. Wished he were there as a tourist instead of this.

"Make a U-turn. We'll park on the other side."

He did, and she pointed to a house directly across from the mission. "Right there."

"Um, just...on the street?"

"Yeah. That's my house."

He took in the squat, concrete building that shared walls with the houses on either side. There was no driveway, no sidewalk. He pulled over where she directed, and they both stepped out and stretched after the long drive.

"Quiet town," he said.

"People work hard here. They sleep at night."

"Of course. It's...quaint." Well, he thought it might be, anyway.

"The people are wonderful."

She pushed open the door and flipped on the overhead light, which glowed yellow in the dark space.

"It's not locked?"

"It doesn't have a real lock." She stepped inside and showed him a jury-rigged lever that pivoted into a wooden support on the door frame.

"At least you're safe when you're at home."

"*Normalmente.*"

He smiled at her slip into Spanish.

"Sorry. Usually."

"I figured it out."

She squatted on the floor and lifted one of the rotting boards. She dug inside the hole and handed him the items she retrieved. A passport, a wallet that held her expired New York driver's license, and some old credit cards. He checked the passport, just in case. Not expired, thank God.

She stood and brushed off her dress. "I told you."

"Just double-checking. Were you planning to come home?"

"I always hoped... I never imagined this, not in my worst nightmares."

He couldn't tell if she was holding in her emotion or had become numb to the situation. "Why don't you get some clothes and whatever else you need? I can buy you another bag on the way."

She stepped into the bedroom, flipped on another overhead light that bathed the space in gloom, and crossed to a tiny bureau.

He stepped into the doorway. One bed, a double. They must have shared it. Above the bed was a beautiful landscape, a mural of the sun rising over the old mission that stood across the street. It was painted right onto the stucco wall. The rest of the scene appeared different from what he'd made out in the dark. Verdant fields of crops, smiling people, and well-kept houses.

"The village as it should be," Marisa said.

He turned to see her watching him. "It's beautiful. You're so talented."

She pivoted back, opened the middle drawer of the short bureau that looked like a garage sale find, and dug through it.

"Can I help?"

She tossed a pair of jeans and a sweatshirt onto the bed. "I don't think so." She added underwear and bras to the pile. He turned away and surveyed the living room. Well, living, dining, and kitchen. Like a great room, only about the size of a normal dining room. If that. The kitchen consisted of a two-burner stovetop, a tiny sink, and a refrigerator about Ana's height. They ate on a rickety table for two. The living room consisted of a futon that looked like it was about to fall over. From behind, he could see it was supported not by legs, but by concrete blocks. There was no TV, but a small radio stood on top of the bookshelf. The other shelves held books, notebooks, pens, pencils, and paints. Lots of paints.

And he could see why. The walls were nearly papered in paintings, some of local vistas and people, but there were plenty of New York. Manhattan and Queens and what looked like scenes of upstate. And portraits. Leslie with an older woman who looked like her—their mother presumably. A handsome dark-skinned man. Probably Marisa's father—she looked like him. Lots of portraits of Ana and other folks Nate assumed were friends here. There were a few of Vinnie. And on the bookshelves, stacks of canvases. He stepped closer, saw they also held paintings. He lifted the one on top—two little Mexican children arm-in-arm. He flipped through the portraits until he reached one that had him pausing.

It was his own image, staring back at him. His hair was longer, like he'd worn it when he and Marisa had met. He was seated on a bus, his eyes concerned, his mouth turned down at the corners.

It was probably exactly how he'd looked the day they'd met. And she'd remembered every detail.

The way he'd always remembered her.

"It's my therapy," she said.

He set the paintings back on the shelf and turned. "I'm sorry. I was curious."

"I don't mind. How do you think I did?"

He shrugged. "Very good, considering how little you had to work with."

She nearly smiled, but it faded fast. She found a plastic sack in the dingy kitchen and returned to the bedroom.

Was painting how she'd survived here? Not just survived,

but from all accounts, she'd thrived. His respect for her grew even more.

He went back to the bedroom door. "Did you get socks and warm shoes?"

"Don't have either. I gave a lot of stuff away. Is it cold there now?" She stuffed her things into the thin plastic bag.

"It's March. Do you have more warm clothes?"

She shook her head.

"We'll figure it out."

"I have no money."

"Don't worry about it, Marisa. Just grab what you need."

From the bottom drawer, she pulled out a small, carved box, which she rested on the bed and opened. She lifted out the engagement ring she'd been wearing when Nate had met her. She closed the lid and shoved the box in her canvas bag. "My valuables."

"Anything else?"

She looked around the space, shook her head. He stepped back into the living room, and she passed him and headed for the kitchen.

"You need a bathroom?" She pointed to a door on the far side of the kitchen. "It works, most of the time."

"That's okay. I'll wait."

She spun slowly, obviously wondering if she'd missed anything.

The door banged open, and a man stepped inside. He wore dark jeans and a T-shirt that stretched across his overly large muscles.

Nate stepped between Marisa and the door, facing the man. His legs itched to run, but he wouldn't leave her unprotected.

A second man stepped in behind the first. Smaller, beady-eyed and mean-faced.

Not exactly how Nate had planned to die.

The first man crossed the room and stopped a foot from Nate. "*¿Quién es usted?*"

Nate knew enough Spanish to answer. "I'm a friend of Marisa's. Who are you?"

"Marisa." The man sidestepped Nate. "*¿Estás bien?*"

"I'm fine." She turned to Nate. "It's okay. Ramón is a...friend."

Nate could tell the word *friend* had been a stretch. He feared Ramón had heard the hesitation, too.

Nate crossed his arms. "You always barge into women's houses in the middle of the night?"

Ramón stepped toward him until they were nose-to-nose. "You no belong, gringo."

"Like I said, she's my friend."

"Ramón," Marisa said, "it's fine."

He turned back to her, eyes narrowed. "You want I take care of him?"

"Please... I'm okay. Nate's doing me a favor."

"*¿Necesitas algo?*"

"I don't need anything. But thank you."

"*¿Dónde está Ana?*"

Nate turned and saw tears fill Marisa's eyes. "Ana's been...taken. I have to get—"

"*¿Quién se la llevó?*"

"I don't know who took her." She sighed, started again. "*Por favor, habla Inglés.* You're making my friend nervous." At Ramón's scowl, she added, "He's helping me."

"Sí. Okay." He turned to Nate. "You helping?"

Nate's gaze darted from the small man back to Ramón. "I'm trying."

Ramón turned back to her. "I will help. We will have her back by tomorrow. You no need this gringo."

"They've taken her to America."

"Sí. *Tengo*"—he glanced at Nate—"I have friends. Where you going?"

"It's okay, Ramón." Marisa nodded as if she were confident.

"You think I cannot help? I can help. I know many people. Give me paper."

Nate got the distinct impression that Marisa didn't want his help. Nevertheless, she scooted past Ramón and Nate and took a sketchbook and pen from the bookshelf. She handed them to him.

He wrote something on it and handed it to her. "You call me if you need me. Also, I put Julio, a friend in New York. His phone number is there. You need anything, you tell him Ramón said give you whatever you need. Money or..." He glanced at Nate. "Whatever. Sí?"

She took the paper. "Gracias."

With a nod to Nate, Ramón and the other man left.

"Seems like a nice guy," Nate said after the door closed. "I can see why you lock the door."

"He's my protector, so I don't fear him. Well, I don't *only* fear him, if that makes sense."

"Can I have that sheet of paper?"

Marisa dropped the sketchbook on the table. "We don't want his help. He's the drug dealer—"

"I gathered," Nate said. "You never know what kind of help we'll need."

"Fine." She grabbed the sketchbook, tore the paper out, and handed it to him. He slipped it in his pocket.

She wrote something in the sketchbook, tore out a second sheet, and stepped outside. He watched her jog across the street. She folded the note and slipped it under the mission door before she jogged back. "A note for Carlita, so she doesn't worry."

"What'd you tell her?"

"That I was going to be gone longer than I'd thought, and

that I'd call her soon. And to pray for us." Marisa looked at the bookshelf, then toward her kitchen. "I don't need anything else."

"You sure?"

She shrugged. "I'm not sure about anything. I just want Ana back."

EIGHT

THE FLIGHT from Acapulco to Mexico City took barely long enough to take off and land again. Marisa couldn't help thinking about the last time she'd been on a plane, when Vinnie had flown her to Montreal to celebrate the anniversary of their first date. That's where he'd proposed. She'd only been twenty at the time, probably too young to get married, but she'd been in love, and Vinnie had been the perfect man. Kind, generous, handsome. He'd lavished her with gifts the same way her father had.

In retrospect, he hadn't lavished her with his attention—also a lot like her father. He'd always been working, but she'd overlooked that. It would all be different when they married, or so she told herself. And maybe it would have been.

Vinnie's admission that he'd broken the law hadn't changed her decision to marry him. She'd agreed to stand by him, and at least he'd planned to do the right thing.

His murder had shattered her life. No, not exactly. His murder had shattered her heart. When she'd run, though, that had ended her life. With Vinnie, she'd been somebody's everything. And even after he'd died, Marisa had had Leslie, she'd had friends and coworkers and fellow students, people who liked her and cared about her. Marisa had mattered to those people.

After she'd had to escape, it was as if she'd disappeared. She had still existed, still taken up just as much space in the world, but people had stopped seeing her. They often noticed the pretty face—when she didn't hide well enough—but they didn't know her.

She remembered standing on a corner in Mexico City, surrounded by hoards of people and wanting to scream, "Look at me! I'm right here." Not that she would have, not with her fear of Charles and his goons. Even if she had, though, they wouldn't have looked, wouldn't have cared. She was one of millions and millions of people. She might as well have been a ghost.

When she'd started teaching at the orphanage, that had changed a little. Even then, though, she could imagine what would have happened if she'd vanished like so many people in this part of the world did. What would they say about her?

Remember that lady who taught English? She disappeared.

Oh, how sad. What's for lunch?

It hadn't been until Marisa found Ana, the baby who'd always been meant to be hers, that Marisa felt corporeal again. Suddenly, she wasn't just the English teacher. She was somebody's mother, and that somebody needed her like Marisa had never been needed before.

Now Ana was gone. Marisa could feel herself vanishing, even as she sat on the airplane and headed home. Without Ana, she would disappear. Without Ana, Marisa wouldn't matter at all. Without Ana, she wouldn't want to exist, anyway.

At the airport in Mexico City, Nate bought breakfast and two coffees. Rather than eat at the food court, they continued to the gate to wait for their next flight.

Seated in one of the many leather-like chairs scattered around the gate area, Marisa eyed the sack Nate had set on the seat between them. "I won't be able to eat. Not until I know where Ana is."

"Starving yourself won't help."

When Nate handed her the egg sandwich, her stomach growled. She ate the whole thing, then teared up for the thousandth time that morning. Had Ana eaten breakfast? Had she slept? Had they mistreated her?

Thirty minutes later, they were seated near the back of the jet, passengers still filing on and filling the rows in front of them. The engine humming below, the murmur of other passengers, and the slamming of overhead bins gave the scene a sense of normalcy.

As if anything was normal.

"Why Boston?" Marisa asked.

"I was surprised when you didn't ask me earlier."

"I thought about it, but..." She'd been too tired, too worried, to think about anything but what she was doing. She'd focused on getting her stuff, getting to the airport, and getting to Mexico City.

The truth was, she'd been relieved to turn over the decision-making to Nate. She'd had no idea what to do. She'd been muddling through life for eight years. And what a job she'd done, taking care of herself. Adopting a child who was now in harm's way because of her. If only she'd ignored her sister's email. If only she'd never looked at the computer that day. If only she'd stayed in her safe little village, none of this would have happened.

Her decisions had gotten her here. They'd gotten Ana and Leslie kidnapped. Marisa never wanted to make another decision as long as she lived.

But.

But she couldn't follow blindly. Ana was Marisa's responsibility, and all that had happened was her fault.

Now that they were about to take off, Marisa needed to know Nate's plan. "You said to do the next thing. So that's what I've been doing."

He shifted to face her. "There are still people looking for you, right?"

"Who do you think kidnapped them? The people who were looking for me obviously followed you guys. They must've found me."

"Maybe," he said. "Maybe not."

"Wait, what do you mean? Of course it was them."

"It could have been Charles and his people, but there were a lot of other people at G&K who might've had a bone to pick with you. It wasn't just *his* money that was stolen. The business account was emptied, too. Everybody lost their jobs. They couldn't even negotiate with the feds to keep their doors open. They were broke. They were in debt."

"That wasn't my fault."

"They think it was. Anyway, I'm not willing to take the chance that, while we're searching for Ana, somebody else doesn't try to hurt you."

"You think I care if something happens to me? As long as Ana's safe."

"And what happens to Ana if you're killed? Do you want her to grow up without a mother?"

"Leslie will take care of her."

"Assuming she survives."

"Don't say that."

"And you'd want that, to leave Ana in Leslie's hands? How would Ana feel to lose you? How did you feel when your mother died?"

"You don't..." She faltered. Her parents' deaths had been

devastating, and she'd been an adult, theoretically.

So she knew what he was saying, but Marisa needed to be close to Ana. "Don't you think they're in New York?"

"They could be in Florida or California or Nebraska. They didn't say we'd make the trade in New York. And even if they are in the city, how do you propose we find them?"

"At least we could try. From Boston—"

"We're not going to Boston. I couldn't get a flight from Mexico City to Manchester without a wicked layover. We're going to New Hampshire."

"To your hometown?"

"We'll be safe, and nobody will know where to find us. We can figure out where to go from there."

"But..." She wanted to argue, because she felt in her bones that Ana was in New York. She wanted to be near her little girl. But Nate's argument was sound, and anyway, she couldn't think straight enough to plan.

"Go to sleep, Marisa." He stepped out of his seat, searched in the upper compartments, and came back with two pillows and two blankets. "Here." He handed her one of each. "We both need to sleep."

"I won't be able to."

"Please, try."

She stared out the window until the flight took off, trying not to think about Ana and unable to think about anything else. After they'd leveled off, she draped the blanket over her jeans and sweatshirt, which she'd changed into in the airport in Mexico City. She slid her braid over her shoulder and propped the pillow against the window. She closed her eyes. The trip to her village, this flight, the airports—it all felt surreal. Just two days earlier, she and Ana had hitched a ride to Chilpancingo. And now... How had she gotten here? Tears dripped down her face and off her chin.

"Hey." Nate touched her arm.

She opened her eyes to find him watching her. He lifted the armrest between their seats and patted his shoulder. "Try this. It's soft."

She shifted, leaned against Nate. The tears kept coming, but finally she drifted to sleep.

AT LOGAN INTERNATIONAL IN BOSTON, Marisa reached for the duffel Nate had purchased for her, but he lifted it from the baggage carousel first and slung over his shoulder. He pulled his and Leslie's suitcases toward the doors.

"I can help with that," she said.

He turned, his eyes kind. "I got it."

The area was packed with people, most speaking English. Any feeling of joy at being home was tempered by the circumstances.

She followed Nate, who still looked as good as he had that first day despite so little sleep. They'd both slept much of the nearly seven-hour flight.

The door to the street opened automatically. He let her go first and followed her to the sidewalk.

She shivered and folded her arms. "I'd forgotten how cold the air could be."

He just smiled and led her to a bench. "My friend will be here soon."

"I feel bad he had to drive so far."

"I didn't want to rent a car. We could be tracked that way. Bad enough they can track us to Boston through our flights. From here, we shouldn't be easy to find."

She looked around. "You think we're in danger?"

"The guys who kidnapped Ana have no reason to hurt us. They want their money. Theoretically, nobody else would know you were coming today. But it won't be long before they do. Information like that tends to spread."

A shiny black truck pulled to the curb in front of them. A man as built and nearly as handsome as Nate circled the front of it and approached them. He had dark brown hair and warm eyes.

Nate greeted him with a hug and a slap on the back. "I can't thank you enough, man."

The man stepped back. "I still owe you."

"I did nothing," Nate said. "Nothing good, anyway." He turned to her. "Marisa, this is Brady Thomas."

She stepped forward and shook his hand. "Thank you for coming."

"No problem." He slung Nate's suitcase in the bed of the truck. Nate followed with the rest. He said to Marisa, "You want yours back here or with you?"

"Back there is fine."

He set the duffel in the bed and opened the back door of the pickup. "Are you okay to sit back here? If you'd prefer—"

"It's fine." She climbed in the backseat and inhaled the new-car smell she hadn't experienced in forever.

"Nice truck," Nate said.

Brady pulled into traffic. "I needed something big enough for a car seat."

"How is Johnny?"

Marisa could see the man's smile in the rearview mirror. "He's perfect. Crawling all over the house now."

"Wow. Can't wait to see him. And Rae?"

"Feisty, as always."

Marisa said, "You two were school friends?"

They both laughed. "Actually," Brady said, "Nate is much older than I am."

Nate turned to face her. "Like three years. Brady tried to fill my shoes on the football team."

"Tried to? We went to the state championship."

"And lost, if I remember."

"Closer than you got."

Both men laughed, and Marisa sat forward, intrigued. "So you weren't high school friends?"

"Nope," Nate said. "I barely knew him, and then, for a while, I kind of hated him."

"Fair enough," Brady said. "I kind of hated you for a while there, too." He met Marisa's eyes again. "See, there's this woman."

"Ah," she said.

"Your wife now." Nate turned to her. "They were married the Saturday between Christmas and New Year's."

"You had a thing for her?" Marisa asked, ignoring a pang of jealousy. As if she had time for that.

"We were together a few years when she lived in New York, a million years ago. Before I met you."

"Ah. And you were angry at Brady for stealing her away?" Marisa asked.

"Nah," Nate said. "I was angry because the whole time I was with Reagan, I knew she still had a thing for Brady. I never could make her forget him."

Marisa couldn't imagine any woman choosing another man over Nate.

What was wrong with her? What kind of mother thinks of men when her daughter is missing? Missing, maybe dead. The kidnappers hadn't called back. She hadn't heard her daughter's voice in nearly twenty-four hours. Had Ana eaten? Had she slept? Were they being kind to her? Had they hurt her?

"Hey." Nate reached over the seat to grab her hand. "You okay? Where'd you go there?"

She just shook her head.

He pulled off his seatbelt and climbed into the back.

"What are you doing?" she said.

Brady angled away but didn't say a word as Nate settled in the seat beside her. "She's okay," he said.

"You don't know that."

"Until we know she's not, we're going to assume she is."

Tears filled her eyes. She'd cried more in the last day than she had since Vinnie died. "I don't know how to do that."

"They get nothing from you if she's not okay."

"You mean if they kill her, but they could hurt her. They could..." All the thoughts of what they could be doing to her daughter, to her sister, hit her.

Nate wrapped his arms around her and held her. "They have no reason to hurt her."

"They have no reason not to."

Brady cleared his throat. "From the little Nate told me on the phone, it sounds like these guys are after money. In my experience... Did he tell you I'm a cop?"

Nate had said that, though she'd forgotten. She nodded.

"Anyway," Brady continued, "in my experience, most people, even bad guys, don't hurt kids. Most people value children and care for them, even hardened criminals. So unless these guys are kidnappers and...something worse, your Ana is probably okay."

But maybe they were the *something worse*.

Brady stopped in traffic and turned back to her. "You know, they say fewer than five percent of men are..." He faltered, looked at Nate, and turned back at her. "Like little kids in an inappropriate way."

Perverts. Pedophiles. That's what he was trying to say.

"Less than five percent," Brady repeated. "Not bad odds."

Those weren't bad odds. Brady was right. But she wasn't in the habit of gambling with her daughter's life. Odds seemed irrelevant.

"And Leslie's with her." Nate squeezed her shoulder. "Leslie's taking care of her."

"What about Leslie, though?"

"Your sister's tough," Nate said. "She can handle it. And don't you remember the way she took to Ana, held her hand, took her shopping? Leslie won't let your daughter get hurt."

The traffic moved, so Brady turned to the front again. "We're going to find her, Marisa. We won't stop until we do."

Tears stung her eyes. She reached forward and touched Brady's shoulder. "Thank you." She turned to Nate. "And thank you. I can never thank you enough. You didn't ask for any of this."

"Neither did you," Nate said. "We have to play the hand we're dealt."

"You don't have to play it, though. You could walk away."

He shook his head. "You think I'd do that?"

"No. I know you wouldn't. But that doesn't mean I don't appreciate your help."

She wiped her eyes, but the tears kept coming. "I don't know what we're going to do."

"All we have to know is the next step."

"And what's that?"

He nodded toward Brady in the front seat. "We start with my friends."

∽

MARISA YAWNED as Brady turned onto a narrow side road. She caught a glimpse of a lake between cabins and tall trees. One day, forever ago, Nate had told Marisa about the lake in his hometown. She never thought she'd see it. On this late afternoon in March, the oaks and maples were still bare of leaves, but the pines stood tall and colorful against the pale blue sky and reflected in the sparking water. The light dripped between the branches, reflected off the white birch bark, and was soaked into the trunks of oaks and maples and pines, nearly sucked dry before it reached the leafy bracken on the ground.

Her fingers itched for her paints. "It's amazing."

"I've been all over the world," Nate said, peering out the window on her side of the truck, "and I've never found anyplace as beautiful as this. You ever been to New Hampshire before?"

Marisa shook her head. "Upstate New York a few times."

Brady turned into the driveway of a little one-story woodsided cabin and parked beside a blue truck. "Sam's not here yet, but I have the key."

"Isn't that your old truck?" Nate asked.

"Thought you'd need some wheels." They climbed out. Marisa stretched, tired of sitting, and joined the men at the back of Brady's pickup.

"And you didn't tell my father we were coming," Nate asked.

"No sense involving your folks. Only Sam and Rae know."

Marisa looked at Brady. "Rae is your wife, right?"

"Right. And Johnny is our son."

"Aren't you worried about getting your wife involved?" Marisa asked.

"I'm always worried about her," Brady said. "But if you knew Reagan, you'd know it's never a good idea to try to keep something from her." He opened the tailgate, reached in for Marisa's duffel, and gripped Leslie's suitcase.

Nate grabbed his own while Brady led the way up the steps to the cabin. "Anyway," Brady continued, "Reagan finds out everybody's secrets. And I'd hate to think what she'd do to me if she discovered Nate needed our help and I hadn't told her." He shuddered, and Marisa smiled.

"If you say so. But I'd rather keep your family as far from my troubles as possible."

Nate nodded for her to follow Brady. "They'll be fine. Rae can take care of herself."

Marisa followed Brady up the three steps to the front porch. It was beautiful outside, and she wanted to stay out and enjoy the view. The chilly temperatures changed her mind.

Inside the door of the cabin, Marisa stalled. The word *cabin* should never be used to describe this place, not with its gleaming hardwood floors and floor-to-ceiling stacked stone fireplace. The couch and chairs looked both chic and comfortable. Across the great room stood a narrow island that separated the living room from the small kitchen. It had granite countertops, and three barstools had been pushed beneath it. The kitchen was furnished with stainless appliances. On the far side of the cabin, a glass sliding door led to a deck, where a round table was surrounded by six chairs. Beyond the table, a dock jutted out from the deck and over the lake, so that it looked as if the cabin were built nearly on top of the glistening waters. The vista was beautiful. "Wow."

Nate cleared his throat.

"Oh, sorry." She stepped to the side so he could enter.

He entered and spoke to Brady. "Two bedrooms?"

Brady pointed to the two doors on Marisa's right. "The one in the back is the master. Has a bathroom in there. That's hers. The other one'll do for you."

Marisa took her duffel from Brady and went into the master.

She couldn't remember the last time she'd been someplace this nice. A tall, king-sized four-poster bed took up the bulk of the space. There were nightstands on either side, a bureau at the end of the bed, and a flat-screen TV mounted on the wall.

Marisa set her bag down and crossed to the bathroom. More granite and pretty tile. And a huge soaking tub. Ana would love it.

Ana.

She squeezed her eyes against the threat of tears and returned to the great room, where she joined Brady and Nate, who were leaning against the granite counter.

"Sam and Rae will be here any minute," Brady said. "You need something to eat? Sam said there would be some basics in the fridge." He circled into the bar and opened the refrigerator.

"I'm not hungry," Marisa said.

Nate touched her elbow. "Maybe you should try. You haven't eaten since Mexico City."

"I ate the peanuts on the plane." She looked at Brady. "I would love a cup of coffee."

"Okay." He pushed a button on a weird, black appliance she didn't recognize and slid a rack of little plastic things across the counter. "What kind?"

She eyed the rack and the appliance, which seemed to be steaming or something. "What in the world?"

"Uh..." Brady looked from Marisa to Nate, who laughed.

"She's been out of the country for a while." Nate turned to Marisa. "Ever heard of a Keurig?"

"No. Wait, maybe. I think I've seen a picture online. I never really looked to see what it did."

"It's a coffee maker that makes one cup at a time," Nate said. "They're pretty cool." He spun the rack. "Pick one."

Marisa read all the different choices. Regular, decaf, mocha, vanilla.

She selected one. "What does Christmas coffee taste like?"

Nate looked at it. "Oh, I've had that. It's really good. It tasted like, well, coffee. If you don't like it, we can get you another one."

She turned back to Brady. "You're sure it's okay? Your friend won't mind?"

He took the coffee from her and put it in the machine. He pushed a button, and a minute later, the coffee was brewing. When he handed her the full cup, she said, "I want one of those."

"We'll see what we can do," Nate said.

She shook her head. "No. That would definitely blow a fuse. The power in my house is not very reliable."

But maybe she wouldn't be going back to Mexico, not to live, anyway. Maybe she and Ana...

She couldn't think about the future. She lifted her gaze to Brady. "Sugar?"

"Right." He searched the cabinets and returned with a little glass cup filled with various types of sweetener packets. She chose sugar, poured it in the cup, and stirred with a spoon Brady handed her. She'd become accustomed to drinking coffee black in Mexico, but it was much better sweet. And Nate was right. Although there was nothing particularly Christmassy about it, the flavor was delicious.

Just imagine. Twenty different varieties of coffee in your own house. The luxury.

She looked back at the rack. "It even has hot chocolate. Ana's never had that. She would love it. Anything sweet..." Her words trailed off.

Nate wrapped his arm around her. He'd been doing that a lot, and it felt more and more comfortable every time. She should probably pull away. She'd have to be careful not to let it progress. She leaned into him and sipped her coffee.

Someone knocked on the front door. Nate crossed the room, opened the door a crack, then opened it all the way.

A woman stepped inside and set a bag on the floor. She was much shorter than Nate and had long, light brown hair pulled back in a ponytail. She wore a business suit that showed off her curves, the kind of curves Marisa had always envied. Nate pulled her into a long hug and said something Marisa couldn't hear.

Behind her, another woman stepped in. She was taller than the first and had reddish-blond, shoulder-length hair. She wore jeans and a light green sweater and carried a giant patterned purse. When Nate had finished hugging the first woman, he turned to the second and hugged her. After a few seconds, Brady said, "Okay, that's enough."

Everybody laughed, and Nate led the two women across the room. "Marisa, I want you to meet my good friends. He indicated the redhead and said, "This is Rae Thomas."

Marisa stepped forward and held out her hand, but the woman passed right by her outstretched hand and hugged her. "I'm glad to meet you, but I'm very sorry for what you're going through."

Marisa felt the tears again. She blinked them back as Reagan stepped away and said, "For a couple of hours, I thought I might lose my son. I cannot imagine what you're feeling right now."

Marisa didn't know what to say and probably couldn't have formed words anyway. She nodded. The other woman stepped forward and hugged her, too.

Behind her, Nate said, "And that's Samantha Messenger."

"I'm praying like crazy," Samantha whispered in her ear.

Marisa sniffed. "Thank you." They stepped apart. "Thank you for letting us stay here."

Sam flipped her hand. "It's nothing."

Marisa let out a short laugh that sounded as much like a sob. "I thought you were a man."

The woman's eyebrows lifted, and Marisa sniffed and wiped her eyes. "They kept calling you Sam. I just assumed..."

Sam turned to Brady and Nate and shook her head. "What am I going to do with you two?"

Nate said, "Sorry. I didn't think."

Rae lifted the bag Sam had left by the door. "Enough chit-chat. We have a little girl to find. Let's get to work."

THE FIVE OF them sat at the round table. Sam pulled out a laptop, and Rae slid a folder and pen from her huge purse.

Brady nodded to Nate. "Why don't you give us the background information?"

"We already know about the mortgage fraud." Reagan nodded to Nate. "We downloaded your old stories and read a few others, so we're caught up on what Gray & Kinnison did. Tell us what happened to bring it all to light."

Nate nodded to Marisa.

"Vinnie told me about the fraud," she started. "He said—"

"Wait." Rae opened her file and flipped through it. "Vinnie is Vincent Depalo, your boyfriend. Right?"

"Fiancé," Marisa said. "Some FBI agent had cornered him and told him they were investigating G&K for fraud. He suggested Vinnie cooperate with the investigation or go down with the rest of them."

"Why him?" Brady asked.

Marisa shrugged. "Maybe because he'd made the least money off of it. I mean, he was making plenty, but not like the guys on top."

"And he was the newest person to get involved," Nate

added. "And the youngest. Plus, the FBI wanted to bring down the guys on the top. They didn't care about small potatoes like Vincent Depalo." He turned to Marisa. "Not that he wasn't—"

"I know what you mean." She reached out like she might touch his hand, then pulled it back. "You're probably right."

Brady focused on her. "Do you know the name of the agent?"

"Garrison Kopp."

"His last name is Cop?" Rae raised her eyebrows.

Marisa nodded. "But it's K-O-P-P."

Rae smiled. "Appropriate."

Brady glanced at Rae while she wrote something on her notepad. He turned back to Marisa. "I'm guessing this agent tells Vinnie to cooperate, or he's going to bring him down, too."

"Yeah." Marisa could still remember the fear in Vinnie's eyes when he'd relayed the information to her. And the shame. She'd been horrified to discover her fiancé was a crook. She'd told him that if he didn't come clean and straighten up, they were finished.

Not that the threat had been necessary. Vinnie had known what he had to do. He was a young man, not even thirty. Why spend his life as a felon?

"Okay," Brady said. "Then what happened?"

"Vinnie contacted Kopp, and they set up a meeting for a week later. But a few days after that, Vinnie was beaten to death." For the first time, those words barely raised any emotion in her. Right now, all she cared about was getting Ana and Leslie back.

"I'm sorry," Brady said. "That must have been terrible."

"I was convinced Charles and his men had done it to keep him quiet. Vinnie thought he was being followed and even talked about running away. He was going to try to meet Kopp earlier, but before Vinnie could work it out, he was killed."

Reagan was taking notes but looked up and gave her an encouraging nod.

Brady leaned forward. "The question is, who told Charles Gray about the meet?"

Marisa opened her mouth, closed it again.

"What?" Nate said.

"I can't be sure, but..."

Nate turned to face her, leaned forward, and said very quietly, "You need to tell us everything, Marisa. Now is not the time to hold back."

She nodded. Swallowed. Said, "I know. You're right. It's just... I'm not sure."

Nate waited.

"Leslie." There, she'd said it. She'd never had the courage to confront her sister all those years ago, and she would never have told the FBI her suspicions, but now, with both Leslie and Ana kidnapped, the secret no longer seemed to matter.

Nate sat back, looked at the table. "Leslie." He met her eyes again. "I can see why you didn't say anything. You probably should have, but—"

"Who's Leslie?" Brady asked.

"My sister."

"Oh." Rae made a note. "She's the one who was taken with Ana?"

"Yeah." Marisa turned to Nate. "If it was her, I'm sure she didn't mean any harm."

"Of course." Nate's words didn't match his expression, though. His eyes had narrowed, his mouth pinched shut like he was working to keep his thoughts inside.

"Wait," Rae said. "Explain how that happened."

Marisa explained Leslie's business and the cleaning contract for G&K, how she'd known Charles Gray and Vinnie and a lot of the guys up there.

"The night Vinnie confessed it all to me, Leslie had been out. But at some point while we were talking, she came home. I never knew when, never knew what she'd heard. But I always found it odd that I hadn't heard her come in. Later, she told me we looked like we were in a serious conversation and she didn't want to interrupt. I believed her, of course. Why wouldn't I? But when it all happened, and that FBI agent kept asking me who I'd told... I wondered."

"Why didn't you tell him?" Brady asked.

She shrugged. "I didn't know for sure. And even if Leslie had heard, why would she tell Charles or any of them anything?"

Sam spoke for the first time since they'd sat. "But now, you think maybe your sister told your fiancé's boss what she overheard? Why would she do that?"

Marisa sighed. "I can only guess. She liked Vinnie okay, but she didn't want me to marry him. I was really young, and we only had each other at that point, and I think she was jealous. And it didn't matter how much money Vinnie made, Leslie thought I could do better."

Rae looked up from her notebook. "You think maybe your sister told Charles what was going on to... What? Break you two up?"

Marisa shrugged. "It's just a theory. Maybe somebody else did it."

"Did Vinnie tell anybody?" Brady asked.

"No. He was adamant that neither of us could tell. He was terrified Charles would find out before he had a chance to meet with the FBI guy."

"If you didn't tell, and Vinnie didn't, then either the leak came from the FBI"—Brady's expression told them what he thought of that theory—"or your sister told someone."

Sam reached across the table and laid her hand on Marisa's.

"If she did it, I'm sure she had your best interests at heart. And I know you don't wish her ill."

Marisa teared up again and nodded.

"Okay," Brady said. "Go on."

"And then Vinnie was murdered." Silence settled on the room at the word. She let a beat pass. "Then I went to Nate."

Brady glanced at Nate. "Why him?"

"He used to ride the same bus as I did. I recognized him from his picture in the paper."

"At the *Times*?" Brady asked.

Nate shook his head. "I was working in Queens. I wrote a column occasionally on the financial market, and they ran my photo above the column."

"Oh." Brady turned back to Marisa. "You picked him because you recognized him."

"And because of the finance column. Seemed he'd understand what G&K was up to. I sat next to him on the bus the next day and told him I had a story, but I needed help. I gave him the gist of it, and he put me up in a hotel. He hid me. I thought they would try to kill me, since they killed Vinnie."

"I still think they might have," Nate said.

"I told him the story. He protected me while I tried to figure out what to do next. He encouraged me to call the FBI and tell Kopp what I knew about Vinnie's murder. I met with Kopp and told him everything. Kopp was working on getting me in witness protection. The next morning, the FBI stormed the G&K offices."

"That fast?" Brady asked.

"Remember," Nate said, "they'd already been working on bringing G&K down. They just needed proof. Marisa knew just enough to convince Kopp he'd find it in the files. And Kopp didn't want to lose the opportunity."

Rae looked up from her notes. "But Charles knew they were after him. Why didn't he hide the evidence?"

"It's not that simple," Nate said. "We're talking about years of documents that probably looked fine at a glance, but under the FBI's microscope? I'm sure Charles was working on it, but remember, all this happened very quickly. And Charles thought he'd bought himself some time by having Vinnie killed."

"By the time the FBI got there," Marisa said, "both Charles's personal account and the company's operating account had been emptied."

"How much money?" Rae asked.

Marisa looked at Nate, and he shrugged.

"I never learned the actual numbers, but the man who took Ana demanded two million."

Brady looked at Marisa. "And you didn't take it?"

Familiar rage rose in her chest. "I didn't care about their money. I wanted justice for Vinnie's murder. Besides, even if I'd wanted to, it's not like they kept the account codes posted on the wall. How could I have?"

"Okay."

The rage turned to confusion. She studied Brady. "You believe me, just like that?"

"If you had the money, you'd give it to the kidnappers, right? To get your daughter back?"

"Of course! I'd do anything to get her back."

"Besides, Nate told me about your house. That's not the way someone with that much money would choose to live."

She turned to Nate with a raised eyebrow.

He lifted both hands in surrender. "I just wanted Brady to know you didn't steal the money."

"He said it was small and sparse," Brady clarified. "Nothing bad."

"It is those things."

"Okay," Brady said. "But like you say, they didn't keep the account numbers and passwords just lying around. So how do they think you got access?"

"I have no idea." Marisa looked at Nate. "Do you?"

"I'm not sure they know how. Only that, as far as they knew, Marisa was the only one who knew the feds were on to them. I know they figured Vinnie's murder was her motive."

"But they must have a theory about how," Brady said.

"They didn't share it with me," Nate said.

Brady stared off, shook his head slightly, and frowned. Finally, he focused on Marisa again. "What else?"

She couldn't think of anything to add.

"That's all we know," Nate said. "After that, Marisa went from the FBI's best witness to their number one suspect."

"Charles's, too." Marisa still couldn't believe how it had all backfired. "Even my own sister doesn't believe me."

Nate pulled her hand into his and held it on his knee. "I knew Marisa hadn't stolen it."

"How?" Brady asked.

"I just knew. I'd gotten to know her, and I couldn't believe that of her. And I was right."

"But it didn't matter, because they all thought I had. Charles, Kopp—they were all after me. I thought if I exposed myself to the FBI to try to clear my name, Charles would find me and have me killed."

"Or worse. Whatever it took to get his money back." Nate squeezed her hand. "The way Vinnie was killed...the man was vicious."

"You helped her escape?" Brady clarified.

Nate sat up straighter. "You have a problem with that?"

Brady glanced at his wife, whose eyebrows rose, before focusing on Nate again. "I wish more people trusted the authorities. It stands to reason that whoever stole the money knew the FBI was on to them. Who knew?"

"Just Nate and I," Marisa said.

"And maybe Leslie," Nate added. "And Charles."

"Well, yeah," Rae said, "but Charles wouldn't steal his own money,"

"Why not?" Nate looked at Rae. "He's in prison, but for all we know, all that money is in some offshore account, just collecting interest."

Brady shook his head. "But we don't think Charles knew the FBI was coming that night. Or else he'd have been destroying evidence."

"Maybe he knew the jig was up." Rae tapped her pen on her yellow pad. "Maybe he knew he was going to prison, so he hid the money."

Brady conceded that with a nod. "Possible. Put him on the list."

Rae wrote on her tablet.

"Who else?" Brady asked.

"As far as I know," Marisa said, "nobody else."

"But if Leslie knew, she could have told someone," Nate said. "Charles got the hit man involved, which proves he knew. Maybe he told someone else at the company. Even Kopp—"

"You think the FBI agent did it?" Brady's eyebrows rose.

Rae chuckled. "Because cops are never bad."

He glanced at his wife. "It's not usually the cop, despite what you see on TV."

"We're just brainstorming here, Brady."

He nodded once. "Fine. Put him on the list."

"Already did." Rae winked at Marisa. "We'll need the names of the rest of G&K's employees."

"On it," Sam said, tapping away on her keyboard.

Brady looked at Nate. "Anyone else?"

Nate looked at Marisa. She shook her head, a little shocked at the turn of events. Nate had told her his friends would help. She didn't know what she'd expected, but not this. "I can't think of anyone else."

They were silent, digesting what they knew so far. After a minute, Brady said, "Well, despite the fact that he's a"—he cleared his throat and glanced at this wife—"suspect, I think our next step is to talk to Agent Kopp."

"Agreed," Rae said.

Nate looked at Marisa. "What do you think?"

Were they crazy? "He'll throw me in jail."

Nate squeezed her hand. "We don't have to tell him where you are. We just want to have a conversation with him. Surely he has more information than we have."

"But what if he finds me?" She looked from Nate to Brady. "I'm a fugitive."

"We'll take it one step at a time. First, we have to find him."

"I got him."

They all looked at Sam.

"Already?" Rae said.

She looked up from her screen. "It's not like *Kopp* is a common name."

A moment of stunned silence was followed by Brady's chuckle. "Why do I ever doubt you?"

"Because you're a slow learner," Sam quipped.

His jaw dropped, and he covered his chest with his hand. "Me? I'm like...like..." He leaned toward his wife and said, "Quick. Think of somebody smart."

Marisa nearly giggled.

Rae smacked his arm and turned to Sam. "Is Agent Kopp still working in New York City?"

"He retired two years ago."

"Retired?" Marisa said. "He was like thirty."

Sam click-clicked. "According to this, he's forty-two. He was commissioned in the Air Force at twenty-two, so he had twenty years in."

Nate leaned sideways to look at her screen. "How in the world do you do that?"

She lifted her shoulder in a no-big-deal shrug. "I did a little digging. He lives on Long Island. I have a phone number for him."

"His phone number isn't unlisted?" Nate said.

"It is," she said.

"But how—?"

"Don't bother asking," Brady said. "She won't tell."

Sam ripped a piece of paper from Rae's notebook. "You'd probably throw me in jail."

"Did you do something illegal?"

"Can I plead the fifth?"

"That's enough." Rae looked at Marisa. "I'm sorry. They've been like this since third grade."

This time, Marisa did giggle. The sound seemed foreign and wrong and she immediately squelched it.

Sam wrote something on the paper. "Here's the number. Who's making the call?"

"Brady should do it," Rae suggested. "He could probably get the most information, being a cop."

"Actually, I'd rather not. Since we're harboring a fugitive here, I think I need to step out." He looked at Marisa. "I believe you, but I am still a cop. I can only go so far."

"I understand." Marisa swallowed a lump of emotion. "I appreciate what you've done so far." She looked around at the rest of them. "All of you. I can never repay you."

Rae reached past Sam and touched Nate's elbow. "You're Nate's friend. And we'd do anything for him."

Marisa looked just in time to see his cheeks turn pink. "I

didn't do anything. I nearly..." He looked at Marisa, then at the table. "I didn't do anything."

Rae squeezed his forearm. "You did, and I'm forever grateful."

Marisa was definitely missing something. She'd ask Nate about that later.

"Okay." Rae pulled her hand back. "I can call the guy."

"I'll do it." Nate snatched the paper from Sam's fingers. "We've met before. He'll talk to me."

NINE

Nate stood and pulled his cell phone from the charger on the kitchen island.

Marisa stood, eyes wide. "Wait. Are you calling right now?"

"The sooner we talk to him, the closer we'll be. You okay?"

Marisa looked behind her as if Agent Kopp might have just sneaked in the back door.

"It'll be fine," Nate said. "I'm not going to tell him where you are."

Brady pushed back in his chair. "Be careful what you do tell him. You're guilty of harboring a felon. If he believes you know where Marisa is, this could backfire."

All true. But Kopp was their best bet for more information. They'd have to expose themselves to someone if they were going to figure out who stole the money—or who kidnapped Ana and Leslie. Kopp seemed like the safest place to start.

Brady, Rae, Sam, and Marisa were staring at him. "I'll be careful." He smiled at Marisa and pushed out the back door.

The air felt brisk and clean, cool—fifties, maybe—but the sun shone through the bare branches overhead and warmed him. He crossed the patio onto the dock, where he wandered the twenty feet or so to the end. He stared out at the clear water and inhaled the loamy scent of the forest all around him. It was good to be home.

He typed the number Sam had found into his phone and hit send.

Two rings later, the call connected. "Earl's Pizza and Grinders." The voice sounded like it belonged to a teenager.

So much for Sam's magic touch. "I'm afraid I have the wrong number."

"Oh, wait. Uh... Who's this?"

Nate said, "I'm looking for Garrison Kopp."

"Oh. Sorry, dude. Hold on a sec." There was a muffled sound, a bang, and a laugh. "Dad! Hey, Dad. Telephone."

Another muffled sound, then Nate heard, "Sorry. I was sorta messing around."

Nate clearly heard the sound of a sigh on the other end before an older male voice came on the line. "Hello?"

"Agent Kopp, this is Walter Boyle of the *New York Times*. Do you have a minute?"

"It's Nate, right?"

"You remember."

"Hard to forget a guy who harbored a fugitive."

If only he knew. The retired fed had a memory like a crypt. "Allegedly. What I really did was protect my source. It's that pesky freedom of the press. And as a matter of fact—"

"Hold on." His voice was professional, a contrast to the laughter Nate heard in the background. The laughter got quieter, and a door slammed. "You calling to tell me where I can find Marisa Vega?"

"Do you really think she stole that money?"

"I think she's wanted in connection to a federal case."

"She gave you the information you needed to bring down G&K."

"Are you calling about that?"

Nate paced back toward the cabin. "I've had contact with Marisa. Her daughter's been kidnapped."

The squeak of a chair came through the phone. "She has a kid?"

"Adopted. Four years old. She was with Marisa's sister, Leslie. They were both snatched from...a city in Mexico."

"She report it?"

"Kidnappers told her if she did, they'd kill them both."

"Hmm. And rather than call the cops, she contacted you."

"She trusts me."

"Because you always believed she was innocent."

"I know she is."

"How?"

Nate couldn't very well tell Kopp about the house where Marisa had been living. And Kopp wouldn't be impressed by Nate's gut instinct. He went with the same argument he'd made years before. "First, she was afraid to leave the hotel."

"Or so she told you."

"Second, she wouldn't have gone near that building for all the gold in Ft. Knox. She was trying to stay alive."

A snort from the other end.

"Third, she wouldn't have had access to the bank account numbers. She was a nighttime cleaning lady."

"She had access to Vinnie."

"You think Vinnie, the smallest cog in the machine, had Charles Gray's personal bank account information?"

"Somebody stole that money."

"Yeah, and somebody wants it back."

"Meaning?"

"She was told to get the money in exchange for her daughter and sister. In fact, the kidnappers said they wanted her to turn over the money or tell them who stole it."

A long pause. "The kidnappers want the money or—"

"Proof she didn't steal it."

"How peculiar."

Nate let the information simmer and hoped Kopp would say something helpful. After a minute, he said, "Well, all I can do is refer you to somebody at the FBI. I'm retired."

"If she goes to the cops, Ana and Leslie are dead. I'm only talking to you."

"Why? 'Cause we're such good friends? As far as I'm concerned, you're harboring a fugitive."

Nate's pacing became more like stomping. "For the thousandth time, I didn't know where she was."

"*Didn't* know," Kopp said. "Past tense."

Crap. "Don't put words in my mouth, Kopp. Marisa took off as soon as she knew you'd arrested Gray."

"As soon as the money was stolen. Interesting coincidence."

"Not her fault the money was stolen before you guys stormed the place. For all I know, you took it."

A humorless chuckle. "If you could see this house, you wouldn't wonder about that anymore."

Nate pictured Marisa's shack in Mexico. Wherever Kopp lived, it was a mansion compared to that.

"What do you want from me?" Kopp asked.

"I want to meet. Maybe we can compare notes, figure out who stole the money."

"I'm not in the city. And I don't have my notes. They're with the FBI."

"I have mine."

No answer.

"Just tell me where and when," Nate said. "I can be there tomorrow."

"Are you in Manhattan?"

Kopp was coming around. Nate considered lying but

changed his mind. "No. I resigned from the *Times*."

"And when you introduced yourself as Walter Boyle, *New York Times*—"

"Just trying to jog your memory. And besides, it's not a felony to impersonate a journalist, is it?"

Another chuckle. Apparently under the Men-in-Black shades, Kopp had concealed a sense of humor.

"I'm moving back home," Nate said. "I'm in New Hampshire, but I could be in New York in just a few hours."

"New Hampshire, huh? That where Marisa is?"

"Yeah. She's been hiding behind the *Old Man on the Mountain* for eight years."

"Thought that thing fell."

"She probably knocked it down."

The man chuckled again. "Okay, I hear what you're saying." He stopped talking, and Nate waited through the silence. He wasn't going to speak again until Kopp told him yes or no. One thing he'd learned, once you make a request, you keep quiet and make the other person turn you down. Most people didn't like to disappoint, though he doubted Garrison Kopp cared much about that.

Finally Kopp spoke. "Look, my son's going to his mom's after school tomorrow. He'll be gone all weekend. Why don't I come up there?"

"I just need an hour of your time." The last thing Nate needed was Kopp hanging around, scaring Marisa. "I hate for you to drive all the way up here."

"It'll give me something to do. And it'll take us more than an hour, if you really want to learn anything."

"I could meet you in Boston."

"I'm happy to come to you."

How could Nate refuse? He dug deep, trying to find an excuse, but whatever he said at this point, Kopp would take as confirmation that Marisa was nearby. "Great. I'm in a little town called Nutfield."

"Never heard of it."

"There's a restaurant in town called McNeal's. What time can you be there?"

"I drop my son off at eight-thirty. About how long will it take me?"

"Five hours, give or take."

"Fine. Two o'clock. See you then."

THE LUNCH CROWD had mostly headed home or back to work by the time Nate got to McNeal's the following afternoon. The remodeled restaurant smelled of today's special—corned beef and sauerkraut. He asked for a booth near the back.

The TVs over the bar displayed college basketball, and the hum of one of the games played over the speaker.

He'd just given his drink order to the waitress—her name tag read *Bonnie*—when Sam walked in. She pointed to the table she wanted, the one adjacent to his.

She smiled when she walked by and slid into the booth right behind where Kopp would sit. Nate didn't get up. "You don't need to be here."

She didn't turn when she answered. "I'm here for Marisa. She wants to know what's going on."

That made sense.

Sam pulled out her laptop. Apparently she planned to work —or maybe email updates to Rae and Marisa—as she eavesdropped.

He didn't like having an audience, but Sam was probably right—and the rest of them, too. Kopp's insistence on coming to New Hampshire was suspicious.

So Nate pretended she wasn't there and checked his watch and watched the door.

Garrison Kopp stepped inside like he owned the place. He was a few inches north of six feet tall. He'd worn a crew cut when Nate had last met him, but now his light brown hair had grown out a little. Very little.

He stood straight, hands in fists at his side, and within a second of walking in, his gaze landed on Nate. He said something to the hostess, who giggled and blushed. She didn't take her eyes off Kopp as he approached Nate's table, whispering to the waitress who stood beside her.

"You found it okay," Nate said.

"Can't hide anything from the FBI."

There was that sense of humor again. Nate hadn't remembered that from his last encounters with Kopp. "Former FBI," he corrected.

Kopp slid into the booth across from him, hiding Nate's view of Sam. She hadn't even looked up when the guy walked in. Town clerk turned James Bond.

The waitress approached, slid Nate's drink on the table, and set a menu in front of Kopp. "What can I get you to drink?"

"Just water." His fingers tapped the menu. "You have a Reuben?"

"Best in the world."

"I'll take that and french fries."

"Good choice." She looked at Nate. "How 'bout you."

"I'm good with my drink, thanks."

She took their menus and stopped at Sam's table.

Nate had brought all the notes he and his friends had compiled the previous day. He opened the file on the table. "Here's what I have. I guess all your information is stored in your head."

"Yup."

"So, where shall we start?"

Kopp leaned forward. "Why don't you tell me where Marisa Vega is."

Nate set his pen down. "I told you, I have no idea. She called me and told me what happened with her sister and her daughter. I agreed to try to help her."

Kopp rested his arms on the table between them. He folded his hands and leaned back. He didn't say a word.

Nate had used a similar tactic a thousand times on people he'd interviewed. Keep silent, get them talking. He smiled and sipped his Coke.

A minute passed before Kopp said, "You know I'm way ahead of you, right?"

"You don't seem that quick to me."

Kopp cracked a smile and leaned forward. "How was Mexico?"

Nate and Brady had talked about this, but Nate hadn't taken the threat that seriously. What were the chances that Kopp would check flight records, especially if he wasn't still in the Bureau? Apparently, very good.

"A little hot for my taste," Nate said.

"And Marisa? Was she a little hot, too?"

Nate tamped down a flash of irritation. Kopp was trying to throw him off-guard, and Nate couldn't let him. "I haven't seen her."

Kopp nodded slowly.

Bonnie returned with his drink and a fresh Coke for Nate. Kopp thanked her while Nate's brain spun. If Kopp knew Nate had gone to Mexico, what else did he know? Probably way more than Nate had bargained for. Had Kopp come to New Hampshire in hopes of finding Marisa? One last collar, for old time's sake?

Nate had to keep the focus on Ana. "Her daughter and her

sister were kidnapped. She can't turn herself in, and she can't get caught."

"The kidnappers know where she is?"

Nate shook his head.

"I'm not a cop anymore. You can tell me."

"So you can arrest her?"

"If she didn't do anything wrong, what are you afraid of?"

An idea popped into Nate's mind. He tried to come up with a better one. Nothing. He slipped his iPhone out of his pocket and tapped the photos app. A photograph filled his screen. "I saw Marisa and her daughter in Mexico, because she needed my help." He handed Kopp the phone.

Kopp studied it.

"That's Ana. She's four years old. She was an orphan, dumped at the orphanage where Marisa teaches English to the kids. Marisa fell in love with her and began adoption procedures almost immediately."

Kopp scrolled through the photographs. Rude, but Nate didn't say anything. There were photos of Marisa and Leslie on there. At this point, the biggest priority was getting Ana and Leslie back. Nate would worry about getting rid of the photos of Marisa later.

Kopp paused on a photo and angled the phone to Nate. He'd stopped on a close-up of Marisa.

"She looks good."

"This isn't about Marisa," Nate said. "It's about Ana and Leslie. They've been kidnapped. We need your help to get them back."

"I heard you the first time."

Nate held out his hand for his phone. Kopp slipped it in his pocket.

"That's mine."

"I don't want you to warn her."

Nate thought of Sam sitting behind Kopp, furiously typing on her laptop. With luck, Marisa had already been warned.

"I do have more information," Kopp said. "I kept working the case for months after you printed your stories and moved on."

"What can you tell me?"

Kopp leaned back and crossed his arms. "Nothing until I see her."

Nate folded his file and stood. "I guess we're done here. My phone please."

"I don't even have my sandwich." Kopp nodded to the waitress, who was walking toward them across the nearly empty restaurant.

Nate stepped out of the way so the waitress could serve Kopp.

"What else can I get you?" she asked.

"This is perfect. Thanks."

Nate just stood there, feeling stupid.

"Sit down." Kopp tapped some ketchup on his plate before he took a bite of the sandwich. "Wow, that's delicious."

Reluctantly, Nate slid back into the booth. "Not a sauerkraut man myself."

"You don't know what you're missing." Kopp wiped his fingers on a napkin.

"I can't tell you where she is," Nate said.

"Hmm. Looks like I'm going to have to arrest you."

While Kopp dipped a french fry in the ketchup, Nate's stomach dipped to the floor. He'd planned for a lot of contingencies, but this one hadn't even entered his mind. "Arrest me for what?"

Kopp popped the fry in his mouth. "You want some? They're really good."

"Not hungry."

"Suit yourself." Kopp ate another fry.

"How can you arrest me? You're retired."

"I just need to make a call, and we can get someone over here straight away to take care of that. You ever been arrested?"

"Haven't had the pleasure."

Kopp bit the sandwich and took his time swallowing.

Nate's heartbeat was racing. He had no idea what to do here.

"You tell me this is your hometown?" Kopp asked.

Nate imagined how it would feel to be perp-walked out of McNeal's into downtown Nutfield. Enough people knew him as the eldest son of Gordon Boyle, Attorney-at-Law, that it would no doubt create a spectacle. Heck, Nutfield was a quiet tourist town. Anybody getting arrested created a spectacle.

Nate shook off the images. Whatever he had to do to protect Marisa. "Look, I thought you came here to help me. If you're just here to make idle threats—"

"Not idle. I know you and Marisa flew into Logan yesterday. I haven't alerted my old friends at the Bureau yet, but—"

"Why not?"

Kopp shrugged. "I don't think she stole the money. And I don't want to get that little girl—or the sister—killed."

A surge of hope. "Then help me! You said—"

"Not until I see her. Fact is, the Bureau is good at hostage negotiation. They'll probably have a lot better luck saving her sister and her kid than you will. But it's not your decision to make. It's hers."

Maybe Kopp did think Marisa innocent. Maybe he would help them. But maybe those were just more lies to get Nate to give up her location. He wouldn't give Marisa up for anything. They'd just have to find another way to get Leslie and Ana back. Nate blew out a frustrated breath. "Forget it."

"You don't have a lot of choices here, man."

Man. Like they were friends.

"I'm trying to help," Kopp said.

"Fine. Give me my phone and let me make a call."

Nate hoped to at least get his phone back long enough to destroy it. Dropping it in his fresh Coke should do the trick. He wasn't sure what else was on the iPhone, but the updated photograph of Marisa alone would be a good first step to getting her caught.

"Don't think so."

"You're really going to do this? Put two people's lives in danger?"

Kopp tilted his head to the side. "You're really going to go to prison to protect a fugitive?"

"She's not guilty." His voice had been loud enough the hostess turned in their direction. He lowered it. "And I'm not going to prison."

"It's a gamble. You may, you may not."

"I thought you feds were supposed to protect the weak."

Kopp leaned forward. "I already told you, I don't think she's guilty. I have my suspicions about who took the money, but I never thought it was her."

"Could've fooled me."

"I know you don't believe me, but I'm trying to help you."

"So help."

"I need to see her."

"Why?"

Kopp took another bite of his sandwich. Nate had the irrational urge to toss the plate across the room like a Frisbee. Instead, he kept his hands still and waited.

"You tell me her daughter and sister have been kidnapped. But for all I know, she's the one in danger—from you. You knew everything everybody else knew. Maybe you're behind all of this."

"You're crazy."

"You just quit your job, right? Sold your house?"

"How did you—?"

"Not a state secret, man." He sipped his water. "So all of a sudden, you don't need a job? Found a way to make money on the side? Like by kidnapping for ransom."

"I didn't take them. Are you insane?"

Not only did the waitress and the hostess look that time, but Sam turned around and glared at him. Nate looked at the table. It was over, and there was nothing Nate could do. At least Marisa wouldn't have to wonder what happened to him. Sam was there, reporting everything.

A familiar feeling of hopelessness washed over Nate as he stood. He held his hands out in front of him, wrists together. "Go ahead. Arrest me."

Kopp took another bite of his Reuben while Nate stood beside their table. He dropped his hands to his sides. He could run, but the only thing worse than getting led out of McNeal's in handcuffs on a Tuesday afternoon in front of God and everybody would be to do it after being tackled attempting to flee.

Sam had turned back around, but he could see her shaking her head violently. He could imagine what had happened. Sam had messaged Marisa, and Marisa didn't want him to get arrested. Unfortunately, Nate didn't see any other options.

Kopp wiped his mouth with his napkin. "Why don't you see what your friend thinks before we do this?"

"What friend?"

Kopp slid to the end of his seat and looked up at him with raised eyebrows. Nate sidestepped, and Kopp stood and turned to Sam.

Her eyes registered shock—and something else that had Nate rolling his eyes.

Okay, fine. Kopp might be considered *attractive* in some

circles. Female circles, mostly. Based on her reaction, definitely in Sam's circle.

"Your voice sounded older," she said.

Right. Flirt with him, Sam. That'll help.

Kopp smiled and held out his hand to shake. "Garrison Kopp."

She took it and shook. "Samantha Messenger." Was she blushing?

Nate blew out a breath loudly. "Are you two done?"

They ignored him. "What does Marisa want to do?" Kopp asked.

Sam glanced at Nate before she answered. "She doesn't want Nate arrested. He's trying to help her."

"Do you think she can trust me?"

Sam swallowed. "Let me ask her." She turned to type on her laptop while Kopp turned back to Nate. "Sit down."

This meeting had spun so far out of Nate's control he almost laughed as he slid back into the booth. Kopp sat and slid to the inside end of the booth. When Sam turned to speak, he patted the space beside him. "Why don't you join us?"

She gathered her laptop and her bag and slid in beside Kopp. "I asked her. I'm waiting for a reply."

"Good. You want some fries?"

Sam smiled and took one off his plate. "Thanks."

Kopp met Nate's eyes. "Seriously, man. Help yourself."

Nate just sipped his soda and waited.

A moment later, Sam's MacBook dinged. She read the message and looked at Nate. "She said to trust him. She wants you to take him to the cabin."

Well, at least Nate wasn't getting arrested today. He hoped he could say the same about Marisa.

TEN

MARISA PACED BEHIND THE SOFA. Her eyes were scratchy from lack of sleep, her muscles achy. The night before, the soft mattress had wrapped her in luxury while her thoughts had wrapped her in dread.

How was she supposed to sleep without her daughter by her side?

Would Marisa even be able to keep Ana? She hadn't considered the danger when she'd decided to adopt the newborn. At the time, Marisa had thought she'd spend the rest of her life in Mexico. Oh, sure, she'd hoped to come home, but not as a fugitive. And now... Would Ana have a mother in prison, or would the adoption fall through entirely?

Assuming Ana survived.

Rae stepped through the front door, little Johnny on her hip. Marisa had tried not to cry—and failed—when she'd first seen the seven-month-old. He smiled and cooed, his dark hair and skin so like Ana's. Marisa physically ached for her child. How could she survive if she didn't get Ana back?

Now, Johnny was desperately trying to grab the phone from

his mother, who held it to her ear. "Okay, I'll tell her." She paused. "Love you, too."

She ended the call and slid the phone into her pocket. "Brady's headed this way."

Marisa stopped. "No. We don't need to pull him into this. He could lose his job. And you should go, too. You don't need the trouble."

Johnny squealed and squirmed, and Rae set him on the floor. He immediately crawled away. Marisa could remember when Ana had been that age, just itching to walk, to run, to explore her world. Marisa had been terrified every minute, more in Mexico than she would have been in a safe place like this. Mexico had never seemed as dirty as when Ana was sticking everything in her mouth.

Where was that sweet girl now? What kind of environment had the kidnappers taken her and Leslie to? Was it clean? Were they feeding her?

Eat your eggs. She'd said it every day, hoping her daughter would grow up strong and healthy.

Now she just wanted her to grow up.

"We're not going anywhere," Rae said.

Marisa had to blink to return to the conversation, the room.

"Kopp doesn't know we know you're a fugitive," Rae continued.

"Do you think I'm doing the right thing?"

Rae watched Johnny as he tried to pull himself up at the coffee table. The pause told Marisa she was taking the question seriously, which Marisa appreciated. Finally, Rae said, "I don't know how Nate getting arrested would help anything. Brady was right about that—it would just put the authorities onto the fact that you were in the country, and Kopp already knows that. Nate wouldn't give you up."

"I always trusted him."

"But the police would be looking for you everywhere. You'd have to flee, and how could you figure out who stole the money on your own?"

"But what if Kopp arrests me? What if the people who took Ana...?"

Rae wrapped her arms around Marisa and pulled her into a hug.

Marisa barely knew the woman, but Rae's arms felt like a lifeline in a stormy sea. Rae patted Marisa's back. "Brady knows what he's doing. You have to trust him. And Nate."

Marisa stepped away. "And the federal agent who wants to arrest me?" Marisa started pacing again. "I don't even care at this point. I just want Ana and Leslie safe."

"I know. Why don't you sit?"

The sound of tires on gravel sent Marisa to peer out the window. Nate parked Brady's blue truck in the short driveway, and he and Sam stepped out. A black sedan stopped on the narrow road in front of the cabin.

Marisa had the overwhelming urge to bolt. She turned, spied the back door. Right, and then what? Jump in the lake?

She stepped back and stood between the breakfast bar and the sofa. Rae picked up Johnny and joined her.

The door opened, and Sam and Nate stepped inside. "I'm sorry," he said. "This isn't what I thought would happen."

"I know," Marisa said.

Sam and Nate flanked them, Nate sliding Marisa's hand into his. They must look ridiculous, four people and a baby lined up as if they were facing a firing squad.

Nate had left the door slightly ajar. Still, Kopp knocked.

"Come in," Marisa said.

He stepped inside. Kopp had aged in the eight years since she'd seen him last, but he still looked good. Tall, strong jaw, blue eyes, and light brown hair. The guy was still handsome.

He closed the door behind him, turned, and smiled. "Marisa, are you okay?"

She nodded. Her voice wouldn't work.

"Nate, step away, please."

Nate squeezed her hand, and she remembered what Sam had messaged to her earlier, that Kopp was suspicious of Nate.

"Nate's helping me."

"Humor me," he said. "Let's step outside and talk. Just you and me."

"If you're going to arrest me, just do it."

Kopp blew out a breath. "Fine. Everybody else step outside, and Marisa and I will stay in here. I want to talk to her privately."

Nate shifted forward, and the group formed a circle. "We've come this far," Nate said. "I think we have to trust him." He looked at Marisa. "What do you think?"

She swallowed and walked past Nate to join Kopp.

"Outside?" he clarified.

She nodded and led the way.

The screen door slammed behind them. She stopped by the blue truck. "Okay," she said. "Now what?"

"Tell me what happened in Mexico."

Her voice shook as she told him the story, beginning when she first got the email from Nate and ending at that moment.

When she was finished, Kopp nodded and stared into space. "Don't you think it's suspicious that Leslie and Nate showed up, and right after that, Ana and Leslie were kidnapped?"

"Nate doesn't believe I have the money."

"He says he believes you, but—"

"Not once has he suggested I confess and turn the money over. Not once."

"Okay." He processed. "Have you considered going to the FBI? They're very good at this kind of thing."

She shook her head, terror filling her. "He said not to. He said he'd kill them. I can't take that chance."

"You're not keeping quiet so you don't get arrested, right? Because I can help with that. I can't guarantee anything, but—"

"I don't care what happens to me." Her voice rose, and she could feel the panic rising like a flood. "I just want them back. Don't you get that?"

"I do," he said. "It's okay. I'm not going to do anything without your permission."

She swallowed and wrapped her arms around her middle, trying to hold herself together.

Birds chirped and squirrels ran across the dry leaves that littered the ground beneath the trees. Marisa turned and took a few steps between the cabins to look at the lake. Her fingers itched to sketch it. To paint it, even. Painting, drawing, sketching. Those had been her escape for years. Others turned to alcohol or drugs or food, but not Marisa. Those things held no pull for her. But to paint, to recreate something beautiful on a stretched canvas or a crisp white drawing pad.

She hadn't had a good set of paints in years. Hadn't wanted to spend the money, when she needed all her savings and more to pay for the adoption.

Ana.

Tears filled her eyes. They were wasting time. If Kopp wasn't willing to help her, what would she do?

She just wanted her daughter back.

He stepped beside her. "Sure is pretty here."

As if that mattered. As if anything mattered, without Ana.

"Are you going to arrest me?"

MARISA STEPPED INSIDE and found Sam and Nate standing in roughly the same spot as they'd stood when she'd stepped out.

Rae came from Nate's bedroom. "Johnny was late for his nap," she said. "I just laid him down. What happened?"

Marisa wiped the tears still flowing. "He's going to help us. He just had to get something out of his car."

"Thank God," Sam said.

Nate swallowed hard. "Let's sit."

A minute later, Kopp joined them at the table carrying a thick manila envelope. Brady was right behind him. Apparently they'd made introductions outside.

Kopp stopped behind the chair next to Sam and reached across to Rae. "Garrison Kopp."

She shook his hand. "Nice to meet you, Agent Kopp. Reagan Thomas."

Kopp pulled out the chair and sat. "I'm not an agent anymore. Call me Garrison."

"Okay," Rae said.

Garrison looked around the table. "That goes for the rest of you, okay?"

They all nodded, and Brady sat beside his wife.

"What you got there, Garrison?" Nate asked.

"Information." He reached in his front pocket and pulled out a cell phone. He held it out to Nate. "You can have this back."

Nate took it. "Thanks." He nodded to the fat envelope. "Thought you didn't bring anything."

"I had to be sure Marisa was okay." He unclasped the folder and slid out a half-inch stack of papers. "These aren't official FBI files. Not allowed to take those. But I had a few unresolved cases when I retired. I typed up my own notes to help me remember, in case anything ever happened on them."

"Lucky for us," Marisa said.

"That's a lot of papers," Rae said. "You must have remembered a lot."

"This is also stuff I've collected in my spare time."

"Like?" Nate prompted.

He picked up the first section, bound with a paperclip. "I told you I had new information, and I do. Nothing earth-shattering. I'm not sure how much you remember, but only a couple of guys at the firm were aware of the fraud. Charles Gray, Vincent Depalo"—he nodded to Marisa—"and two other middle-management guys."

"And Jeremy Kinnison," Nate said. "But he cashed out before they got caught. He might have had access—"

"Wasn't Kinnison," Garrison said. "He was in the Bahamas when the money was stolen, and our computer geniuses proved the transfer was made from a desktop in the G&K offices."

"Whose computer?" Nate asked.

"Charles's, and we know he didn't do it. His whereabouts is accounted for that night." He flipped through his papers, then looked up. "Whose place is this? Could I have a glass of water?"

Sam stood. "Anyone else?"

Nobody spoke. She stepped around the bar into the kitchen. "Keep talking. I can hear you."

Garrison continued. "I've kept my eyes on the other two guys ever since. Burns managed to plead to a misdemeanor. He got another job right away and seems to be doing fine. I have no reason to believe he stole the money.

"Anderson was deeper in it. He skirted prison but pled to a felony. He couldn't get another job in banking. He bounced from lousy job to lousy job and finally ended up working at an auto body shop. He got a divorce. I assume his wife dumped him when he lost his job."

"You keep that close tabs on people?" Rae asked.

"I kept my eyes open. But also, I did some digging last night. I have no reason to believe Anderson stole the money. But he might have a good motive for kidnapping. A little payback for what it cost him."

Rae wrote the name on her notepad while Nate nodded. Maybe they were getting closer. A tiny surge of hope rose in Marisa's heart. Calling Garrison Kopp had been a good idea.

Sam slid the glass in front of him and took her seat.

He smiled. "Thank you."

"Sure."

Garrison turned to Marisa. "Have you thought of anything else over the years? Anybody else who might've had access?"

Marisa wanted to protect Leslie, but her sister needed their help now—and Ana, too. She'd want Marisa to do whatever she had to do to get her back home and safe. "My sister overheard Vinnie when he confessed to me. At least I think she did, but I don't know how much. Maybe she told Charles."

Garrison nodded and stared beyond her. After a minute, he said, "Huh."

"What?" Marisa said.

He said nothing.

Marisa looked at Nate, who shrugged.

"Okay," Garrison finally said, "your sister's the missing puzzle piece. Why didn't you tell me?"

"I wasn't sure. I'm still not."

"How close are you and your sister?"

She sat straighter. "We were very close."

"But you suspect her." Not a question.

Marisa recounted the conversation she'd had the day before around this very table while Garrison nodded silently.

"Sounds like she's a good bet," he finally said. "Who else might she have told?"

"Like, you mean besides Charles?"

"Friends, boyfriend?"

"Leslie didn't have close friends. Just me. And no boyfriend. She's engaged now. I don't know the guy's name, but it doesn't matter. He wasn't in the picture back then."

Garrison looked past Marisa to Nate. He shrugged.

Rae wrote something on her notepad.

"What?" Marisa said.

Garrison turned back to Marisa. "I wish we could question her. I wish she'd come forward at the time. Any idea why she didn't?"

"I don't know anything more than I told you. I mean... If she did tell Charles, she'd inadvertently gotten my fiancé killed. I think she was scared I wouldn't forgive her."

"Maybe. When she came to Mexico to see you, she still didn't confess?"

"No."

"I see." Garrison looked back at Marisa. "It's too bad she didn't. Let's say you're right and your sister's the one who told Charles what she overheard. Maybe somebody else overheard that conversation? I could have asked her who else she saw in the office that day. If Charles got any phone calls while they talked. If he made a phone call as she was leaving. But I didn't get to question her, and now all those details are lost to us."

"If she did it, she didn't mean any harm," Marisa said.

Garrison looked at Nate. "When did she ask you to help find Marisa?"

He blinked, thought for a moment. "Gosh, was it just four days ago? Seems like forever."

"You didn't report that new information to the authorities?"

"We got on a plane a few hours later," Nate said.

"Otherwise you would have?" Garrison's smile said he knew better.

"It honestly didn't occur to me."

Garrison turned to Marisa. "I think you need to talk to Charles Gray next. I'd go with you, but I doubt he'll open up to me."

"Why him?" Sam asked.

"Based on the information we have, the only people who knew we were investigating G&K were Leslie—though how much she knew is unknown—and Charles. Since Leslie appears to be a victim at this point, and she's not available to interview, Charles is your next best bet."

Marisa could remember very well how it felt to be in Charles's crosshairs. Back then, she'd been too afraid to set foot out of her hotel room for fear he or his men would do to her what they'd done to Vinnie. She'd not seen her fiancé's body, but she'd heard enough. No clean execution for Vinnie. He was beaten to death. If Charles's men had taken Ana and Leslie, would they hurt them the same way? A picture filled her mind, her beautiful daughter, battered and beaten.

"Hey." Nate scooted closer and wrapped his arm around her shoulders. "It's okay. I'll go. Charles is behind bars. He can't hurt you."

"I'm just..." She shook her head, afraid to even voice her fears for her daughter and sister.

"I'm not going to tell Charles where you are."

She turned to face him. "But what about you?"

Nate swallowed hard. "I'll be fine."

ELEVEN

Sing Sing Correctional Facility squatted uncomfortably on the east bank of the Hudson River about an hour's drive north of New York City. Nate parked in the visitor lot, dread settling in his stomach as he looked up at the guard towers overhead and imagined the rifles perched there. He took his driver's license and his keys. He'd left his wallet with Marisa at the Dunkin' Donuts a few miles away, where she waited with Garrison. He wasn't sure why they'd both insisted on making the trip. Marisa he could understand. As she'd explained to him rather loudly that morning, it was her daughter and her sister in danger. But Garrison?

Nate stepped out of Brady's blue pickup and surveyed the view of the Hudson River. The sun reflected off it, making the gunmetal gray waters shimmer. He turned back to the prison. Amazing the difference a hundred-eighty degrees could make. All concrete and barbed wire.

After the rigmarole of getting checked in and searched, Nate left his ID, his keys, and his hope with the guard. When the door closing him off from the free world slammed behind him, he had the sudden urge to turn and bang on it, beg them to let him out. The terrible fear rose in his stomach until his entire body trembled. He rubbed his wrists, felt the skin where ropes had once held him, fought the urge to scream. Finally, the next door clicked open, and he walked into a metal and concrete hell.

He was led to the visiting area, an overlarge room where he chose a table near the door and sat with his back to the wall. There were a lot of tables, which he figured were crammed on the weekends, considering Sing Sing's two thousand prisoners. Just a few other prisoners and visitors were there today, far from where Nate sat. The room wasn't bad, all things considered. No discernible scent apart from cleaning solution and coffee. Vending machines stood along one wall, and trash cans were scattered throughout. Though Nate didn't go to get a closer look, it seemed there were toys and playthings in one corner for children who visited.

Who would bring a child there? And what would it be like to visit your father in a place like this? To visit his own dad, the town lawyer and solid citizen? He couldn't comprehend such madness. Even though his mother had died when he was a teen, he'd still been dealt a good hand where his family was concerned.

Nate had visited a prison before—a minimum security federal institution that housed mostly white-collar criminals. That had been Nate's beat—financial markets, mortgage fraud, and SEC violations. This was so far out of his league, he felt like a little leaguer at Fenway Park.

Sing Sing had opened back in the early eighteen-hundreds, and though much of it had been updated and remodeled, there was still an air about the place, like it had known every kind of evil in its nearly two hundred years, and it wasn't impressed.

The door opened, and Charles Gray walked in. Nate had never met him, but he'd seen photographs of the man who'd once been a force on Wall Street, welcomed in the finest clubs.

He'd been silver-haired and distinguished before. After nearly eight years in a maximum security prison, he was barely recognizable.

Charles scanned the room until his eyes rested on Nate, the only visitor without a prisoner. He shuffled toward him and stopped at the table. "You're the reporter, right?"

Nate stood and held out his hand. "Nate Boyle."

Charles shook his hand and sat, back straight, eyes piercing through his black-rimmed glasses. He exuded confidence, but the years in prison hadn't been good to him. Gray was no longer just his last name. The man's skin matched his hair as if one had seeped into the other. He looked far older than his sixty years, and for a moment Nate wondered if the prisoner needed a doctor.

"Bad ticker," Gray said, as if he'd read his mind. "And being surrounded by these people doesn't help."

"I can imagine. Are the doctors taking care of you?"

"They keep me alive. If I die in here, there's a mountain of paperwork."

"Good to know they care."

Charles nearly smiled, but it faded fast. "What can I do for you, Mr. Boyle?"

"Nate, please." Not that he wanted to make friends with this guy, but he did need his help, and he had nothing to offer in return. "I have a problem."

"Don't we all?"

"You remember Marisa Vega?"

Charles hunched slightly, as if a weight suddenly rested on his upper back. "Is she okay?"

Nate's question faltered on his lips. Was that genuine concern? "Last I heard, you wanted her dead."

"No." His head shook, seemed to shake his whole body, and Nate worried something was wrong. He was about to call the guard when Charles let out a strangled sob. "No. I never meant..."

Nate waited until the man regained control. After a moment, Charles continued.

"I never meant for any of it to happen. It was just... It seemed like such an easy way to make money. It didn't hurt anybody. At least, I didn't realize people were getting hurt. We were helping people get into houses."

"Which they couldn't afford."

"I know, I know. And when it all went sideways, most of those people lost everything. I didn't... Who knew the housing market was going to implode?"

"Some say you and people like you caused it."

"Maybe we did. We just wanted to make money."

Nate nodded but kept his mouth shut.

"I didn't pay William Buckley to kill Vinnie. I just wanted him to scare him, that's all. I never would have hurt that girl."

"Like every other guy in here, you're innocent?"

Charles's shoulders hunched even more. "I'm as guilty as any of these guys. It took me a couple years in here to realize that. At first, I was angry at the injustice of it all. But I got to thinking about Vinnie. He was a nice kid. Young and enthusiastic. And smart. You have no idea how smart that kid was. He hadn't had a lot of opportunities, not like I had. He was the third son of a single mother, went to college on a needs-based scholarship. But he made it worth something. Straight A's. I hired him right out of college.

"Vinnie saw me as a father-figure. Truth is, I wasn't a very good dad to my own kids, especially Richard. By the time he was a teen, I was... Well, I was busy with other stuff. And his mother was no better. And Richard... He wasn't like John and Andrew. They were like me, you know? Ivy League attitudes and brains. But Richard, I never knew how to connect with him.

And he never seemed to like me very much. I love him. Love all my kids, though I never see them."

"They don't visit?"

He looked around. "Would you want to visit this place?" After a minute he said, "Doesn't matter. They have their own lives."

He looked down, seemed to slump a little more. "Doesn't matter."

Nate prompted, "But Vinnie...?"

Charles looked up. "I loved Vinnie. I taught him the business and helped him succeed. I never should have gotten him involved in the other stuff. Because Vinnie would have done anything I asked of him. He was desperate for somebody to tell him he mattered."

Charles wiped a tear. "He did matter. He trusted me, and I betrayed him."

"He was about to betray you."

"My fault," Charles said.

Of all scenarios Nate had prepared for on his drive down that morning, this one had never crossed his mind. "Did you have some sort of religious experience in here?"

Charles nodded. "You could say that, yeah. I can never undo what I did, but I'm sorry for it. I wish I could tell the girl that. I ruined a lot of lives, but what I did to Vinnie, to her—that still plagues me."

Nate wasn't sure if Charles was sincere or just a great actor. "If that's true, I might be able to help you get some redemption."

"Only God can offer redemption, but I'll do whatever I can."

It was unsettling how much the murdering felon suddenly sounded like Nate's father and step-mom. "After Marisa fled for her life, she ended up working in an orphanage in...a foreign country. A baby girl was left there, and Marisa fell in love. She adopted the girl."

"Good for her."

"That was four years ago. She stayed hidden and made a life for herself there. Three days ago, that little girl was kidnapped, along with Marisa's sister."

"Leslie?"

Charles remembered the cleaning lady's name? After everything that had happened? Nate made a note of that. "Leslie and Ana were snatched from a shopping center, and Marisa was given an ultimatum. Return the money stolen from you"—Nate nodded to Charles—"or her daughter and sister die."

Charles leaned forward. "Why doesn't she just return the money? Surely she hasn't spent it all. Unless she was living like a princess—"

"She doesn't have it."

"Bad investments?"

"Charles, she didn't steal your money."

He blinked, tilted his head to the side. "Of course she did. Nobody else could have done it."

"I'm here because I hoped you'd have some idea of who else might've stolen it."

Charles opened his mouth, snapped it shut. "But, if she didn't steal it, why did she run?"

"Weren't you going to kill her?"

"I just wanted my money back."

"She didn't steal your money."

"But nobody else—"

"We're talking in circles, Charles. It's irrelevant what you thought."

"Cops thought it, too."

"They were wrong. Marisa didn't take your money. She ran because she was afraid for her life, and because the feds thought she was guilty. She ran because she felt she had no other options. Frankly, I agreed with her on that."

"You helped her?"

"Just kept her hidden until she could make a plan. And gave her some traveling money."

Charles cleared his throat. "You're sure she doesn't have it?"

"They took her daughter. Don't you think she'd give them the money to get the girl back?"

"Maybe she likes the money—"

"I saw where she's been living. Trust me, she doesn't have it."

He took a long breath. "What do you want from me?"

"How did you find out Vinnie was planning to cooperate with the FBI?"

Charles's gaze settled on the wall behind Nate. "I guess it doesn't matter now. I was careful to keep quiet before, because she begged me, but..."

Nate waited, fairly certain what he was about to hear.

"Leslie told me she'd overheard Vinnie telling his girlfriend about the stuff he'd been doing, the system we'd been working."

"Leslie knew about the fraud?" Nate clarified.

Charles shook his head. "No details. I think Leslie just... G&K was her first sizable contract, and she wanted to keep in my good graces. And I think she didn't want her sister to marry Vinnie, though I always believed they made a good match, and Marisa was loyal to him."

Nate's next words faltered as he considered that phrase. "What do you mean, Marisa was loyal?"

Charles shifted in the chair, focus downward. "Just that there were a lot of guys up there who'd have, you know, liked to get to know Marisa better. She's, you know." He looked back up. "She's gorgeous. Guys with a lot of money and influence made her a lot of offers. But she never strayed from Vinnie."

The information didn't surprise Nate. "Leslie told you Vinnie was considering going to the FBI?"

"She didn't know for sure. She said she overheard him say

something about the FBI, but she didn't know exactly what he'd said. Anyway, I—"

"Just a second." Nate needed to process that. Maybe Leslie had had a bigger role to play in what had happened eight years earlier than Nate and Marisa had ever comprehended. "Sorry. Go on."

"Everything okay?"

Nate nodded. "You thought Vinnie was considering going to the FBI—"

"I wasn't sure what Leslie had heard, but the FBI's involvement—that scared me. On the other hand, Vinnie had always been loyal to me. I wasn't sure I even believed her. I figured he'd just confessed what he'd been doing to his girlfriend. That's what I'd hoped, anyway." Charles took off his glasses and cleaned them on his drab shirt.

He kept his gaze downward when he continued. "I hired Buckley to scare him into keeping quiet. He wasn't supposed to kill him."

"That's not what Buck says."

Charles looked up, met Nate's eyes. "He got a reduced sentence for turning against me. But he knows." Charles nodded and looked at the wall. "He knows."

"You have no idea who else could have stolen the money."

"I didn't tell anybody. I figured I could keep it quiet, protect Vinnie—"

"Protect him?"

"From Anderson."

"Russell Anderson?"

"Right. He'd taken over the operation at that point. Another smart guy from the wrong side of the tracks, but unlike Vinnie, Anderson hadn't always kept his nose clean. He'd been in some scrapes as a young guy. He was a little rough around the edges and still had contacts with... He's the one who introduced me to Buck."

"You told him Vinnie had confessed?"

"No, no. Just that I needed someone to do me an unpleasant favor. I gave him the impression it was a family matter. I didn't want Anderson anywhere near this. I didn't know what he'd do. I was trying to protect Vinnie."

Protect him? That seemed a stretch, considering Vinnie ended up dead.

"But maybe Buck told Anderson who he was really after," Nate said. "Maybe Anderson convinced Buck to kill him. Or, after the fact when Vinnie turned up dead, maybe Anderson put two-and-two together. Maybe Anderson's got the money."

Charles seemed to consider that. "I never have figured out how Marisa"—he nodded toward Nate, possibly in deference to Nate's opinion—"or whoever it was got access to my personal account. The business account, maybe. But mine? Made no sense."

"But somebody did. Anderson had access to the building, and he might've known something was going on."

Charles shrugged. "Maybe. I don't know anymore."

Okay, so maybe Anderson knew more than Charles gave him credit for. It was something.

"Your wife," Nate said. "She had had access to your bank account, right?"

"But why would she steal from me?"

"You still married to her?"

Charles's smile was sad. "She divorced me when I was convicted. Said she couldn't fathom visiting a place like this. I don't blame her. This isn't what she signed up for."

So much for *for better or for worse*.

"Maybe she got wind something was happening at your firm, and she took the money to safeguard it."

"My money, maybe. But the firm's? Why would she destroy the very company that financed her lifestyle?"

"If she knew what was going on—"

"She didn't."

"You didn't confide in her."

Charles looked at the table. When he looked back up, his eyes were sadder. "I was not a good husband. There were a lot of other women. My wife and I hadn't been close in a long time."

"Maybe she figured out about the other women—"

"She always knew," Charles said. "Didn't seem to care, as long as the money kept coming in."

"Let me just confirm. The kidnappers are asking for two million. Is that what was in your personal account?"

He looked toward the ceiling, paused a moment, and met Nate's eyes. "You have to understand, I knew something was up. I was planning to transfer it offshore first thing the next morning, try to shield it. So I gathered as much as I could, to protect it. Yes, it was about two million."

"But if your wife took the money in your personal account—and everything in the business's—she wouldn't need you anymore."

"Wasn't just the money. Being associated with me made her part of the top echelon of New York society."

"Not after you were arrested."

"But she can't have known that was going down."

"Okay." Nate made a mental note to check out Charles's ex-wife. "These other women... Did you confide in any of them?"

"Not everything, but I was pretty serious with a woman at the time. I was in love with her." He rolled his eyes. Nate wasn't sure if Charles considered himself a fool for falling for this woman, or if he thought love itself was foolish. "I was trying to figure out how to extricate myself from my marriage without making an enemy of my wife. Jessica was far too young for me, but she cared for me."

"Jessica what?"

Charles paused, seemed to weigh the pros and cons of answer. "English. Jessica English."

"You no longer believe she cared for you?"

"The fact that she's never come to visit tells me something."

"This is a pretty scary place, Charles. Maybe she's afraid. Maybe she has no idea how to handle it."

"She never answered when I called, either."

"Oh." How could Nate actually feel sorry for this guy? "Did she know what you were up to?"

"I told her a little bit. It's been a long time, though. I don't remember exactly how much."

"Do you think she might've had something to do with the money being stolen?"

Charles was shaking his head before Nate finished the question. "She'd never set foot in G&K's offices. She wouldn't have the foggiest idea how to go about something like that."

"Maybe she met somebody who did."

"I told her I was worried about Vinnie, but she didn't know there was anything illegal going on. I can't see how she could have been involved in any of it."

Nate wasn't convinced, but he didn't argue with the guy. He stood. "Thank you for your time. If I have any more questions, is it okay if I come back?"

Charles stood, too, and shook his hand. "Anytime. Not like I have anything better to do. You're in contact with Marisa Vega?"

Nate nodded.

"Tell her I'm sorry. Tell her... I know it's nothing, but I'm sorry for all I did to her. I wish I could do more to help."

Strangest thing was, Nate believed him.

NATE STEPPED into the Dunkin' Donuts to see Marisa and Garrison huddled together on a bench with their backs to the window. Two half-empty cups sat on the table in front of them. They watched something on Garrison's cell phone and laughed.

The sight of her laughing warmed him.

She looked up and smiled.

He crossed the room. "What's so funny?"

"Could you hear us from there?" She nudged Garrison in the shoulder, and he moved to the chair across from her. "Garrison was showing me some funny videos."

Garrison lifted his smartphone. "We have access to all the information known to man on these phones..."

"And we use them to watch cat videos." Marisa laughed, and Garrison joined her.

Nate chuckled with them. "Did you two eat?"

"A while ago," Garrison said. "Grab something, and you can tell us how it went."

He ordered a bagel sandwich and returned to the table, where he slid into the booth beside Marisa.

"Well?" she prompted.

"A few possibilities. First, Charles wanted me to tell you how sorry he is." He relayed Charles's insistence that he'd never wanted Vinnie to die, and that he'd never had any intention of hurting her. "He just wanted his money back and thought you had it."

"Right," Garrison said. "Every guy in Sing Sing is innocent."

Between bites of his sandwich, Nate flipped through his notebook. He'd written down everything he could remember from the conversation as soon as he'd gotten to his truck. Now, he detailed the information Charles had given him. He left out the part about Leslie. Marisa knew, but Nate had a niggling idea that there was more to the story than they'd uncovered yet. He needed more information before he shared that. He'd tell Garrison in private later, see what the cop thought.

When he'd finished the report and his lunch, he said, "I think we should go see Anderson." He looked at Garrison. "You said you know where he works?"

Garrison took his thick file from the chair beside him. "I have it in here somewhere. But I don't think he stole the money."

"But if we can figure out who kidnapped Leslie and Ana," Marisa said, "maybe we can find them."

Her expression looked hopeful. Nate nodded. Whatever it took to keep that look on her face.

"It's been three days," Marisa said. "Why haven't they called back?"

Nate glanced at Garrison, who was still flipping through his file. "It's a good question."

"Maybe something terrible has happened." Her expression faded back to the look of terror she'd worn so often since the kidnapping.

Nate scooted closer and took her hand. "There's no reason to believe that."

"But why wouldn't they call back?"

Garrison looked up from his file. "They gave you a week."

"Still..."

Garrison nodded slowly. "Nobody knew you'd adopted Ana until Nate and Leslie got to Mexico, right?"

"She didn't tell us until we got there," Nate said.

Garrison looked back at Marisa. "So let's say these guys followed Nate and Leslie to Acapulco. I'm not sure how that happened, but it seems it did. Otherwise, they wouldn't know about your daughter. They see the girl, they see their opportunity, and they come up with a plan. They snatch Leslie and Ana. Then they call you and say they'll be in the States."

"Why wouldn't they just take me?" Marisa asked. "Ana and Leslie are innocent."

Nate had no answer. He looked at Garrison, who shrugged. "Maybe they thought you'd need to be free to get to the money. Maybe they didn't want to take on Nate."

That answer didn't satisfy Nate, but he didn't have a better one. Marisa didn't look convinced, either.

"Why do you think they wanted to return to the States?"

Garrison shook his head. "Because they're idiots. If you're going to kidnap someone, Mexico is a far better place to do it. Happens there all the time. The authorities don't have nearly enough resources to follow up on every disappearance."

"Exactly," Marisa said. "So why?"

Garrison shrugged. "They're not very smart. They didn't feel comfortable there, so they wanted to come home. The guy on the phone was American, right?"

"Sounded like a New Yorker. But the guy who grabbed me was Mexican."

"Probably a hired gun. The guys in charge are American. Whoever they are, they're arrogant and think they won't get caught. In any event," Garrison continued, "they put their plan together on the fly. They can't have had forged papers before they snatched Leslie and Ana, because they'd need good photographs. Did Leslie have her passport on her?"

"No." Marisa looked at Nate to confirm, and he nodded. "We found it in her stuff at the hotel."

"If the kidnappers planned to fly out of Mexico, they'd need to have gotten papers to do it. That would take time."

"Good point," Nate said. "How long would that take?"

"Maybe their Mexican accomplice could have gotten them papers to fly out. But they couldn't guarantee that you wouldn't go straight to the cops." Garrison leveled a gaze at Nate. "Which you should have."

Marisa said, "But they told us—"

"I know what they told you. Still, that would have been the right play. Because if you had, the authorities would have looked for them at the borders. If they were coming back to the States, they had to leave from somewhere and go in somewhere else. All those somewheres are crawling with cops."

Good logic. Nate wished he'd thought of it.

"My guess," Garrison continued, "was that they didn't want to risk all that. They found another way into the country. Either they drove and smuggled Leslie and Ana through, or they headed to the Gulf and secured passage on a ship."

"That makes sense," Marisa said. "How long would that take?"

Garrison shrugged. "Days. If I were you, I wouldn't worry. They're probably still traveling."

Nate studied Garrison's expression. He couldn't tell if the guy really believed it, or if he'd just wanted to make Marisa feel better. Either way, she seemed relieved, which left Nate thankful for the FBI agent.

NATE AND GARRISON left Marisa in the pickup a few streets over from the auto body shop where Russell Anderson worked. She'd argued that she wanted to go with them, but Nate adamantly refused to take her to visit the former G&K employee. Even if Anderson'd had nothing to do with the kidnapping or the stolen money, there was a good chance he blamed Marisa for what had become of his life. No point in subjecting her to that.

When Garrison took Nate's side, Marisa agreed to hang back.

After the first block, Garrison said, "What'd you leave out?"

"What do you mean?"

"There was something else you learned from Charles Gray, right? Something you didn't want to tell Marisa?"

Nate glanced at the man beside him. "How did you know?"

Garrison shrugged "Instinct, maybe."

Instinct indeed.

"Well?"

Nate told Garrison what Charles had said about Leslie.

"Marisa's theory is correct," Garrison said. "Leslie set the whole thing in motion."

"The question is, why?"

"Any guesses?"

He thought about the woman he'd spent so much time with. "Leslie's a bit of an enigma. She's rough around the edges, very argumentative. She admitted she'd always been jealous of her sister. But she seemed legitimately sorry for that now. I didn't get the impression that she'd want to hurt her, but then I didn't know her back then. Maybe she was trying to protect Marisa from Vinnie, from marrying someone involved in that kind of thing."

"Maybe," Garrison said. "But why not tell the truth when the FBI stepped in? Like I said to Marisa, it would have helped us a lot if we'd known."

"It's possible she was afraid Marisa wouldn't forgive her. Even if it had been inadvertent, she got Vinnie killed."

"You believe that?"

Nate couldn't seem to force words past the niggling suspicion in his gut.

"It's possible."

Garrison didn't sound convinced, and Nate wasn't either. Leslie might have helped clear her sister's name, if she'd been honest. She hadn't done anything illegal, and surely putting up with her sister's anger would have been better than never seeing her again. Even if she hadn't come forward at first, when suspicion turned to Marisa, Leslie could have given the cops more information, kept her sister out of their crosshairs. But she hadn't. Nate couldn't help but think they were missing a big piece of the puzzle.

Nate waited for the former FBI guy to at least hazard another guess. Instead, Garrison remained silent for the rest of their walk.

The body shop wasn't far from the entrance to the Lincoln Tunnel. Hell's Kitchen was like a plumber at a cocktail party. Manhattan might need its goods and services, but she hoped her guests wouldn't get a glimpse of the crack in their sophisticated facade. Although they were just a handful of city blocks from the New York Times building and Times Square, this corner might have been in a different city all together. A warehouse on one side, a couple of unmarked brick buildings on the other, and in front of a backdrop of skyscrapers, a one-story brick building with a blue-and-white sign above that read Acme Auto Body.

"Whenever I hear the word *Acme*," Garrison said, "I think of Wile E. Coyote."

Nate could picture the coyote beside an Acme invention—and the explosion that often followed. "Not the image you want of the place fixing your car."

"No kidding." Garrison stopped in front of the door. "Look, let me do the talking, okay?"

"Why?"

"Like you said, I have an instinct for people."

"You said that. I think you just got lucky. And I have an instinct, too. I interview people for a living."

"I've been collaring criminals for nearly twenty years. Trust me, okay?"

Nate started to argue, but this wasn't a competition. "Fine. What's your strategy?"

"Ask a bunch of questions, hope for the best."

Some strategy.

They pushed through the door of the Acme Auto Body.

Nate was surprised at the interior. He'd expected to see a bunch of bays with cars suspended in midair. Instead, they stepped into a nice lobby area with upholstered chairs and magazines on the tables. Two men sat in the chairs, both wearing business clothes. One was typing on a laptop, the other scrolling on his phone. A faint scent of paint mingled with air freshener coming from one of those plug-in things on the wall between the two men. A receptionist looked up from her desk behind a glass-fronted partition.

"Can I help you?"

Garrison stepped forward. "Looking for Russell Anderson."

"Sure thing." She picked up a phone, spoke into it, and hung up. "He'll be out in a sec. Have a seat. You need something to drink? There's coffee in the corner and sodas in the mini fridge."

"Great. Thanks."

Garrison chose a water bottle out of the fridge. "Want something?"

Nate sat in one of the chairs. "I'm good."

Garrison unscrewed his water and sipped it. He'd barely gotten it re-screwed when a man opened the door that separated the lobby from the area beyond. He wore a pair of khakis and a blue golf shirt. His hair was neat and cut short, and his face was clean-shaven. Nate had assumed the guy worked on cars. Obviously not. The man stepped out and looked around. His gaze landed on Garrison.

Garrison stood. "Russell Anderson. You remember me?"

"Unfortunately."

Nate stood. "I'm Nate Boyle."

"We'd like a few minutes of your time." Garrison stepped toward the man. "It won't take long at all."

Anderson looked at the other men in the waiting area, who were watching the exchange. "Fine. Come on back." He turned and led the way.

Through the door, the scene changed. The left-hand side of the long hallway was lined with windows showing men working on cars in various states of disrepair. The scent of paint and the sounds of pounding and drilling and shouting drifted through the glass. On the right, past the receptionist's office, Anderson stepped into a small, cluttered room that held a big wooden desk. He sat in a leather chair on the far side. Garrison took the chair that faced the desk. With no other seats, Nate closed the door behind them and leaned against it.

"Whatever it is you think I did," Anderson said, "you're wrong."

"That's what I hear," Garrison said. "And you should know, I'm no longer with the FBI."

"Oh. What's this about?"

"Marisa Vega."

Anderson's perplexed expression turned to a scowl. "What about her? They find her yet?"

"Somebody found her," Garrison said. "Any idea who it might have been?"

"How would I know?"

Garrison didn't answer. Instead, he took in the windowless office. Posters of muscle cars had been tacked to the walls. A few awards Nate couldn't read hung behind Anderson's head. Files were stacked on the desk, and a black computer monitor sat on the far corner, angled toward the chair.

"What is it you do here?" Garrison asked.

"I'm the manager. I keep the books, make sure the customers are getting what they want, and deal with the employees."

"That must be a challenge," Garrison said.

"They're good guys. The ones who aren't don't last very long."

Garrison nodded. "Far cry from Wall Street."

"What's going on here? What do you think I did?"

"Nothing." Garrison settled his long frame back in his chair, which creaked. "Ever talk to any of your old friends?"

"You mean from G&K?"

Garrison shrugged.

"You think they want me around? I'm a felon."

"You're doing okay, though."

Anderson looked beyond Garrison for a moment. "There was a guy who worked in the same building as me back then, a stockbroker a few floors down from G&K. We used to get drinks together, hit on women. Played golf a few times. We were friends. He brought his car in a couple months ago. A BMW or some such thing. He looked right at me and acted like he'd never seen me before."

"That must've made you mad," Garrison said.

"What are you, my therapist? Yeah, I was mad. But geez." He slowed his speech as if talking to a dimwit. "I'm a felon. I wouldn't want to be friends with me, either."

"So nobody else?"

"I don't keep in contact with any of them. Charles is in prison. Vinnie...well, you know what happened to Vinnie. Burns got off with a slap on the wrist. He's still working on Wall Street. I haven't tried to contact him."

"Lot of people lost their jobs. You don't hear from any of them?"

Anderson seemed about to snap. He blew out a long breath. "I don't see anybody. I don't want to. Look, I've got a life now, okay? My wife left me, and I was pretty ticked off for a long time. Now, I've got a good job. I help people with their taxes on the side for extra money. I bought a place in New Jersey. I got a

woman who lives with me. My daughter comes over on weekends. We're doing good."

"Glad to hear it," Garrison said.

"I never belonged on Wall Street. I think Charles brought
me on because he knew about the trouble I'd gotten into as a kid.
Figured I had...questionable morals."

"And he was right."

"That's in the past."

A cell phone rang. Garrison reached into his pocket and
pulled his out. He swore and stood. "I have to take this."

"Go ahead," Nate said.

Garrison passed him on his way out. Nate slid into the chair
and pulled out his notebook.

Anderson seemed to relax when Garrison was gone.
"What's going on?"

"Marisa Vega."

"So he said. What about her? They find her?"

"They who?"

"Whoever. The feds. Weren't they looking for her?"

"Why would they be?"

"'Cause of the money, of course." He threw up his hands.
"She stole millions of dollars."

"Why are you so sure Marisa did it?"

"She disappeared, didn't she?"

"She thought your friend Buck was going to kill her, like he
killed Vinnie."

Anderson narrowed his eyes. "What's this about?"

"Did you know Buck was going after Vinnie?"

Anderson lifted his hands, palms out. "I knew nothing about
that. Charles said he needed a guy to do him a favor. He told me
his kid was getting in with the wrong crowd."

"You believed that?"

"Why wouldn't I?"

"Buck was your friend. He didn't tell you the truth?"

Anderson stood abruptly, and his wheeled chair hit the wall behind him. "This is... Buck was not my friend. He was a guy I knew, that's all. A guy from my neighborhood."

"He never told you who his target was?"

"I went over all this before. I never talked to Buck. I just gave Charles his number. That's it."

Nate settled deeper in the chair. The way the office was configured, there was no way Anderson could get out without passing Nate, who purposely took up a lot of space, unless Anderson wanted to climb over his desk like a gorilla. "And you had no idea Vinnie was talking to the feds."

"Not a clue." Anderson looked at the door, glared at Nate, and sat back down. "Don't you think if I knew, I'd have sheltered some of my money? The feds confiscated everything. If I'd known, I would have emptied my accounts, stuck my money overseas like Charles did."

"So you think Charles took the money?"

"That's not what I meant. But he has other money, accounts the feds never found. You should see how his wife still lives. Obviously, there was more money."

"His wife's living large?"

"Like nothing changed."

Nate made a note of that. "Why do you think it was Marisa who stole the money?"

"Who else? She knew what was going on. She knew the feds were coming. She was ticked her boyfriend got killed. And I don't blame her. Except why not just steal Charles's money? Why destroy the whole business? Why make it so everybody loses their jobs?"

"One thing I don't understand," Nate said. "Marisa was just the cleaning lady. I can see how she might have been able to dig through paperwork, get access to the business accounts. But how do people figure she stole Charles's money, too?"

"You don't get it? That's the easiest part of all. Obviously, she was sleeping with him."

"As in...you mean Vinnie right? But how would he—?"

"Charles."

The very thought of Marisa with that gray man. Nate couldn't imagine. "You think Marisa and Charles—?"

"Obviously. How else would she have gotten the money?"

"You assume they were sleeping together because she stole the money. And you assume she stole the money because they were sleeping together. And at the same time, you assume she stole the money because she was mad her fiancé was killed, all while she was sleeping with his boss, the guy who had him killed. That doesn't make sense."

"Why, because you can't screw one person and love another?" He looked at Nate like he felt sorry for him.

"You don't have any other evidence for this supposed affair between Charles and Marisa? Because Charles told me the name of his mistress."

"Jessica English. Yeah, everybody knew about her. She shot her mouth off all over town about her relationship with Charles. But you have to understand Charles... I don't want to say anything bad about the guy. I mean, I hate that we got caught, but I was right there with him. I don't blame him for what happened. Not anymore. But the guy was like a horny rabbit. He cheated on his wife, cheated on his mistresses, cheated on the girls he cheated with. Any willing woman, Charles was there. Call it an addiction if you want. I think he just liked sex."

Nate tried to put together the image of the man he'd met in prison with Anderson's information. Of course, when Charles was in his heyday, making boatloads of money and throwing it around like confetti, there'd probably been plenty of willing women.

But had Marisa been one of them?

"You don't believe it," Anderson said.

"I spent a lot of time with her. I never got that impression."

"Like she'd have told you. She was grieving her dead fiancé."

"The thing is, Marisa Vega didn't steal the money. So your theory is flawed."

"Not just *my* theory. Everybody assumed she was screwing him."

Nate's temper was rising like the tide. He needed it to roll back. "Let's just assume everybody was wrong. Because Marisa didn't steal the money. But somebody thinks she did. That somebody kidnapped her four-year-old daughter. Now she has to figure out who took it, or the kidnappers are going to kill her child."

Anderson's jaw dropped. He sat back in his chair and closed his eyes. "It's never going to be over, is it?"

"Any other bright ideas?"

He opened his eyes and shook his head. "I'm sorry. I have no idea. Is Marisa around, then?"

"She's hiding."

"You're sure she didn't take the money."

"Positive. And Garrison Kopp agrees. The feds stopped looking at her a long time ago."

Anderson swallowed. "Man, I had no idea. I wish I could help, I really do. My daughter's a lot older than that, but... Sheesh, four years old. Who would do that?"

Nate wondered the same thing. He stood, and Anderson did, too. "If I have any more questions, do you mind if I come back?"

Anderson handed him a business card. "Just call, if you

want. I'm happy to help. Even if Marisa did steal the money, nobody deserves to have their kid snatched."

Nate was halfway to the door when Anderson said, "You know what I never understood?"

Nate turned. "What's that?"

"The money was stolen from two accounts and sent to two different accounts. I always figured maybe the person was hedging his bets—maybe the feds would get to one, but he'd always have the other, too. But maybe... Maybe two different people did it."

TWELVE

MARISA YANKED the keys out of the ignition, climbed out of the pickup, and slammed the door. She'd been waiting half an hour, and she couldn't sit still another minute. The problem was, Nate hadn't told her the address of the auto body shop. She could start walking in the direction he and Garrison had gone, but what if she couldn't find it? And what if Nate and Garrison got back and she wasn't there? Would they worry?

It would serve them right.

She crossed her arms and rubbed her shoulders. It was chilly and overcast, and it smelled like rain. She'd always loved that scent, like the air was charged with some invisible force. When she'd been a little girl, her father had told her that the smell of rain meant God was close. "He's always near, but when you smell rain, he's trying to remind you, to bring you peace. When you smell rain, God is right beside you."

For all her father's faults, he'd been a believer. He'd taken their family to the Catholic Church faithfully every Sunday before he and Mom had divorced. And Marisa knew that tradition hadn't fallen away over the years. He'd believed in a good, kind God. And then, he'd been killed. He'd been back in Puerto

Rico visiting family—people she'd never met—when he'd borrowed a cousin's motorcycle to take a ride. Family reunion one minute, funeral the next.

Would Marisa ever get to keep anybody she loved, or would they all be taken from her? Her mother, her father, Vinnie, Ana, Leslie. Would Nate be next?

The scent of rain wasn't bringing her the peace her father had promised.

Where were Nate and Garrison? Would Nate take her back to Nutfield today, or would they stay in New York? Despite the fact that New York reminded her of all she'd lost, and all she feared, she wanted to stay. Ana was nearby. She could feel it. Or maybe she just wanted desperately to believe it. She felt the phone, still in her pocket. She hadn't walked away from it for a second since it had been dropped in her bag in Acapulco. Why hadn't the kidnappers called back? Garrison's theory had made sense at the time, but in retrospect, she wondered if he'd just been trying to placate her.

She paced on the sidewalk beside the truck. Past a pizza place, a plumber's shop, a coin-operated Laundromat, and a place called Freedom Tax Preparation—*Be Free to Keep More of You're Cash.* She read their stupid sign every time she walked by. Apparently they only employed math geniuses. The English geniuses were probably working at the Laundromat.

Was this what it felt like to lose your mind? Marisa couldn't take it anymore. If she'd had a smartphone, she'd have figured out where Acme Auto Body was, just to give her something to do. With Ana and Leslie gone, Nate and Garrison doing who knew what, Marisa wanted to scream. She was trapped here, dodging the little foot traffic there was on this street and scowling at the signs.

"Marisa?"

She spun and saw Garrison standing beside the truck, watching her.

"Where's Nate?"

"I left him with Anderson. I have to go."

She returned to the truck to see Garrison squeezing the life out of his keys. "What's wrong?"

"Nothing to do with you. My son..." He shook his head. "I'm sorry. I have to go."

"Is he okay?"

"He will be. You got a pen and paper?"

"Uh..." She opened the truck and looked inside. The thing was spotless. She turned to tell Garrison she didn't, but he'd returned to his sedan, parked a few car-lengths down. She locked Brady's truck and joined Garrison as he placed a pad of paper on the roof of his car and wrote something down.

He ripped the paper out of the notebook and handed it to her. "That's my cell phone number. Have Nate call me when he gets back."

"Anderson was there?"

"Yeah. Nate'll tell you. I'm sorry, but I—"

"It's fine. Go. Thank you for your help."

He glanced at his car door. "Please, tell Nate to call me."

She nodded, but tears pricked her eyes.

"Hey, it's going to be okay."

She tried to smile. "I appreciate your help."

He placed his huge hand on her shoulder. "You know what Sam said?"

Sam had said a lot in the time the woman had spent with them, but Marisa couldn't seem to focus on anything right now.

"She said God knows exactly where your daughter and your sister are."

The scent of rain, and now this. Like a big cosmic joke. "You believe in God?"

Garrison paused, looked at nothing. "I do. I think I do. How about you?"

"I just want my family back."

"Yeah." He glanced at his car door again.

She stepped away. "Go. Thank you for your help."

"Don't forget to have Nate call me."

Marisa watched as Garrison drove away. She'd kept the tears at bay, but now they streamed down her cheeks. She'd been praying. If God knew where her family was, she needed him to tell her. Now.

She climbed in the truck to wait for Nate, and mercifully, just five minutes later, he knocked on her window. When she opened the door, he said, "You want to drive?"

She slid to the passenger seat. "I haven't driven in years, Nate. You don't want me to drive."

He seemed relieved but didn't say anything as he climbed into the driver's seat.

"Well?"

"I don't think he had anything to do with it."

Nate started the truck but didn't shift into drive. He turned to tell her what happened, but she stopped him.

"Why don't you call Garrison? He wanted to hear, too."

"You talked to him?"

"He had to go." She handed Nate the folded piece of paper. "He wants you to call."

Nate dialed, and the sound of ringing came through the speakers. Bluetooth cars. Another new thing she'd heard of but hadn't experienced in Mexico.

Garrison answered a moment later, and Nate told them both what Anderson had to say.

"He has a theory. He says a lot of the people at G&K share it."

"What's that?" Garrison asked.

"That Marisa was able to gain access to Charles's accounts because they were"—he glanced at Marisa—"sleeping together."

"What!" Her whole body vibrated with rage.

Garrison said nothing.

Nate ignored Marisa's outburst. "You heard that, Garrison?"

"A few of them expressed that theory to me, yeah."

The very idea that people thought she and that...that terrible man had been together turned her stomach. She looked at Nate.

He met her eyes.

"Do you believe it?" Marisa asked.

"No." Nate's gaze never left hers. "Not for a minute."

Garrison said, "I didn't know you from Adam's cousin, Marisa. I kept my mind open to the possibility."

Charles had been such a pig when he'd come on to her. And that was after she'd started seeing Vinnie. He'd even bought her a bracelet, as if a few precious gems would convince her to cheat on her boyfriend. And to think, all those people she'd run into from time to time at the office, their smiling faces—they'd all thought she was a whore.

Had Vinnie heard the rumors? Had he ever considered it?

"How could they think that of me?"

"They didn't know you," Garrison said. "You were just the cleaning lady."

Nate took her hand. "It's circular reasoning. You had to have stolen the money, therefore, you must've gotten access because you were sleeping with Charles."

"And if you were sleeping with Charles and found out he'd killed your fiancé," Garrison said, "obviously, you stole the money to get back at him."

"Or because you found out you weren't his only mistress." Nate went on to explain about what he called Charles's "propensity for intimacy."

"Sexual addiction?" Garrison said.

"Probably. Apparently, there were a lot of women."

"But Jessica English," Marisa said. "I thought she was his mistress."

"Did you know her?" Garrison asked.

She shrugged. "Didn't know her. Saw her one night, slipping into Charles's office."

"Huh." Nate rubbed his temples. "But Charles said she'd never set foot in the office."

Marisa shrugged. "I just assumed it was her. I guess because I'd heard her name before."

"From?"

"Leslie. She always knew the office gossip, everywhere she cleaned. I never knew how she did it."

"What did the woman you saw with Charles look like?" Garrison asked.

"Tall, pretty, and blond. She was wearing a gray suit with a bright blue shirt and carried an expensive purse. She had on... What were they called? Those really expensive, gorgeous, but sort of slutty stilettos."

"Jimmy Choo?" Nate suggested.

Garrison chuckled. "Got a pair in your closet, Nate?"

"I don't have to own them to know them," Nate said. "Unlike some of us, who buy our clothes at Walmart."

"How could you tell?" Garrison asked.

Marisa almost smiled. "They looked like Jimmy Choo's. Maybe they were knock-offs. She was sophisticated, but the shoes... At the time I remember wondering if she'd worn them all day or just slipped them on to visit Charles."

"That sounds like Jessica English, if I remember correctly." Garrison was all business again. "She was working for an advertising agency, a graphic designer."

"The woman I saw looked more like...I don't know, somebody who'd *own* an advertising agency."

"They say to dress the part," Nate said.

"And tall, blond, and sophisticated," Garrison said, "could describe a lot of women. We'll want to confirm it was English, because if she was at G&K's offices, that means she lied to me when I questioned her."

"And Charles lied to me," Nate said.

"Right." A horn blared through the speakers, and Garrison muttered, "Idiot driver."

"Where are you?" Nate asked.

"On my way back to Long Island. Did Anderson tell you anything else?"

"One thing I never knew. He said the money was transferred at two different times to two different accounts. Is that true?"

"It is."

"At two different times?" Marisa glanced at Nate. "Why would somebody do that?"

Garrison said, "We never could solve that mystery."

"Anderson theorized that if Marisa didn't steal the money, maybe it was stolen by two other people."

"On the same night?" Garrison said. "That's quite a coincidence."

That it was, but things had all happened fast. "I didn't steal it, but whoever did, Garrison, they knew you guys were moving in."

"We think so."

"Okay, hold on." Nate let go of Marisa's hand, pulled out his notebook, and wrote something down. "Garrison, you said back in Nutfield that you'd quit suspecting Marisa. Why was that?"

"It didn't add up. If you'd stolen the money, Marisa, why hang around? Why not steal it and run? But you hung around awhile longer."

"I was trying to figure out what to do," she said.

"Of course," Garrison said. "But if you'd stolen the money, you'd have had a plan, right?"

She shrugged. "I never had much of a plan. I just took off."

"That makes sense, though." Nate nodded to the steering wheel as if Garrison could see him. "She would have been prepared, because the money being stolen wouldn't have been a surprise."

"Instead," Garrison said, "you were still hoping for witness protection until you found out we suspected you. And you didn't know we were going to raid G&K that day. You only knew we were going to arrest Charles, and you didn't know when. And if you were going to steal it, why that night? Why not earlier? You'd known what was going on for weeks."

"That's true." She glanced at Nate, who was still taking notes.

"The whole thing never added up," Garrison continued. "Your running—that made you look guilty."

"I thought Charles would kill me."

"Exactly what I said to my partner," Garrison said. "It took me a while, but I eventually convinced him we were on the wrong track."

"Where was the money transferred to?" Nate asked. "Two different accounts in the same bank?"

"Not even in the same country," Garrison said.

"Huh."

"Charles's money went to an account in Grand Cayman. The firm's money went to an account in Switzerland."

"So you always knew two different people had stolen it."

"No," Garrison said. "We figured one person had two accounts, because it seemed too much of a coincidence, unless they were working together."

"If that's the case, why was the money taken at two different times?" Nate asked.

Marisa pushed her hair back from her face. "We're going in circles."

Nate sighed. "You're right."

"I agree," Garrison said. "Was there anything else, Nate?"

"That covers it."

Garrison cleared his throat. "Nate, can you take me off Bluetooth for a minute?"

Nate glanced at her, and she glared. He gave her an apologetic look. "Sure."

He tapped his phone and spoke into it. "What's up?"

Marisa strained to hear what Garrison was saying.

Nate stepped out of the truck and closed the door behind him.

She had half a mind to drive away and leave him standing there. Except she was a little scared to drive. And it was his friend's truck. And her license was expired. And Nate had done nothing but help her.

She tried and failed to wait patiently. Fortunately, less than a minute later, Nate opened the car door and slipped the phone in his pocket.

"Well?"

"It was nothing."

"Please don't lie to me."

He blew out a breath. "He has a theory about...something. I promise I'll tell you if you need to know. Right now, you don't."

"I need to know everything!"

He looked in her eyes. "Please, trust me." He squeezed her hand. "Let's go see Jessica English."

～

"ARE you sure it's the right Jessica English?" Marisa asked.

Nate turned onto 9A and headed north as the map program on his smartphone directed him. Marisa was continually amazed at what the little devices could do.

"As sure as I can be," Nate said. "Garrison told us she was a graphic designer. This Jessica English owns a graphic design business. You read her website—it said she worked on Madison Avenue before she opened her doors. Why are you convinced it's not?"

"Because..." She stared out at the Hudson on her left as she considered her answer. Finally, she said, "Because the woman I saw didn't seem the suburban type."

"Maybe she's miserable in White Plains." Nate glanced at her and smiled.

"I wish we'd asked Garrison to help us track her down. He'd be able to tell us for sure."

"You're the one who said not to call him."

"He seemed distracted, and he was driving. But what if this is a fool's errand?"

"We're already on our way. It'll take us less than an hour. If this isn't her, we'll regroup, figure out our next step."

"Any idea what that'll be?"

"I think Jessica English is our next step. If this isn't her, we'll call Garrison. He'll be able to find her."

"What if she's moved out of the country or something?"

"Remember what we said back in Acapulco? Do the—"

"Next thing. And then the next thing." Her voice rose. "And then the next. We're just going to keep doing the next thing until Ana and Leslie are dead."

"We have to trust—"

"What? Trust what?"

He seemed to falter. A moment passed before he said, "Trust that it's going to be all right."

"Why would I believe that?"

"Because if you don't, the worry will drive you crazy. And we need to think straight if we're going to figure this out."

Right. Except they weren't going to figure it out, and even if they did, why would the kidnapper release Ana and Leslie? Marisa wouldn't be able to give him the money he obviously wanted. Would proof of who stole it really satisfy him? And how could Marisa and Nate figure out something the FBI had failed to learn in eight years?

They continued north until the road turned inland. The landscape changed from the pretty view of the river to the ugliness of the harbor buildings, warehouses, then apartment buildings. Millions of people, millions of places to hide.

Ana could be anywhere.

A phone rang.

Nate glanced at her, and she fumbled for the phone in her pocket as Nate exited the highway.

She took a deep breath and connected the call. "Hello?"

"You got the money?" The man's voice was clearer than it had been the day of the kidnapping. And scarier. His local accent came through perfectly. As if that narrowed the search.

Nate screeched into a parking lot and slammed on the brakes. He leaned over to hear.

"We're working on it," Marisa said.

"Don't tell me you spent it all."

Marisa hands shook, and she pulled in another breath and forced it out, trying to push down the frantic fear. "I didn't take the money. I never had it."

"I thought you loved your daughter."

"I do." She swallowed a sob and looked at Nate.

He pulled the phone closer. "Even the feds don't think she has it."

"You talked to the cops?"

"No!" Marisa shouted.

Nate laid his hand on her knee. When she looked at his face, he put one finger over his lips. The universal sign for *shut up*.

"I told the agent I was working on a follow-up story," Nate said. "You said that if we could prove Marisa didn't steal it, you'd let them go. We're trying to figure out who stole it."

"Right." The man drenched the word in sarcasm. "She has the money, and you're probably in on it."

"If we had the money," Nate said, "We'd give it to you with interest to get Ana and Leslie back."

"Please, you have to believe us," Marisa said. "We're trying to find it."

Nate met her eyes. He wanted her to keep quiet. But how could she?

"Why don't I believe you?"

"Because you want the money"—Nate ignored the man's obvious sarcasm—"and you've paid a high price to get it. You've kidnapped two people. You've made yourself an international criminal. But you've targeted the wrong person. Marisa doesn't have it, and she never did. We're doing our best to figure out who does. And you'll let them go. Right?"

"You don't ask the questions," the voice said.

"You're already a kidnapper. A kidnapper who lets his victims go might escape. A kidnapper who treats his victims well, the courts might have mercy on him. You don't want to become a murderer. A child killer. Nobody has mercy on that guy."

"Nobody's going to get hurt if I get my money."

My money. Marisa met Nate's eyes, and he nodded. "We need to speak with Ana and Leslie."

"You need to get the money."

"We're working on it. Please put them on the phone."

"Screw you. Get the money."

"We're not doing anything if we don't hear Ana's voice right now."

The man swore a blue streak, which was followed by silence. On the other end of the line, Marisa could hear scuffling, some banging. And crying.

Ana's crying.

"Shut up, kid. Talk to your mother."

A moment passed while tears streamed down Marisa's face. She couldn't move, afraid to break the connection and the only link to her little girl.

"Mama?"

"Oh, baby." Marisa stifled a sob. "Are you all right?"

"I want to come home now." Her voice was strong, just like always. Marisa wanted to hug her confident little girl so badly, her limbs ached.

"I know, pajarita. I miss you so much. I'm trying to get to you."

"Aunt Leslie has been really nice to me, and they let me have ice cream. Chocolate. But this place is yucky. Rats and cockroaches and spiders. And there's a—"

"Hey." The man's voice was too loud and too close.

"I love you," Marisa said.

The man answered. "Yeah, I'll tell her. You have 'til Friday to get me the money."

"You said a week," Nate said. "That gives us until Sunday."

"I changed my mind."

"We can't do Friday." Nate said. "If you want your money—"

"Fine. Saturday I want my money."

"Or proof of who stole it," Nate said. "That was the deal."

A second ticked by, two, then three before the man said, "If she doesn't have it, I need to know who does."

"Let's make the trade in New York," Nate suggested.

"I decide where and when."

"You'll have to give us a hint or some time to get there. We're not staying in the city."

Another moment of quiet. "Where you staying?"

"You want to stop by for a visit?"

"Just trying to figure the plan."

"You tell us where and when," Nate said, "and we'll be there. And remember, if you hurt the woman or that little girl, money's going to be the least of your problems."

"The girl's fine. Leslie's fine. Four days."

The line went dead.

Marisa held the phone in her hand long after the man hung up. She stared at it, willing her daughter's voice to come through again. Ana had sounded scared. But she was okay, and Leslie must've been, too, if she was taking care of Ana. Marisa should take solace in that.

But it had already been three days, and they were no closer to finding out who stole the money than they had been the day of the kidnapping.

Nate took the phone from her hand. He pushed up the armrest between them and wrapped his arms around her. She wept on his shoulder.

"They're still alive. The man wants his money. We're going to figure out who has it."

"What if we don't?"

"One step at a time, Marisa."

She sniffed and sat back. "If we don't, we have to say we do. We'll have to trick this guy into exposing Ana and Leslie. I'm going to get them home safely, or I'm going to die trying."

THIRTEEN

LESLIE. The kidnapper had called her *Leslie*. Not *that woman*. Not even *your sister*.

Nate didn't know what to make of it, but he couldn't get the thought out of his mind as he turned onto a quiet suburban street in White Plains, New York, just an hour outside the city, and stopped in front of a two-story blue Colonial with black shutters and a wide front porch. The yard was well kept, and evergreen shrubs lined the front of the house. A BMW was parked in the narrow driveway.

He stepped out of the truck and inhaled the crisp scent of approaching rain. The sun would set in a few minutes, though with the low blanket of clouds, there was no colorful show.

In front of the house next door, four boys—maybe eight or nine years old—played a two-on-two game of soccer. They were using a minivan parked in the far driveway for one goal, and, if he had to guess, two trees on the other edge of the property for another. Their shouts and laughter filled the evening air.

Nate walked around to open Marisa's door. Unlike most women, she'd waited until he got there. He wondered if Vinnie

Depalo had displayed good manners. He hoped so—Marisa deserved to be treated like a lady.

She stood beside him and sniffed.

Nate wiped an errant tear from her cheek. She'd managed to pull herself together, though he'd noticed her wiping tears on and off during the traffic-laden drive. "You okay?"

She nodded and took a deep breath. "I have to be, don't I?"

He took her hand, and they walked up the concrete sidewalk to the house. He rang the doorbell, and they heard the muffled chime from inside.

A woman's voice called, "Just leave it on the porch."

He looked at Marisa, who shrugged. He knocked.

"I said leave it on the porch!"

He called, "I'm not the pizza guy."

A moment later, the door opened. On the other side stood a woman who looked nothing like the person Marisa had described. She wore pink and black fleece pajama pants and a black sweatshirt. Her blond hair was pulled on top of her head in a messy bun, and she had a pair of glasses pushed up, holding back escaping strands. She wore no makeup. When he looked past the outfit, though, he could see that this Jessica English was a beautiful woman. High cheekbones, dark blue eyes, well-shaped lips.

Still, he doubted this was the right person. She seemed nothing like the sophisticated New Yorker Marisa had described.

She eyed them and said, "Can I help you?"

"We'd like to speak with you," he said.

"What about?"

"Charles Gray."

She stared silently, and he might have believed he'd been right about having the wrong woman, if not for the slight narrowing of her eyes. After a couple of beats, she said, "What about him?"

"May we come in?"

She stepped outside, looked at the boys next door, and peered in the other direction. Was she afraid they'd been followed? He'd found her address online, so surely she hadn't been trying to hide.

She looked at her wrist as if checking the time, though there was no watch there. "I have a lot of work to do."

"We won't take up much of your time," Nate said.

Marisa added, "It's very important we speak to you."

She sighed. "Fine. Come in."

They followed Jessica to the living room. Hardwood floors, dark purple floral sofas, and a flat-screen TV on a dark wood stand in the corner. A small fireplace filled the far side of the room. Above, a mantle painted gray was adorned with photographs. The room was nicely decorated and tidy, though when Nate peered through to the kitchen, he saw snack wrappers and soda cans on the counter.

Marisa sat on the couch, and he sat beside her. Jessica chose a chair catty-corner. "Is Charles in trouble again? Last I heard, he was still in prison."

"He is," Nate said. "We're on a bit of a quest."

Her expression told him what she thought about quests.

"You and Charles were an item before he was arrested, isn't that right?"

"Are you a cop or something?"

He shook his head. "No. I'm sorry, I should have explained. This is Marisa Vega"—he nodded in her direction—"and I'm Nate Boyle. I'm a reporter. I wrote a series of stories about the fraud at G&K."

"You're the guy who took the company down."

"No, not at all. I just wrote a few stories. The feds took them down."

Jessica jutted her chin in Marisa's direction. "Why is your name familiar?"

"I was engaged to Vinnie Depalo."

"You're the one they think stole the money!"

Nate noted the qualifier—*they* think, she'd said. Maybe Jessica would be more helpful than Anderson had been.

Marisa sat straighter. "I didn't steal it."

"We're trying to figure out who did."

Jessica yanked her glasses off her head, pulling a few hairs with it. "Everybody thinks you did it."

"I didn't," Marisa said.

"Didn't you escape the country or something? Why are you back?"

"I ran because I thought Charles would try to kill me, the way he killed Vinnie."

Jessica's gaze softened just a bit. "Charles can't have meant for your boyfriend to die. At the trial, he said he was only trying to scare him."

"You believe that?" Nate asked.

"Charles was no killer. Sure, he broke the law, but mortgage fraud isn't murder."

"People will go to great lengths to stay out of prison."

"Not Charles." She shook her head, and the bun on top wobbled. "Not that."

Nate nodded and leaned forward a bit. "You two were pretty close."

She didn't say anything. Nate didn't either, and the moment got uncomfortable. After a minute, he said, "Do you keep in touch with him?"

She scoffed. "Are you kidding? The guy's a felon."

"He was a felon when you were with him. He just hadn't been convicted yet."

"I didn't know. He was rich. How was I supposed to know he was breaking the law?"

"So he never confided in you?"

"Nothing like that."

"Even when he feared he might be in trouble? Even after Vinnie died, he never told you anything?"

She yanked the elastic holding the bun, and her hair fell around her shoulders. Nate imagined all those shampoo commercials where women let their gorgeous locks fly free. This was nothing like that. She finger-combed it, but clearly it was too snarled to get her fingers all the way through.

"Sorry." She looked at Marisa. "Your hair ever start to hurt when you've had it up all day?"

"All the time." Marisa smiled, though Nate could tell it was forced.

Nate tried again. "So did he ever tell you—?"

"I had no idea what was going on. I thought maybe... I mean, Charles mentioned he was afraid they were going to be audited or something. I had no idea they were involved in fraud. Not the go-to-prison kind, anyway."

As if mortgage fraud were perfectly acceptable. "When did you find out?"

"Same as everybody else. When he was arrested."

"Did he tell you anything about Vinnie's murder?"

"Of course not! You think I'd want to marry him after that?"

Nate sat back, unsure of where to go from here. She hadn't given them any information that would help, and Marisa was right—they weren't getting at all closer to the truth.

Marisa stood and walked to the fireplace mantle. "Is this your son?"

Nate watched as Jessica's face paled a little. "What about him?"

Marisa turned and smiled. "He's adorable. Is he one of the boys playing next door?"

"Every kid in town plays soccer," she said.

Defensive. Interesting.

Marisa lifted one of the photographs and peered at it closely. "Is this his father?"

Jessica's laugh was more snort than giggle. "That's his soccer coach. One of them, anyway. He's a great guy, always hanging out with the boys who don't have fathers." She looked at Nate. "With supervision, of course. I'm not an idiot."

"Of course," Nate said.

"How old is your son?" Marisa asked.

She took a deep breath. "I could lie."

Nate shrugged. "I'm sure there are records, though, and I'm really good at ferreting out the truth." When Jessica said nothing, he said, "Does Charles know?"

She shook her head. "And he doesn't need to."

Marisa set the photograph down and resumed her seat. "You don't think he has a right to know he has a son?"

"I'm not taking Hunter to see him in that place. Ever. And by the time Charles gets out—if he survives Sing Sing with that heart—he'll be too old to play the doting daddy."

"Still," Nate said, "I'd want to know."

"He has other kids. And anyway, I doubt Hunter is the only one he doesn't know about." She turned her attention to Marisa. "You know how he was, right? You were one of his... What did he used to call them? Dalliances?"

"I was not," Marisa said. "Never."

"Whatever." She turned her attention back to Nate. "I knew he'd had a lot of affairs before me, but I thought we had something special. I thought he loved me. And then I found out the truth. The guy would screw anything in a skirt." She looked at Marisa. "Or a maid's outfit. Did you wear one of those little white aprons? I bet he really liked that."

Marisa's face turned bright red. "I was never with him. He was..." Her voice trailed off, and she looked at Nate.

"Marisa didn't sleep with him," Nate said, "not that Charles didn't try."

"You don't have to lie to me," Jessica said. "Did you have the braid before? I bet he loved that." She closed her mouth in a straight line and shook her head. "I know how he was. He could charm his way under the queen's skirt, if he had five minutes alone with her."

"I was in love with Vinnie," Marisa said. "Charles tried, I said no. The end."

"Right." She rolled her eyes at Nate, as if the very thought of telling Charles *no* was akin to a fat kid turning down a Kit Kat. "Besides, it wouldn't matter. I thought all that stopped with me. Apparently not."

"How'd you find out the truth?"

"The other cleaning lady, the ugly one."

"Leslie?" Nate suggested. He ignored Marisa's glare, but he could feel it.

"Right," Jessica said. "Her. I was up there—"

"At G&K? In the offices?"

"Yeah, I went there sometimes after the place closed. He didn't like people to know I went there, but they knew. He had a couch in his office." She shrugged. Nate was glad he didn't have to hear the details. "He'd left the room to take a phone call, and the lady came in. She told me he met girls up there all the time."

"When was that exactly?" Nate asked.

"Right before he got arrested. I knew I was pregnant, and I'd even thought I might tell him that night. But she told me about the other women, and I wasn't so sure. After that, Charles was busy night after night for, I don't know, a week or so, and I figured the maid was right—he was seeing other women. And then he got arrested."

Marisa leaned forward. "Leslie told you that? You sure it was her?"

"I don't know her name."

Marisa turned to Nate. "Leslie always told me to keep my nose out of everything. Just clean and keep your mouth shut. So it doesn't make sense."

Leslie obviously broke her own rule more than once. She'd told Charles about Vinnie's contact with the FBI, and now this.

Nate pulled out his cell phone and flipped through his photos until he got one of Leslie. They'd taken it at dinner that night in Mexico, before she and Ana had gone for their walk. She had leaned closer to Ana, so the shot showed them both. Leslie wore a wide smile, rare for those days in Acapulco when fear had clung to her like sweat. He turned the camera's screen to Jessica. "That her?"

Jessica looked at it. "You two friends or something?"

"She's my sister," Marisa said.

"No joke? You sure got the better genes." She leaned closer. "Yeah. That's her. The frizzy hair—has she ever tried to tame that?"

Nate thought the woman was pushing it to criticize Leslie's hair, considering the state of her own.

Marisa ignored the question. "You're saying that woman, Leslie, told you Charles had women up there all the time after hours."

"Yeah. Acted like it was a nightly thing. She's the one who told me you and him—"

"That's a lie. My sister wouldn't have told you that. She knew better." Marisa looked at Nate, and he shook his head. They'd talk about it later.

"Why would I lie about that?" Jessica asked.

Nate turned to Marisa. "There has to be an explanation. When we find Leslie, we'll ask her." He turned back to Jessica. "This is a nice house. You like living in the suburbs?"

She looked around and smiled. "After Charles was convicted and Hunter was born, I decided it was time for a change. Everybody knew Charles and I'd been together, and suddenly, it was like he had some communicable disease and I was a carrier. My boss at the advertising agency suggested I *take some time*"—she made air quotes around those words—"which was code for find yourself a new job. So I sold my condo in the city and moved here."

"Pretty nice place for a woman with no job."

"I made a good profit on my condo. We lived in an apartment for a while, but this house became available. And..." She sighed and said, "Oh, what difference does it make now? Charles had given me a lot of money, and a lot of jewelry and stuff. I sold it all. The profits from that crap paid the mortgage the first year, until I was able to establish myself. Now, I own my own business working for a lot of those same agencies on Madison Avenue that wanted nothing to do with me eight years ago. I'm cheaper and better than their in-house people. And I work right here." She looked down and laughed. "Usually, in my pajamas."

"Seems like a good gig," Nate said.

"It isn't what I thought I wanted for my life. I never imagined I'd be a single mother—never in a million years. Which is kind of stupid, in retrospect. Truth be told, I got pregnant because I thought that would be the final push Charles needed to leave his wife. I never even thought about the fact that there'd be a baby." She shook her head. "When Charles got sent to prison, I got stuck with the kid. Except once he was born and I looked in that tiny face, I fell in love."

Marisa sniffed and swallowed.

"You have a kid, Marisa?"

"A daughter. She's"—Marisa looked at Nate, and he nodded —"the reason we're here. She's been kidnapped." Tears streamed down her face, but she didn't falter. "They're holding her for ransom because they think I stole all that money from G&K."

Jessica glanced at Nate as if he might dispute the facts. "I can't imagine."

"No, you can't," Marisa said, "so if you have any information—"

She lifted both hands. "I swear, if I knew anything, I'd tell you. I was never convinced you took the money. I always thought..." She looked at Nate. "Have you been to see Charles's wife?"

"Ex-wife," Nate corrected. "Not yet."

"That's right. I heard she finally divorced him. Apparently screwing everything that moved was fine, but going to jail— probably too embarrassing for the old bat." She shook her head. "Anyway, I always thought she did it."

"Why?" Marisa asked.

"Because she knew about me. Knew he was in love with me. He'd been to see a divorce lawyer, and I think she found out. And she probably knew a lot more about what was going on up there than he ever said. I bet she did it just to get back at him."

NATE AND MARISA drove off the quiet street in White Plains and stopped in a gas station parking lot. After Nate wrote down everything he could remember about the conversation with Jessica English, he called Garrison from the car, and Nate and Marisa filled in the former FBI agent on the conversation.

"I figured about the kid," Garrison said.

"How did you know?" Marisa asked.

"I worked the case long after you disappeared. I knew she was pregnant. But it didn't seem relevant. It's...unbelievable."

"Why do you say that?" Marisa looked at Nate with raised eyebrows.

"She's twenty years younger than Charles." Garrison said. "It's just..."

"I'm with you," Nate said. "Apparently being rich is very attractive."

"Apparently." Garrison's one word dripped with sarcasm.

Marisa sighed. "We're not all like that. And she's certainly paid the price for it."

Nate turned off the car, and Garrison's voice suddenly seemed too loud over the car speakers. "Did you guys believe her?"

Nate turned the volume down. "She certainly had an answer for everything."

"Not a lot's changed," Garrison said. "The mistress thinks the ex-wife did it. When you talk to Pamela Gray, she'll tell you Jessica did it."

"Speaking of," Nate said, "do you have a phone number for her? And her address?"

They could hear shuffling. "You got a pen?"

Nate poised his pen over the notebook. "Go ahead."

Garrison rattled off a number. "That's the house phone. I never got a cell for her."

"Maybe she can't afford one," Nate said.

Garrison chuckled. Marisa barely cracked a smile.

"We'll call her. Thanks."

Nate ended the call and dialed Pamela Gray's phone number. A women with a heavy Spanish accent answered.

"This is Nate Boyle calling for Pamela Gray."

"I'm sorry. Mrs. Gray is not here."

"Can you tell me when she'll be back?"

"May I take a message?"

Marisa whispered, "Take it off Bluetooth and give it to me."

Nate said, "Hold one moment, please." He handed Marisa the phone, and she spoke into it in rapid Spanish.

Nate's high school Spanish classes proved useless, as he'd argued to his mother at the time they would. The two women talked, then Marisa said to Nate, "What's your phone number?"

Nate told her, Marisa translated it into Spanish, and the two chatted for a couple of minutes. Marisa even laughed once before she hung up and handed him the phone.

"Pamela Gray has gone to Chicago to attend a charity board meeting. She won't return for two days. I told the housekeeper it was an emergency, and she promised to give Mrs. Gray your phone number and tell her we need to speak with her. I told her it was a matter of life and death."

"Did the housekeeper think she'd call?"

"She said unless it was Pamela Gray's life on the line, I shouldn't expect a response. However, I did get Rosa to agree to call or text us when Mrs. Gray returns on Friday. It's her under-standing the woman will be home late morning."

"Well done."

"*Gracias*." Marisa smiled, but it faded fast. "What do we do now? We're out of leads."

They weren't, not really, but Nate wasn't about to tell her his theory without backup. He needed his friends. "We're going back to Nutfield."

She shook her head. "I want to stay in New York. We can go to Leslie's—"

"Absolutely not. We have to stay hidden."

"We can hide in New York."

"We could, but we're not going to. We're going to the cabin to get a good night's sleep and regroup. All our stuff is there, and we have two comfortable beds. If we need to, we can come back tomorrow."

"But Ana—"

"Could be anywhere," Nate said.

Marisa turned and crossed her arms. "She's in New York."

Maybe she was, but staying in a hotel was not going to get them to her any faster, and Marisa needed peace and rest, not the hubbub of New York. And so did he. And besides, they both needed to know what Sam had found out, though Marisa didn't know that yet.

FOURTEEN

Marisa woke the next morning to the scent of coffee wafting beneath her door. As much as she wanted some, she needed a shower first. She checked the clock on the nightstand.

No way she'd slept until ten.

They'd arrived home after eleven the night before. No amount of arguing with Nate had persuaded him to turn the car around and stay in New York. Once she'd fallen into bed, she'd realized he was right. Now, after sleeping ten hours, she was even more convinced. She'd needed a good night's sleep, and this cabin in the woods was much more peaceful than any hotel could have been.

She showered and slipped on clothes she'd found folded on her bed the night before. Probably Rae's, because Sam's clothes would have been too short for her. She chose a dark pair of jeans from the few folded there. They were a bit baggy but long enough, and with the belt Rae'd supplied, they worked fine. She looked outside at the drizzly day and chose a sweatshirt from the pile. Soft and cozy. How she'd missed sweatshirts.

She'd live with a million stifling hot days if only she could get her daughter back.

Hair wet and braided, she stepped into the great room and stopped.

Nate, seated at the bar, turned and smiled at her. Sam waved from her perch at the end of the counter. Rae was behind the counter, sipping from a mug. She said, "You're up. We thought we heard the shower."

Marisa blinked at all the faces, noted the tray of baked goods on the kitchen table, and turned when the back door opened. Brady stepped inside carrying a few logs. "Good morning."

"Hi," Marisa said. "I'm late to the party."

Nate walked toward her. "We didn't want to wake you. Did you get a good night's sleep?"

"Very."

He urged her to the bar. "Here, take my seat."

As Marisa slid onto the barstool, Rae set the coffee caddy in front of her. "What kind of coffee today?"

She selected one. Rae set it in the machine and pushed the button to start it brewing.

Marisa turned and watched Brady tear a newspaper into strips and shove the strips in the bottom of the fireplace.

"Is it cold enough for a fire?"

Nate nodded. "It's dropped into the thirties out there, and it's raining."

"I saw that." A thought occurred to her. "What if it turns to snow? We'll never get back to New York."

Before she'd finished speaking, Nate shook his head. "It's not supposed to snow. It's supposed to warm into the forties today. We'll be fine."

"But it could have, and we'd be stuck—"

"I checked the weather, Marisa. You have to trust me."

Brady lit the fire, and she stared into the flames for a moment as the paper burned. The twigs he'd stacked caught, and one of the logs started to flicker and hiss.

How long had it been since she'd seen a fire in a fireplace? A very long time.

Sam approached and slid the tray of baked goods and a plate in front of her on the counter. Marisa turned and met her eyes.

"It's good you came back here," Sam said. "You needed your rest."

"I need to know my daughter's okay."

Sam and Nate shared a look, and the bottom dropped out of Marisa's stomach. Ana was dead. They'd found her body, and nobody'd wanted to tell Marisa. It was over. She whipped round to face Nate. "What didn't you tell me? Is she—?"

"Nothing happened," he said. "Nothing's changed."

She studied his face. "Why are you lying to me?"

"As far as we know, Ana and Leslie are fine. And I'm not lying. I just want to wait until you have some coffee before we get into it."

"Get into what?"

He sighed.

Rae slid the coffee across the bar to her. "Cream? Sugar?"

Marisa ignored her and stared at Nate.

"Get your coffee, eat some breakfast, and we'll talk."

"I don't want to eat."

"It's not optional."

She could tell by the set of his mouth that he wasn't kidding. She could throttle him or eat. Eating was faster, even if the food tasted like cardboard. She snatched a muffin off the tray and took a bite. When she'd swallowed, she said, "Satisfied?"

"Is it good?"

She's hadn't noticed. Banana nut, she thought. She set it on the plate. "It's fine."

He nodded to the sofa in front of the fire. "Let's go where it's warm."

She sat on the end of the long sofa nearest the fire. Sam

chose a club chair opposite her, and Rae perched in the love seat across from the fireplace. Nate followed a minute later with Marisa's coffee and muffin and set them on the table before he sat beside her.

Brady futzed with the fire another minute before he sat beside his wife.

When Brady moved out of the way, Marisa could feel the heat from the flames. She stared at them, wondering what terrible news Nate had for her and trying to figure out how she'd ended up in the middle of a fire herself. She'd built a life. She'd fallen in love with the people in Mexico, tried to serve them well.

She imagined the ancient chapel in the orphanage, where the priest had come every week to teach the kids about God. "God is on your side," he'd said. How she'd wanted to believe it. But Ana's kidnapping had taught her better. If God existed, he didn't care about her. She was on her own.

She tore her gaze away from the flames and looked at Nate. "What happened?"

"Yesterday when I saw Charles, he told me something that got me thinking. I told Garrison about it, and he agreed it was suspicious."

"But you didn't tell me."

"I needed more information."

She looked at the faces gathered around her. Ten o'clock Thursday morning, and everybody was there. For the first time she realized that little Johnny was missing. People had taken off work, Rae had gotten a babysitter, all for this news.

Marisa looked back at Nate. "You might as well tell me. It can't be worse than what I'm imagining."

He took a deep breath. "Your guess about your sister was right. She's the one who told Charles what Vinnie was up to. He confirmed that yesterday."

Marisa let that sink in. She'd never known for sure, but she'd always suspected. Leslie hadn't wanted Marisa to marry Vinnie. Marisa could imagine that her sister had seen the information as an opportunity to break them up. Leslie would have justified it, if she'd been caught. *I was only trying to protect you. I only want what's best for you.* And Leslie would have believed her own justifications.

Marisa looked back at Nate, glanced at the rest of the faces, all studying her. She focused on Nate. "Leslie set this whole thing in motion."

"Looks like it. I told Garrison—"

"Is that what you two were talking about yesterday when you stepped out of the car?"

"He'd had time to process it. He told me that he was going to do more digging. And after you and I met with Jessica yesterday, my theory sort of blossomed. When we stopped for gas and you stepped into the restroom, I texted Garrison."

Marisa's anger at being left out was slightly overpowered by her desire to know the rest of the story.

Sam cleared her throat. "Garrison called me last night and suggested Leslie's finances might shed some light on the mystery. It took time, but I managed to figure out where she banks and looked at her transactions."

Brady shook his head and looked down. "I don't even want to know."

"The hardest part," Sam said, "was figuring out where she banks. After that, it was pretty simple. It's not that I hacked the bank. All I had to do was go to her bank account and request a password reset. Then hack her email."

"What part of *I don't even want to know* did you not understand?" Brady asked.

"Anyway." Rae gave both Sam and Brady a look that had them clamping their mouths shut. She nodded at Nate. "Go on."

"Sam looked at her banking habits in the last seven years."

"That was as far back as the records went," Sam said.

"Every few months," Nate continued, "she has a small influx of cash. A couple thousand here, a couple thousand there. Sam checked the business account and doesn't see any reasonable explanation. And it's always from the same bank account."

"An overseas bank account," Sam said.

Marisa met Sam's eyes, but the woman immediately gazed at the table. Marisa turned back to face Nate. She didn't like where this was going. "Maybe she has a client that pays her from that overseas account?"

Nate looked at Sam, who looked up, her expression almost pitying. "Your sister emails her invoices to her clients. I matched most of the incoming money to invoices. But these large deposits —there are no invoices that match. Plus, the invoices aren't usually round numbers. You know, they're exact, like eight hundred thirty-seven—numbers like that. But these are big, round numbers—two thousand or twenty-five hundred."

Nate reached for Marisa's hand, but she yanked it away. "What are you saying?"

Sam looked at Nate, and Marisa turned to him.

"Leslie knew about the fraud," he said. "She knew about the FBI, and she told Charles about Vinnie's plan. She knew you were talking to me. Did you contact her when you were in the hotel?"

"She didn't know where I was staying." Marisa had promised not to contact anybody, but of course she'd contacted Leslie. "I called her once, just so she'd know I was okay. When I ran away, I met up with her. She gave me some money."

"The first time you contacted her," Nate said, "you told her what was going on?"

"Yeah. Of course. She's my sister, she needed to know."

"That's what I thought."

Marisa scanned the rest of the faces. They were all watching her. She focused on Nate. "That doesn't... I don't understand what you're trying to say."

"From Jessica English," Nate said, "we learned that your sister told her about all the other women. Did you see Charles with a lot of women in the office?"

Marisa shook her head. "No. Just Jessica, that one night."

"No other women?"

Marisa looked back at the flames, mostly because their compassionate gazes were making her angry. "It makes no sense. Why would Leslie tell Jessica that?"

"I don't know exactly," Nate said. "And I don't know why she'd say you and Charles had been together. And you said yourself, it went against what she always told you—to mind your own business. To keep your head down and not get involved."

"She was angry at me for dating Vinnie, even more so because we met there. She even threatened to fire me."

"Did you consider breaking up with him?"

"We were in love. Like I was going to give up the man I loved for a night job cleaning office buildings. I just worked there to pay my way through school. She paid well, but not that well."

"She wanted you to keep your distance from the G&K employees. But it seems she was very involved in what was going on there."

Marisa stood and stepped to the fireplace. She stared at the flames consuming the logs, one simmering spark at a time. She spun and faced Nate. "What exactly are you trying to say?"

Brady cleared his throat. "All that evidence... It points to something. If I were investigating your sister, I'd be pretty convinced at this point that she had done something wrong. People don't go against their own standards for nothing."

Marisa turned to Nate and crossed her arms. "Just say it."

"Your sister stole the money from at least one of the accounts."

"The company account," Sam clarified. "Garrison checked the bank accounts the money was transferred to eight years ago against the one your sister's been getting money from. It's not the same account, but it's at the same bank."

"There's no doubt your sister stole that money," Nate said.

"I don't understand," Marisa said. "Why that night?" Nate opened his mouth, but she lifted her hand to stop him. "I'm not saying she didn't do it. I'm just trying to understand. You're saying she somehow got the bank account information."

"She had plenty of opportunity to go through people's drawers. She probably found the account numbers and passwords written somewhere."

"Fine. So she maybe could have gotten that stuff. Why did she steal it that night—exactly the same night Charles was arrested? If she had the access, she could have done it any time."

Nate started to speak, but Rae beat him to it. "I don't think we can answer that for sure. But I have a theory."

Marisa was almost sorry she'd asked the question, because whatever Rae and the rest were going to tell her, it was going to make perfect sense. And she wasn't sure she wanted to know. She steeled her courage and said, "What's your theory?"

"Your sister knew the feds were coming, right?" Rae asked.

"She knew everything," Marisa said.

"I think your sister had a thing with Charles."

Rae's pronouncement hung in the air. Sam's dropped jaw mirrored what Marisa was thinking. Brady, on the other hand, nodded slowly, as if all the pieces were falling into place.

Marisa turned to Nate, who had closed his eyes. He slowly lowered his head, so she couldn't see his face. But she could guess what expression he wore.

Marisa turned back to Rae. "Why do you think that?"

"She told Jessica about the other women. Why would she do that? What other motive except jealousy?"

"But Leslie never said..." Marisa tried to remember something that would have hinted at an affair with the boss. "I think she would have told me if she'd been in a relationship with the boss."

"Would she, though?" Rae asked gently. "After grilling you about keeping your distance from the business people you worked for, after trying to break you and Vinnie up, would she have confided in you that she was doing the same thing?"

Marisa tried to imagine that conversation, but the picture wouldn't come. No, Leslie wouldn't have told her, not after all the lectures about Vinnie. About how she could do better. About how he would never see her as anything more than the cleaning lady. Marisa had always wondered if Leslie's biggest objection to their engagement was that she had been wrong.

And to admit Leslie'd been duped into the same kind of thing? "You're right. She wouldn't have told me. But still, why that night?"

Nate finally looked up. His expression was...sad. "When did you tell her Charles had come onto you?"

Marisa remembered that conversation well. Leslie'd been furious. The truth hit her, and she staggered back to the sofa and sat. "After Vinnie died, when I was at the hotel. A week or so before he was arrested. She was trying to tell me that Charles probably hadn't meant for Vinnie to die. That he was probably a decent guy who'd just gotten in over his head." Marisa's admission that Charles had come on to her—that's what had prompted Leslie's decision to steal the money.

"I hate to say it," Brady said, "but your sister doesn't have your looks. You were used to men fawning all over you, but your sister... Maybe it was a first for her. She just got sucked in."

Nate said, "And she gave you money to help you escape.

Nice, of course, but it made you look guilty. It was kind of the perfect plan. Because Charles wasn't going to tell the feds he was sleeping with the cleaning lady. He underestimated her."

"He probably never even considered her," Sam said. "If what Anderson said was true. Sounds like he had a sexual addiction. Maybe there were too many to think about."

Marisa looked at the flames as she let the information settle in. Her sister had stolen at least part of the money. All those people had lost their jobs, the mortgage company closed down, because Leslie had used the information Marisa gave her to steal that money.

Leslie had been her big sister, her protector. She'd given Marisa a job to help her get through school. She'd paid all the household bills so Marisa could focus on tuition. And Marisa had always pitied Leslie. Poor Leslie had no father and had lost her mother. Poor Leslie had to play the caretaker to Marisa when their mother died. Poor Leslie wasn't blessed with good looks like Marisa, with a talent like Marisa's. Poor Leslie.

Poor Leslie was a liar and a thief.

Marisa considered the money Leslie had given her to escape. A few thousand dollars, a drop in the bucket compared to what she'd stolen, but because of it, Marisa had been able to escape.

And because she'd run, she'd looked guilty. And Leslie had gotten off scot-free. She'd continued to build her business, and she'd been smart, never taking too much. It was as though she'd taken the money not to get rich, but to prove something. To get back at the world for dealing her such a rough life. To get back at Charles for using her and discarding her. To get back at Marisa for what?

It didn't add up.

Marisa turned back to the room. "If Leslie has the money, why doesn't she just tell the kidnappers, offer to pay them off in exchange for their freedom?" She looked at Sam. "She hasn't spent it all, right?"

"Assuming this is the only bank account she's using, she should still have plenty."

Marisa couldn't sit still. She stood and stepped back to the fire, warming her hands in the heat. She turned to Nate. "How do you explain that?"

Nate looked at Brady before he stood and joined Marisa by the fire. He took her hand, and she resisted the urge to yank it away.

"What I'm about to suggest—it's sort of good news for Ana."

"What?"

"We believe"—he nodded to his friends—"that your sister always believed you had stolen Charles's money. Remember what she said back in Mexico—'just give it back to them, and I'll be safe.'"

She did remember. "Okay."

"For whatever reason, your sister decided she wanted to get her hands on the rest of the money. I don't know why. I don't know what prompted it. But I think your sister lied about those people in her room that night. I think...we think her kidnapping was staged."

Marisa tried to step back, bumped into the hearth, and stumbled. "No." She righted herself, pushed past Nate, and stalked to the bar. She turned to look at them, all watching her.

"No."

Nate stood and started to step toward her, but Brady shook his head, and he stopped.

Nobody else moved.

"Leslie wouldn't do this," Marisa said. "She wouldn't..."

Marisa stomped to the back door, yanked it open, and stepped outside. Cold damp air shocked her system, but she didn't care. She couldn't be inside with those people, with Nate.

Couldn't listen to their terrible lies about her sister. Terrible lies that, God help her, made too much sense.

No.

Maybe Leslie was a thief. The facts lined up like chisels, chipping away at her battered heart.

But to kidnap a four-year-old girl, to smuggle her out of the country? To terrify Marisa? To harm a helpless child, all for the sake of money?

No, Leslie couldn't sink that low.

Marisa pulled the arms of the sweatshirt over her hands and hugged herself. The back deck extended a few feet beyond where she stood, but she stayed where the house's overhang protected her from the steady rain. The lake was gray, the raindrops splashing and creating a layer of mist that rose up like ash from the fires of hell.

Leslie wouldn't have done this. Leslie had never loved anyone except Mom and Marisa. And sometimes, Marisa had wondered about her sister's feelings for their mother. But she'd never doubted Leslie's love for her. She'd cared for her, protected her, guided her.

But even if Leslie hadn't been behind the kidnapping, she had stolen the firm's money. And because of that, Marisa had run away. Her life had been ruined because of something Leslie had done. Was it possible? Had Leslie done this, too?

The door opened, and a moment later, someone stood beside her.

"You okay?"

Nate, of course. She glanced at him, but he kept his gaze on the lake beyond the trees.

Marisa sighed. "I'm cold. Let's go inside."

He opened the door, and she stepped in. Brady, Rae, and Sam had moved back to the kitchen. They all looked at her.

"I'm fine." She went to the fireplace and warmed her hands. Stared at the flames. Tried not to think.

A moment later, Nate wrapped an afghan around her shoulders. "Cold out there."

"Yup."

"Probably feels pretty strange after so many years in Mexico."

"Yup."

She watched the flames, itching for a pencil and paper. To escape the nightmare for a few minutes with her fingers and her imagination. A picture filled her mind. A cabin, water dripping down the siding, the gray lake beyond, and the fire flickering through the windows. A figure entered the picture in her mind's eye, a little girl with dark hair and joyful eyes, her face lifted to the sky to catch the raindrops.

Tears dripped down Marisa's cheeks, but she couldn't move to wipe them. She let the moment fill her, overwhelm her, until a sob rose in her heart and burst out.

Nate turned her to face him, and she leaned against his sweatshirt and wept. He held her, silent, until the latest round of tears was spent. When she looked up and sniffed, Nate stared into her eyes, and she stared back. If only things could be different and she could stay with him, right in that spot, with Ana adding the music of her laughter. If only.

Nate wiped her tears with the sleeve of his sweatshirt. "You okay?"

She turned to see Brady, Rae, and Sam getting coffee, picking at muffins, and generally trying not to watch. Polite. A little awkward. She nearly laughed. "It's okay," she said to the room in general, and they all looked up. "Sorry about that."

Rae nodded gently. "You're entitled to fall apart. We don't mind. Right?" She nudged Brady, who nodded.

"Yeah. It's fine. Uh..."

"Let's sit back down," Rae said.

The five of them took their seats, and Marisa laid the blanket over her legs and sipped her coffee. Someone must've microwaved it while she'd been outside, because it was hot. She was thankful as it warmed her.

"Are you with us?" Nate asked.

"You're saying the kidnapping was staged. Leslie staged it."

Nate looked at Brady, who shook his head. "Just to be clear, your daughter was kidnapped. That wasn't staged. Your sister wasn't a victim, though. She's the kidnapper."

Leslie had kidnapped Ana. How could she have sunk so low? And more importantly, why? Marisa faced Sam. "But you said Leslie still has plenty of money."

"As far as I can tell," Sam said.

"Why would she do this?" Marisa asked. "And why now?"

Sam shrugged. Marisa turned to Nate. "You spent time with her. Did she give you any indication—?"

"That she was lying about everything? Of course not. I knew she was jealous of you, that maybe she wasn't convinced you didn't steal the money. But if I'd thought her capable of this, I never would have helped her find you."

"Of course." Marisa touched his hand. "I didn't mean to imply..."

Nate squeezed her hand. "I know."

"You asked the right question." Brady looked at Marisa. "We might not be able to figure out her motive, but let's focus on the other half of it—why now? What's different now from, say, a year ago? According to Sam, her business is thriving."

Sam nodded. "She picks up new accounts all the time, bought a new car with cash about a year ago. Her house is paid for—"

"Our inheritance," Marisa said.

"If there are gambling debts, I'm not seeing them," Sam said.

"But even if there were, why not just pay them out of the money she already has?"

Rae leaned forward. "Maybe we can't figure out why, but something prompted her to do this. What's different in your sister's life now from before?"

The answer was obvious. "There's a guy. She's engaged." She looked at Nate. "She wasn't wearing a ring, but she said he was going to get her one soon. She talked about him a lot, said he was handsome and sweet, and she couldn't believe he wanted her."

"Did she give you a name?" Brady asked.

"Rick."

"No last name?"

Marisa shook her head. "I never thought to ask. We didn't have that much time to visit, honestly. We spent the one night together, but she was exhausted after all the travel, and she was sick the next day. We talked a little before bed that night, but..."

"It's okay," Rae said. "Rick is a start."

Sam was already tapping on her laptop's keyboard. "I'm looking at your sister's Facebook profile. Her relationship status says she's in a relationship. She doesn't mention the guy's name, though. I'll scroll through her friends..." Her voice trailed off as she studied the screen.

"Maybe this Rick she's involved with is her accomplice."

Marisa turned to Nate, a new thought occurring to her. "Or maybe he was just using her to get information, to find me. Maybe he threatened her, and she didn't have any choice."

Nate nodded slowly. "Maybe."

The rest of the room was silent. Clearly, nobody thought that seemed plausible, but the idea took hold, a lifesaver in this ocean of doubt. "Maybe she really was threatened that night, and they think I have all the money. She went to Mexico to get me to give it to her. Maybe she's been caught up in something she can't control."

"That's very possible, Marisa," Nate said. "We'll just have to wait until we find her and we can ask her."

"But you don't believe it."

He shook his head. "Why wouldn't she have just given them the money she stole? To protect herself, to protect you, why not just pay them off to get them to go away?"

Marisa had no answer to that.

"Remember what Nate said?" Rae asked. "In a weird way, this is good news."

Marisa turned to Nate as the memory of his words from a few minutes before came to her. "Why is it good news?"

"Your daughter is with your sister." Nate adjusted in his seat to face her. "Don't you see? She might be guilty of all these things, but she's not a psychopath. She wouldn't be cruel. I don't know your sister like you do, but from what you've told us, and from what I've seen, she has a strong instinct to nurture. Don't you think she's taking good care of Ana?"

The tightening in her chest loosened just a tad, and a tiny flicker of hope lit. Marisa remembered Leslie with Ana, remembered how they'd walked hand-in-hand through the market. Remembered the gifts Leslie had bought her, the way they'd laughed together, how Leslie had protected Ana on that Acapulco street. Leslie wouldn't hurt Ana.

Marisa met Nate's eyes. "Leslie will take good care of her."

"I think so, too."

"Thank God." Marisa looked up, saw only the ceiling, but imagined some strong force up there. For the first time, she allowed herself to believe this might work out. She looked back at the faces around her, all watching for her reaction. She smiled. "You're right. That's good news."

Nate squeezed Marisa's hand and turned to Brady. "We have the information. What do we do with it?"

"I know what I'd say," Brady said, "but Garrison probably has more experience with this kind of thing than I do. Let's catch him up and see what he says."

"What would you do, though?" Marisa asked. "I'm curious."

"If it were me, I'd stay the course, see if you can discover who stole Charles's money. For all you know, they're watching you. You don't want them to know you're on to them."

Nate was nodding with Brady's words. "I agree. I'll call Garrison and get him up to speed." Nate stood and walked into his bedroom, dialing on the way.

Marisa sipped her coffee, picked up the muffin, and took a bite. It was delicious. She hadn't noticed before.

"More coffee?" Sam asked.

She looked inside her cup, finished the last sip, and nodded. "Let me. I want to play with the machine."

Sam laughed, and she and Rae joined Marisa in the kitchen, where Marisa figured out the Keurig. "I really missed America."

"I know what you mean," Rae said.

Marisa turned to the tall woman. "You've lived abroad?"

"Nate didn't tell you?"

Marisa looked at the closed door of his bedroom. "We haven't had a lot of time to catch up."

"We were colleagues."

More than colleagues at one point, but Marisa didn't quibble about the details.

"I'm a reporter, too," Rae said. "I lived in Tunisia."

"What brought you home?"

Rae looked at Sam, who lifted her eyebrows.

"It's a long story. You should ask Nate about it."

"I've tried a couple of times to ask him why he left the *Times*, but he always changes the subject."

Sam took Marisa's hand and squeezed. "Ask again. I think you need to know."

Their expressions were too serious. Seemed these two women knew a lot more about Nate than she did, and they felt she needed to know. Why, though? Would it affect their ability to find Ana and Leslie? Or did they think there was more going on between her and Nate?

Was there?

Marisa slid her coffee across the counter, took her muffin from the coffee table, and perched on a barstool. She ate the muffin, sipped her coffee, and wondered about the man who'd come to mean so much to her.

FIFTEEN

AFTER NATE FILLED Garrison in on all they'd learned, he stepped back into the living room to find Marisa chatting with Rae and Sam. Her plate held crumbs, and her coffee was half full. She was laughing at something, and the sound was more beautiful than a symphony at Carnegie Hall.

She turned when he walked in, her smile fading. Not the effect he wanted to have on her, but it couldn't be helped.

"Garrison thought our theories were sound," he said. "In fact, he was a little annoyed he'd never put it together before."

Brady stood in front of the fire, where he'd been adding more logs and probably avoiding all the estrogen in the kitchen. "He didn't have all the information." He brushed his hands off on his jeans.

"That's what I told him, but you know how those law enforcement guys are. All ego."

"Watch it," Brady said.

Marisa giggled, and Nate's heart did a little backflip. He'd made her laugh. The realization sent him a thousand stupid ideas, silly things he could do to elicit the same reaction. Good grief, he was thinking like a middle-schooler. Maybe he should tug on her braid to get her to notice him.

The thought of children brought his mind to Ana, which sobered him. He walked around the bar into the kitchen. Not that he needed more coffee, but putting space between him and Marisa seemed a good idea, if he wanted to think straight.

Rae swiveled on her barstool. "What did he suggest?"

"Same thing as Brady—keep looking for the truth, because it might be our only leverage. The only way we can use the information is if we can either figure out who Leslie's accomplice is or get her on the phone alone. And even then, it would be risky to say anything. What if he's listening?"

Marisa said, "We could ask—"

"But why would she tell us the truth?" Nate leaned toward Marisa. "If he's listening in, she could say he's not. If we could be sure she was alone, we could confront her, suggest she give herself up and work with us to put her accomplice away. But if he's listening, or if she tells him we know…"

Marisa's face paled. "We could put her in danger."

"Or they could just run," Rae said. "Use her money and take off."

Marisa looked at Nate. "And what would they do with Ana?"

Rather than guess the answer, he said, "We keep going forward, searching for the money, and hope your sister and her friend keep their end of the bargain. Maybe an opening will come, and we'll get the chance to talk to Leslie alone. We'll just have to go where the circumstances take us."

Marisa sighed. "Nothing's changed, not really."

Brady stood behind Marisa and put his hand on her shoulder. "We know more than we did before. You know what they say—knowledge is power."

Rae nodded. "We'll figure out a way to use it. You never

know how these things will work out." She met her husband's gaze, and they shared a moment that had Nate's heart beating wildly. He knew what they were thinking. It brought back a thousand bad memories.

Sam said, "What do we do now?"

Nate looked at her, thankful for something else to focus on besides Brady and Rae. "Any chance you could hack into Pamela Gray's accounts, see if she stole the money?"

"It's not stealing if it was her husband's money," Brady said.

"True," Nate said, "but she claimed she didn't have it. If she does, the mystery is solved." He looked back at Sam. "Can you do it?"

"I haven't been able to yet. She's better about security than most people."

"We'll just have to ask her," Marisa said. "Maybe if she knows the stakes, she'll help us."

Nate doubted it, but he didn't say that. "She's not going to be home until tomorrow. In the meantime, I think we need to figure out who Leslie's fiancé is. Did you find anything on her Facebook page?"

Sam shook her head. "It says she's in a relationship, but there were no Ricks or Richards."

"Maybe she lied about his name," Marisa said. "If he's an accomplice, why would she tell us the truth?"

"Maybe," Sam said. "The problem is, she has five hundred friends, about half of them men. I can scroll through them, see if I can narrow it down, but it'll take time."

"Five hundred friends?" Marisa couldn't imagine her sister connecting with that many people. Must be friends from her business. "Don't you have to work? I hate that you're all taking time off for this. Maybe I can do it."

"Don't be silly," Sam said. "It's just a job. I can catch up next week. This is more important."

Rae patted Marisa on the back. "I work freelance. My time is my own."

"But Johnny—"

"Is fine," Rae said. "Whatever you need, I'm here to help."

Brady nodded. "I'm a detective. This is what I do."

Marisa looked at Nate. He reached across the counter and took her hand. "There's no place I'd rather be than right here. I'm with you in this."

"I know." She held his gaze. Something warm and electric passed between them. Something terrifying and beautiful. He cursed the counter between them.

She looked away first. "Thank you. All of you. I can't imagine doing this alone."

NATE OPENED the door for Marisa, who climbed into Brady's truck Friday morning just as the night faded to gray. After a stop at McNeal's for coffee and breakfast sandwiches to go, they aimed for I-93. They were mostly silent until they slowed slightly as traffic picked up nearing 495.

"Where are all these people going so early in the morning?" Marisa asked.

"Most are trying to beat the traffic into Boston."

She looked at the clock. "I would still be sleeping back in Mexico. Our commute was a walk across the street."

"Different lifestyle down there."

"There were plenty who left for Chilpancingo before dawn. Ana and I were fortunate."

Nate glanced at her profile in the brightening light. Even this early in the morning, she was stunning. "Not a lot of folks would consider your circumstances fortunate."

She shrugged and sipped her coffee.

He'd managed to eat his sandwich before they'd hit London-derry, before the traffic really slowed them down. Her sandwich lay on the paper it had come wrapped in, resting on her lap. She'd been picking at it for twenty minutes. She took the final bite, balled up the paper, and dropped it in the McNeal's sack. After she'd finished the bite, she said, "Thing is, it could have been much worse for me, but since I already spoke Spanish and I'm half Puerto Rican, moving to Mexico was easier than it would have been for someone like your friend Rae, for instance. Trying to fit in with her complexion and red hair—that would have been tough."

"You'd be surprised, though. Rae's able to fit in about anywhere she goes. She dyed her hair dark brown when she lived in Africa. It wasn't very pretty, but she stood out less."

"Tunisia, she said."

"Right." A little ball of apprehension settled in his stomach.

"She told me I should ask you about why she moved home. She gave the impression there's a story there."

His palms started to sweat just from the thought of sharing the story. He wiped his right hand on his jeans, then his left. He adjusted the heater. It suddenly seemed very warm.

"You don't want to tell me."

He glanced at her, saw a flicker of hurt in her eyes, and focused on the road. They were moving faster now, but it would take another three hours before they got to Queens. Not like he could pretend there wasn't time. He took a deep breath. "It's not easy to talk about."

"Okay." The one word held both question and resignation. She wouldn't push it. Which made him feel worse. Could he get through it without losing his breakfast? More importantly, what would Marisa think about him when he'd finished the story?

He could hear his therapist's voice echoing in his ears. *Your prison bars are only as solid as your secrets.* Fine. If Marisa thought less of him, at least she'd know the truth about the person she'd trusted to help her through this. Maybe she'd decide to leave him out of it, and he could go back to the solitary life he'd planned.

He glanced again and saw her watching him. What would she think of him? But it couldn't be helped. She'd learn the truth eventually. Rae or Brady or Sam—one of them would certainly tell her before this was all over. Of course, if he let one of them tell it, Nate would come out looking like a hero instead of the coward he was.

So yes, he should tell her. But, under the circumstances... "It's a pretty ugly story, Marisa. It has nothing to do with the people who have Ana, but I don't want to make things worse for you."

"I think I can handle it."

He took another deep breath. "Rae married a guy who turned out to be an arms dealer, part of an international crime family that makes our local gang activity look like child's play. She didn't know what he did for a living. He'd lied to her about everything, but..." He forced a breath. So far, so good. "A lot of this story is hers. I'll only tell you my part in it. Before I go on though, this isn't something I'm really supposed to talk about outside of therapy. It's all hush-hush, which means you have to keep it to yourself."

"You can trust me with your secrets."

He nodded once. "After Johnny was born, she left the guy and went back to Nutfield to hide. I was the only person he'd met from her past, so he..."

Nate paused, swallowed, and loosened his grip on the steering wheel. He took a deep breath and willed his voice to stay steady.

"He and his bodyguard grabbed me. And there was a

woman, too. They stuffed me in the trunk of a car and took me to a hotel room in Connecticut."

"Oh, my God."

"The guard was..." She didn't need the details. "I knew where Rae was, but I refused to tell them."

"Did they hurt you?"

He nodded.

"Did you escape?"

If only he'd had the courage. "The guard was working against Rae's husband. Julien found out and shot him. Twice." Nate swallowed the nausea that always rose with the memory. "I watched it happen."

He focused on the road, the white lines whizzing by on each side, the sedans and minivans and SUVs and eighteen-wheelers all around him. It was a normal day, and he was surrounded by normal people. He was safe.

"That must have been terrifying," Marisa said.

"I just thought... You're in that situation, and you think, this is how I'm going to die. Just like that. And you start to wonder about inconsequential stuff, like will I soil my shorts? Will it hurt when the bullet enters my brain, or will I die instantly? Should I try to run and get shot in the back instead? At first, I kept trying to figure out how to get away, but there were three of them, just one of me, and they had the guns. The woman was adept at tying my ropes. And then I was badly beaten, I couldn't imagine how I could ever get out of the ropes, much less fight to get away. After a while, I don't know. You just decide, *whatever*. I guess I'll die."

"Oh, Nate."

"I got angry. I thought, screw 'em. They're going to kill me anyway. I'm not telling them anything."

"But everybody breaks. That's what they say on TV, anyway."

He nearly smiled. "Yeah. I would have, eventually."

"But you didn't?"

"Rae called. I should have..." His eyes stung, but no way was he going to cry. He waited until the feeling passed. "I should have answered the phone with, 'They have me. Run.'" But I thought they'd just figure out I'd been lying and try to get me to tell where she was. I never imagined she'd give herself away. When she did, I should have warned her."

"But there was a reason you didn't."

He could still feel the gun pressed to his temple. All his thoughts about being ready to die had come to that moment, and he hadn't had the courage to go through with it. "I was afraid." At least he didn't have to look at her as he admitted this most shameful moment of his life. He might never be able to look at her again.

Marisa reached across the truck and touched his hand, which had a death grip on the steering wheel. He looked down, saw her hand there, palm up. An invitation. He considered ignoring it, wanted to ignore it. But he cared too much for her to hurt her. He took her hand.

"We're all afraid, Nate. That's what it means to be human."

"I should have protected her."

"But she's all right. It worked out."

"No thanks to me."

"What happened?"

He sighed. "The rest is really her story to tell."

A few moments passed, and he hoped the conversation was over. Marisa scooted closer. "How long did they have you?"

"About thirty-two hours."

"A long time."

"Nothing, really. Think of POWs and what they have to endure. My situation was nothing like that. And still I couldn't hold out."

"You didn't tell them where she was."

"Eventually, I did. He threatened to kill my family, and at that point, I couldn't figure out what the point was in not telling them. They knew the town she was in; it was just a matter of time before they figured out her real name and where she lived. I didn't want them hunting down my parents or my brother to get the information."

"They put you in an impossible position, Nate. You did the right thing. The only thing."

"You say that because Rae and Johnny survived. If they'd died..."

"But they didn't. And Rae and Brady obviously feel very differently about what happened, based on the things they've said to you. And to me about you."

"Rae blames herself for what I went through. I wish she wouldn't. She didn't have any control over the situation."

"And you did?"

He didn't answer. He knew what Marisa would say, the same thing his therapist said, the same thing Rae and Brady and Sam had said so many times. He hadn't had any control. Maybe it was easier for the rest of them to say it, but to realize the truth of it? That was a whole different ballgame.

Nate had felt a lot of terrible emotions in his lifetime, but none hit that depth of powerlessness. He'd never considered himself a control freak, but having everything removed from his control, from when he was able to use the bathroom to the number of sips of water he was allowed between beatings. Being tied to a chair, unable to wipe the dripping blood, unable to scratch an itch. Some people found peace in knowing the world was out of their control. Nate found only torment.

Marisa moved their joined hands to her lap, where she laid her other hand over his. "I can't imagine how awful it was for you."

No, she couldn't imagine it. And he wasn't going to tell her any more. She had enough of her own torment right now. She didn't need to worry about his.

"Is that why you quit your job?"

"I needed to escape the chaos. Escape the job, escape New York." He needed to control his environment, and there was too much in New York that was out of his control. A quiet life. That's what he longed for. A life where he would never, ever feel that powerless again.

And if that were the case, what was he doing here?

"I believe I've ruined your plans," Marisa said.

Was she a mind reader? "Nobody ever plans for something like this."

"I would never have guessed you'd gone through that. Did you have PTSD?"

"Did. Still do, I guess."

"Yet, here you are."

A sucker for a pretty face. He glanced at Marisa and smiled. A beautiful face, a beautiful heart. He squeezed her hand. "Like I said yesterday, there's no place I'd rather be."

"How are you handling it, the...the fear? Because after I escaped eight years ago, I was skittish all the time. And nothing had really happened to me. I'd just been afraid, and it was awful."

"I feel like I'm in AA. Maybe I should be—do they have AA for control freaks?" The joke fell flat. "I'm worried I won't be able to handle it, yeah. That's why I need my friends and Garrison to stay involved. You need somebody you can count on if things get dangerous."

"I can count on you."

"No, you can't. You think you can, which is why I'm telling you this. I am..." He really didn't want to go on, but she needed to understand who he was. Even if it painted him in an ugly light. She needed to know he was not worthy of her trust. "Remember when that guy grabbed you in Acapulco?"

"Not the kind of thing a person forgets."

"Ever ask yourself why it took me so long to react?"

When she didn't say anything, he glanced at her face. She seemed more confused than anything. "You were there right away."

"I wasn't. I paused. I stood on the bottom step and stared for, I don't know, a few seconds, anyway. The instinct to help seems to have been replaced with the instinct to run away like a little kid."

"A second, two seconds—that's normal."

"It's not. A real man—"

"Don't be ridiculous. You think you're not a real man because you paused for a second? After what you've been through, a lot of people would have bolted. But you didn't. You rescued me."

"Not really. The guy took off as soon as he heard me. And anyway, he'd only been trying to stick the phone in your bag and create a diversion. He ran when he heard the tires squeal. I did nothing. Just like last time."

She sighed. "You're insane."

"There's that, too."

"That's not... Nate, the man you describe, this *coward* you think you are, would not have stuck with me through all of this. He wouldn't have gotten involved from the very start. He'd never have left Queens."

He wasn't sure what to say. He'd just been caught up in it, but he wouldn't be able to convince her of that. At least he'd told her the truth. Funny, though. His prison bars still seemed just as solid.

SIXTEEN

Marisa stared at the house as Nate parked the truck on the street. This had been home for most of her life. Leslie'd taken good care of it. The wood siding had recently been repainted. It was yellow now, and it looked pretty with white window casings. The windows looked new. Leslie had kept the small front yard in good shape, and the rhododendron bushes looked bigger and healthier than ever.

"How will we get in?" Nate asked.

Marisa stepped out of the car and shivered. The previous day's rain had passed, but the sun had brought a cold front with it. She crossed her arms and walked up the short walk that cut the tiny yard in half. At the front door, she peered at the same lock had been there since Father had bought the deadbolt when Marisa was little. She could still remember the conversation about "my girls' safety" as he'd installed the lock. That had been just a few months before he'd moved out. Maybe he'd known they'd need something to count on besides him.

"I still have a key," Marisa said. "I've kept it in my wallet all these years."

"A talisman of hope."

She smiled at him. "Something like that." She pulled her wallet from the bag Nate had bought her in Acapulco, found the key in the coin purse, and unlocked the door.

They went inside, and she looked around. The house looked so different, she hardly recognized it. Apparently this was what Leslie had done with at least some of the money she'd stolen. The hardwood floors had been refinished, the old wooden banister that led to the second floor had been replaced with ornate wrought iron. She stepped into the living room. The old, ugly fireplace had been updated. Gray stacked stone had replaced the old brick, and a new dark stained mantle sat above it. Over that, a black-and-white abstract drew the eye.

The furniture was different, too. A taupe low-profile sectional surrounded a square table with a few magazines, a modern, unused ashtray, and a vase filled with some sort of dried twigs. Leslie had no decorating ability, which meant she'd hired help. Add decorator's fees to the list of costs.

Marisa continued into the kitchen. Granite countertops, stainless appliances, and even a dishwasher. If only they'd had that growing up, their evenings would have been much more pleasant. The room had been completely remodeled. She turned to Nate, who'd followed her through the house. "Leslie's been busy."

"It looks brand new."

"If not for the address, I might not have recognized it."

"It's nice."

She supposed, though she'd been looking forward to seeing the white appliances their mother had bought, the old pictures on the walls. Even the kitchen wallpaper had been removed, replaced with pale blue paint that stretched into the living room and entryway. "She changed everything."

"Does that bother you?"

Marisa looked for some sign of herself, of their mother, but saw only Leslie's fingerprints. She didn't answer Nate's question.

"You look down here," she said. "I'll head upstairs. Let me know if you find anything."

"Will do."

After spending hours looking through Leslie's Facebook friends the day before, Sam, Rae, and she had decided their best chance for discovering the name of Leslie's fiancé would lie in the house. They'd found a handful of guys among her Facebook friends who weren't married, but most were either clients—which Sam had discovered using Leslie's invoices from her email—or lived too far away. Maybe they'd have more luck in the house.

At the top of the stairs, Marisa entered what used to be their mother's bedroom. Why she'd thought her mother's things would still be there, she didn't know. Instead, Marisa found that Leslie had moved into the space. New paint, new bedroom furniture, new everything. She stifled a sigh as she crossed to the bureau and the many photographs there. Leslie with a host of people, all wearing the logo of Leslie's office cleaning business. In these photos, she looked different than she had when Marisa had lived here. She looked different than she had in Acapulco, too. She'd never spent a lot of time on personal grooming. Maybe the new boyfriend had encouraged her to try a little harder. In the pictures, her hair was sleek, and she wore more makeup than Marisa was used to seeing on her. Leslie wore nicer clothes fitted to her shape. She looked...pretty.

She hated that the thought of her sister as *pretty* had come as a surprise. She'd always thought of Leslie as kindhearted and honest, if not a little homely.

Seemed she'd been wrong on all counts.

Marisa studied the photos again. There were none of Leslie with a man.

Interesting.

She perused the rest of the room. It seemed perfectly normal. Normal except for the fancy clothes, jewelry, shoes, and handbags, which hadn't been normal for Leslie eight years before. In the adjoining bathroom, Marisa found makeup galore, not to mention various hair styling implements—a curling iron, straightening iron, and blow dryer, along with expensive hair gels. It seemed that frumpy Leslie had transformed. Funny how she hadn't bothered with any of that stuff when she'd gone to Mexico. Marisa would have assumed her lack of grooming had been due to fear, but now she knew better. She hadn't been afraid. She'd been...what? Maybe trying to look the part of the grieving sister? Maybe trying to pretend nothing had changed? Marisa took in the updated bathroom and thought of the designer clothes hanging in her sister's closet. Leslie had apparently changed everything.

Marisa went through the drawers in the bathroom. Mostly Leslie's stuff, but one drawer held a man's razor, a can of shaving cream, a toothbrush, and a box of condoms. Lovely.

She returned to the bedroom to search. Aside from Leslie's things, she found a drawer filled with men's clothes. T-shirts and sweat pants, all larges, along with boxers and white socks. Seemed the man didn't live here, but he stayed over often enough to need his own drawer.

Marisa crossed the hall and checked out Leslie's old room, which had been converted to an office. Marisa dug through the drawers and file cabinet looking for something, anything that might shed some light on what was going on. No photographs of any mystery man. No files labeled *kidnapping scheme*— wouldn't that have been convenient? Nothing to give her a hint about what her sister was doing.

With a deep breath, Marisa left the office and headed to her closed bedroom door. She could still picture the double bed, the white furniture her father had bought for her thirteenth birthday, the pink walls and white lacy curtains. She could imagine the easel, the pads of paper and charcoals and watercolors and markers she'd used to create every kind of artwork, the pictures she'd tacked all over the room. She'd been such a girly-girl, and her father had spoiled her long after he'd moved out. She remembered the scent of the cheap perfume she'd gotten from a friend for her fifteenth birthday. She'd thought it was the sweetest smelling stuff in the world. She could imagine the thin layer of powder and blush and eyeshadow covering the top of her makeup table. This room had been hers, and she was afraid to find out what her sister had done with it. After a deep breath for courage, she stepped inside.

A workout room. A high-end elliptical machine and a treadmill both faced a flat-screen TV. The walls were white. The curtains black. The crappy artwork as dark as her sister's heart. Hoping to find some trace of herself, Marisa opened the closet. Workout clothes and a cache of DVDs. She slammed the door and headed back downstairs.

Nate stood at the door, looking outside. He'd been nervous about coming here, and she didn't blame him. If the bad guys— whoever they were—were looking for them, they'd certainly have eyes on this house. Marisa was ready to face them, face her sister and tell her what she thought of her. But nobody came.

He turned when she hit the landing. "You find anything?"

"Nope."

His head tilted to the side. "You okay?"

"I always thought..." She shook her head. "Did you find anything?"

"Nothing really to see. Some photos on the bookshelves in

the living room, more in the kitchen, but no guys. We're sure your sister was engaged to a man, right?"

"Not a woman, if that's what you mean."

He shrugged. "You never know."

She told him about her discoveries upstairs, and he nodded. "Definitely a man, then." He walked to the photographs on the bookshelves in the living room. "She has a lot of pictures."

"Yeah. She always liked to take pictures of herself with everybody she ever met. I think it makes her feel important or something. Like if she knows all these different people, it must mean she matters."

Nate nodded slowly. "Okay, but where's the guy?"

"I know, it's weird. If they're that close, I can't imagine it never occurred to her to get at least a snapshot with him."

"Maybe he refused?"

"Maybe he imagined this very scenario," Marisa said. "What does that tell us about him?"

"If he thought we might start to suspect Leslie, it tells us he didn't care that much about her getting caught. That he was trying to save his own ass."

"Sounds like a keeper." Marisa glanced at the photos again. Each had Leslie and at least one other person, if not many more. She recognized some as clients they'd served way back when Marisa had worked there. Her sister garnered loyalty, that was for sure. Leslie'd kept the photos with employees upstairs, the photos with clients down. Marisa'd like to think that was because she was closer to the employees and wanted their photos in a more intimate place. She'd like to think it, but she didn't. Leslie kept the client's pictures downstairs because they made her look good.

"Do you recognize any of them?" Nate asked. "Might they be friends?"

"A few. Clients."

"No friends?"

"She never had many friends." Marisa returned to the door. "This was a waste of time."

He stepped to the window in the living room and pushed the heavy curtain aside. "I want to show you something." She joined him at the window and looked at the casing as he pointed. "These are really good windows. New, with excellent locks. See?" He showed her the double-locking system. "No reason why she'd have them open in March, and if you look around, you'll see they're all locked. There are none that look like they've been tampered with." He crossed to the back door and opened it. "No scuff marks on this lock."

She looked. He was right.

"And there are none on the front door, either," he said.

"You're saying nobody broke in."

He shrugged. "I don't see any signs of it."

"Great. Just proves what we thought."

He closed and locked the back door, then gestured toward the front. "Shall we?"

She led the way, ready to leave.

She climbed into the truck. When he joined her, he started the engine and drove a few blocks, glanced at her a few times. He pulled over and put it in park.

"What's wrong?" he asked.

She sighed. "It's my house, too."

"Okay."

"She changed everything. I mean... Everything. Every light fixture, every cabinet, everything."

"That bothers you?"

"She made my bedroom into a workout room. All my stuff is gone."

"I looked in the basement. There were lots of dust-covered

cardboard boxes. I didn't check, because they seemed to have been there a long time. Maybe your stuff is down there."

"Maybe she didn't give it all to Goodwill."

"It's something."

She sighed and stared out the side window. "It's like she never believed I'd come home. Like she just wrote me out of her life. Like I never existed. There wasn't even a photograph of me." She turned to look at him, wanting him to understand. "No photographs of Mom, either."

He nodded slowly, his brown eyes intent as he studied her. He reached across the seat for her hand. "It seems your sister is not who you thought she was."

"I don't know if she was always like that and I never saw it, or if something changed her. Maybe I was wrong about her feelings all those years. I thought she loved me, but now...everything's wrong." She stared at nothing while she tried to imagine the girl her sister had once been. "I guess it doesn't matter. When I was a little girl, Leslie was kind to me. Despite everything, I still don't think she'll hurt Ana, and right now that's all I care about."

"You're right. But at the same time, I think the questions you have about your sister do matter. She's your family, your history. Just remember, what your sister thinks about you—what anybody thinks about you—that doesn't define you."

"What does define me?"

He shrugged. "That's a good question. I don't know the answer. I do know that you're an amazing woman. I always thought you were beautiful—nobody could deny that."

She'd heard that her whole life, as if it was something to be proud of. As if she'd sculpted her own face and spun her own hair. As if she was supposed to feel proud of her beauty instead of recognizing it as the accident of genes that it was.

Nate continued. "But it's who you are on the inside that I find beautiful now."

That was the sentiment she'd longed for, always. "You're a good man, Nate Boyle."

He looked out the windshield and watched a passing car before turning back to her. "At least we can be sure of one thing."

"What's that?"

"Ana is with Leslie, so she's still safe. Your sister's a lot of bad things, but nobody is all bad. You saw her good qualities growing up, and those are still there. She'll take good care of Ana."

But what about the man Leslie was working with? He was a wild card. Who knew what he'd do?

MARISA WATCHED her childhood neighborhood grow smaller and disappear in the rear window.

Nate headed toward Pamela Gray's Upper West Side brownstone to wait for the woman to get home from her trip. Why wait for a call from a maid when they could watch the front door? They'd just turned onto Grand Central Parkway when his cell phone rang. He answered it, and Garrison's voice came through the speakers.

"Where are you guys?"

"Queens," Nate said. "We're on our way to Manhattan. What's up?"

"Can you meet me? We need to talk."

The solemn tone in his voice made Marisa's heart pound. "What happened?"

"Nate," Garrison said, "what's your location."

"Almost to the Triborough Bridge."

"Okay. Hold on."

Marisa glared at the dashboard as if that would make Garrison explain himself. She glanced at Nate. He kept his eyes on the traffic-heavy road.

What was going on? Garrison sounded serious, and not happy. If it were good news, he'd just tell them. Which meant it was bad. What would be so bad that Garrison would get involved? He was no longer with the FBI. Whatever was going on, how did he find out? She was about to blurt out her questions when he spoke.

"Can you meet me on Randall Island? You know where that is?"

Nate nodded. "I've seen it."

"There's a park right under the bridge. Meet me there."

Marisa couldn't wait. "What happened?"

"I gotta go," Garrison said. "I'll be there soon."

The line went dead.

She looked at Nate. "Ana's dead. He doesn't want to tell me over the phone, but—"

"Let's not jump to conclusions."

"Why wouldn't he just tell us?" Her voice was rising. "If Ana's fine, why wouldn't he—?"

"Maybe it's not about Ana. We were working a lot of angles. Maybe he got a lead." Nate reached across the car for her hand, but she shifted away.

"Don't. I need to know what's going on."

"Garrison is working. He's in FBI mode. It doesn't necessarily mean good news or bad. Just news. News is good."

"Not always." Not usually. She thought of the moment she'd learned Vinnie was dead. His mother had barely been able to speak through her tears. A moment later, another woman's voice came on the phone. Vinnie's sister explained that his body had been found. He'd been beaten to death.

That was the moment Marisa's life had shattered. She'd spent eight years trying to put it back together, and now it was about to shatter again.

She wasn't sure if she'd survive this time.

Nate followed the traffic onto the bridge. She'd been on this road a thousand times—happy moments with her mom and Leslie, commuting to college and work, going on dates with Vinnie. A thousand times she'd seen the New York skyline from here. A thousand times she'd ridden beneath the steel towers, passed between the thick cables that ferried millions of cars from one side of the East River to the other. Today, those cables seemed pretty thin. One snap, and it would all be over.

They exited onto the Bronx Shore Road on Randall Island. A few minutes later, Nate parked, stepped out of the car, and opened her door.

"Let's walk until Garrison gets here."

She didn't get out of the truck. She felt nearly paralyzed with fear. "What is he going to tell us, Nate?"

He took her hand and squeezed. "I have no idea. Let's try not to worry."

"Easy for you to say."

He met her eyes. "No. It's not."

She blinked and looked down. Nate had done nothing but help her. Whatever was going on, it wasn't his fault. She looked back up. "Sorry."

"No reason to be sorry. Come on."

He helped her out of the truck and closed the door behind her. He kept her hand in his and led the way along the paved path toward the foot of the bridge they'd just crossed. A cold breeze blew up from the river, and she folded her arms and looked out over the water.

"My dad played in a softball league when I was a kid,"

Marisa said. "I used to come down here for his games sometimes."

"Must be good memories."

"Long time ago."

They walked in silence. Marisa couldn't make conversation, and it seemed Nate had no idea what to say. The world seemed in suspension, just like the bridge overhead.

Finally, Nate's phone rang. He answered.

"We're in the park." He told Garrison where they'd parked and slipped his phone back in his pocket. "He's going to meet us in the lot. He's not here yet."

Nate set the pace, which was the only thing that kept her from running back. They leaned against the bumper. A moment later, Garrison's black Camry parked beside the pickup.

Marisa met him as he stepped out of his car. "What happened?"

"Let's find a place to sit down."

"I'm freezing," she said, "and I don't want to sit. What happened?"

Garrison looked over her head at Nate with a pleading glance.

Nate said, "Why don't we just—?"

"Fine. Whatever."

Nate opened the tailgate to Brady's truck, and she lifted herself onto it. The cold of the metal seeped through her borrowed jeans. "Please tell me what happened."

Nate stood beside her, and Garrison stopped in front of them. "I called my old partner last night. I figured it was time to get him up to speed on what was going on."

Her heartbeat, already racing, sped up. "The guy said no cops."

"Relax, Marisa." Garrison wore a patient smile, which made her want to smack him. "My partner's trustworthy. With our theory about your sister, I thought maybe he and I could figure out who she's working with."

Marisa glanced at Nate, who nodded to Garrison. "And?"

Garrison shook his head. "Nothing on the partner yet. But..." He took a breath and blew it out. "He called me this morning."

She waited through a long pause, knowing what was coming was bad news and almost not wanting to hear it. Almost.

Garrison's expression softened. "Your sister's body was discovered this morning. She was murdered."

SEVENTEEN

HE HADN'T MEANT to kill her.

The scent of that morning's burnt toast mingled with the stink of old garlic and bad cheese, the remnants of a thousand meals previous tenants had prepared here. The sound of his footsteps joined the noises beyond the thin walls. A slamming door. A distant TV. The traffic out front. He paced past the gouged and discolored laminate countertops, past the stovetop grimy from decades of misuse, past the cheap, fiberglass table and its fake leather chairs. He swiveled at the wall, trying not to see the faded wallpaper, sure that if he accidentally touched it, his hands would come away dirty, and paced back. Maybe if he could think about something else, anything else. But despite the apartment's assault to his sense of aesthetics, all he could think about was Leslie.

He hadn't loved her. Hadn't cared at all about her. He'd found her because he believed her sister had Charles's money. He'd convinced her he loved her, convinced her that all that stood between them and their eternal happiness was the money Marisa had stolen. They'd been fiddle-farting around about how to get the money from her when Leslie'd phoned him one day and announced they had to move soon. She'd seen a Pod in the reporter's driveway. If Boyle moved, Leslie might never be able to find her sister. They'd cobbled together a plan and set all this in motion. Leslie had been as desperate for that money as he had. Or maybe she'd just wanted to please him.

But she'd gotten cold feet. Started worrying maybe her sister was telling the truth.

He hadn't wanted to kill Leslie. Not just because now he had to take care of the kid. Not just because he hadn't yet gained access to her overseas account. Yeah, he knew Leslie had stolen the firm's money. He'd still been figuring a way to get his hands on it.

He looked at his hands, remembered what they'd done. The blows. The knife. He hadn't meant to do it. He'd never be able to undo it.

To bring her back. To get the cash.

Whatever.

Leslie's money was lost to him. She was dead. Now, more than ever, he needed to find Charles Gray's money.

At least Leslie had paid off his gambling debts. A couple thousand here, a couple thousand there. She'd helped him.

He hadn't meant to kill her.

He punched the mustard-yellow refrigerator, and the pain in his fist traveled up his arm. Stupid move. He shook out his hand. The fist had already been bruised and cut from his fight with Leslie. And now the fridge was dented, too. The landlord would probably keep his security deposit.

As if that mattered.

What had he done?

He'd killed her.

The kid started crying again. He could hear her high, whiny voice through the walls. He didn't want to hurt the girl, but he was running out of options. He stalked out of the kitchen and across the living room. He'd kept the shades down and the lights off. He pounded on the bedroom door on the far side. "Shut up!"

Her little voice responded, "I want—"

"I don't give a flying..." He stopped short of the word and shook his head at his own stupidity. Murder, sure, but God forbid he should swear at a child. He pounded the door again, finished his sentence, and added, "Shut up, or I'll shut you up."

The girl's cries turned to whimpers. At least he wouldn't be able to hear the muted sound in the kitchen.

He couldn't stay in the living room. The sight of the blood brought it all back.

If Leslie had just kept her stupid mouth shut. But no, she decided—long after it was too late—that maybe her sister didn't have the money after all. She'd been sure. Completely convinced. And then she'd gotten cold feet. She'd started talking about how to give the kid back without getting caught. He'd screamed at her. "It's my money."

And the waterworks had started. "You never loved me at all, did you? It was all about the money." When she'd started for the kid's room, he'd had no choice. She'd have ruined everything.

He'd had to kill her.

He stomped back to the kitchen, leaned against the sticky countertop, and looked at his hands. Had he always been capable of murder? Or had the circumstances changed him?

If he didn't move and strained to hear, he could still hear the kid crying.

What was he going to do with her?

EIGHTEEN

LESLIE. Murdered.

The words weren't making sense, because her sister couldn't be dead. She couldn't be. Leslie had been Marisa's caretaker, her confidant, her companion. The idea that she could be gone...

Thank God it wasn't Ana.

Ana.

"Oh, my God. My baby."

"There's no sign of her," Garrison said.

"He's going to kill her."

Nate reached for her, but she angled away and focused on Garrison. "Did they find anything that made them think...?" She closed her eyes to block out the image of her daughter's beautiful body, dumped in an alley, dead and deserted. Gone.

Nausea rose to her throat, and she jumped off the truck and stepped a few feet away before losing her breakfast. After emptying her stomach, she staggered further into the grassy area and fell to her hands and knees.

Leslie was dead. Dead, dead, dead.

Forever.

And maybe it was Leslie's own fault for getting involved

with that guy. Maybe she'd let greed and envy rule her. Maybe she'd gotten in over her head.

No chance for redemption now.

Dead, dead, dead.

And Ana... Sweet Ana, if she was still alive, she no longer had someone to care for her. What was that man doing to her? Had Leslie died trying to protect her? From him? From pain? From death?

Marisa sat up, stared at the park, imagined the city beyond it, the state, the country. Her daughter was out there somewhere. They were no closer to finding out who stole the money than they had been at the beginning of this nightmare, and even if they did figure it out, would the kidnapper—the murderer—really exchange Ana for information? And risk being caught?

Why would he, when the only person left alive who could identify him was a four-year-old girl he couldn't care less about? A little Mexican girl, just a pawn with no value. A pawn who could destroy him.

And there was nothing Marisa could do. She'd adopted Ana to give her the best chance for a good life, and all she'd done was sign her death warrant. A Mexican orphanage was no place to grow up, but at least her daughter would've had the opportunity to grow up. To fall in love and have children. To learn and live and laugh. Now, Ana would have none of that. And Marisa... Marisa wouldn't survive this blow. She didn't want to.

The men waited behind her. She heard a car door open and close a minute later. Neither of them spoke.

Marisa didn't care. She just wanted to lie down on the cold grass and drift away. She ignored the moisture seeping through the denim. The soft blades of grass beneath her fingers seemed a perfectly good place to rest. Should she? How long would she be able to lie there before she froze to death? Was it cold enough at night to kill her?

If only she could run away from it all. Not face it. Like she'd run away eight years before. Except now... Now, the child of her heart, her love, would be the one to bear the burden. Marisa couldn't run. She could only go forward and face it. Ana was worth whatever price she had to pay.

Marisa would find her daughter, or she'd die trying. Right now... Right now, she just had to do the next thing, like Nate kept saying. Stand up. Wipe her tears. Breathe.

Keep going.

She returned to the truck, brushing slivers of grass off her hands and onto her wet jeans along the way.

"You okay?" Garrison asked.

It was a stupid question. She didn't answer.

He held out a stick of Trident and a bottle of water. She took the gum and popped it in her mouth.

"Why don't you sit down again?" Nate asked.

She would argue, but her knees were too weak to support her any longer. Nate and Garrison lifted her onto the tailgate. Garrison popped his trunk, found a fleece blanket, and slipped it over her shoulders. "I usually keep it with me, just in case."

She didn't know what to say.

Nate said, "You probably have all sorts of emergency preparedness supplies in your trunk, too, right?"

"Flashlight, first aid kit, auto-repair kit, jumper cables, and flares. And granola bars and bottles of water."

"I knew it."

"Hungry? Thirsty?"

Nate glanced at Marisa. "We're okay right now."

They were kind to make conversation while she regained her sanity. She feared they'd need to talk a lot longer, but sane or not, she had to go on. "I'm okay." She looked at Garrison. "When did she die?"

"Their first guess, sometime last night."

Nate touched her hand tentatively. She gripped his back like it might keep her from slipping away. She felt a modicum of comfort.

Nate squeezed her hand. "Let's give her time to process—"

"No." She shook her head and nodded to Garrison.

Garrison continued. "They found her body in an alley in Chelsea, but that's not the murder scene."

"How did...?" Marisa's voice was weak. She cleared her throat and continued. "How did she die?"

"Again, it's just a guess right now, but based on...it looks like she bled to death."

She tried to process that. Bled to death. "From a wound, or...?"

"You don't need the details, Marisa."

Garrison was probably right. Still. "Was she shot?"

He shook his head and looked at Nate, who sighed. "Why don't we just—?"

"Please just tell me."

"She was beaten and stabbed," Garrison said. "A couple of times."

An image of her sister's body, bloody and broken, filled her mind. Garrison had been right. She hadn't needed that information. Nausea rose again, but she swallowed it back.

Garrison turned to Nate. "I thought you could identify the body."

"Of course. How did your partner find out about it?"

"Her fingerprints gave the cops her identity."

Nate considered that. "Why would they have her fingerprints?"

"She had a Certificate of Conduct for herself and all her employees. It's like a background check for NYC employees. I assume so clients would know they could be trusted."

"Ironic," Marisa said.

Nate glanced at her, and she looked away.

Garrison said, "My partner wants you two to come in and tell him everything."

Marisa shook her head. "This guy..." She swallowed hard. "We know now that this guy's a killer. No way I'm taking that chance."

Garrison looked at Nate. "Okay. You'll want to wait to ID the body, because they'll hold you up, and you don't want to lie to them."

"Do they know I'm involved?"

"My old partner, Simon, does, but he hasn't told the NYPD anything about the kidnapping. He's staying involved. If the police can figure out who killed her—"

"We'll have our kidnapper," Nate said.

"At that point, Simon will get involved."

Nate tilted his head. "Why isn't your partner handling the investigation?"

"He can't unless he tells them about the kidnapping, which I asked him not to do. He's pretty irritated with me for tying his hands like this."

"I bet."

"He understands the stakes. He expects me to contact him if we get any more information."

"Will you?" Marisa asked.

"The FBI is good at finding people. They might be your best bet."

"But this kidnapper just became a murderer," Nate said. "He'll do whatever he has to do to keep from getting caught."

"Yeah." Garrison turned to Marisa. "I know you don't want the feds involved, but I can't hold out much longer. If we don't get some information soon, Simon's making it official."

She kept her voice even, rational. "Then he'll kill Ana."

"Not if we find him first."

"But—"

"I know," Garrison said. "It still might be our best bet to catch this guy."

"I don't care about catching him." Marisa wiped a single tear. "He can escape to the outer rings of Saturn for all I care. I just want Ana back."

Nate was studying her, probably waiting for her to lose it. She sniffed and sat taller. Maybe she was in shock. Maybe she didn't care.

Nate sat on the tailgate beside her, and she cringed with the truck's movement. Tentatively, he scooted nearer and wrapped his arm around her. Part of her wanted to tell him to back off. Mostly, she needed his nearness.

Garrison said, "You okay?"

She stared beyond him. "We should go."

"Go—?" Nate asked.

"To Pamela Gray's house."

"I think you need—"

She pulled away from him. "I need to find Ana." She jumped off the tailgate, and Garrison stepped back just in time to avoid a collision. "Let's go."

"I don't know if..."

Her look silenced Garrison. "I don't have time to grieve my sister. My daughter is in the hands of a murderer. We have to find her. Now."

She walked to the passenger side of the truck and waited for Nate to unlock the door.

Nate stepped closer to Garrison and whispered something.

Garrison angled his body so his voice wouldn't carry to her ears. They spoke quietly for a few moments.

Marisa stalked back to where they stood. "What?"

"Nothing," Nate said.

She could call him on his lie, but she didn't have the energy. "Are we going?"

Nate glanced at her. "Just making sure we have all the information."

She looked at Garrison, eyebrows raised.

"Pamela Gray's as cold as they come. She won't give you anything if she doesn't see an angle in it for her."

"Even if she knows Marisa's daughter's been kidnapped?"

"She didn't care about Vinnie's murder. Maybe the years have softened her."

"Not according to her maid," Marisa said. "But it doesn't matter. We have to do the next thing. Right?"

Nate thanked Garrison and turned to her. "Let's go."

NINETEEN

N ATE PARKED across the street from a brick brownstone in Carnegie Hill on the Upper East Side and glanced at Marisa for a reaction. She didn't seem impressed.

In Nate's days covering the financial world for the *Times*, he had been to some swanky areas. This neighborhood ranked among the nicest. Just a couple of blocks from Central Park, the five-story house had to be worth close to ten million. A drop in the bucket for too many Wall Street types.

Back in the day, Gray'd had another house in the Hamptons, an apartment in Manhattan, and a vacation home in Colorado. During Nate's investigation of the mortgage scandal, he'd learned that the federal government had seized all of those properties. Pamela had managed to hang onto this brownstone because she'd brought it into the marriage, and because the house had been owned by a trust. Her wealthy grandfather had fixed it so that Charles had never had access to it. Maybe the old man had known something the rest of them had missed.

Marisa opened her door and stepped out before Nate could stop her.

He jumped out of the truck and called over its bed. "If she were here, the maid would have called."

She glanced at the house. "Maybe she forgot."

"It's not even eleven yet. She was flying in today. Let's not spook Rosa."

Reluctantly, Marisa slid back into the truck. "Can you at least call?"

He slid in, closed his door, and unlocked his phone. He found the woman's number in his notebook and dialed. When the Hispanic housekeeper answered, he took the phone off Bluetooth and handed it to Marisa.

While she conversed with the woman in Spanish, Nate's mind drifted to the events of the morning. Leslie was dead. Nate tried to wrap his mind around it. A week ago, Leslie had shown up in his house, battered from the purse thief and desperate for help. Or so he'd thought. And now, she was gone. Just like that.

Life was fragile, even for a tough woman like Leslie. What had happened? Had the kidnapper simply grown tired of her? Had they fought? Had Leslie been trying to protect Ana?

Nate glanced at Marisa and wondered if she'd had the same idea. He hoped not. She was right to keep moving forward. Her forward motion was probably the only thing keeping her sane.

A few tears dripped down her cheeks. What was she telling this housekeeper? Could the woman be trusted?

Could anybody? Leslie had trusted the man who'd pulled her into this charade. Was the kidnapper the same man Leslie had said was her fiancé? That was the theory they'd been working under—assuming the fiancé was real. If he was, Nate had a strong suspicion he was the kidnapper. Otherwise, why hide his identity? Not a single photograph of him had been displayed at Leslie's house. Leslie must've believed he'd loved her, believed it enough to be convinced to betray her own sister. In those moments before the life seeped from her body, what had she felt? Fear? Shock? Regret?

Resignation?

Nate understood all of those. The memories came before he could stop them. His torturer's sudden, powerful blows. The realization that Nate's life was no longer in his control. That he would die in that crappy hotel room, in a pool of his own bodily fluids. He'd imagined the police finding him tied to the chair, imagined his father's face when he identified Nate's body. The hopelessness poured over him like thick tar.

Nate forced himself to look beyond the truck's dashboard to the street. A young woman with a child holding each hand skipped down the steps from a brownstone a few doors away. Probably a nanny. Folks in this neighborhood could certainly afford them. The little girl on her right was pointing at something, and Nate turned to see an old man walking a dog. The man stopped, and both the children fawned over the creature. One of those yappy little lapdogs with a bow on its head. A shih tzu, he thought.

Cars lined the street on both sides. Lots of luxury vehicles. A taxi idled in front of a house down the block.

Nate took a deep breath and blew out the memories of his own personal trauma, picturing the hopelessness dripping off of him and settling in a pool on the bottom of Brady's truck. A stupid visualization exercise his counselor had suggested. He'd never been willing to admit it worked. He rolled down his window, heard the birds singing and Marisa's rapid Spanish. He breathed in the air, safe for now. And Marisa was safe. They just had to get Ana home. Then he could get back to his real life and finish his move to New Hampshire.

And do what? Live alone, hide from the world? That had seemed a really good plan at one point, but now... He glanced at

Marisa beside him. The thought of leaving her behind, of never seeing her again, was a whole different kind of torture.

But what if they weren't able to rescue Ana? Garrison had been right earlier. The FBI would have more resources and better instincts than he did. What did Nate know about chasing a killer? Nothing. Absolutely nothing. Maybe he should insist they step back and let the FBI handle it.

He imagined how that conversation would go. Not well, he knew. But maybe the FBI could rescue Ana.

Maybe not. There were a thousand ways Nate could fail. The myriad options were overwhelming.

If they got the FBI involved, and Ana still died, could Nate live with having talked her into that decision? Would Marisa ever forgive him?

If they continued going Marisa's way and they failed, she wouldn't blame Nate. He could be with her, help put the pieces back together. Otherwise, she'd be all alone in the world.

Nate wanted desperately to find Ana, but Marisa was right. With Leslie dead, the situation looked bleaker than it had that morning. Chances were good Ana wouldn't survive.

Once again, Nate would have failed to protect someone he loved. How could he live with himself after that? What accusations would the image in the mirror hurl at him then?

And what difference would that make? He couldn't imagine that sweet, precious child hurt, killed. Ana was so full of life, so energetic and joyful. If she didn't make it through this, Marisa would never be the same, and neither would Nate.

Marisa hung up the phone and handed it back to him.

Nate pulled in a deep breath and turned to her. "You told her everything, didn't you?"

"Not everything, but about Ana, yeah."

"And?"

"Pamela Gray's flight landed a half hour ago, and she's on

her way. I tried to get Rosa to let us in, but she said she couldn't risk her job." Marisa shook her head. "She said Pamela Gray considers the help expendable. She said Mrs. Gray would fire her on the spot and not think a thing about it. The woman's a fool. Maids, cleaning people—they know everything about their clients' lives. They see what's in the trash, they overhear conversations. Mrs. Gray's just lucky she hasn't been ripped off or worse if she treats her employees like that."

A spark of passion lit Marisa's eyes. Despite everything, she still cared about people. He loved that about her.

The thought had him swallowing and leaning toward his door. Until he got his head screwed on straight—as if that would ever happen—he'd better put the L-word away. And with Ana still missing, there was no time for such foolishness.

If only he could dictate to his heart how to feel. Just one more thing he was powerless over.

"Will she call us when she arrives?" he asked.

"Rosa said we wouldn't be able to miss her."

They settled in to wait. Nate hoped Pamela Gray had answers, because if she didn't, they were out of options. He didn't know how, but one way or another, he had to get Marisa's daughter back to her, safe and sound. If he didn't...

He couldn't fail to be a hero twice and survive the fallout.

TWENTY

Two SECONDS LATER. Two FRIGGIN' seconds, and his plans, his life, would have all been over.

He'd shifted Leslie's Impala into park and had almost climbed out when he saw the woman step from a pickup truck parked a few car lengths in front of him. He'd stared. Surely, it wasn't her.

But when she turned to talk to the man who climbed from the driver's side, he got a good look at her. He hadn't met Marisa Vega, but he'd seen enough of Leslie's photographs to last him a lifetime. She'd removed all the pictures of her sister and her mom from the house, but she'd kept plenty in that giant purse of hers. Snapshots and portraits in that little photo album she'd carried with her everywhere. Who knew what she'd been thinking when she stared at her sister's face. He should have asked. Not that it mattered now.

If he'd had any doubt, one look at the man with Marisa brushed them away. He recognized Walter Boyle from the million times he'd considered punching the man square in the face. Maybe pummeling him until he died. Not that he'd ever had it in him.

But there was Leslie. So, he was capable of almost anything. Who knew?

Walter Boyle's newspaper articles had ruined Charles Gray's life. Pamela Gray's, too, and his own. And Walter—Nate, as Leslie had said he preferred to be called—had gone on to get a job with the *Times* and have a great career as an investigative journalist. No punishment for what he'd done.

Marisa and Nate got back in the truck, but the truck didn't pull away. Good thing. Now that he had them in his sights, he wasn't about to lose them. Maybe he could turn the tables. He'd been convinced that snatching the kid would get Marisa to give up the money, but apparently she didn't care about the little Mexican brat as much as she'd claimed to, because she still insisted she didn't have the cash.

But Leslie had known differently, and he did, too. Never mind that Leslie had changed her mind. Stupid, sentimental sister stuff.

The thought of her made his hands shake, and he clasped them together and forced the memory of the previous night from his mind.

He'd come to this house on a whim, not sure what to do with the Mexican brat he'd stuffed in the trunk. At least the sedative seemed to be working. She hadn't made a peep. He'd given her a pillow and blanket, and he'd cracked the space between the trunk and the backseat to get fresh air in there. The kid should survive.

He'd thought maybe Rosa or one of the other maids might help him with her. But now...

And what in the world were Marisa and Nate doing here?

He had no idea, but they'd made it impossible for him to go inside, even after they left. Too risky. Much too risky.

How to use this chance encounter to his advantage?

He could follow them. Leslie's car was much more ordinary

than his, so they'd probably not notice the tail. Who remembered a silver sedan? And even if somebody did, it would trace back to Leslie, not him. As long as he wiped it down carefully, he should be fine.

But where would Marisa and Nate go after this? How long could he conceivably follow them before they hit open road and got suspicious? And with the kid in the trunk...

That wouldn't work.

What could he do?

The answer was obvious, and he laughed out loud. Duh—he was in Leslie's car. He'd been tracking her since he'd started seeing her. He'd been watching her on the iPhone app, too, but that wasn't as reliable, and he had to keep an eye on it all the time. The car's tracker kept records. With it, he could check it every once in a while and see what she'd been up to. That was just one way he'd confirmed that she was indeed on his side and not working with the feds.

Their pillow talk was the other way he'd known. Make a woman feel loved, and she'd do anything for you.

Now he just had to get the tracker on Nate and Marisa's truck. Eventually, they had to get out of it, if not here, somewhere. He'd just follow until they did. When the truck was empty, he'd grab the tracker from beneath Leslie's car and secure it to the truck. The magnet would keep it in place, and he'd know where they were.

For the first time since this all had begun, luck was on his side. He'd get what was coming to him, one way or another.

TWENTY-ONE

NATE GLANCED at his watch when the limousine stopped in front of the brownstone. Thirty minutes had passed. Thirty difficult minutes during which Marisa had more than once opened the door of the truck. He'd barely kept her from getting out.

"I just can't sit here," she'd finally said. "I have to move."

"You don't want her to see you when she pulls up."

Marisa had stayed in the truck, though every muscle in her body seemed poised. Her legs jiggled, her hands folded and unfolded. Her eyes darted up and down the street, over and over.

Finally, the chauffeur opened the rear door, and a thin, silver-haired woman stepped out. She wore a wool coat and carried a red leather bag big enough for a laptop. The chauffeur followed her up the stairs with her suitcase. A moment later, they disappeared inside.

"Let's go." Marisa opened her car door and headed for the house.

Nate caught up with her at the foot of the steps, and they

climbed together. The door was still open. The chauffeur brushed past them on his way back to the limo.

Pamela Gray stood in the entry beside a round table that held a vase of fresh flowers that filled the narrow room with their sweet scent. Beside the vase lay the laptop case Mrs. Gray had carried. Beyond her was a sitting area, probably reserved for guests. On the far side, a wall of windows looked out on the small garden beyond.

"May I help you?" She still wore her coat. Nate had never met her, but having seen Charles, he'd expected her to look older. Perhaps she'd had a facelift. Her eyes were dark brown and deep set. Her skin was darker than he'd expected, as if beneath the aristocratic facade, she had Italian or Hispanic roots. Her face wore a polite scowl.

A noise shifted his attention to the staircase that led to the second floor. A Hispanic woman descended the last few steps and froze. He'd assumed Rosa was older, but by the look of fear on her face, this young woman was the housekeeper Marisa had just spoken to. She wore a tan uniform that looked more like hospital scrubs than a maid's outfit. Nate flicked his gaze away from Rosa. He wouldn't give her away.

"I'm Nate Boyle. This is Marisa Vega."

Her eyes narrowed as she studied Marisa. "You're the one who stole the money."

"I didn't," Marisa said. "And I need your help."

"Why should I help you?" She looked about to order them out when Marisa interrupted.

"My daughter's been kidnapped."

Mrs. Gray turned to her. "And this concerns me how?"

"The kidnappers are demanding the money they think I stole. But I didn't steal it. I'd give anything to get my daughter back. Anything."

"Mrs. Gray," Nate said, "we were hoping maybe you could help. And maybe we can give you some information, too."

"What do I care? My ex-husband's in prison, and I've moved on. If you'll excuse me." She pointed to the door. "I've just arrived, and I don't have time for this."

"We just need five minutes."

"Sorry. I can't help you."

Marisa stepped closer to the woman. "My sister was murdered last night."

Pamela Gray's eyebrows shot up, and she stepped back. "Murder? Kidnapping? All the more reason for me not to get involved."

"It has to do with Charles and the money that was stolen."

She regarded Marisa with narrowed eyes. "You really didn't take it?"

Marisa was about to answer, but Mrs. Gray continued.

"I knew it. Charles knew the feds were coming. I bet you anything he transferred it overseas to some secret bank account. It was either him or that whore he was sleeping with. Or maybe one of the other whores. There were so many."

"That's not what happened." Nate let the words hang in the air.

She looked at him and licked her lips.

"I can tell you who stole the money from the G&K business account," Nate said, "if you agree to help us."

She looked back and forth between them for a minute. "Please"—she indicated the seating area behind her—"be seated. My housekeeper will get you a refreshment. I need to get out of these boots." She snatched her laptop case and swept up the stairs.

Nate and Marisa followed Rosa into the sitting area. A family portrait hung over the fireplace. Pamela was in the center. On her right stood a man in his mid-thirties with his arm around

a woman about the same age. Two miserable looking boys
around ten or eleven years old stood at their feet. On Pamela's
other side stood a man in his early twenties beside an older,
shorter man. Beside him stood another woman who was holding
an infant. A little girl of about four stood in front of them. The
two older men looked like Charles. The man who seemed the
youngest and lacked a wife and children favored his mother,
though with the dark brown goatee, it was hard to tell for sure.

Nate focused on that one. He looked vaguely familiar,
though Nate couldn't figure out why.

The portrait had been professionally made—and within the
previous eight years, considering Charles wasn't in it.

Marisa was staring at the photo, too.

"Something to drink?" Rosa asked.

Nate looked at Marisa and shook his head quickly in warning, but it hadn't been needed.

"I'll have a glass of water." Marisa's smile was the only hint
that she'd ever spoken with Rosa before.

Nate winked at the woman and said, "I'll have the same.
Thanks."

Rosa's tense shoulders relaxed as she walked away.

As soon as she was gone, Marisa crossed to the portrait.
"Can you take a picture of that?"

"Why?"

She shook her head quickly, eyes wide. She seemed excited.
He took out his phone and snapped a photo of the portrait.
Marisa pointed to the man with the goatee. The same guy Nate
had been looking at. "A close-up of him, please."

He snapped a few. At the sound of footsteps, he slipped his
phone in his pocket.

Rosa reappeared carrying a tray with two glasses of water.
She set the tray on the coffee table and went upstairs.

"What are you thinking?"

She whispered, "I'll tell you after."

Nate had originally asked for the water simply because Marisa had, but now he realized how thirsty he was. They hadn't eaten or drunk anything since they'd driven down from New Hampshire early that morning, and it was nearly lunchtime. He sat on the love seat and patted the space beside him. Marisa joined him. They sat in silence, though Marisa seemed to be nearly bouncing. Her eagerness made his heart race. He was definitely missing something.

When Pamela Gray returned, she'd removed the boots and slipped on black house shoes. The casual choice surprised him—she'd seemed so buttoned-up. She sat in the wingback chair with her back to the windows and caught Nate looking at her feet. "I'm convinced dress shoes were invented by some misogynist to get back at powerful women." She looked at Marisa's canvas slip-ons, which she'd borrowed from Rae. "I like those. They look comfortable."

Marisa was coiled like a spring, and Nate tensed at the talk of shoes, afraid Marisa was about to explode in frustration, but she attempted a smile. "I borrowed them from a friend. They're a little big, but they work. All my shoes are back in Mexico, where I've been living."

"Hiding, you mean."

She nodded and stared at the portrait again. "That's your family?"

The woman looked up. "My three sons. Two are married, as you can see."

"What are their names?"

Pamela sighed. "On my right, that's John and his wife, Tricia. On my left is Richard. He's the youngest. Next to him is Andrew. His wife is Jana."

"Richard's not married?"

Pamela shook her head.

"Do they live close by?"

Mrs. Gray looked at the portrait again, and the hint of a smile transformed her expression, if only for a moment. "John and Andrew have relocated their families to the suburbs. They both work in the city, of course, and the commute is difficult. But it's a better place to raise children."

Marisa nodded, seemingly interested. "And Richard? What does he do?"

Mrs. Gray's expression shifted. "Richard is still *finding himself.*" By her tone, it was clear what she thought of that. "A luxury only young men with trust funds can afford." She sighed. "But he was much younger than his brothers when his father was sent away. It's been hard for him." She angled away from the portrait.

"Does Richard live here?"

"Heavens, no. When he decided not to work, I decided not to provide for him any longer. I have no patience for sloth. Nor do I have time to waste. Miss Vega, why run if you didn't take the money?"

"I thought Charles was going to kill me the way he killed Vinnie."

Unfazed, Mrs. Gray turned to Nate. "But you're saying you know who took it?"

"The G&K money. We have reason to believe Marisa's sister, Leslie, stole it. We're trying to figure out who stole your husband's money."

"Ex-husband," she said.

"Of course." Nate continued. "The people who kidnapped Marisa's daughter believe Marisa has it, but she doesn't. They want their money, or they want to know who has it. Since Marisa doesn't have it, we're hoping that if we tell them who does, they'll let the little girl go."

Mrs. Gray looked at Marisa with narrowed eyes. "Your sister's a thief, but you're completely innocent."

"I didn't take anything. I ran because—"

"Don't repeat yourself." She turned back to Nate. "And what do you need me for?"

He could dance around it, but perhaps the straightforward approach was best. "When Charles's money was taken, a few people believed you'd taken it. That wouldn't have been a felony, of course, because it was your money, too. But by not telling anybody, you didn't have to pay taxes on it, and who knew how much the feds would confiscate—"

"Charles protected our personal assets. Much of his money was untouchable, thanks to great lawyers and accountants."

The benefits of the rich. "If we can figure out who has Charles's money, we can negotiate to get Marisa's daughter back." He pulled out his phone, tapped on the photos, and quickly navigated away from the one of the Gray family, swiping until he found a photograph of Ana, the sun shining off her black hair, her gaze one of wonder as she studied a flower they'd discovered on their walk. He leaned toward Pamela to show her. "That's Ana. She's four years old, incredibly precocious, speaks English and Spanish. She loves every kind of flower, but her favorites are the blue ones."

Pamela studied the photograph. "Who's her father?"

Marisa's voice was clear when she answered. "She's adopted. Her parents abandoned her at the orphanage where I work in Mexico."

The older woman looked Marisa up and down. "I see."

Nate met Marisa's eyes and nodded before he turned to Pamela. "If you have any information that'll help us rescue Ana, we'd be eternally grateful." An uncomfortable silence filled the space.

Finally Pamela said, "I have no idea what happened to

Charles's money." She glanced at Marisa. "Maybe your sister stole that money, too."

"She was one of the kidnappers looking for it."

The woman's eyebrows lifted. "You don't garner much loyalty, do you, Miss Vega?"

"My sister was disillusioned. And she's paid the price with her life."

"As you said." She shook her head. "I'm sorry about your sister and your daughter. I really am. I wish I could help you."

Nate was about to press her further when Marisa stood. "Thank you for your time."

Pamela seemed just as surprised as he was. She stood and shook Marisa's hand. "I wish you luck finding your daughter."

"If you think of anything, please call us." Marisa turned to Nate. "Would you give her your phone number?"

He pulled a business card out of his pocket and handed it to her. "I'm no longer with the *Times*, so that number won't work, but my cell's on there. Anything you remember, anything at all, please give us a call."

TWENTY-TWO

Marisa all but ran to the truck. It was all she could do to contain her excitement while they'd questioned Mrs. Gray.

Nate climbed in beside her. "What was that all about?"

"The man in the picture. Richard. He's the same guy from Jessica's house."

Nate's eyes narrowed. "From Jessica's—"

"The soccer coach. Remember. I asked if he was the father? And she laughed and said no, he was her son's soccer coach. It was Richard Gray."

He hadn't looked at the photograph at Jessica's, but the man had seemed familiar to him, too. "You're sure?"

"We have to ask Jessica, but I'm almost positive. Call her."

"Wait a second. Let's think this through. What if she's in on it?"

Marisa excitement waned. What if she was? "But would she have a photograph of him in her living room if they were doing something illegal? You saw her face when I asked about him. She wasn't at all nervous."

He nodded as if he agreed. "We should call Garrison, see what he thinks."

"No." Marisa had been thinking a lot about Garrison since they'd left him that morning. "He's a good guy, and he's been really helpful, but his loyalties lie with the FBI. I told the kidnapper no cops, and I'm not about to let Garrison get the feds involved."

"But maybe—"

"She's my daughter, Nate. If you don't want to help me—"

"I didn't say that." He blew out a frustrated breath. "I just don't want to misstep here, and I think Garrison could help us."

He was right, of course. Garrison could help them. He had a lot more experience than either of them did. Why didn't she want to call him? He'd done nothing but help. But he'd also told them he'd have to get the feds involved soon. And she couldn't risk that. "I know he wants to help, but the last time the FBI got involved in my life, I had to flee to Mexico. They were wrong about everything. And I'm not saying they would be again. But I just... I don't trust them to make Ana a priority."

"They would, though."

"Maybe. But—"

"Okay. She's your daughter. We do what you want. We can always bring Garrison in later."

She nodded as if she agreed. "Should we go straight to White Plains?"

"Let's call Jessica. If she agrees to see us, if she's cooperative, that'll tell us a lot." He pulled out his notebook and flipped through it until he found the numbers and dialed. A moment later, her voicemail picked up.

Nate left a message.

"What if she doesn't call back?"

He put the car in drive. "We'll give it an hour, then we'll drive up there. Okay?"

An hour was a long time to wait. What would happen to Ana in the next hour? "Maybe we should just—"

"Eat. I'm starving."

"But—"

"And you have to be, too. It's been hours since breakfast."

She'd left her breakfast in the grass at the park.

"Greek food? I know you love it."

She sighed. "Fine. As long as it doesn't take too long."

"Honey, you're in good hands."

Nate drove to a garage in midtown, where he had a friendly conversation with the attendant. Marisa watched, amazed, as Nate talked the Middle Eastern man into letting them park for free. "Just for an hour, though," the man said in a heavy accent. "And if my boss finds out—"

"Your boss loves me," Nate said.

The man laughed and nodded. "Is true."

Nate waved and drove up to the second floor. "I interviewed him and his boss a year or so ago."

"Do they owe you?"

"'Course not. I just let them tell their story."

"How come they're so willing to do you a favor?"

He shrugged. "I treated them with respect. Unfortunately, I think that's rare, especially for guys like him and his boss."

She regarded this man she'd spent so much time with and thought about how he'd treated her, all those years ago. A crazy woman on the bus, but he'd listened to her. He'd taken her at face value when a lot of people might've just written her story off as the ramblings of a crazy person. "You're a good guy, Nate Boyle."

He opened his door, came around the car, and opened hers. "Shall we? I'm starved."

SHE WAS HALFWAY through the best Greek salad she'd had in

years when Nate's cell rang. He looked at the number and said, "It's Jessica."

She swallowed a black olive while he answered the phone. The little shop was loud, crowded with customers, and she didn't blame him for not putting it on speaker, but she wished she could hear the woman's voice.

"We had another couple of questions for you," Nate said into the phone. "We thought we'd head your way..."

He listened, nodded as if the woman could see him, and said, "That'd be great. Where do you want to meet?"

He told her where they were eating lunch, then waited through another pause, writing something in his notebook. "Perfect. See you soon."

He ended the call. "She's in Manhattan with a client. She said she could meet us in half an hour."

Marisa pushed back from the table. "Let's go."

"We have time to finish our lunch. We're meeting at a park about five minutes from here."

She sat reluctantly. "What if she doesn't show?"

"We know where she lives, Marisa. It's going to be okay." He nodded to her salad. "You need to finish your lunch."

MARISA AND NATE paced near the fountain in Bryant Park. Marisa had never been to this little green haven in the middle of midtown. Under different circumstances, she'd enjoy it. The sun was shining, and it seemed everybody who could be out today was taking advantage of it. She'd always loved springtime in New York, when even the hardest folks would thaw from their winter gloom, crack a smile occasionally. People in suits and jeans and skirts and all manner of attire munched their lunches at the many round tables that rimmed the grassy area. A few children played tag, and two rode small bikes with training wheels. The sounds of birds chirping and children laughing and cars passing and people talking all mingled in a discordant symphony, while the scents from the hot dog vendor on the corner brought back memories of happy times. All around them, buildings stood like sentinels. The sun was shining on the park for now, but the skyscrapers would block it soon enough.

The scene was perfect, and her fingers itched to sketch it. Anything to take her mind off the truth, if only for a second. The sounds, the scents, they should all calm her nerves. They didn't.

She looked at Nate. "What time is it?"

He glanced at his wrist patiently, though she'd asked the question three times already. "She was coming from an appointment."

"Where was she?"

"With a client on Madison Avenue."

Marisa turned toward the famous street. "That's just a block from here."

"It's a long street. Let's not worry yet."

"Easy for you to..." She glanced at his raised eyebrows and stopped. "Sorry."

Nate led her to a nearby table. "Shall we sit?"

"I can't. We're close. Don't you feel it?"

He nodded slowly. "We shouldn't hang all our hopes on this. You could be wrong."

Adrenaline pumped through her veins, and she clenched her fists. "You think I'm wrong?" She couldn't be wrong. She couldn't. Wrong meant they were no closer to Ana. Wrong meant her daughter would die.

Nate pulled out a chair. "I'm just saying—"

"We have nothing else! If I'm wrong..."

He reached for her hand, but she stepped away. He

dropped his arm. "I don't think you're wrong. I'm just saying, let's not get our hopes up too high."

When she didn't sit in the chair he offered, he leaned against the table and pulled out his phone. She couldn't see what he was looking at, but his eyebrows scrunched up, and his mouth formed a frown. She'd been with him enough to know he was thinking pretty hard about something, and she was about to ask what it was when she spotted Jessica.

The woman was still a block away, walking quickly toward them. Her blond hair was down, fluttering in the breeze. She wore a fitted gray business suit with a teal camisole beneath and carried a leather laptop case. Makeup made her pretty features striking, the perfect image of a Madison Avenue executive. Such a contrast to the pajama-clad, messy-bun-sporting woman they'd seen two days before. Jessica smiled as she entered the park and approached. "Sorry I'm late. I ran into an old friend. I didn't want to be rude."

Nate looked up from his phone and indicated a chair. "No problem. Thanks for meeting us."

Jessica sat. Marisa did too, though she'd have preferred to stand. Nate chose the third chair.

Jessica settled her bag on the round metal table. "I'm glad you caught me before I headed home. Lucky, I guess."

Lucky? Marisa allowed herself to believe it. She could use all the luck she could get.

"Definitely," Nate said. "And we think we've had another bit of luck." Nate pulled his notebook and pen out of his shirt pocket. "The other day, you told us your son—it's Hunter, right?"

Her smile faded. "What about him?"

"His soccer coach. You said the man had taken an interest in Hunter."

"Yeah. Well, not just Hunter, I think. He hangs out with other boys."

"Not just Hunter?"

"I think my son is his favorite." She glanced back and forth between Marisa and Nate. "What does Rick have to do with anything?"

Rick. Marisa swallowed the name, a morsel of truth in the mess that had become her life.

Rick was Leslie's fiancé's name.

Richard was Charles Gray's third son.

Despite what Nate had warned, her hopes soared.

"Did you ever meet Charles's kids?" Nate asked.

"Of course not." Jessica glanced at Marisa before settling her attention on Nate. "I mean, we would have done that, eventually. But when we were together, I was still, you know..."

Nobody finished her sentence. Jessica continued. "What does any of that have to do with..." Her eyes widened. "Wait. Are you saying...?"

Nate turned his phone so Jessica could see it. "Is that Rick?"

"That's him. Yes. Why?"

She asked the question, but the way her skin had faded to deathly pale told Marisa that Jessica already had an inkling of the answer.

Marisa leaned forward. "You didn't know?"

"What?" She looked back at Nate. "Who is that?"

"Richard Gray."

"No. No way. No." She looked up, shook her head, and swallowed. "No. It can't... Why in the world would he... Charles's son?" She looked back and forth between them. "I don't understand."

Marisa wasn't sure she did, either, now that they'd confirmed it.

Nate said, "Was he the coach before Hunter joined the team?"

Jessica took a deep breath. "No. Actually, I met him. I

thought it was just a chance meeting. I was doing marketing work for the city, and he was there, applying for a permit or something. He started a conversation with me, and at first, it was like..." She brushed her hair away from her face. Her hands were trembling. "He was a bit of a flirt. A charmer. Honestly, he reminded me of.... Oh! Of course he did. He's his son."

The noises of the park seemed to have faded, or maybe everyone had paused to hear the rest of the story.

"I wasn't interested. He was young, and I had Hunter. My son wasn't with me that day, of course. I was working. But I probably told him about him." She blushed and looked down. "He invited me for coffee. It was flattering, really. I spend way too much time alone." Her words faded, and she looked up and started again. "He told me he wanted to get involved with kids, loved working with boys. I told him Hunter's team needed another coach. Rick used to play soccer." She stared beyond them. "Charles's son played soccer. I just never put it together." She met Marisa's eyes. "You have to understand, Richard was just a kid when Charles and I were together. Like, I don't know, sixteen or something. I'd seen photos, but he'd had long hair, and he was little and skinny and"—she waved at Nate's cell phone and the picture still displayed there—"nothing like that. It just never crossed my mind."

"Did you guys talk about Charles at all?" Nate asked.

"No. Never."

"How about money? Did he ask you about that?"

"He came to my house a couple times to pick up Hunter or just to hang out with him. I told him Hunter's father had paid for it, but maybe... I don't remember exactly how I said it, but I often sort of make a joke of it. Like, 'amazing what a few trinkets can buy, if you sell them right.' Maybe I said that. But money is still tight. Always tight, because... Obviously, it's expensive to live in White Plains. So maybe..." She looked at the photo, and her words faded out.

"Maybe," Nate said, "he assumed you didn't have the money because you weren't living as though you did."

"He asked me about my BMW once. I laughed and told him how old it was. Charles bought me that, too. Feels like decades ago."

Marisa marveled at Nate's abilities to cut right to the heart of the issue and get the truth. And do it in a way that made Jessica feel comfortable.

He looked at Marisa. "Maybe Richard assumed Jessica"—he nodded to her—"had the money, but when he saw how she was living, decided she must not."

"At which point, he moved on to Leslie," Jessica said.

"But Leslie did have it," Marisa said. "And considering all the updates Leslie had done on her house, Richard probably figured he'd hit pay dirt. Her business was successful, but *that* successful?"

"Right. But she only had the G&K money."

Only the G&K money? It was millions. "Surely that was more than what Charles had in his account."

"Right," Nate said. "But wouldn't Richard consider Charles's money his?"

Marisa remembered the man's words from their phone call two days earlier. *Nobody's going to get hurt if I get my money,* he'd said. *My* money.

"This isn't just about money," Marisa said. "It's about getting what he believes he deserves."

"Exactly. Which is why he was willing to consider taking proof of who stole it instead of the money itself. For him, in his weird way, this is about justice."

Marisa couldn't help an angry chuckle. "Because there's justice in kidnapping a four-year-old. In..."

Nate rested his hand on her knee, and she stopped before she said too much. Nate was probably right. There was no need to tell Jessica about Leslie's murder.

Jessica looked between them, eyes narrowed. "The thing is, he was good to Hunter. He really seemed to care about him. He hung around, coached soccer, spent time with him. He was like..."

After a moment, Nate said gently, "Like a brother?"

"Oh." She sighed. "Yeah. Just like a brother."

Nate scribbled something in his notebook. "He found you to feel you out, see if you had the money. He stayed because he cares about Hunter."

"I guess," Jessica said.

"Okay. Good. Now we just need confirmation. Do you have the guy's phone number?"

Her eyes widened. "I do, but—"

"If we can confirm who he is, that would make all the difference. Can you call, just make up a story?"

She looked between them. "Like what?"

Marisa reached across the table and took Jessica's hand. "I know it's scary. But if we're right, this could mean the difference between finding Ana or never knowing what happened to her."

"Of course, I understand." Jessica turned to Nate. "But what should I say?"

Marisa pulled her hand back. "Are he and Hunter close?"

Jessica focused on her. "Very."

Marisa swallowed the rising excitement. "Does Hunter ever call him?"

"Yes. I'll have to tell him not to."

"You should, yes. But maybe... Could you call to tell him Hunter is sick? Or maybe to cancel something they'd planned?"

"They have no plans."

"Wait." Nate scrunched up his eyes again. "How much does he care about Hunter?"

"A lot. I think. And maybe more than I realize, because of the brother thing."

"Would he come if you asked him to? What if you told him...?" Nate stared at the park. Another few beats passed before Nate focused on Jessica. "I need to formulate a plan, but right now, can you tell him you're going out of town for the weekend? Maybe tell him something like Hunter wants to see him, maybe next week. Maybe you could do it this weekend, but you're getting out of town. Something like that."

Jessica narrowed her eyes. "Why?"

"We need to plant the idea that you won't be in White Plains."

Marisa tilted her head. "What are you thinking?"

"That I need my friends, and you don't want to tell Garrison."

Brady. Of course. But how would it work? She wanted to question Nate, but first things first. They needed to confirm their suspicions.

Jessica watched the exchange suspiciously. When both Marisa and Nate turned to her, she said, "What exactly do you want me to say?"

Marisa spoke. "Tell him Hunter misses him, and see if he might be able to get together with him next week. Say he'd do it this weekend, but you guys are going out of town. It doesn't matter if he can do it or not."

"But what about the out-of-town thing?"

Nate took a deep breath and leaned toward Jessica. "Are you willing to help us save Ana?"

Jessica swallowed. "I mean, yeah. Of course. I just... I have to protect Hunter."

"Richard loves Hunter," Marisa said. "He's his brother. And he has nothing against you."

"Not now. But what if he figures out I helped you?"

"He'll go to prison," Nate said. "It won't matter."

"Assuming what you're planning works. But what if he gets away?"

Marisa looked at Nate, because that was the question that had been niggling at the edges of her mind since they got here. What if it didn't work out? Ana would die. And what would happen to Jessica? Would drawing her in put her life in danger? Her son's?

Nate kept his focus on Jessica. "If he gets away, he'll know we know who he is. He'll run. And we'll get the FBI involved. They can protect you."

He didn't look at Marisa when he made that statement. Fortunately, neither did Jessica, or the woman might've seen her skepticism before Marisa had the opportunity to hide it.

Jessica nodded. "I'm not sure. I'll have to think about it."

Tears prickled Marisa's eyes, and she turned away. Finally, someone who could lead them to the kidnapper, and she wouldn't help.

Nate's hand settled over Marisa's, but she didn't look at either of them.

"Can you at least call him?" Nate asked. "That way, we can confirm it's him. And you can plant the idea that you're going away for the weekend. If you do decide to help us—"

"I can do that."

Marisa looked in time to see Jessica pull out her cell phone and put it on speaker. "This way you can hear his voice." It went straight to voice mail.

Jessica's tense shoulders relaxed.

"It's Rick. You know what to do." Richard Gray's voice

sounded so pleasant, even lighthearted. Nothing like the killer Marisa knew him to be.

Jessica took the phone off speaker and lifted it. "It's Jess. Hunter was asking about you. We're thinking about getting out of town for the weekend, but I was hoping you could carve out some time for him next week. Maybe just ice cream or something? Call me when you get a chance."

She ended the call and set the phone on the table. Her hands were trembling, but her voice had been steady as spring rain.

She looked at their faces and attempted a smile. "I take it by the look on your faces that was him."

Marisa couldn't speak for the wave of affection that rose for this woman, and the hope that carried it in like a tsunami. Jessica had been afraid, but she'd helped them anyway, and that one phone call might have made all the difference.

Marisa could only nod.

Nate reached across the table and took Jessica's hand. "Thank you. Even if you can't do anything else, you just gave us our first real advantage. Do you mind giving us that phone number?"

"Of course." Jessica showed Nate the phone, and he jotted the number down.

"Do you know his address?" Nate asked.

"I know where he lives, but I couldn't tell you the address. I can drive by it later—"

"That's okay," Nate said. "We can probably figure it out. If not, we'll call you."

Jessica nodded, looked from one to the other. "I don't know if I can do more. If it were just me, I'd do anything to help you, but I have to protect my son."

Marisa took Jessica's other hand. "I know exactly how you feel."

TWENTY-THREE

Rick hefted the little girl over his shoulder while he unlocked the door to the crappy apartment Leslie had rented. He'd given her a hard time about it. Could she have found more of a dump? But she reasoned that nobody who suspected either one of them would frequent that part of town nor live in that kind of building. She was right. Besides, it wasn't home, just headquarters.

He'd considered following the truck after Nate and Marisa left his mother's house, but when he put the car in drive, the kid woke up, freaked out in the trunk. Apparently, she was scared of the dark.

He'd been afraid of the dark when he was little. He could hardly blame her. He headed for the apartment, content in knowing he could find Nate and Marisa again if he needed to.

He dropped the girl on the twin-sized bed in the smaller of the two bedrooms. They'd boarded up the window so the neighbors across the alley couldn't see in. He flipped on the overheads and flooded the dingy room in yellow light.

"Stop screaming," he said.

She looked up at him with wide eyes and nodded. "Where's Aunt Leslie?"

"She's gone, kid. It's just you and me."

She started babbling in Spanish like she did all the flipping time.

"Shut up. You can prattle on all you want, but if I hear you from the other room, I'm coming back in here, and I'll shut you up. ¿*Comprende?*"

The kid nodded, and Rick slammed the door behind her.

What had he gotten himself into? He had no idea how to take care of a kid. He should just let her go.

And then what? Never get his money? Go to prison? No way.

A soft knock sounded on the girl's door.

"What?" He made his voice harsh, better to keep her in line.

"May I have something to eat?"

Crap. He'd forgotten to feed her. Again. "I'll bring you something. Get back in bed."

After he delivered her a granola bar and one of those squeezable yogurts—both Leslie's idea, because they were healthier than the toaster pastries he'd picked up—he slammed the door on her again and returned to the kitchen.

He still couldn't look at the living room. Eventually, he'd have to get the blood stains off the sofa and wood floors. Eventually, but not right now.

He was bored, missing his real life. He pulled out his real phone and turned it on. A message.

From Jessica. He listened to it quickly, scrolled through his other messages, and powered it back off. He couldn't answer any of the messages right now. He'd told his boss he was going out of the country and would be impossible to reach. He'd told his friends the same thing. So answering calls or texts would only show he wasn't where he said he'd be. No need to make anybody suspicious about anything.

When he'd first manipulated events to meet Jessica—not an easy task considering the woman hardly left her house—he'd thought he might seduce her, get her to spill the beans about her involvement in the money chase. But she hadn't been the slightest bit interested in him. Too young, she'd said through offhanded laughter. Not that he was that much younger than she was. He had to hand it to the old man, getting a looker like her into his bed. He'd still been planning her seduction when he'd agreed to coach her kid's soccer team. Everything changed when he'd met the kid.

Rick could still remember the jolt of recognition when his father's eyes had looked back at him from the little boy's face. All thoughts of seducing Jessica fled, and he'd poured himself into becoming friends with the little guy.

His brother.

He liked the role of big brother. He was a lot better at it than his own brothers were. Andrew and John had never had any feelings for him beyond disdain.

They'd probably be surprised Rick knew the word *disdain*.

Andrew and John never gave a crap about Rick, not the way Rick cared about Hunter.

Coaching soccer had come easily to him, too. Rick had established himself as integral to the team, and he and Jessica had settled into a friendly acquaintance. Rick had grown close to Hunter and his friends, buying them ice cream, playing basketball with them in the off-season, taking them to the movies sometimes. Always, there was a group. Always, there was at least one mom tagging along to make sure he wasn't some child molester. As if.

Often, he and whatever mom had tagged along hit it off, and more than one of them had landed softly in his bed.

But never Jessica. Once he'd met Hunter, he decided to

keep that relationship pure. In the process of getting to know her, he'd become convinced she didn't have Charles's money. That's when he'd moved on to Leslie.

According to Jessica, Hunter missed him and wanted to see him. He hadn't seen his brother in a few weeks, and he missed the kid, too. Next week should work fine. He'd finish the business with Marisa and Nate this weekend, and by next week, he'd have his money secured in an offshore bank account where nobody would ever find it. He'd hang around for a few more weeks, just to make himself look innocent. If anyone ever came sniffing around, he'd act like he had no idea what was going on. If he had the money, he'd just ask the cops why he'd still be there if he was a crook. And what did he need the money for, when his family was loaded?

It was true, too. Mom still *was* loaded. She'd just cut him off. Told him to make his own way in the world.

Look, Mother. I'm making my own way. Not what you expected, is it?

He swallowed the rage. Focused on the plan.

When the hubbub died down, he'd move away. Southern California had always beckoned him. He'd buy a place on the beach and spend the rest of his life sipping cocktails and meeting blondes. If anyone asked him about the money, he'd remind them about his trust fund. Not that the money in there could ever have afforded him the life he wanted to live. But nobody else knew that.

And maybe he'd coach soccer for fun, give back a little. Though he'd been shocked to discover it, he really enjoyed hanging with the kids. And who'd suspect a volunteer soccer coach of all this?

It wouldn't be long now before he enjoyed the life he'd planned before his father got sent away. The life Rick deserved.

A far cry from the life he was living right now. The stink of dried blood filled his nostrils and turned his stomach. As soon as he knew where his targets were headed, he'd get out of this dump for good.

TWENTY-FOUR

NATE OPENED the cabin's front door the next morning for Rae, who stepped inside carrying a diaper bag big enough to carry three small children and their tricycles. Behind her came Brady with the car seat and a sleeping Johnny.

"He looks peaceful," Nate whispered

"Don't get used to it." Rae set her bag on the sofa. "He's busy these days. And mischievous."

Brady set the baby's seat on the coffee table. "We'll be at the kitchen table, right?"

Neither of them had kept their voices down, and the baby hadn't stirred. "Yeah." Nate rounded the bar to the kitchen. "Coffee?"

While Rae and Brady made their coffees, Marisa trudged out of her bedroom, hair wet from the shower, braided as usual. Dark rings surrounded her bloodshot eyes.

Nate left his friends and joined her. "You holding up?"

She nodded, though she looked haggard.

"You didn't sleep well."

"How could I?" Marisa had seemed hopeful when they'd left Jessica the day before. He'd called Brady, given him Rick's phone number. Brady had been trying to ping it. It had only come on for a moment the day before, not long enough to get a read on it. According to Brady's text an hour earlier, the phone had been off ever since.

As they'd driven back to New Hampshire, her hope of finding Ana had drifted off, replaced by despair, which seemed to have nested on Marisa's shoulders, heavier by the minute. By the time they reached the little cabin, she'd been curled up on the seat, weeping.

Not that he could blame her.

Nate wrapped her in his arms, and she folded against him as if he could fix it all. If only it were true. He rubbed her back and whispered in her ear, but there was nothing he could say to alleviate her fear. He waited until the latest round of tears was spent, knowing there were more.

Tears were the world's only unlimited resource.

"Come on." He stepped away and took her hand. "Let's get you some coffee and figure out what to do next."

He walked Marisa to the bar, made her coffee, and chose a muffin from the assortment Sam had brought earlier in the week. She shook her head.

"You haven't eaten since the salad yesterday."

"I'm not hungry."

"You want me to warm it up for you?"

Her eyes filled. "Is Ana eating?"

Rae stepped behind her. "How will starving yourself help your daughter?"

Nate set the muffin on a plate and slid it across the bar. "Eat."

She sighed and broke off a tiny bite.

At the sound of a knock, Brady answered the door, and Sam came inside, her laptop case over her shoulder. "Sorry I'm late. Been busy."

Brady took her coat and tossed it across a sofa. "Did you learn anything?"

She headed for the kitchen table. "A little." She set up her laptop. Rae set a notebook and pen on the table, and Nate slid his little notebook from his breast pocket. Brady probably stored everything he needed to know in his brain, and if he forgot anything, Nate figured his wife would gladly fill him in.

Marisa's hands were clenched together and white-knuckled.

Nate bumped her shoulder. "We're going to figure it out."

A glimmer of hope sparked in her eyes, but it faded fast. He couldn't blame her. Her daughter had been gone for six days. A long time. Too long.

Why had the kidnapper given them so much time? Nate thought the whole thing must have been planned on the fly. How much of it had been Leslie's idea, and how much Rick's? And what would Rick do, now that Leslie was gone?

There were too many unknowns.

Brady looked at Sam. "What'd you learn?"

"Richard Gray manages a copy shop in White Plains. He has an apartment not too far from there that he leased a couple of years ago."

"A copy shop?" Nate looked at Marisa. "Doesn't seem like the ideal place to 'find yourself.'"

Rae asked, "Which means?"

"That's what his mother told us, that Richard was finding himself." Nate turned back to Brady. "Maybe that was her way of saying that he wasn't doing anything worth mentioning. She seemed proud of her older boys, but Rick was definitely the sheep wearing the black suit in the family."

"Right, but..." Marisa's voice trailed off.

Sam was furiously typing on her computer. "Looks like his oldest brother, John, followed in their dad's footsteps. He's a banker, and a very successful one, according to this website."

She typed some more. "Andrew's an attorney who specializes in"—she scrolled down, reading the screen—"business and finance law." She looked up. "Again, a lot like their dad."

"But Mrs. Gray told us Rick didn't work." Marisa looked at Nate. "Remember. She said something like, 'When he decided not to work, I decided not to support him.'"

Nate nodded, impressed. "She did say that." He turned to Sam. "But you're saying he does work?"

She typed, then maneuvered her mouse. "Yup. The copy shop's website lists him as the manager, and according to his bank account, he gets paid every two weeks."

"He didn't tell his mom he has a job," Rae said. "He probably figured she wouldn't be impressed."

"And maybe the fact that he was sniffing around Jessica wouldn't have made her happy either." Brady addressed Nate. "You suppose she knows where Jessica lives?"

Nate looked at Marisa, who shrugged. "No idea." He turned to Brady. "What about the car. Did you—?"

"You asked me to look for a silver sedan, right?"

Marisa turned to him, eyes wide. "Why? What didn't you tell me?"

"I didn't think of it until you'd gone to bed. I couldn't figure out why Rick looked familiar to me. Even before you asked me to snap his photo, I was trying to place him. Last night, I realized that he was the guy who was trying to steal your sister's purse. It was all a set-up."

Marisa's eyes filled. "From the very start. Of course it was, but still... I never knew she could be so devious."

"Wait, though," Sam said. "Why would she go to all that trouble? Why not just knock on your door?"

Nate shrugged. "We'll never know for sure, but what better way to get me on her side than to have me rescue her first? Not only did I help her, but I brought her into my house. I was tending her wounds when she told me she was there to see me. She set herself up from the very start as the victim. It's pretty ingenious, if you ask me."

"Diabolical," Marisa said. "And you know what else? Leslie came to Mexico with that frizzy hair and no makeup, baggy clothes, but at her house, I saw high-end clothes and all sorts of makeup and hair stuff." She looked at Nate. "She wanted us to see her as this... Well, victim is the right word. A frumpy, powerless victim. When really... And now she's dead."

Nate squeezed her hand and looked at Brady. "What's next?"

Brady said, "Richard Gray owns a red Audi A5."

Sam typed quickly and turned the computer so he could see the photo she'd pulled up on Google.

"Definitely not the car I saw that day."

"Your sister, though"—Brady nodded at Marisa—"owned a Chevy Impala." He looked at Nate. "Silver."

Sam typed again, turned the computer so Nate could see the sedan. Looked just like it.

Brady cocked his head at Nate. "That's the car you saw?"

"Yup."

"Good," Brady said. "Good thinking. Helps to know what we're looking for. About the job... We should call and see if he's there."

Rae stood. "I'll do it. You guys keep talking."

Nate watched as Rae glanced at Johnny, found her phone, and dialed. Seemed a waste of time. Obviously, the guy wasn't at work. He turned back to Sam. "The apartment's probably our best bet. Can you see if he has a landline?"

She shook her head. "Already checked."

"We need to get somebody there to check on it." Nate looked at Brady. "Know anybody in that area who could see if anybody's home?"

Brady shook his head. "I don't. Never been to that neck of the woods. I could call the police department—"

"No!"

Brady nodded at Marisa. "Figured you'd say that." He looked around the table, waiting for ideas. When nobody supplied any, he said, "We could call a private investigator."

Nate started to agree when a memory filled his mind. Two very scary men in a minuscule house in a tiny village in Mexico.

He looked at Marisa. "Would your friend help us?"

She tilted her head.

"Ramón. Remember, he gave us a phone number of a guy in New York. Said the guy could help us."

"Oh. I don't know. Should we get them involved?"

"Ramón's on your side, right? He wants to help you find Ana. All we need is for someone to knock on the guy's door and see if he's there. If he's not there, maybe he could go inside, get a look around." He looked at Brady. "An investigator probably wouldn't do that for us, but I bet this friend of Ramón's knows somebody who would. They could see if Ana's there, or if there's any trace of her."

Rae slid back into her seat, and Nate looked at her. "Just hung up with the assistant manager, who said Rick took a week of vacation." She lifted her eyebrows. "Who are we talking about?"

Brady cleared his throat. "Someone Marisa knows." His gaze flicked from Marisa's to Nate's.

"He's a man from my village," Marisa said. "We saw him the night..."

The night Ana was kidnapped, but Nate didn't supply the words.

"Before we came here," Marisa said. "He runs the local drug cartel. He gave us the name of a man he works with in New York."

Brady grimaced. "Doesn't seem like the kind of guy we want to be involved with."

Rae said, "Exactly. Which makes him a perfect candidate." She looked at Marisa. "Would you be willing to call him?"

Marisa sat a little straighter. "I'll do whatever I have to do to find my daughter."

"I have his number." Nate stood and headed for his room. "Be right back."

When they'd been in line for security back at the airport in Acapulco, he'd found the note in his pocket and shoved it in his wallet. He pulled out the paper and read it. Both names and numbers had been printed in neat, block letters.

Was this a good idea? What if this Julio or one of his men actually discovered Rick at the apartment. What should they do? Maybe Julio could tail him or put a tracker on the silver sedan or something. Or just call the police. Marisa wouldn't like that idea, but it was the best choice. They'd take it seriously— the guy was a murderer.

He carried the paper back to the table, where he picked up on his friends' conversation.

"Whatever you do," Brady was saying, "don't let on that you know who he is."

Marisa nodded as Nate slid into his seat. "We talking about when Rick calls?"

"Yeah." Brady met Nate's eyes. "Why do you think he gave you this much time?"

"I've been thinking about that. I think the first few days, like you said, they were trying to get back. And then, they didn't really have a plan."

"And Leslie was probably urging him to be patient with me," Marisa said.

"Right." Nate found himself pulling her hand into his. She rarely shrank away from the physical contact, and if he wasn't mistaken, it helped her relax. He could hardly help touching her. Maybe when this was all over... He couldn't even let himself think it. If they got Ana back, and if he didn't screw it up in his attempts to help, maybe Marisa might see him as more than just the guy who'd led the kidnappers straight to her. But there was no way to know right now, and even if he could trust his own feelings, hers were all out of whack. No, Nate needed to support Marisa with his feet firmly planted in the friend-zone.

He squeezed her hand. "You ready to call Julio?"

Marisa turned her attention away from Brady and onto him, and even with her eyes red and puffy, no makeup, and grief etched on her face, he barely kept himself from wrapping her in his arms.

"What should I ask him to do exactly?"

They'd been over this a few times already, but Marisa seemed to be having trouble concentrating. No sleep, drenched in fear and worry, it was no surprise. "Knock on the door, see if Rick's there. If he's not, and if Julio doesn't object, maybe he could step inside, see if he sees anything fishy, anything that might tell us where he is now." Nate looked at Brady. "Can you think of anything else?"

"I'm not about to endorse breaking and entering."

Sam shot Brady a look. "The man's a kidnapper and a murderer."

"I know that. But if this Julio gets caught, he'll be guilty of a felony. I'm just saying—"

"If he's willing," Sam said, "we should let him do it."

"Aren't you supposed to be the Christian here? All moral and..."

Sam glared at Brady, and he shut up.

Rae addressed Marisa. "Do what you think is best, but I'm with Nate and Sam. If he's willing to step inside and have a look around, that'd be great. Just encourage him to wear gloves and not to leave a trace."

Marisa pulled her hand away from Nate's and slid her chair back. "Can I borrow your phone? I don't want to use the one Rick gave me. Just in case."

"Of course." Nate handed it to her, and she walked away. She'd chosen a different pair of jeans and a lightweight sweater that hugged her curves. She silently paced on the hardwood floor in the living room as she waited. A moment later, he heard her melodic voice, though aside from Julio's name and hers, he didn't understand a single word. If he were going to stay with this woman, he might have to take Spanish lessons.

Stay with her? Sheesh, Nate. Get a grip.

"Are you okay?" Sam asked.

Nate realized he'd been staring and turned back to the table. "I'm fine. Just worried about her. And Ana."

Her face took on some sort of knowing glow, and Rae's matched it. Nosy women. He pushed back in his chair and stood to refill his coffee mug. The coffee had just finished brewing when Marisa disconnected the call.

"He said he'll do it. He's leaving the city now."

Brady, Rae, and Sam joined them around the bar.

"How did he sound?" Nate asked. "Like he was helping because you used Ramón's name, or—"

"Actually, Ramón contacted him a few days ago and told him to expect my call. He also said that Ramón told him he owed me a great debt because of my service to his town and that Julio should do whatever I asked." She shook her head as if she couldn't understand the man's attitude, but Nate got it. Wherever she went, Marisa would be a blessing.

"Julio sounded"—she tilted her head to think—"honored. And eager to please."

"Good news," Rae said.

"Not only that." Marisa shifted to face her. "But I'd sort of expected him to sound like a thug. He's one of Ramón's colleagues, and Ramón is... Well, he's well respected, but he's a criminal." She turned to Nate. "You know what I mean?"

"I do."

"But Julio sounded educated. In fact, he answered in English, and his accent was nearly perfect. We just spoke in Spanish because I offered."

"Drug dealers need lawyers and accountants, too," Brady said.

Rae gave him a look that had him clamping his mouth shut. She turned to Marisa. "I'm glad he's going to help."

"He said he'd call back as soon as he was finished." She handed the phone back to Nate.

He made sure the ringer was on and slid it in his pocket. "Now we wait."

Nate could see by the anguish in Marisa's face that the last thing she wanted to do was wait for Julio to call back. "How about we take a walk?"

"But if he calls back—"

He pulled his cell phone from his pocket and wiggled it. "It works outside, too."

"Let me just get some shoes on."

To be polite, Nate turned to his friends. "Anyone else?"

Sam and Rae shared a look and smiled. "You two go ahead," Rae said. Seemed they thought there was something romantic going on between Marisa and him. Not likely. Not ever.

He turned to Brady, who shook his head. "I have work to do."

Marisa returned wearing the jacket and shoes Rae had loaned her. "Thanks again for the clothes."

"Don't mention it. Least I could do."

"I don't think so. I think you have all done far more than anybody could have asked."

Rae joined Marisa by the bedroom door. "I know how hard it is to have to depend on others in a situation like this. Just know, we wouldn't be anywhere else."

A lump of emotion rose in Nate's throat as he watched his friends encourage Marisa. How had he gotten so lucky, to call these people his friends?

He didn't know what he'd do without them. Amazing, considering a year before, he'd barely known Brady and wouldn't have been able to pick Sam out of a lineup.

Funny how life worked out.

Marisa squeezed Rae's hand and looked at him. "Ready?"

"Yeah." He slid on his coat and pushed open the back door for her.

The air was crisp. The sun glittered off the glassy lake like a sea of jewels. The birds twittered a frivolous melody. Under different circumstances, today would be the perfect March day. Marisa stepped onto the dock. Not much of a walk, but Nate didn't care. As long as he was with her.

And that was the kind of thought he needed to banish.

The cabins on either side had similar docks, but this was the only one connected to the patio and the house. The other cabins hadn't been built so close to the water. He imagined a summer evening when everybody was out. Kids swimming, grown-ups sipping cocktails, a radio piping nostalgia across the airwaves, the scent of grills and burgers tickling noses and setting stomachs to grumbling.

None of that today, though. Just he and Marisa and the singing birds.

Marisa leaned her elbows against the railing and looked out at the lake beyond. The water reflected the deep blue of the sky. The tall pines joined maples and oaks that stretched empty arms to the sky. Puffy clouds drifted on a slight breeze above. In the distance, the zzzm of a motorboat barely reached them.

"It's beautiful," Marisa said. "I wish I had a sketchbook. I'd love to try to capture this place."

"Try to? I've seen your work, Marisa. It's amazing."

"It's just a faint reflection, though. Nobody knows the real colors, the true shadows and lines. We see it through our own..." Her words faded, and she turned to face him.

All the beauty around him, and he couldn't take his eyes off her.

"We see the world through our own prisms," she said, "separating perfect oneness into different categories like a prism separates light. Doing that helps us understand things, I think. But it also takes away from the whole. Back in art school, professors would teach us techniques for capturing what we saw and transferring it into whatever medium we were using. It was helpful—don't get me wrong. But it was separating a beautiful still life into lines and colors on a palette. That's what we do as humans."

Nate tried to concentrate on what she was saying and ended up staring at her perfect lips as they formed the words. He shook his head and looked at the railing, the water. "I'm not sure I follow."

She turned her focus back to the lake. "Vinnie took me to Paris once, just for a few days. We were walking across one of the bridges near the Notre Dame, and there was this line of artists, all sketching the great cathedral. I looked at their canvases. They were all different, every one. As if the artists were seeing completely different scenes. But they were all painting the Notre Dame." The wind picked up a few tendrils of her dark hair and blew it in her face. She combed it back. "Nobody really knows what anything looks like." She looked out at the water and chuckled. "Carlita would say only God knows."

"Do you believe in God?"

She turned and looked up at him. "I believe... I believe in Ana. I believe in you and your friends and Garrison. The way you've all helped me. I believe in the way I feel about my daughter. I believe... I believe in love."

He hadn't planned to pull her into his arms, but a moment later, there she was. He paused an instant to memorize her wide eyes, her slightly opened mouth. And then he brushed his lips against hers.

He knew she'd pull away. Of course she would. But she didn't, so he drew her closer and deepened the kiss, allowing his heart to lead. He slid his fingers over her silky braid, which he'd longed to touch for a week. When Marisa touched his own curly strands, his body nearly exploded with desire. He never wanted to let her go.

She tensed, and he ended the kiss, but he didn't release her. He leaned back to study her face, but she looked down. "Hey. You okay?"

When she looked up, tears filled her eyes. "What kind of mother—?"

"No." With all his will power, he let her go. "What kind of man takes advantage like that? I'm sorry."

"It's not..." She turned toward the cabin, seemed to falter. Poor thing had nowhere to go to get away from him and his mauling mitts.

"I'm sorry," Nate repeated. "It won't happen again."

He expected to see anger in her eyes, though she hadn't fought the kiss, and if he had any instincts at all, he'd say she might have even enjoyed it. But when she finally met his gaze, it wasn't anger he saw. Only sadness. "I hope..."

Her words trailed off. Nate desperately wanted to know what she'd been about to say.

"Hey." She held his hand, and her soft skin felt perfect there.

"We're okay, right?"

"Of course." Nate leaned against the railing and tried to calm himself. Every nerve seemed on fire, every synapse begging for answers. For her. He took a deep breath and tried to remember what they'd been talking about. Art. Right. "Do you remember the picture you gave me?"

She nodded. "This was the lake you described? The place you'd escape to, if you had to?"

The place he'd been planning to escape to just nine days before. Nate looked around at the quaint cabins. "Yeah. This is perfect."

"I agree."

"What about Mexico?"

"It was fine. I could have lived there forever. But it wasn't ideal. Too hot."

Nate imagined the little village she'd lived in. "And the poverty."

"I didn't mind that. That's how most of the world lives. And the people there have food and shelter. It wasn't the poverty that bothered me. It was the crime. The drugs. The disappearances. There are people who volunteer every weekend to comb through fields known to be dumping spots, looking for human remains, so they can tell the families what happened to their loved ones. As if that'll bring them peace."

Nate swallowed the disgust that rose. He didn't know what to say.

"But what peace can there be?" she said. "The families of those who'd disappeared, they want their loved ones back. Knowing they're dead... It just kills hope."

"But maybe not knowing is torture, too."

"It is." She sighed, and her shoulders slumped a little. "It is. But at least... To think Ana's still alive. It's all I'm living for right now."

He let go of her hand and slid his arm around her back. The move was so natural, but he worried she'd pull away. Would the kiss they'd shared change things between them?

He hadn't needed to worry. She leaned into him. He waited for sniffing or tears, but she seemed spent.

"If Mexico wasn't your ideal place to live, what is?"

She took in the vista, the tall trees on the small mountain in the distance. She turned and stared, for just a moment, into his eyes. Then she dropped her gaze. "Wherever Ana is, that's where I want to be."

TWENTY-FIVE

MARISA STARED in silence at the scene in front of her, hardly seeing it.

Nate had kissed her. And she'd kissed him back. And she'd liked it.

What kind of mother thinks of romance when her daughter is missing? If she never got Ana back, could she ever open her heart to anyone again? Eight years had passed since Vinnie died. She hadn't kissed a man, hadn't even been on a date, in eight years. And then Nate had walked into her life, and she suddenly felt like a foolish schoolgirl.

While her daughter was missing. While her sister rested in a morgue.

But Nate had been with her through it all. He'd held her while she'd cried, strengthened her when she'd been on the verge of crumbling to pieces, and dug into the truth with her, for her, to find a little girl he barely knew. This thing with Nate didn't feel like some random romance. It felt like...like safety.

Kissing Nate hadn't been about fun or even escape from the evil reality she was living. Kissing Nate had felt as natural as crying for Ana. Nate felt like home.

How she'd love to ponder a future with him, the three of them living here, skipping rocks in the lake, tucking Ana into bed, reading her a book together. She'd love to dream about a safe world for the three of them.

A cloud covered the sun, and the breeze increased. She crossed her arms and shivered, thankful Nate couldn't read her thoughts.

"You want to walk?" he asked. "It would warm us up a little."

The last thing she needed was to spend more time alone with him.

She turned, looked around, and sighed. "I don't have the energy."

Nate led her to the door, his arm still lightly around her back, as if she might collapse at any moment. Or maybe as if he didn't want to let her go any more than she wanted him to.

And there she went again. She couldn't help those thoughts. She felt connected to Nate. It was wrong, and if the worst happened, she'd never forgive herself. But she didn't have the will to fight it right now.

Inside, she slipped off her coat and draped it on the hook near the back door. Somebody had cleaned the kitchen. She should have done that. They probably all thought she was the laziest houseguest ever. She just couldn't seem to think of anything but Ana.

And Nate, apparently.

She sighed and pushed the thought away. Brady and Sam were seated in the living room. Rae was feeding little Johnny in his car seat, which she'd set on the kitchen table. The adults had been talking but quieted when Nate and Marisa walked in. The only sounds came from little Johnny, happy sounds that belied the situation.

"Beautiful out there," Nate said. "But chilly."

Rae scraped green baby food off Johnny's chin with the tiny spoon. "No news yet?"

He shook his head and met Marisa's eyes. "Can I get you anything?"

"I'm fine." She couldn't look at Johnny. He reminded her too much of her own daughter. She settled onto the love seat, slipped off her shoes, and pulled her feet up beneath her.

"Coffee would warm you up," Nate suggested.

He was always thoughtful. "I'll make it."

"You look comfortable. Let me." He was in the kitchen before she could protest.

The others made small talk until Nate returned with two cups of fresh coffee. She sipped hers, tasted the sugar, and smiled at him. Perfect.

Brady leaned forward. "Nate, you think we could use this Jessica woman to draw the kidnapper out. What's your plan?"

Nate sat beside Marisa. "Jessica said Rick is really attached to Hunter. I thought if she could tell him Hunter was hurt or injured, maybe even up here, we could get him to come up—"

"To Nutfield?" Brady asked, eyebrows raised.

"Well, you're here, and I thought—"

"You want to bring a murderer to my town?"

"To catch him, yeah," Nate said. "I thought we could set a trap."

"I think it's a good idea," Sam said.

"You would," Brady said.

In the kitchen, Rae sighed, and Marisa almost smiled at their predictability. Brady and Sam seemed close enough to be siblings.

Rae cleaned her son's face with a washcloth. "Nate, the problem is, how do we guarantee he'll bring Ana? If he doesn't and something happens to him—"

"We'd never find her." The thought had Marisa's hands trembling. She set her mug down.

"I hadn't quite worked that out yet," Nate said. "I can't imagine how he'd leave her unattended."

"It's not like he's going for parent of the year," Rae said. "He could tie her up."

"Or lock her in a closet," Brady suggested.

Marisa stifled a sob, and Nate took her hand. He met her eyes. "I'm sure he's taking good care of her. Remember what Brady said? Most people, the vast majority of people, treat children with tenderness and care."

Yes, but Rick was a murderer. She swallowed and looked down. Nate was sweet to try to alleviate her fears, but she knew the truth. There was no way to know if Ana was being cared for, or if she was even still alive.

How could Marisa go on, never knowing the truth? Suddenly, the fields of bones in Mexico and the volunteers who combed through them made sense to her. *God, please...*

Rae settled in next to Brady, the baby over her shoulder. "Sorry, Marisa. We're just—"

"It's okay." She met Rae's eyes. "I understand."

Rae patted Johnny's back. "Chances are good we could set a trap for him. We could get him to tell us where Ana is."

"The cops could get the DA to reduce his sentence," Sam said.

"So he doesn't pay for Leslie's death?" Marisa slid her feet to the floor and sat up straighter. "He gets away with what he did?"

"Not completely," Sam said. "It's not like they'd set him free. And you'd get your daughter back."

Marisa would do anything, agree to anything, to get Ana back.

"We may not have another choice," Nate said. "This can't go

on much longer."

Marisa turned to Nate. "Why don't we set a trap for him when we're supposed to make the exchange? He'd definitely have Ana with him."

"But we lose the element of surprise," Nate said. "He'll be expecting that. But if he came up here to see Jessica, he wouldn't be expecting us."

"It's a risk," Brady said.

Nate ran his hand over his curly hair. "Whatever we do, it's a risk. I've been round and round this same line of reasoning all night. There are no guarantees."

No guarantees. Marisa tried to imagine a scenario where Ana was returned to her, safe. Unscarred. She pictured setting a trap, somewhere near here. Pictured a trade. A thousand images, possible scenarios, flitted through her mind. But in not one of them did Ana emerge alive and healthy.

"You need to get the police involved," Brady said.

His words seemed to come from far away as more thoughts assaulted Marisa. Her daughter and that...that evil man. What was he doing to her? Maybe the best scenario would be that her daughter was locked in a closet. Maybe at least then he wouldn't hurt her. But her sweet pajarita, afraid of the dark, crying and alone.

Nate twisted to look into Marisa's eyes. "Hey, why don't you go lie down for a while?"

She tried to shake the fears off, though the awful images wouldn't go away that easily. "I'm fine." She glanced at the coffee. No way she could pick it up without spilling it every-where. She focused on Brady. "No cops. Please."

"Your choice, but..."

Nate's phone rang. He slipped it from his pocket and checked the caller ID. "It's Julio." He held the phone to her, but she shook her head. "Put it on speaker. I can't think. I need you guys to hear."

Nate did and then set the phone on the coffee table. Marisa answered.

"He wasn't there," Julio said in Spanish.

"Can we speak English? My friends are here."

"Okay." He shifted the language. "I knocked, and nobody answered. I gave it a few minutes, but when nobody came, I let myself in."

Brady's frown told them what he thought of that. Marisa didn't care. "Did you see any sign of my daughter, any clues—?"

"I took many photos. The place was pretty clean. There were two bedrooms. The master bedroom was normal. But the other one he used as an office. Lots of photographs of a young boy in there. Also, a lot of information about a company called G&K, newspaper clippings, financial statements, stuff like that."

"That makes sense," Marisa said. "This whole thing goes back to that scandal."

"I didn't see anything that made me think a kid was there."

Marisa's heart sank.

"Except the stuff in the trash can." Julio sounded curious suddenly. "See, the guy's kind of a health food nut. Had all sorts of grains and seeds and crap. Even had kale in the fridge. And those fruit drinks that health food stores sell. But in the trash, there are wrappers from those frosted things that go in the toaster, and more wrappers from packaged cookies. Oh, and a spent cup and napkins from an ice cream shop."

Marisa turned to Nate. His eyes were as wide as hers must be. Ana had told them she'd had ice cream. "They were there."

"Yeah," Julio continued, "looks like it. And there's one scrap of paper. I mean, this is why I shred everything. It's amazing what you can learn from a trash can."

Brady's eyes narrowed.

"What was on the paper?" Nate asked.

"Maybe an apartment?" He rattled off an address. "I checked it on my phone. It's in Chelsea."

Chelsea. Marisa and Nate looked at each other again.

Brady said, "What?"

Nate shook his head and nodded to the phone.

"Can you read that address again?"

Julio did, and Nate and Rae wrote it down. Sam typed on her laptop.

"Otherwise, the apartment was just what you'd expect. I will send you the photos."

"That'd be..." Marisa's voice faltered as something rose in her heart. Hope. She swallowed. "You've helped us so much, Julio. How can I ever thank you?"

"No need to thank me. A friend of Ramón's is a friend of mine. Call if you need anything else."

She disconnected the call and looked at Nate.

"Well?" Brady said.

"Leslie's body was found in Chelsea."

Brady slapped his thigh, started to stand, but settled back down. He looked across the table at Marisa. "We have to call the police. They can raid that place and get your daughter back now. Like in the next few minutes."

She turned to Nate, who nodded and said, "It's the best plan."

The police. If Rick found out she'd gotten them involved, would he kill Ana? But if they didn't involve the police, he could be gone before she and Nate were able to get there. And even if they could get there, what were they going to do? Go in, guns blazing? She didn't even know how to shoot a gun.

"Marisa?" Nate's voice was so patient and tender.

She looked at Brady. "Okay. Call the police."

Marisa felt like, if she did anything to disrupt the moment, it would all fall apart.

This could be it. They could find Ana. Soon.

Brady stood and pulled his phone from his pocket.

If it went well, Richard Gray could be arrested in the next few minutes. If it went well, Ana could be released, and it could all be over.

If the address led them to Richard.

If Richard was there.

If that's where he was keeping Ana.

Too many if's.

Maybe in a few minutes, Marisa would learn that Ana was safe and sound, had indeed been well cared for. Or maybe she'd discover she'd lost her daughter the way she'd lost her sister and her mother and her father and Vinnie.

Nate's phone chimed, then again, and again.

He picked it up and tapped the screen. "Photos from Julio." He shifted so she could see. She turned toward the screen, though she felt nearly in a trance with fear and anticipation.

Nate took her hand. "It's going to be okay."

"How do you know?"

He shrugged. "Hope." He nudged her shoulder with his. "Let's see these photos." He scrolled through the pictures. The apartment looked just like Julio had said. He'd snapped a few of the boy in photos in Rick's office.

"Hunter," Marisa said.

"I thought so," Nate said.

He scrolled through more. An ordinary bed, an ordinary kitchen, an ordinary living room. Nobody would guess a murderer lived there.

Ana had been there.

They got to the photos of the trash. A Ben and Jerry's cup and crumpled napkins. There was the photograph of the paper with the scrawled address. It had a brown smudge on it. Chocolate ice cream, presumably.

Ana loved chocolate.

And just like that, they had something to go on.

Nate reached the end of the pictures. "I didn't see anything else, did you?"

She shook her head. "I haven't had Ben and Jerry's in years."

"I'll get you some."

She'd like that. Maybe. With Ana.

Rae scooted over to see what Sam was looking at on her laptop. She pointed at the screen and looked at Marisa.

"Want to see?"

"What is it?"

"The apartment building," Sam said. "I can't get pictures of that exact unit, but I found another unit in the same building for rent."

Marisa nodded, and Sam stood and rounded the coffee table. She knelt beside Marisa on the floor and turned the laptop to face her.

On the screen, Marisa saw what looked like an average red brick building. Six stories. Nothing remarkable at all.

She thought of the moment they'd been driving from Manhattan to White Plains, of all the buildings. Structure after structure. Millions of corners and alleys and rooms. She'd believed they'd never find her daughter. Yet, somehow, they'd located Rick's hideaway.

It seemed like...like a miracle or something. If only Ana would be there, safe and sound.

Sam placed a hand on her knee. "I'm still praying. Constantly praying. We have to trust God."

Marisa had been praying, too, desperate for help from somewhere, anywhere. Would God help her now? Maybe not for her sake, but for innocent little Ana's? She could only hope.

Sam clicked the laptop. "This is a different apartment in the building." She scrolled through the pictures.

Empty rooms. Wood floors, old appliances. White walls. Few windows.

There were probably closets just big enough for a four-year-old, though the pictures didn't show them.

When they reached the end, Sam closed the laptop. "I don't know if it helps, but..."

"It does." Marisa covered her mouth to hold in the emotion. "If that's where she's been kept... I mean, who knows how the man has...what he's done. But that place looks normal."

"It's kind of dingy," Sam said.

Marisa couldn't help her laugh. "You should see my house in Mexico. That"—she nodded at the closed laptop—"that was luxurious. They had a microwave and everything."

She chuckled again and looked at Nate. "What's wrong with me?"

"You know we're close. We're finally close. I can feel it."

Brady stepped back inside, phone to his ear. "Yeah. As soon as you..." He listened, gave Marisa a thumbs-up, and turned toward the kitchen, speaking into the phone. "Promise me. The second you know anything." He paused again. "Okay, thanks." He ended the call.

"Garrison's on it. Coordinating with his partner, and they're working with the NYPD. They should know something soon."

"If only we could see what's happening," Marisa said.

Sam tilted her head to one side. "Hmm. We could if we—"

"You're not hacking the NSA." Brady glared at her, and she laughed.

"I was just kidding." She turned to Marisa. "I wouldn't have the slightest idea how to redirect a satellite."

Brady's heavy sigh made Marisa giggle. Nerves, she knew.

"One of these days, you're going to get caught." Brady sat

beside his wife. He set his cell phone on the coffee table.

Sam batted her eyelashes. "Will you testify at my trial? Tell them I only use my powers for good?"

He cracked a smile.

Little Johnny leaned toward his father, and Brady pulled him into his lap and lifted him in the air over his head.

"I wouldn't do that," Rae said. "He just ate."

Brady set the boy on his lap. "Good point." He turned his attention to Marisa. "How you holding up?"

"Am I holding up? I'm not sure."

"You're doing great." He bounced Johnny, whose squeals of delight filled the room.

Marisa stared at the boy's pretty face. She'd heard enough of the story to know Johnny wasn't Brady's son—not by blood, anyway. That was clear in the kid's caramel coloring. He had some of his mother's features, but Rae's fair freckled skin and red hair weren't among them. But in every way that mattered, Johnny was Brady's son. Like Ana was Marisa's daughter.

The baby giggled and cooed, and Marisa couldn't help but smile.

"When did you adopt Ana?" Rae asked.

She forced her attention away from the baby. "I've had her almost since she was born. But the adoption's not final yet. Who knows when it will be? Assuming I even go back to Mexico. Now that we're out, the government won't miss one little girl."

Sam returned to her chair. "Really? Won't somebody report her missing?"

"Only Carlita cares enough about any of the orphans to miss her, to even know she exists, and she's complained more than I have about how long it's taking. It's a strange situation—an American adopting a Mexican, but not taking her back to America. I think they're trying to figure out how to get more money out of me."

"There's not like a set fee or something?" Sam asked.

Marisa couldn't help the chuckle. "There's really not a set *anything* in Mexico. Everything's up in the air."

"And who's Carlita?" Rae asked.

"She runs the orphanage where I work. She's a saint. Truly."

"And a friend?" Sam asked.

"Yeah. My closest friend there."

Rae asked, "When did you decide to adopt Ana?"

Marisa returned her attention to Rae. She appreciated them trying to make small talk. Maybe it was helping. "She was left on the doorstep when she was an infant. She weighed about six pounds that day. And the first time I held her, I knew. She was mine."

"Was there a waiting list or something?" Sam asked.

Marisa shook her head. "Nobody even knew she existed. She came with nothing but a piece of paper tucked beneath her bottom that said her name was Marifer Ana Elbertina."

"Elbertina—that's her last name?" Sam asked. "Could you not find her family—?"

"That's a given name." Marisa laughed at Sam's grimace. "Not the prettiest first name in the world. And maybe it's a last name, too. I don't know. Didn't matter, though. Her family didn't want her. Probably couldn't feed her. They left her at the orphanage for a reason."

"Did you ever fear they'd come back for her?"

"It's a small village. Whoever left her wasn't from there. If she had been, we would have known, you know? Somebody's pregnant one day, not pregnant the next, and there's no child... You just know. But that didn't happen to anybody in our village. Whoever it was had probably heard of Carlita's kindness and dropped her off. I never worried her mother would come back to claim her, and even if she did"—Marisa shrugged—"she didn't really have any claim on the child, did she? At the orphanage, we have a lot of children whose parents brought them because they can't feed them. We care for the kids, make sure they go to school, but their parents are still involved. Ana's mother clearly didn't care about keeping in contact." Marisa sighed. "Truth is, I never worried, because from that first moment, Ana felt like my child. I hardly ever think about her birth parents. Now, I wonder what they'd think of me, putting their child in danger—"

"This isn't your fault." Nate leaned forward and faced her. "You didn't do this."

She wanted to believe him. Marisa had thought they were safe in Mexico. And they had been. Until Leslie had drawn her out.

She looked at Brady, who looked at the phone on the table in front of him.

Marisa stared at it, too. Willed it to ring.

A minute passed with no sounds but little Johnny's cooing.

She couldn't stand it any longer. She leaned forward. "Why haven't they called?"

"It's only been a few minutes," Brady said.

Nate wrapped his arm around her back, and she settled against him.

The clock ticked, the baby cooed, and the phone remained silent.

A hundred years passed.

And then, it rang.

TWENTY-SIX

N<small>ATE WANTED</small> to hold Marisa close, to shield her from whatever bad news might come through that ringing telephone. But Marisa pulled away and stood.

Brady handed Johnny to Rae and snatched the phone. "Brady Thomas." A pause. "Okay."

Marisa scooted past Nate and paced in front of the breakfast bar while Brady listened. Her gaze kept darting to his face.

Brady gave no thumbs up. No smile. No reaction at all.

Aside from Brady's occasional cryptic words, the room was silent. Even Johnny seemed to be holding his breath.

Nate stood and leaned against the arm of the sofa so he'd be close if Marisa needed him. Not that he could do much if the news was bad.

He couldn't do anything to help her. A few weeks ago, all he'd wanted was security. Now he'd give everything, even his own life, to see Marisa reunited with her daughter. To see them both happy and healthy and protected. To heck with his own security. To heck with his own future. To heck with everything, as long as Marisa and Ana were safe.

Marisa paused in front of him, arms crossed, staring at Brady.

Nate pushed himself up and opened his arms. If nothing else, at least he could offer comfort. It seemed like such a little thing. Such an insignificant thing. But Marisa stepped into his arms and allowed him to hold her while Brady spoke.

Finally, Brady said, "Thanks. Let me know," and hung up the phone.

Marisa pulled out of Nate's arms and turned to Brady. "Well?"

"Why don't you sit?"

"Just tell me."

"They weren't there."

Marisa's hope seemed to crumble.

Nate guided her to the sofa.

Brady continued. "But it was definitely where he'd been holding her. Thing is, the place has been emptied out. Either the guy never had any personal stuff there, or he cleaned it all out. No clothes. No food except some yogurt in the fridge. No shaving cream or soap or any of the stuff a man would need if he were living there."

Marisa nodded. Tears streamed down her cheeks, but she made no move to wipe them away.

Nate snatched a tissue from the box on the coffee table and held it out to Marisa.

She looked at it like she had no idea what to do with it. "Did he know they were coming?"

"Doubtful," Brady said. "The cops only had the information for forty-five minutes before they acted on it. I think he just moved on."

"We're never going to find her."

"We know who he is," Brady said. "We know what he wants,

and we can get in touch with him. Through the mistress, Jessica. Through his mother. Don't lose hope."

She stood and hovered in the space between the coffee table and the sofa.

"Where you going?" Nate said.

"I feel..." She wrapped her arms around her stomach, and her face paled. She bolted into her bedroom and slammed the door behind her.

Nate stood, stepped toward the door.

"Wait."

He turned to see Rae lift Johnny and stand. "I'll check on her." She laid the baby on a blanket on the floor, where he fussed in the silence. Rae snatched a rattle out of her giant bag and handed it to him. "Here you go."

Johnny grabbed the rattle and shook it and smiled.

Rae faced Nate. "Okay?"

Nate stared after Marisa. "Yeah. Okay."

Rae disappeared into the bedroom, and Nate sat back down.

He knew how Marisa felt. They'd been close. But they were too late.

Brady cleared his throat. "I didn't want to say this in front of Marisa, but there was blood all over the living room. That's the murder scene. And maybe that's why he left. He hadn't made any effort to clean it up. Maybe he couldn't."

"What do you mean?"

"The murder was gruesome. Not the work of a cold-blooded killer. He lost his temper and stabbed her. And then he had to live with it. Maybe he just couldn't stand to be around the reminders."

Nate looked at the closed door before turning back to Brady. "Do they think...?" He could hardly say the word. "Is there any evidence that he hurt Ana?"

"They're analyzing the blood now. Garrison's partner's there, and he says that, at first glance, based on the spatter, he thinks all the blood came from a single victim in the living room. There's no reason to believe Ana was involved."

"But they don't know for sure."

Brady's lips thinned. "It's not an exact science, and they haven't had enough time."

"Poor Ana." Nate tried to imagine what it had been like for the little girl. Had she witnessed her aunt's death? Had she heard the screams, the violence?

Brady continued. "Thing is, it was a two-bedroom place, and the smaller of the two bedrooms had fresh urine stains on the mattress. Could be Ana's."

The girl was potty trained, of course, but under those circumstances... What child wouldn't regress?

"Fresh urine means she's alive," Brady said, "or at least she was when they left. That's good news."

"You need to tell Marisa that," Nate said. "But not the rest." He glanced at Sam, who'd been oddly quiet throughout the exchange. Her elbows were on her knees, her head in her hands. Her eyes were closed, and tears dripped off her cheeks. He slid to the far end of the couch and touched her knee. "Hey, you okay?"

She looked up and swiped a tissue. "My heart just breaks for them."

He couldn't speak for the emotion. He nodded and dropped his head.

Sam lowered her head and resumed praying. If there were a God—and Nate had never wanted more to believe—then if anybody could reach him, it was Sam.

They needed all the help they could get.

TWENTY-SEVEN

Marisa brushed her teeth, sat on the bathroom floor, and leaned against the wall, spent. She hated vomiting. She'd rather have fever and chills for a week than throw up once.

But she'd trade her health, her hope, her everything if only she could get her daughter back.

"Knock, knock." Rae stood outside the open bathroom door and peeked in. "You okay?"

She started to nod but stopped. She wasn't okay. She'd never be okay.

"Stupid question." Rae stepped inside. "What can I do?"

"Nothing."

"Water?"

"Maybe in a few minutes."

"Okay." Rae sat beside her and folded her legs. "All is not lost."

Marisa sighed. "I know. Intellectually, I know. But it feels... I thought they were going to get her."

"Yeah."

Marisa waited for Rae to encourage her, to offer platitudes. She didn't, though. She sat with her and waited. A few minutes passed before Marisa said, "What are they talking about out there?"

"I'm sure they'll fill us in."

They would. At least whatever Marisa insisted on knowing. Which, at this point, might be very little. She couldn't take any more bad news. Unless they had some hope, maybe she didn't want to know.

She thought again about Mexico's fields of bones. Oh, to never know your loved one's fate. What did she want more—hope or closure?

Neither. She wanted Ana. And she wasn't going to get her daughter back by hiding in the bathroom.

She pushed off the floor and stood. "We need to figure out what to do now."

Rae stood beside her. "Agreed. Let's go."

When Marisa stepped into the living room, Brady, Sam, and Nate all looked at her. Nate's concern was palpable from across the room.

"I'm okay. My stomach..."

"What can I get you?" Nate asked.

She sat beside him and patted his knee. "I'm okay. Really. We just need to make a plan."

"I agree." Nate turned to his friends. "The kidnapper said he'd call today. We haven't really talked about what to say. I guess we'd hoped..."

When he didn't finish, Brady said, "You need to quit putting him off. You'll have to tell him you have the money."

"Or I can get it," Marisa said. "Maybe I should say I can get access to it on Monday. That gives us two more days. And it is Saturday."

"Some banks are open. And they all have online banking," Nate said. "What would be your excuse?"

She didn't know. She looked around the room for advice.

Brady glanced at Rae, who opened her mouth before snapping it shut. Sam started tapping on her computer as if all the answers could be found on that screen. If only.

It was Nate who finally spoke. "The money is tied up in a mutual fund, and the account has been closed and the money sent, but it won't be in your account until Monday."

"That could work," Sam said. "And it would make sense, I think."

"That I'd bought a mutual fund with stolen money?"

"Not you," Nate said. "You've maintained all along you didn't have the money. You need to stick with that. Tell him the person who has it is giving it to you."

"Okay. But still, stolen money in a mutual fund?"

Rae leaned forward. "In this story, you're just telling him what the person who really stole the money told you. If he questions you, you can tell him that. You're just passing on what you've been told."

"Not only that," Nate added, "but this guy doesn't have the same skills as his brothers. Does he know anything about that stuff? He's the manager of a copy shop."

"True." It seemed like a good plan. She turned to Nate. "Good idea. But what if he asks me who stole it?"

A moment of quiet while the group thought. Then Sam suggested, "Tell him you can't say, that it's a condition of getting the money."

Nate angled to face her. "And be sure that you don't let on that you know about your sister. We don't want him figuring out we're talking to the police."

"Right." She squeezed his arm. "Thank you for reminding me. There's too much to think about."

"You've got it," Nate shifted to look into her eyes. "And I'll be with you."

Thank God for that. She wasn't sure if she'd survive without Nate by her side.

Brady cleared his throat. "Okay, let's talk about our plan. How are we going to draw this guy out?"

She turned her attention to the group. "Are we going to ask Jessica for help?"

"I think that's the best plan," Brady said. "But instead of trying to lure him up here, I think we should just let the cops take him down in White Plains. If he doesn't have Ana with him, the FBI can squeeze him until he gives up her location." He nodded toward Marisa. "She's your daughter. Does that work for you?"

"Yeah. Now that they're involved, there's no point in trying to push them out."

"I agree." Nate turned to her. "Shall I call Jessica?"

"Please. I don't think I could get through the conversation."

"Actually," Brady said, "let me set it up. I'll talk to Garrison's partner, and they can make the call and work with her." When Nate started to protest, Brady pinned his friend with his gaze. "They know what they're doing."

"Yeah." Nate nodded slowly. "Of course."

Marisa knew how Nate felt. It was hard to give up control of the situation. As if they'd ever had it. "Sounds like a plan."

TWENTY-EIGHT

Rɪᴄᴋ ʜᴀᴅ ʙᴇᴇɴ ᴡᴀᴛᴄʜɪɴɢ the cabin all day. Boyle and Marisa had come out earlier, but since then he'd only seen the big man who'd arrived with the lady and the baby that morning.

It was that big man Rick kept thinking about. Rick had a bad feeling about him. He carried himself like a soldier.

Or a cop.

Rick didn't like him. But the lady and the baby he'd arrived with made him wonder. And the other lady. Maybe they were relatives or something. Rick had researched Boyle while the tracer app on his laptop showed their car passing into New Hampshire. This place, Nutfield, was Boyle's hometown. Probably the big man and his family were his friends or something. And the other woman. Maybe a sister. Maybe just another friend. They were probably all in there right now, talking about Rick and the brat.

She was in the bedroom of the empty cabin Rick had found. Just a few doors down from Marisa's. He'd broken in, then he'd jumped back in his car and driven down the road to watch. When no cops arrived, proving there was no silent alarm, he'd returned and made himself comfortable.

It wasn't the nicest cabin on the lake, that was for sure. Which was why he'd picked it—why get an alarm to protect a dump like this? Needed updating. Brown carpet, ugly plaid couches. But it was better than that rat trap Leslie had found them. And it had this nice deck.

The deck had been empty of furniture, but he'd dragged a padded rocking chair out from the living room, along with a kitchen chair to use as a footrest. Not a bad deal for a couple of hours of spying.

He had to admit, this wasn't the worst part of his adventure, sitting on the back deck of a cabin, sipping water with one hand, watching through his binoculars with the other. He wished he could see the front of their cabin from here, too. But it was quiet on the lake. He had heard car doors slamming earlier and been out in front in time to see everyone get there. He was sure he wouldn't miss anything as long as he stayed outside and stayed vigilant.

The problem was, he was bored to tears.

When Nate and Marisa had come out earlier, their voices had traveled across the little cove. Not that he'd been able to make out what they were saying. And the big man had come out twice, once just a few moments before, to make phone calls. Again, Rick couldn't make out the man's words. Too bad he didn't have a listening device. He'd love to hear what was going on over there.

He pulled out his real cell phone. He shouldn't turn it on. Didn't need to get in contact with anybody or hear from anybody. Ever since he'd lost his temper with Leslie, ever since he'd...

Nope. Wasn't going to think about that.

But ever since, he'd been paranoid. But he could turn it on for a second, right? See if any of his friends had texted him.

He powered it on and checked the texts. Nothing important. A couple missed calls, one from Jessica. Odd for her to have called again.

He powered off the cell and thought about that. Why would Jessica call him again? Either Hunter was really eager to see him, or something was wrong.

He needed to call her back. But he wasn't going to leave his real phone on, and he couldn't use his burner. Someone was probably trying to trace it. He didn't know how that stuff worked, but he wasn't taking any chances. So. What to do?

He stared at the lake and was considering driving to town for a fresh burner when the answer hit him. He'd taken all of Leslie's stuff when he'd left the apartment, including her purse. And in her purse was her cell phone and her burner phone. He wouldn't use the cell—the cops were surely monitoring that one. Only an idiot would use the cell phone of a dead person.

But the burner... He was the only one with that number.

He jogged outside to his car. He'd left Leslie's car near the apartment in Chelsea and had switched to his own, kicking himself for being stupid enough to choose hers in the first place. As soon as the cops found her body, they'd look for her car. Duh.

His car was clean, except for all the crap inside it. Most of it was Leslie's stuff that she'd had at the apartment. He dug through her purse, found her burner, and powered it on.

There was just enough juice in the battery to make the call.

He dialed Jessica's number.

When she answered, he said, "Hey. Sorry I didn't get back to you yesterday."

"Oh. I didn't recognize the number."

He jogged back to the house. "I'm having trouble with my phone. I borrowed a friend's. What's up?"

"It's Hunter." Her voice sounded strained.

"What's wrong?"

"We didn't end up going out of town. He's sick."

Rick closed the cabin door behind him. "Sick how? Like, really sick, or..."

"Doctors aren't sure what it is yet. They ran a bunch of tests. They're worried, because the fever came on really fast."

"Is he at home?"

"In the hospital. I thought..." She sounded like she was about to cry. "I know it's a lot to ask, but he's asking for you. Any chance you could stop by tonight?"

Rick raked his hand through his short hair. Tonight was impossible. Tomorrow would be difficult. If he could wrap this up... "I'm out of town. I should be home tomorrow or Monday."

"Are you sure you can't get here...?"

"You know I'd do anything for Hunter. Tomorrow's the best I can do."

"Okay. I'd really appreciate it." Jessica sounded relieved. He'd never known her to be that much of a worry-wart. Something must be really wrong with his little brother.

"Anything for Hunter." Rick meant it, too. His older brothers were big, boring turds. But Hunter, even if he was only Rick's half-brother, meant more to him than Andrew and John combined. That was his only regret about moving to SoCal. He'd miss the kid. "Hey, can I talk to him?"

"Oh. Actually, he's asleep right now, and he's really weak." There was a pause. "But if he's feeling better when he wakes up, I'll have him call you."

"Okay. Use this number. Maybe he just needs to get some rest."

"I hope you're right," Jessica said. "Listen, just call when you're on your way. I don't know if we'll be in the hospital or home, so—"

"Sure. I'll give you a ring when I'm on my way, let you know when to expect me."

"Thanks, Rick. I really appreciate it."

After he finished the call with Jessica, he powered Leslie's burner off. Hunter, sick. That wasn't okay, not at all. Rick would try to step up the timeline to get there as soon as possible.

He'd been waiting for Boyle's friends to leave most of the day, and he couldn't wait any longer. Who cared if they were there when he called? Maybe that's exactly what they were waiting for. If that was the case, they'd leave when the call came in.

Might as well give them what they wanted. Make them feel like they had some control.

He snatched his burner phone and dialed.

TWENTY-NINE

MARISA'S PHONE RANG.

She pulled it out of her pocket while the others gathered around the kitchen table where they'd been eating an early dinner.

The few bites Marisa had taken of the lasagna Sam had brought turned in her stomach as she met Nate's eyes.

"Go ahead," he said.

She connected the call. "Hello."

"Did you get my money?"

"Almost."

"Almost doesn't cut it."

"I want to speak with Ana."

"You talk to her when I say."

Her heart raced, but she wasn't backing down. "You won't get a penny if I don't talk to my daughter."

"Have you forgotten who makes the rules? I do. You don't speak to your daughter until—"

"If you want to see one red cent of that money, you'll put my daughter on the phone. Now!"

Her entire body trembled. She glanced at her friends. Their wide eyes and open mouths told her she'd gone too far.

Silence on the other end of the phone. Had he hung up? Had she killed Ana?

"Whatever," Rick said. "Hold on."

Marisa's heart restarted. Barely. She met Nate's eyes and nodded.

His hand slid around her back, and he leaned in to listen. Marisa glanced at the expectant faces around the table and attempted a smile. She stared back at the table and begged God as she listened to sounds coming through the phone. A door closed—sounded like a screen. Then it was quiet. Then a door creaked.

"Come here, kid. Talk to your mother."

"Mama?"

Ana's little voice drifted from far away.

The man's voice came back. "Did you hear that?"

Marisa wasn't settling for that. It could have been a recording. "Put her on the phone."

"You can talk to her when I get my money."

"Put her on the phone right now, or you'll get nothing. For all I know, you recorded her voice."

"Pretty demanding for someone holding none of the cards."

Her ire rose. She waited until she knew she could speak calmly. "I'm holding two million cards. Put my daughter on the phone."

Nate met her eyes and mouthed, *good job*.

She looked back at the table and waited. Just a second passed before she heard the most beautiful voice in the world.

"Mama?"

"Ana, baby, are you okay?"

"I want to go home. I don't know where Aunt Leslie is. The

man said she left. Why would she leave without me?"

Marisa's eyes filled with tears at her daughter's sad voice. "I'm sure she didn't want to, pajarita."

"Mama, he says I have to go. I love you."

"Love you, too."

Nate tapped her back, and she turned to him. He mouthed, *Leslie*.

She nodded as, through the phone, a door slammed. The man's voice came on. "Satisfied?"

"Where's my sister?"

"Like your kid said, she had to go."

"What did you do to her?"

"Your daughter's all right. If I were you, I'd focus on that."

Marisa let the moment drag, let the man think she was considering that.

"So you got my money?" Rick asked.

She took a breath and rehearsed the story they'd decided to tell. "I spent most of the morning at the bank trying to get it today, but there are rules about these things. It's in a mutual fund—"

"You put my money in a mutual fund?"

She swallowed and looked at Nate. He seemed to be asking if she needed help, but no. She could handle this.

"I never had the money," she said. "The person who took it put it in a mutual fund."

"Right. And they're just giving it to you out of the goodness of their heart."

She tempered her reply. "Some people care about children."

"I care about children. Just not little Mexican brats."

Her blood pulsed through her veins. She'd never been a violent person, but if this man were standing in front of her right now, Marisa would kill him. She tamped down the rage and said nothing.

"You spent the morning at the bank?" he asked.

"The money will be deposited into my account on Monday, they said first thing in the morning."

"I thought you wanted your kid back ASAP. You couldn't get them to expedite it for you?"

"Probably, if we'd called the police. But you said not to do that."

Silence. It stretched until Marisa started to say something else. Nate shook his head. *Wait.*

So she waited.

After a minute, he said, "Fine. I'll be in touch Monday."

"Are we going to make the exchange in New York?"

"Like I said, I'll be in touch."

The line went dead.

THIRTY

RICK NEARLY THREW the burner phone in a fit of rage.

Spent the morning at the bank? They hadn't left the cabin.

They were playing him. They were trying to set a trap for him. They had no idea who they were dealing with. No idea.

Lucky for him, he didn't have to wait for Monday to get the information he needed.

This whole thing would be finished tonight.

THIRTY-ONE

NATE SHUT OFF THE LIGHT, pulled up the covers on the queen-sized bed, and stared at the ceiling. He hadn't left the house all day, had barely left the great room, but he was exhausted. All he wanted was to close his eyes and sleep, knowing the next day this would all be over. If their plan worked, Richard would go to visit Hunter, and the FBI would catch him in their net. Richard had kept her alive all this time. Surely, he'd keep her alive until he got his money. And once he was in custody, he'd have no choice but to tell the agents where Ana was.

It was all going to end well. Nate was sure of it. Or as close to sure as he could be, when so many things could go wrong. Things he didn't want to think about right now, when he needed to sleep. He hadn't slept well since this whole ordeal started, and who could blame him? He didn't know how Marisa was handling it.

Marisa.

They'd kissed. In that moment, he'd felt all his fears crumble away, felt all his hopes return. In that moment, he'd felt at home in a way he never had before. In that moment, he'd known he would never be the same.

But she'd pulled away. Had he ruined everything, in that moment?

What kind of a man took advantage of a woman going through the trauma Marisa was facing? He was lucky she hadn't slapped his face. There'd been no tension between them all afternoon, but what would happen when Marisa got Ana back? Would they return to Mexico? Or would she choose to live in her house in Queens and raise her daughter and leave Nate behind? Marisa didn't need Nate. Once this was all over, she'd thank him profusely and walk away.

He'd had his heart broken before. Rae'd broken it pretty soundly all those years ago. But the feelings he'd had for Rae had been nothing, nothing compared to how he felt about Marisa. Maybe the situation was making everything feel stronger. Maybe when Ana was back and there was no life-or-death situation hanging over their heads, maybe his feelings would fade.

He wouldn't count on it.

He shifted to his side and squeezed his eyes closed. He had to sleep.

But sleep wasn't coming.

A soft shuffling sounded near the door. He opened his eyes and watched in the dark as a tall, slender form moved into his room.

"Are you awake?" Marisa's voice was a whisper.

He propped up on one elbow. "Are you okay?"

"I can't sleep, and I thought...I mean...I just can't be alone."

Thank God he was wearing pajama pants.

"You want to lie down in here for a while?"

"Would you mind?"

He flipped the covers back on the opposite side of the bed,

and Marisa tiptoed across the room and slipped in. "You sure it's okay?" Her voice came from the pillow. He could hardly see her face, but her dark hair lay in contrast to the white sheets. She'd taken the braid out, and he itched to run his fingers through her long strands.

He swallowed to keep his voice level, to hide the reaction the rest of him was having to her being in his bed. He shifted to face her and propped his head on his hand, as if this were a perfectly normal situation. "You want to talk, or do you just want to sleep?"

"I'm a little talked out."

"Yeah. Me, too."

"I want..."

Her voice trailed off, but he understood. "Turn toward the wall, okay?"

She did, and he settled behind her—close, but not too close —and wrapped his arm around her. He could feel the thin cotton of her pajamas, the warmth of her skin beneath. His arm and chest picked up the rhythm of her breathing. "Is this okay?" His voice sounded husky and had probably given away too much of what was going on in his mind. In his body.

Sweet torture.

"Yeah. It's..." She sobbed, and he could feel the slight trembling of her body as she let out even more tears.

"Shh." He held her close and inhaled her scent and told himself how he'd feel in the morning if he took advantage of the situation. How he wouldn't be able to look at her. How anything more than just holding her would ruin any chance for a relationship. The reminder helped.

Her sobs didn't hurt. They brought tears to his own eyes.

A few minutes later, her crying ceased. She sniffed, relaxed. Her breathing became steady.

He kissed her hair, inhaled her scent. He made himself comfortable and settled in to sleep beside her.

LIGHT BOUNCED in the dark room.

Nate shifted away from Marisa, trying to figure out the light. He was crazy. It was a dream.

He closed his eyes, opened them again.

It's not a dream if your eyes are open.

The light, a beam of light. A flashlight. He started to sit up, saw a long shaft, a hand gripping the end of it. And the shaft came toward him.

He tried to shift away, but it was too late.

A flash of pain. Everything went black.

THIRTY-TWO

Marisa woke with a start. She'd heard a strange thunk.

A bright light flashed in her eyes, and a wave of terror rose to her throat, choking off a scream.

Before she could react, a hand gripped her arm. "Get up."

It was him. That voice from the phone.

"I said, get up."

She stood on shaky legs and tried to see Nate, to wake him. The flashlight bounced around the room erratically, passing quickly over Nate's face. Just long enough for her to see blood. Had he been shot? Could she have slept through a gunshot?

"Move."

Richard Gray pushed her past the bed and toward the door. She found her voice. "What did you do to him?"

"If he wakes up before we leave, I'll kill him."

Rick could be lying to her, but Marisa decided to believe that Nate was only sleeping. Or unconscious. Either way, as long as he wasn't dead.

"Do you want to see your daughter or not?"

"Yes. Please."

"Then walk."

His hand was tight around her arm, not that she'd fight him now. He had Ana. This man was taking her to her daughter.

He pushed her out the front door, and the wood planks of the front steps were cold on her bare feet. The air blew through her thin pajamas, raising goosebumps on her skin. She'd expected to see a car idling, but no. He pushed her up the driveway, to the street, and turned away from the main road.

Suddenly, he stopped her. The flashlight went out, but the half-moon offered plenty of light to see. He stood behind her, yanked her hair, snapped her head back.

"You'll do what I say, and you'll do it silently. You understand?"

"Yes."

"If you scream, I'll kill you the way I killed your stupid sister. You understand?"

She stifled a sob. She couldn't nod, because he was pulling her hair too tight. She forced out another "yes."

"And then I'll put a bullet between your daughter's eyes."

"I promise I won't scream. Just don't hurt her."

"We'll see."

THIRTY-THREE

NATE COULDN'T MOVE, but from far away, the swoosh of fabric was followed by Marisa's soft gasp.

A menacing voice.

Then Marisa's. "What did you do to him?"

A threat.

Nate had to move. He couldn't make his eyes open. Couldn't make his body obey.

The noises faded.

He had to get up. Dear God, he had to get up.

He forced his head off the pillow. His torso up. His eyes open.

The room spun, and nausea churned in his stomach.

He closed his eyes and pushed to his feet. Stepped forward, nearly fell. Turned and felt around on the nightstand.

There. His phone.

He opened his eyes, squinted in the bright light, and found the number. Dialed.

Staggered forward, nearly fell again, and gripped the door jamb.

"Detective Thomas." Brady's groggy voice.

"He was here. He took her."

"What? Nate?"

"He was here." He couldn't make his voice sound forceful. Could barely make his legs move. His head pounded like the bass drum at a screamo concert, and the accompanying confusion resembled the screeching of the songs. Nate pushed into the living room and supported himself on the back of the sofa as he made his way to the front door.

"Nate, tell me what's happening."

"Please, come. Fast."

"Are you hurt?"

"He took her. Hurry." It was getting better. He could almost see again.

If only the room would stop spinning.

Brady said, "Tell me what's going on."

The front door was open. Nate stopped at the screen and looked outside. How much time had passed? He'd thought, if he hurried, he could get a glimpse of a car. But there was no car.

He almost pushed out the front door but stopped. There they were.

Two forms frozen in the middle of the road. The man was hurting Marisa, and a wave of rage overwhelmed Nate.

The rage brought with it a fresh course of throbbing.

He could hardly move. He took a deep breath.

"Nate?"

"They're..." He watched as the man pushed Marisa, and she walked farther down the gravel road. "They're walking."

"Can you follow?"

"I can try."

"Okay. I'm on my way. Keep the connection open. I'll mute my end."

Nate kept his eyes on Rick and Marisa. He took a deep

breath. His strength was returning. He touched the screen door's latch and worked it silently.

He pushed the door, slowly, slowly. The slightest creak. He froze. Watched to see if Rick turned.

The kidnapper didn't react.

They were a few cabins down the street now, and Nate strained to keep them in sight as they passed behind the trees and shrubs that lined the road.

Nate pushed the door all the way open and stepped outside. He lifted the phone to his lips and whispered. "I'm following."

"Don't do anything until I get there."

Nate kept the connection open and crept down the stairs.

He stumbled to the street and followed, keeping to the edge blocked from the moon's rays, hoping between the trees and the bushes and the darkness, he would be hidden in the shadows.

His head felt like it might explode. Black circled his vision, tried to close in. He stopped, leaned against a birch tree that edged the road, and waited until the feeling passed. When he could see again, he pushed his feet forward.

Marisa and her captor were out of sight. Nate moved faster, desperate, around a bend until he saw them again.

Nate watched as the man pushed Marisa toward a cabin. Past a car. Through a door.

The black came again, pinching his vision. He lifted his phone. Started across the street to get closer. Maybe he could hear. Maybe he could rescue.

"Brady." He whispered the word, hoped his friend could hear.

"Where are they?"

"Beyond..." The black was winning. "A cabin." The world spun. He squeezed out the last two words. "The car."

He hit the ground with a thud.

THIRTY-FOUR

Marisa ignored the gravel digging into her feet, ignored the cold wind blowing through her thin pajamas, ignored the image she'd seen of Nate on his bed, blood trickling from his head. She couldn't think of those things.

Ana.

She was going to see Ana.

One way or another, Marisa was going to see that her daughter made it to safety. Nate would take care of her if Marisa couldn't.

And there was that bloody image of Nate again. Was he still alive, or had he given his life for her, for Ana? She couldn't bear to lose another person she loved.

Loved. The realization made long forgotten pieces of her heart fall into place. She loved Nate. For so many reasons.

She couldn't think about that now, not until this was all over. But if Nate survived, and if Marisa survived, and if they got Ana back safely, she'd think about it. She'd do more than think about it. She'd act on it. Tell him how she felt, and maybe, just maybe...

She thought of the kiss they'd shared.

She thought of the blood trickling from his head.

She had to focus.

And maybe she wasn't going to survive the night. If that's what it took to keep Ana safe, so be it. Nate and Brady and Rae and Sam—they'd take care of Ana, if Marisa couldn't.

But she would do whatever she had to do to save Ana. Her sweet daughter would live.

Marisa stepped onto the first of three rickety steps of a cabin just around the edge of the lake from the one where she and Nate had been staying. The creak of worn wood echoed against the silent night.

The kidnapper reached beyond her and yanked open the screen. The front door was already open. He shoved her, and she stumbled through.

Even with just a dim light coming from over the stove in the kitchen, she could tell it was nothing like their cabin. Dingy walls. Dingy floors. Dingy everything. But it was warm, and Ana was here.

The kidnapper pushed her down on the plaid sofa and locked the door behind them.

He stood in front of her. "You're going to tell me where the money is, right now. Or I'm going to kill your daughter. And you're going to watch me do it."

The threat dripped down her spine like sludge. She had to get her daughter out of there. "I want to see Ana."

He pointed to a hallway on her right. "She's back there. She's asleep." He stalked across the room, and for a moment, Marisa thought he might be going to get Ana. He snatched something off the kitchen table, swiveled, and returned. He set it on the coffee table in front of her and opened it. A laptop. The screen burned her eyes in the dark room. "You can transfer it into my account right now. Then I'll leave, and you'll never see me again. You and your daughter will be safe. You have one minute."

Marisa stared at the screen, at the cursor counting down the seconds. Each lifeless flash was an accusation. Ana would have been better off if Marisa had never laid eyes on the sweet girl.

Rick had called her bluff.

The kidnapper grabbed her chin and yanked her face to his. He bent down until they were nose-to-nose. His breath filled her nostrils, a scent like bad cheese and beer nearly choked her.

"The money." He stood to his full height. Maybe six feet. All muscle. "Transfer it. Now."

She swallowed. Recalled the story. "It's in a mutual fund. It's..."

The blow came too fast for her to react. Her head snapped to the left. The pain was sharp in her face, down her neck.

He grabbed the hair on the top of her head and turned her to face him. "Don't lie to me. I know you weren't at the bank today. I was watching. All day. Where's the money?"

"I don't..." What should she say? What could she say? No stories came. Nothing but the truth.

"I don't have the money. I never had it. I don't know who does."

He gripped her hair tighter, and she lifted, tried to ease the tension. With his other hand, he squeezed her chin. "You're lying. Tell me the truth."

"I never—"

"Don't lie to me!"

She cringed, knew he was about to strike her again, but instead, he pushed her back on the sofa, swiveled, and paced. He walked to the back of the house, looked out the window, and walked to the front door. He looked out the window there. He started to drop the curtain, then pulled it back again.

Swore. Twice.

"Your boyfriend... I should have killed him when I had the chance."

Nate. He was alive. And he knew... Which meant, he'd have called Brady. The police would be on their way.

Hope surged like an electrical current, tingling through her fingers.

The kidnapper returned to the couch and gripped her arm. "Get up."

She stood, and he propelled her toward the back door. She glanced at the opening to the hallway.

"Now that I have you, I don't need the brat. She'd just slow us down."

Thank God, her daughter would be safe. Someone would find her there. "Is she—?"

"Shut up."

He pushed open the back door and shoved Marisa outside. He stood beside her, peered in both directions.

He propelled her off the deck and back toward their cabin and the main road.

THIRTY-FIVE

"Nate."

The word felt whispered from far away. A hand on his neck. "Thank God. You're alive."

Was he?

Marisa.

He tried to get his eyes open. Felt gravel and dirt in his mouth. Spit it out.

"Let me help you."

Brady helped him sit, and it all came back.

"You see it? You see the car?"

"My guys are moving in as we speak."

Nate looked around, saw men in dark uniforms sneaking silently toward the cabin.

"What are you going to do?" The words made Nate's head pound, and he pushed his palms into his temples and dropped his head between his knees.

"I have to go."

"Go."

Nate didn't look up but heard Brady's soft footfalls fade.

He took a deep breath, wished he knew how long he'd been

out. Probably not more than a few minutes. But still, something might've happened. Maybe Rick had taken Marisa and Ana and left while Nate dozed on the roadside.

No. Rick's red Audi was still there. They hadn't gone anywhere.

He stared toward the cabin. Forced his gaze to stay up. Forced himself to his feet. His head was still pounding, but the black cloud around his vision was gone.

He staggered to the side of the road and leaned against a tree. He could be here when Marisa and Ana were rescued. At least he could do that. And he'd made the call.

Yes, he'd done something good. And they would be rescued. Thank God.

He closed his eyes. Countless terrible scenarios flittered through his vision. Shootouts, stabbings. Death.

A sound had his eyes snapping open. A voice.

"Move."

A man's voice. It came from the wrong direction. Nate peered toward the lake, closer to the cabin he'd come from. There, two figures picked their way slowly between the trees and shrubs. A tall man, broad-shouldered, with a grip on a slender woman. Rick pushed Marisa forward. She stumbled, kept upright.

No child.

He didn't want to think about what that might mean.

Nate moved silently along the road, parallel to them. His head still pounded, but the dizziness had passed. The adrenaline helped.

He lost them when they passed behind a cabin. He ran to the other side, peered around it. There they were. He could only see black, one taller than the other, in the light of the hazy half-moon above.

The figures kept moving, and Nate did, too. He reached for

a pocket—nonexistent on his pajamas. He must've dropped his phone on the road.

Another cabin, he raced to the other side, saw the two figures emerge. They passed behind another cabin, and he followed. Nate was keeping their pace easily. Though the trees were sparser between the cabins than they would be in the forest, they were still thick.

Nate felt better, stronger. His head still pounded, but he was regaining his strength.

They reached the cabin where he and Marisa had been staying. Nate crept around the side, stopped at the back corner, and looked into the trees for some kind of weapon. He found a branch, but when he touched it, it felt nearly rotted. He dropped to his knees. There had to be something.

The man said, "Where are the truck keys?"

"I don't know."

Nate dug beneath the bracken. Surely, surely...

The man did something Nate couldn't see, and Marisa answered with a pained gasp.

"Don't lie to me."

Nate's adrenaline soared. He just had to give Marisa a chance to escape.

"Maybe..." she said. "He sometimes left them on the kitchen counter."

Footsteps on the deck.

Nate's fingertips hit a cold, hard something, and he dug it out. A misshapen rock the size of a baseball. Thank God for the granite state.

The back door rattled in its frame. Rick swore. "I don't have time for this." He blew out a breath. "Whatever. I can get in the front."

The deck was nearer Nate's side of the cabin than the other side. He gripped the rock and crept back to the cabin wall. Here he was again, just like before. Terror rose up inside of him. He'd faced evil before, only this time it was Marisa's life in danger. If Nate blew it, it would be Marisa who paid the price.

He leaned against the wall and begged the air and the universe and God for help. He knew himself enough to know he couldn't do this alone.

Nate listened to Rick's footsteps cross the deck floor. Marisa's bare feet were silent, but he knew she was there.

The sound changed. They were on the steps.

Then near silence.

From far away, Nate heard Brady's voice. "Police. Open up."

Banging.

Nate willed Brady to shut up and pressed himself against the wall.

Marisa turned the corner, saw Nate. Eyes wide.

The man was right behind her. He gazed toward his abandoned cabin and the ruckus there. He didn't see Nate.

They passed.

Nate lifted the rock.

The man angled away at the last second. Swiveled toward him.

Dropped Marisa's arm.

"Run!" Nate swung the rock toward Rick, but the man was too quick, Nate's swing too sluggish.

Marisa dashed away.

Rick backed up, reached in his pocket.

Nate didn't want to know what was in there. He barreled forward, tackled, landed on top of Rick. Nate lifted the rock again, aimed at the man's head, brought it down.

Rick dodged, and the rock glanced off his temple.

Rick kneed Nate in the side, and pain crashed through him. He concentrated on keeping hold of the rock. His only chance.

Rick kneed him again.

Nate ignored the pain, shifted to swing the rock a third time when he saw the glint.

A knife.

He twisted. It sliced his back. He stood and scrambled away from the deadly weapon.

Rick stood, too. Nate's back was to the cabin wall. Not that he would run.

Of course he'd brought a rock to a knife fight.

But Marisa was safe. And Ana was probably safe. And this man... He'd pay for what he did, even if Nate wasn't the one to exact revenge.

Rick's gaze darted to the street. He seemed unsure. He turned to run.

Not on Nate's watch. He lunged, tackled, and brought Rick to his knees. Nate was still sluggish. But maybe he could slow him down.

Rick swiveled, thrust with the knife. It sliced into Nate's left side.

The kidnapper stood. "Should have killed you when I had the chance."

"Your mistake."

The sounds of the police just down the road drifted. They were getting closer. A light had gone on in the cabin next door.

"You're not getting away," Nate said. "We know who you are."

"You don't know anything."

"Is that so, Richard?"

The man's eyes rounded like the moon before they narrowed into evil slits. He lifted the knife, aimed for Nate's chest.

Nate parried with his left hand, diverting the knife's aim. Brought the rock down on the man's head. Hard. Then again.

Rick stumbled, crashed into the cabin's wall. Dropped the knife.

Nate grabbed it, stepped back, and raised his arm again. Blood gushed through his pajamas. Reality overpowered adrenaline, making him weak. He couldn't wimp out now. This was for Marisa. And Ana.

But Richard Gray didn't move.

THIRTY-SIX

MARISA RAN toward the police at the other cabin. As soon as she saw a figure, she screamed for help. The sounds of doors opening, men yelling, carried on the still night.

"Brady!" Her shout barely penetrated theirs. She tried, "Help!"

A uniformed officer ran toward her from the cabin. "Ma'am, you need to stay back."

"Help! He's down here."

The cop slowed as he neared her. "Go back in your house."

She gripped his arm. "I'm the woman you're trying to rescue. The kidnapper saw you coming. He's this way."

The man's eyes widened. He spoke into a walkie-talkie, relaying her message. "Backup's on the way."

"You have to hurry." She pulled uselessly on his arm. "They were fighting. He's going to kill him."

Finally, the words seemed to penetrate. "Show me."

Marisa turned and ran back toward Nate, the cop right beside her. She could hear more police officers behind them, catching up.

When she reached the edge of the cabin's property, she

slowed. A man lay on the ground. Another stood over him. But which man was which? It was nearly impossible to tell in the darkness.

"Nate?"

"Stand back, ma'am." The officer passed her, his gun pointed at the two men. "Drop the knife."

The man took a few steps away from the figure on the ground, dropped the knife, and leaned against the cabin wall and slid to the ground. Marisa inched closer. Peered at his face. The blood, now dried, on his scalp. The rock still gripped in his right hand.

Nate. He was alive.

She ran forward, dropped to her knees, and threw her arms around him.

He winced, and she let him go. "I'm sorry. I hurt you." She backed up, searched his face for more injuries. "Are you all right?"

"I'll survive." His eyes met hers.

"Ma'am, you need to step back."

She brushed bits of rock and dirt off Nate's cheek and rested her palm there, soaking in his warmth. She leaned forward, kissed his lips gently, and said, "Thank you."

"I didn't—"

"You did." She kissed him again.

"Ma'am." Police officers swarmed around them now. Some hovering over the man unconscious just a few feet away. Another behind her. "Please step back."

She met Nate's eyes. Even in the darkness, she thought she saw her own feelings reflected there. Maybe, when this was all over, when she had Ana...

"Ana."

"Go."

His word propelled her, and she stood, swiveled, ran back toward the cabin.

Marisa ran until her chest burned. Past one police officer heading toward Nate and the kidnapper. Past trees and bushes and cabins and police cars lining the road. All she could think about now was Ana.

Was she alive?

Had she been hurt?

Would she recover?

Marisa's whole life hinged on this moment. On what she would find back in that dingy cabin. Had she truly rescued Ana from a life of an impoverished orphan in Mexico? Or had she adopted her into an early death?

How would Marisa survive if Ana hadn't?

She reached the cabin and froze at the bottom of the steps just as a figure filled the doorway.

A tall, broad-shouldered figure that could only be Brady.

And on his hip, a little girl in a blue sundress.

"Mama?"

The most beautiful melody in the world could be found in those two syllables.

Through a haze of tears, Marisa rushed up the stairs, and Brady shifted Ana into her outstretched arms. Ana's tiny arms slid around Marisa's neck, her thin legs folded around her torso and clenched as if the girl would never let her go.

Marisa held on just as tight. Focused on the soft skin pressed against hers.

"Oh, baby, I'm sorry."

Ana's tears soaked through Marisa's thin pajamas, and her own tears dripped into her daughter's hair.

Brady whispered, "Are you hurt?"

She shook her head, held her baby closer. "I'm fine."

"Marisa."

His tone had her focusing on him.

"The blood."

"What?"

"On your pajamas."

She had no idea what he was talking about. She adjusted Ana, looked down, and saw the red stain. She'd felt it before, the dampness. She'd ignored it. But now...that was blood.

"Oh, my God. Nate."

"All right," Brady said. "Let's get out of this cold. You want me to get a car to drive—"

"I can walk."

They walked fast down the road to the cabin. An ambulance had arrived, and Nate was lying on a gurney, a paramedic examining him. He must've seen them approach, because he tried to push himself to a sitting position. The paramedic pushed him back down with a hand to his shoulder.

Marisa rushed to his side. Nate's head was bloody, which she'd expected. It was the fresh blood on his shirt that had her gasping.

Before she could form words, Nate said, "Thank God." Tears slid from his eyes. "Is she okay?"

"I think so. Are you all right?"

"It's not serious." He seemed to be trying to peer around her to get a look at Ana.

Not serious. Dear God, let that be true. She turned and bent so Nate could speak to her daughter.

"Hey, pretty girl. Are we glad to see you."

Ana let up her grip just a tiny bit. "Hi, Uncle Nate. Mama found me."

"She sure did."

Marisa faced the paramedic, a tall woman with a no-nonsense stare, who stood on the opposite side of the gurney. "Is he going to be okay?"

"We need to get him to the hospital."

She looked at Nate. "We'll be right behind you."

"No. Take care of her."

"But..." She wanted to argue, but Nate was right. She needed to take care of Ana, and the last thing the little girl needed was to spend the night in a hospital waiting room. "I want to be with you, too."

He reached out, and she took his hand. "Tomorrow. I promise."

Joy and fear bubbled, and she couldn't form words.

"Ma'am, we have to go."

She addressed her question to the paramedic. "What happened to him?"

"It's a stab wound."

She turned back to Nate. "He stabbed you? Oh, Nate—"

"I'm fine. As long as I know you and Ana are okay."

All the joy in Marisa's heart drained like water through a colander. Or the holes in Nate's body.

Marisa held her daughter closer, thankful to have her back. But Nate...

The blood on his shirt, the blood dripping from his head. What if Nate wasn't fine? What if the cost of getting Ana back was Nate's life?

THIRTY-SEVEN

Marisa watched as the paramedics slid Nate into the ambulance. The kidnapper was already on board. She could see him in the bright lights of the truck. He seemed unconscious, but just in case, someone had handcuffed him to the gurney.

A paramedic closed the back doors. A moment later, the ambulance drove away.

Brady stepped beside her. "I've got my guys processing the two scenes."

She turned, confused.

"This cabin and the other one."

"Oh."

"We should be able to get this one processed and opened up in the next hour or so. He just came in, took you, and left, right?"

"As far as I know."

"Good." He looked at the house, and she followed his gaze. A couple of police officers stood inside with two other people, neither wearing uniforms. Brady turned back to her. "I'll give you two a ride to the hospital."

"Do we have to do that?"

"Unfortunately, you do. They need to examine her."

Marisa squeezed her eyes shut at the images Brady's words brought. "You don't think..." She couldn't finish the sentence.

"Let's not guess, okay? Let's just wait, get the facts, and go from there." He nodded toward the truck.

"Can I get some clothes?"

He looked at the house again. "Let me grab you something. Be right back."

She slid in the front seat with Ana on her lap.

A moment later, Brady returned with her jacket. He draped it over them. "She should go in the back."

Ana's legs clamped around Marisa's middle. The little girl wasn't about to let Marisa put her down, and Marisa wasn't arguing. "You can get us to the hospital safely, right?"

He wrapped the seatbelt around both of them and clicked it in place.

"Thank you."

He nodded and closed her door.

Brady had called ahead to the small hospital. A young, perky nurse met them at the door and led her and Ana straight to an exam room.

A gray-haired older man stepped in a moment later and shook her hand. "Dr. Lariviere. Detective Thomas asked me to meet you here."

"Oh. Are you friends with him?"

"I'm Johnny's doctor, so I know Mrs. Thomas better than the detective." Dr. Lariviere peeked at Ana's face. Marisa hadn't looked, but she thought her daughter might have fallen asleep.

"Hey, sweetheart," the doctor said. "You look sleepy."

Ana nodded, held Marisa tighter.

"I'm going to have to lay you down, okay?"

The little girl shook her head, squeezed her arms around Marisa.

The doctor met Marisa's eyes, smiled kindly, and looked at

Ana again. "I bet I can be done in five minutes. What do you think?"

Ana shrugged.

He took his cell phone out of his pocket, touched it a couple of times, and showed the screen to Ana. "I set the timer for five minutes. If you let your mother put you down, you can hold onto my phone in one hand, and your mommy's hand with the other. And you can watch the numbers go down while I work. By the time they're all zero, I'll be done. You want to try that?"

"I'll be right here," Marisa said. "I promise."

There was a pause before Ana nodded.

Marisa gently laid her daughter on the table, held her hand, and let the doctor examine her. Her eyes filled with tears, and she couldn't watch what the doctor was doing, was looking for. Thank God, Ana seemed intent on watching the numbers as Marisa stroked her hair.

As promised, before the time was up he said, "All done." After Ana had scrambled back into her mother's arms, the doctor met Marisa's eyes. "Everything looks fine. Nothing to worry about."

The relief washed over her like a warm rain.

After Marisa got Ana to pee in a cup, they were led back to the waiting room, where Brady met them at the door. "All set?"

She nodded, could hardly speak for the emotions swirling around in her mind. She got them under control enough to say, "She's okay. Have you heard anything about Nate?"

"Not yet. He's being examined. I'll get you settled at the cabin, then come back and check on him."

They climbed in Brady's truck, which he'd left at the door, and returned to the cabin.

"They're done processing it. Just stay out of Nate's room tonight in case they need to go back tomorrow."

"Will do." She undid the seatbelt, and Brady came around to walk her to the door.

"He jimmied the lock. It works, but apparently not so well. I'll keep a uniform outside all night. Okay?"

"If you think it's necessary."

He shrugged. "I doubt it is, but just in case." They stepped inside, and Ana poked her head up and looked around. Marisa had hoped she'd fall asleep on the ride home, but her little girl looked bright-eyed now.

"Where are we, Mama?"

"We're going to stay here tonight." She looked at Brady. "I thought I'd give her a bath." She shifted to look at Ana. "You want to take a bath? You should see the bathtub. It's like a swimming pool."

The little girl nodded.

"Good idea," Brady said. "I'll head to the ER, check on Nate. You have that phone still? The one the guy gave you?"

"Um..." She thought back, remembered setting it on the nightstand in her bedroom. She'd left it there when she'd slipped into Nate's bed in the middle of the night.

The thought had heat rushing to her face. What must Nate think of her? But she'd seen what he thought of her in his eyes before they'd put him in the ambulance.

Nate.

"Is he going to be all right?"

Brady's look didn't reassure her. "I'll find out. If there's anything..." He paused, seemed to search for words. "I promise I'll call you if you need to know anything. What's your number?"

"I have no idea."

"Where's the phone?"

She told him, and he slipped into her bedroom and returned with the phone pressed to his ear. A moment later, his cell rang. He looked at the screen and silenced the call from Marisa's phone. "I have your number now. I'll call you when I have news."

"Right," she said, only half listening. Could Nate's injuries be life threatening? Why hadn't she asked the paramedic more questions? He could die, and she hadn't thought to ask.

And she'd been taken by the kidnapper, yanked out of her bed...

The room spun.

Brady crossed the space and urged her to the sofa. Ana stayed clamped on and still wouldn't let go, though Marisa thought she might pass out.

"Just wait for it to pass." She heard his footsteps but couldn't seem to look up. A moment later, he draped a blanket over her. "You're okay."

She took a few deep breaths and looked up to meet his eyes.

"Why don't I call Sam?"

No. He was right, she was safe, Ana was safe, and Nate was... Well, he was in good hands. "I'm okay. I'm going to give Ana a bath, and we're going to go to bed." She narrowed her eyes. "You have to promise me that if I need to be there, if Nate's injuries are... If it looks bad... I won't be able to rest if I don't think you'll call."

"I promise, I'll call when I know something. Either way. Okay?"

"Thank you."

He turned to the kitchen's bar and pulled a pen and notepad out of his breast pocket. "I'm writing down my phone number, Sam's, Rae's, Nate's, and the hospital's." When he finished writing the note, he said, "I'm taking the keys so Nate can get in when he gets back. Don't hesitate to call me. I'll stay with Nate tonight. If you have any problems or just want to know how he's doing or anything..."

"Thank you, Brady."

He nodded once. "Happy to help." He backed toward the door. "You two will be okay here by yourselves? You sure I can't get Sam—?"

"We're fine." She squeezed her daughter. "Aren't we, pajarita?"

Ana nodded and held her tighter.

"Okay. Tomorrow you'll have to make a statement about what happened."

"Thank you."

Brady walked to the door and bent to examine the outside knob. "This place needs a deadbolt."

"I don't think any of us thought he'd find us here."

"I wonder how he did."

She shrugged, too tired to worry about it tonight. "He's in custody, right? He's not getting out?"

"You're safe. I promise."

Safe. She hadn't felt truly safe in a very long time. Marisa finally had her life back, but what kind of life could it be without Nate?

Exhaustion almost won, but Marisa wanted to wash any remnants of that man's scent from her daughter's skin. When the dizziness passed, she lifted Ana, made sure the front and back doors were locked, and headed into her bedroom, closing the door behind them.

"I know you're sleepy, but let's take a quick bath."

She tried to set Ana on the bed, but her daughter wouldn't let her go.

"You're safe now, baby. Can you sit on the bed?"

She could feel her daughter's head shaking.

Marisa sighed, exhausted, and continued into the bathroom.

Somehow, she managed to bend over and start the water in the giant bathtub, get it to the right temperature, and put in the stopper, all without setting Ana down. Her back would be sore tomorrow, but better her back than Ana's heart.

She gathered the soap and shampoo from the shower, snatched a clean washcloth from the cabinet, and set the items on the edge of the Jacuzzi tub while she waited for the water to fill it.

"You want bubbles?"

Ana's voice was tentative. "Okay."

She feared the noise of the Jacuzzi would frighten her daughter, so instead of turning on the jets, Marisa simply squirted shampoo into the water's stream, and the oversize tub soon filled with bubbles. The scent of strawberries wafted through the room.

"I'm going to have to let you go to give you a bath," Marisa said.

Ana held on tighter.

She couldn't blame her. Marisa didn't want to let Ana go, either. Still... "How about this? How about we both get in the tub. Will that work?"

A tiny shrug.

Marisa didn't mind getting wet. She wasn't thrilled about the idea of soaking her pajamas, but Rae had left a second pair, and these were bloody anyway. She shut off the water, tested its temperature—a little cold for her taste, but Ana would like it—and stepped inside. She sat, let the warm water soak her pajama pants and realized how very cold she'd been.

She eased Ana down, a little at a time, until the girl was sitting on the bottom of the tub between her legs.

"You okay?"

Ana didn't say anything for a moment. Then, "This *is* like a swimming pool." Her eyes were wide as she took in the bathroom. "Is it safe?"

"It's safe. I promise."

The little girl giggled, and the sound dripped like honey over Marisa's soul.

"Mama, you forgot to take our clothes off!"

Marisa smiled. "How could I take our clothes off when you wouldn't let me go?"

Ana's smile faded.

"But it's okay. We can do it right now. Arms up!"

Ana lifted her arms, and Marisa slid the filthy dress over her head and urged off the stained underwear. Had her child really worn the same things for a week? The dress barely resembled the one Nate had bought her back in Acapulco. She squeezed some of the water out and set it on the side of the tub.

She took a fortifying breath and studied her daughter's skin.

No bruises that she could see.

She soaped up the washcloth and set about washing the week of terror off the tiny girl, studying every inch for marks. Except for a small bruise on her arm, Marisa didn't see any evidence that the man had hurt her.

She closed her eyes. *Gracias, Dios*. God had kept her safe.

Ana was thinner than she had been, her little ribs outlined beneath her skin. The thought of her sweet *pajarita*, hungry, held captive...

Tears filled her eyes. She tried to hide them, hoped Ana wouldn't notice. But her daughter was far too observant for that.

She sat opposite her mother and brushed the tears away. "I'm sorry, Mama."

"Oh, sweetie, you have nothing to be sorry for."

"I told Aunt Leslie I couldn't get in the van with that man, but she said it would be okay. That we were playing a trick on you. I didn't want to, but she picked me up, and I couldn't get away."

Marisa held her daughter's hands and looked into her eyes. "Listen to me, Ana. Nothing that happened was your fault. None of it. Aunt Leslie shouldn't have done what she did. This was her fault. And that man's fault. It wasn't yours."

Ana stood and climbed into Marisa's arms. Marisa stroked her slippery back and wept into her hair. "I'm sorry I didn't protect you better."

"I know you didn't want me to go with that man."

"I didn't. And from the second you were taken, I never stopped looking for you."

Ana backed up and looked into Marisa's eyes. "I knew you'd find me."

Marisa convinced Ana to let her get out of the tub. After she traded her wet pajamas for dry ones, she returned to the bathroom with a cup snagged from the kitchen, washed Ana's hair, and rinsed the remains of the soap and dirty water from her skin.

With a towel wrapped around Ana, Marisa lifted her from the tub and was carrying her into the bedroom when she heard a quiet knock, then the sound of the key in the lock. The front door opened.

Marisa froze and stared toward the living room. She was about to search for a weapon when she heard the whispered words. "Marisa? Are you up?"

What was Sam doing there?

"It's okay." She patted her daughter on the back and walked to the living room, where Sam stood beside the sofa.

"I hope I didn't scare you. I thought I'd just sneak in, if you'd gone to sleep."

Marisa started to ask where Sam got the key before she remembered that Sam owned the cabin. "It's fine. We just got out of the tub. What are you doing here? It's"—Marisa looked at the clock glowing on the stove—"nearly three a.m."

"Brady called Rae to tell her the good news, and she called me. A few days ago, Rae and I bought some things we thought Ana might need. Clothes and pj's and stuff." Sam set a giant white plastic sack on the couch. "I didn't want to leave it sooner, because I thought... Well, it seemed wise to wait."

"I was just trying to figure out what I was going to put her in."

Sam dug through the bag and brought out a pair of blue pajamas with princesses on them. "Nate said her favorite color is blue."

Ana turned to look at the pajamas, which Sam held up for her inspection.

"Pretty."

"I'm glad you like them." She crossed the room slowly.

Ana squeezed her tighter.

"You must be Ana," Sam said. "We've been looking for you."

Marisa whispered in Ana's ear. "It's okay, pajarita. This is a friend of mine. She helped me find you. Her name is Sam."

Ana lifted her head slightly. "Sam is a boy's name. Like *Sam, I Am*."

Sam smiled and shifted to meet Ana's eyes over Marisa's shoulder. "That's right. But my name's really Samantha."

"That's pretty."

"You can call me Samantha if you want."

"Okay."

Sam smiled at Marisa before looking back at Ana. "I prayed for you a lot while you were gone."

Ana lifted her head. "You did?"

"I did. Every time I thought about you, which was about a thousand times a day, I prayed that God would be with you and keep you safe."

Ana pushed away from her mother and leaned toward Sam. She placed her index finger on Sam's cheek. "You're not an angel."

Sam tilted her head to the side. "Nope. Just a woman."

"But God listened to you, because Jesus was with me."

"He was?"

"Uh-huh." Ana glanced at her mother. "Every night when it got dark, he came into my room and told me stories until I fell asleep. Not like Mama tells, though. Different stories."

"What were they about?" Sam asked.

She shrugged. "I don't remember. Just that I always fell asleep while he told me stories, just like I do when Mama does."

Sam's eyes filled with tears, and she swallowed hard. "That sounds like Jesus. He loves you very much."

"I know. And you know what else? I could smell him. When I got really scared, I knew he was there, 'cause all of a sudden, I could smell him."

"What did he smell like?"

"Rain." The answer was so matter-of-fact, as if everybody knew that. But Sam's eyes filled with wonder.

Marisa could hear her father's words. *Whenever you smell the rain, that's God's reminder that he's near.*

"What a beautiful gift he gave you," Sam said.

"And he told me Mama would find me, so I wasn't scared." She paused, looked at Marisa, and said, "I was scared sometimes, but sometimes I wasn't. That's okay, right?"

Marisa held her daughter tight, all the words her daughter had said dripping over her like...rain. "Of course, pajarita. You were very brave."

THIRTY-EIGHT

"I TOLD you it wasn't bad." Nate's frustration must have been palpable, because the doctor, a heavyset Hal Holbrook doppelganger, sighed and looked up.

"You'll forgive us for taking stab wounds and head injuries seriously."

"I feel fine."

The doctor ignored the comment and continued stitching the minor flesh wound on his back. After four stitches, he finished and adjusted Nate's hospital gown. "There. Now maybe you won't bleed to death."

"I wasn't going to bleed to death. You guys are just being paranoid."

Brady chuckled, and Nate glared at the man standing in the corner. "And another thing. How come, whenever there's serious crime in this town, I end up in the ER, and you come out without a scratch?"

The man shrugged. "Years of training."

"In avoiding danger," Nate said.

Brady didn't rise to the bait. He addressed the doctor, who

was pulling off his latex gloves as the nurse put away the supplies. "Good to see he's back to his jolly self."

"If this is jolly," the doctor said, "I'd hate to see him cranky."

"I can hear you, you know." Nate wanted to strangle them both.

The doctor straightened. "Because of the head wound, we're keeping you until morning."

"Not a chance."

Dr. Hal peered at him over his glasses. "Son, what's the rush?"

He thought of Marisa and Ana, alone in that cabin. Marisa was probably nervous, and even if she wasn't, it didn't matter. Nate wanted to be there with them, be there when they woke up, be there to eat breakfast. He needed to put his eyes on Ana again, make sure she was okay. He needed to hold Marisa, kiss her, tell her how much he loved her. Because he wanted to be there, with them, forever.

And he didn't want to wait another minute for forever to begin.

He saw Brady's narrowed eyes, knew his friend had been observing the emotions play across his face. Brady turned to the doctor. "See, there's this woman..."

"Ah." The doctor faced Nate. "You have a minor concussion. Rest is the most important thing you can do. If you want to go rest elsewhere, that's your prerogative. Tylenol for pain, and if it gets unmanageable, come back."

"Thank you, Doctor."

The man shook his hand, held it a moment longer. "Good luck with the girl."

"She's probably asleep."

"Obviously. It's nearly five in the morning." Nate hoped Marisa and Ana were both asleep. They sure needed it. He watched the trees speed by outside the car window. Only the white birches were distinguishable in the darkness.

"I called Marisa when we knew you were going to be okay. That was about an hour ago. I told her you were fine and would have to sleep in the hospital. That was before I knew how stubborn you could be."

"Thanks for calling her. And thanks for everything you did. I can't tell you how much I appreciate it."

"Man, you nearly died trying to protect my wife. You think there's anything I wouldn't do for you?"

"Nearly died, and still didn't manage to protect her."

"She's here, isn't she? And so is Ana, thanks to you."

"I'm not a hero."

Brady blew out a breath. "You know, Superman's not real. We're all just people, doing our best. Tonight, you were heroic. You called me. Despite a major concussion, you followed Marisa, told me where she was, fought the guy, and stopped him. Now the bad guy's in custody, and all the good guys—girls —are safe. I mean, what do you think a hero is?"

Nate wasn't sure how to answer that.

"A hero," Brady said, "is a guy who fights to do the right thing despite the dangers to himself. You were a hero tonight. You were a hero last fall. You need to accept that you're human and fallible and scared. But you did the right thing, anyway. That's heroic."

Nate allowed himself to hear Brady's words. To soak them in. Nate was no hero, he knew that. But maybe, tonight, he'd acted like one. Maybe that was all anybody could ever do.

OF COURSE the cabin was quiet when they pulled into the short drive and parked beside Sam's Isuzu Trooper. Nate hadn't thought to bring the keys.

Brady reached for the console between the seats, lifted something, and jingled. "I got 'em."

"Good thinking."

"Figured you'd want to get back in sooner rather than later." He jumped out of the car, ran to the house, and bounded up the three steps like they were nothing.

Nate cursed Brady's ability to move so fast. Despite what he'd told the doctor, his brain was battering the inside of his skull as if trying to get loose. His two stab wounds throbbed. In fact, his whole body ached as he pushed himself out of the sedan and stood.

Brady walked back down the steps. "Need help?"

"I'm fine." He wouldn't allow himself to hunch as he started toward the porch, one slow step at a time. Had the stairs always been that steep?

"You should have stayed at the hospital. They'll still be here tomorrow."

Nate stopped, faced his friend. "Will they? Because they live in Mexico. In a tiny little town I never knew the name of and wouldn't be able to find again on a bet."

"You think she's going to run away?"

Nate shrugged. He didn't, not really, but he wasn't willing to take the chance. He needed to be here. With Marisa and Ana. If they decided to go back to Mexico, then he'd go with them. No way was he returning to his life of solitude now that he'd been shown a better way.

Marisa.

Nate gripped the stair rail, and Brady grabbed his other arm. Together, they navigated the steps.

He made it into the cabin and saw Sam sound asleep on the love seat. She was short, but not that short.

"We talked," Brady whispered. "I told her you were too stubborn to stay in the hospital."

Nate looked at his closed bedroom door and the yellow crime scene tape secured across it.

No matter. He wanted to be out here when Marisa woke, anyway.

He collapsed on the sofa.

Brady pulled a blanket from the chair—Sam must've left it there for him, along with the pillow on the end of the couch—and draped it over him. "You need anything else?"

"No. Thanks."

"You got your phone?"

Nate closed his eyes. "Lost it on the street, I think."

"Okay. I'll check in later today."

THIRTY-NINE

Marisa tiptoed out of the bedroom, careful not to wake Ana as she closed the door gently behind her. There was just enough light coming from outside that she didn't need to turn a lamp on. She crossed the room into the kitchen and started the coffee machine. It steamed and gurgled, and she thought about shutting it off so it wouldn't wake Sam. But she needed coffee, badly. After she'd brewed a cup, she turned and saw a lump on the sofa.

Wait. There was a lump on the love seat, too. Sam was on the love seat.

Who was on the couch?

She crept forward, thankful that her noise in the kitchen hadn't woken either of them. When she got closer, she barely made out the sleeping face.

Nate.

When had he gotten here?

She set her coffee on the counter and sat on the coffee table across from him. His curly hair was tangled, his body mostly hidden beneath his blanket, a landscape of rises and valleys that hid the man who'd nearly sacrificed everything for her. Just one hand was visible, hanging off the narrow couch and nearly touching the floor. His eyes were closed, his lips slightly open.

She looked at the head wound. Two staples. A wave of discomfort flowed over her midsection as if it were she who'd endured that pain, not Nate, this man that she...

Yes, she could admit it.

She loved him. And it wasn't because he'd saved their lives. She loved him for a million other things he'd done. She loved him for the meals he'd delivered to her when she'd been in hiding—Greek salads stuffed in pita bread he refused to call sandwiches, not to mention pizzas and subs and soups and noodles and whatever else she'd requested. She loved him because he'd stayed with her to eat so she wouldn't be lonely. She loved him for flying to Mexico, simply because she'd asked him to. She loved him for the way he'd stood beside her every terrifying moment of the previous week, worked just as hard as she had to find her daughter, and never once lost hope. She loved him for the way his eyes had filled with tears when he'd seen her daughter again. Marisa loved him for the way he'd kissed her on the dock, and then, when she'd climbed into his bed, she loved him for the way he'd not kissed her.

She loved him for all of it, and all of it wasn't enough to describe the reasons she loved Nate.

Her fingers itched to touch him, but she wouldn't risk waking him. She brushed a light kiss on his temple and stood. She lifted her coffee from the counter and headed for the bedroom.

MARISA SAT on a chair on the back porch, Ana asleep in her arms. They were both wrapped in a blanket off their bed. She'd sat beside her daughter for less than an hour before Ana awoke, crying, from yet another bad dream. She'd had them all night. Not surprising, all things considered.

Marisa had pulled her daughter into her arms and tried to get her back to sleep, but Ana had wanted nothing to do with it. Instead, they'd come outside.

Ana had fallen back to sleep within just a few minutes.

The back door opened, and Sam stepped out. She surveyed the scene, smiled, and sat in the other chair. "How's she doing?"

"Considering the week she's had, great."

Sam sipped her coffee. "How about you?"

"I kept waking up to make sure she was really with me. All in all, not a great night's sleep. But the best I've had in a long time."

"I bet." Sam set her coffee on the little table between them. "Nate's sound asleep."

"Yeah. I don't know why he didn't stay in the hospital."

"Really? You don't know?" Sam's smile said the answer was obvious to her.

Marisa shrugged and looked at the calm lake water.

A car's tires sounded on the gravel road in front of the cabin. It had been such a quiet morning, the noise surprised her, as did the slamming of a car door a moment later.

Sam stood. "Bet that's Brady. I'll just get him before..."

Her words trailed off as the sound of knocking came through the house.

"Too late." Marisa stood and followed Sam inside, careful to keep Ana cradled in her arms.

Her daughter stirred. "Mama?"

"I'm right here, pajarita." She kissed her head. "You're safe. I promise."

The girl settled and fell back to sleep.

Marisa smiled at Brady and Rae, then at Nate as he sat up slowly. She ducked into the bedroom and laid her daughter on the bed. She kissed her head and waited to be sure Ana was asleep.

She returned to the living room and looked around. Like every other morning she'd been here, Nate, Brady, Rae, and Sam were congregating in the kitchen. This time, Nate wore scrubs he must've gotten from the hospital. He yawned and turned toward her. "Hey."

"You should sit. You don't look good."

"You look..." He seemed suddenly aware of the others in the room and cleared his throat. "How's Ana?"

"Perfect. Please sit."

Nate hobbled to the sofa, and Marisa got him a cup of coffee and a muffin. Rae must've brought a fresh box of pastries from McNeal's. They'd had enough from the diner in Nutfield in the last few days that Marisa looked forward to going to the place for a meal soon.

As if she were staying right here in Nutfield.

Was she staying? There was nothing for her in Mexico. Nothing for her in New York, either.

A phone rang. Sam hurried to her purse and pulled hers out. "Hey." Her skin tinged a little pink before she turned away. She listened while she stepped on the back patio.

Had Sam been blushing? Interesting.

Marisa sat beside Nate and ate her banana nut muffin. Unlike everything else she'd tasted in the last week, this was delicious. Nate picked at his.

"Would you rather trade? I can eat the blueberry."

"Not hungry," he said, leaning against the back of the sofa.

"You're hurt. Why don't you lie down? I'll sit on the floor."

He took her hand. "Please. Stay."

She did, and Nate scooted closer to her, wincing in pain but trying to cover it with a smile.

Sam stepped back inside and closed the door behind her. "That was Garrison."

"He disappeared on us the other day," Nate said. "Did he ever say why?"

"His son needed him. Teenager."

"Ah. I talked to the kid when I called."

Sam met Marisa's eyes. "He says to tell you he's glad you got Ana back."

"We couldn't have done it without him."

"Agreed," Sam said. "He also wanted me to gently remind you that you need to go to New York."

A little ball of dread settled in Marisa's stomach. "Right. I have to identify my sister's body."

"Yeah. Sorry."

"I can do it," Nate said. "I have to finish packing. I'm supposed to be out of my house by Friday."

"I'd love you to be there," Marisa said, "but I need to see her."

Nate nodded like he understood.

Brady came around the bar and looked at Nate. "You're in no position to carry furniture."

"I'm sure I'll be fine tomorrow."

"I'll drive down with you," Brady said.

"You have much packing left to do?" Sam asked.

"We were almost finished." He looked at Marisa. "Your sister was really helpful while we waited for you to email us back." He took her hand. "I'm so sorry."

It was going to take her a little time to believe her sister was really gone. "I know. Me, too."

A heavy silence filled the room.

Rae broke it with, "So, what else did the hot FBI agent have to say?"

Brady gasped. "Hot? The guy was a total dog."

Nate barked, chuckled, and then groaned.

Sam rolled her eyes, but the blush was back. "Whatever." She took her seat in the living room, and Brady and Rae did, too, as if it were perfectly normal. After all the times they'd done it this week, it felt as if it were.

Brady cleared his throat. "Been at the station a while. I have a few things I can tell you." He shifted toward Marisa. "First, they matched fingerprints at the apartment in Chelsea where"— a slight hesitation before—"Ana was held."

Where your sister was murdered. Those were the words he hadn't said.

"They found Rick's and your sister's fingerprints. They found Ana's in the bedroom."

Marisa let the small relief fill her. "That's good, right?"

"Proves he was there. They haven't finished DNA analysis yet, but when they do, they'll prove it's your sister's blood. It's a mountain of evidence."

Marisa let the little bit of good news reach her heart. They couldn't bring Leslie back, but at least they could make sure her killer paid for what he'd done.

Brady continued. "They searched Rick's Audi and found a purse that belonged to your sister. I can't get possession of it, but I thought you'd like to know what they found inside."

"Something important?" she asked.

He took out his phone. "I took some pictures." He navigated through it while he spoke. "I thought you'd like to see." He reached it toward her, and she took it.

On the screen, she saw snapshots of herself, her mother, and Leslie from when they were children. She flipped through them, tears filling her eyes.

"She had a little album she must've carried everywhere with her. It held photos of you and your mother."

"Yes." Marisa's voice cracked. She kept flipping through the pictures on Brady's phone, seeing her own younger face, Leslie's, their mother's. So Leslie hadn't completely wiped them out of her life after all.

"She showed me that when we first met," Nate said. "I'd forgotten."

Brady added, "I thought you'd like to know."

Marisa looked up and nodded. "Thank you, Brady. It doesn't change anything, but, maybe it kind of does. She wasn't who I thought she was, but maybe she loved us, a little. She got pulled into something she couldn't control, and when she did try to control it..."

"She paid with her life," Nate said.

"Another thing I thought you'd like to know," Brady said. "Garrison's old partner, Simon, has been trying to put the new pieces of the puzzle into place. On a hunch, he went to Pamela Gray's house this morning to deliver the news about Richard. He told her what Richard had done, and the woman confessed that she was the one who'd taken the money all those years ago. Seems she wasn't willing to share the information when it was Ana's life at stake, but when Simon suggested that coming clean might help Richard, she told him everything."

"All this time," Nate said, "the money Richard was trying to get his hands on has been in his mother's bank account?"

"Looks like it," Brady said.

Marisa closed her eyes, let the new information skim off her like rocks on a lake. It didn't matter. None of it mattered, because Ana was safe.

"Their twisted family drama has nothing to do with me," Marisa said. "Never did."

"You were just collateral damage," Rae said. "First to Charles, then to Pamela."

"Just the cleaning lady," Marisa said.

Nate's grip became firm. "You were never *just* anything,

Marisa. And you never deserved to be treated that way."

She turned at the vehemence in his voice, saw it in his narrowed eyes, his set mouth.

"It doesn't matter now. They'll all have to deal with what they did." She turned to Brady. "And I'm free, right? Not wanted for anything? Free to come home? Free to stay in America without fear of being hunted or accused?"

Brady nodded. "You're free. It's over."

FORTY

NATE WATCHED his friends as they drove away. He could never
express to them what their help meant to him. Whatever debt
Rae and Brady had felt they owed him had been paid back with
loan-shark-sized interest in the last week. And Sam... She'd
never owed him a thing.

He could never repay what they'd done for him and Marisa
and Ana. But he'd gladly spend the rest of his life trying. He'd
known a lot of people in his life, had sources and coworkers and
acquaintances in the city, but none could be considered friends
compared to the three who'd just left.

Marisa's voice came from behind him. "Why don't you sit
back down? I'm afraid you're going to collapse."

He turned and smiled at her. "I'm fine."

"You're wobbly."

He laughed, and the movement sent a shard of pain through
his side. He worked to hide it, but Marisa's narrowed eyes told
him he'd failed.

"Fine. I'll sit."

She walked with him to the sofa and sat beside him.

"Ana's still asleep?"

She looked at the clock on the stove in the kitchen. "If she sleeps until noon, I'll wake her. She has an appointment with the pediatrician at one."

"Good idea."

"Sam is sweet to let me stay here for a few days. I can't imagine trying to go to Leslie's house right now, trying to make ourselves at home there."

"It's your house, technically."

"Doesn't feel like it, though. I'm more comfortable here."

Nate knew exactly how she felt. This place felt like home to him, too. Or maybe that was only because Marisa was here.

He shifted to face her and took her hand. "What's your plan?"

"After the doctor's appointment, I thought we'd—"

"Not today. Long term. What are you going to do?"

She looked down at their joined hands, placed her other hand over his, and looked up. "I'm not sure."

"Are you going back to Mexico?"

She stared beyond him. "I find myself in America with this little girl who's mine in every way except legally. I don't know how the adoption will work if I'm here, but if I go back, then anything could happen. I'm afraid if I go back, there'll be trouble for taking her out of the country. What will it take to clear all that up? And anyway, I don't want to go back."

"Good. I don't like the heat that much."

She blinked twice, and a smile he hadn't seen since Acapulco lit up her face.

"My dad's an attorney," he said. "I'm sure he can help you with the adoption."

"Seriously? That'd be great."

"But what about your stuff. You want me to go back and pack up for you?"

She was shaking her head before he finished the sentence.

"Maybe I could have Carlita box up the canvases and send them to me. The rest of the stuff, I'll just let the people there keep. I have all my valuables. I don't need the rest."

"And your job?"

"I'll miss the kids, but I need to do what's right for Ana, for her future. A couple of the older students are nearly fluent in English. Maybe Carlita will hire one of them for my job."

Nate would never have guessed less than two weeks before that his life could turn this abruptly, this perfectly. "Maybe you could stay here, in New Hampshire. Find a place to live. Maybe..."

Her smile widened. "Maybe what?"

"I have an idea."

"What's that?"

"Well, we've spent more than a week together now. We've stayed under the same roofs, traveled together, run together, cried together." Slept together. "In the eight years since we met, we've brought down a crime ring, put guys in prison, and rescued a beautiful little girl. Just this week, we caught a murderer and a kidnapper. The truth is, Marisa, you and I have done a lot together."

Her smile became a lighthearted chuckle, then an all-out laugh. A beautiful sound he could listen to for the rest of his life.

A few days before, he'd thought that tears were the world's only unlimited resource. How very wrong he'd been. Because laughter fueled a lot more action than tears. And love... Love was the greatest resource of all.

"How do we top all of that?" Marisa asked.

"I'm not sure I want to try, honestly. You know what I want?"

Her cheeks turned pink, and he thought maybe she knew exactly what he wanted. "What's that?"

"I want to go on a date with you. Maybe get some Greek

food. The best Greek restaurants outside of Greece are in New Hampshire, you know."

"Is that so?" Her laugh said she didn't believe it, but he knew better.

"Lots of Greeks around here. After dinner, I'd like to see a movie with you. Not an action film, though. Maybe one of those long foreign films. We can share popcorn and hold hands and kiss during the boring parts."

"Those foreign films are almost all boring parts."

He winked at her. "I know."

She laughed again. Oh, that her laughter could be the soundtrack of his life. Then he could die a happy man.

"And after the movie?"

"After that normal, boring date, we could have another one and another one and another one. A bunch of normal days, all strung together." He wrapped his arm around her, drew her close. He looked into those dark chocolate eyes, searched for hesitation, but found none. He lowered his lips to hers, tasted tears and joy and forever.

A shift in the air had him pulling away.

He turned and saw Ana standing in the doorway. She padded across the room in her bare feet and blue pajamas and climbed on her mother's lap.

Nate waited for Ana to push him away, but she just smiled up at him. "Hi, Uncle Nate."

"Hey, pretty girl. How'd you sleep?"

"You were kissing Mama."

"I was. Is that okay with you?"

She shrugged and nestled deeper in her mother's lap.

Marisa met his eyes. "I hope you don't mind if we have company on all those dates."

"I love Disney movies," he said.

"And after that?"

"I don't know. I have nothing to offer you. I'm just an out-of-work reporter, but maybe—"

"You're a hero, Nate Boyle." She reached across Ana, traced the line of his hair to his chin, and rested her palm on his cheek. "Wherever you are, that's where I want to be."

The End

If you enjoyed Nate and Marisa's story, you're going to love Sam and Garrison's.

Turn the page for more about, Generous Lies, book 3 in the Nutfield Saga.

Generous Lies

A single father determined to save his son. A teenage boy who doesn't think he needs saving. A damaged woman afraid to risk her heart. And a tiny package that could destroy them all.

He had no idea it was so bad.

Former FBI agent Garrison Kopp suspected his teenage son was in trouble, but a midnight summons to the ER reveals the drug problem is more serious than he thought. Desperate to get his son away from negative influences, he asks a beautiful and kind new friend who owns rental properties for a place to stay.

She'll help, as long as she doesn't have to risk anything.

Vacation homeowner Samantha Messenger is happy to provide Garrison and his son a lake cabin where they can regroup. She helps him search for a good rehab facility and tries not to hope for more than friendship. After what she's been through, more isn't an option, no matter what her heart wants.

Big trouble comes in tiny packages.

Sparks fly between them as Sam and Garrison work together to help the resistant teen. But that becomes the least of their problems when a package planted in Garrison's car lures enemies to the idyllic cabin on the lake. With their lives—and love—on the line, can they protect all they hold dear?

Get swept up in romance, danger, and intrigue. Order GENEROUS LIES today.

ALSO BY ROBIN PATCHEN

The Coventry Saga

Glimmer in the Darkness: Part of the Dangerous Deceptions Boxset

The Nutfield Saga

Convenient Lies

Twisted Lies

Generous Lies

Innocent Lies

Beauty in Flight

Beauty in Hiding

Beauty in Battle

Legacy Rejected

Legacy Restored

Legacy Reclaimed

Legacy Redeemed

Amanda Series

Chasing Amanda

Finding Amanda

Standalone Novellas

A Package Deal

One Christmas Eve

Faith House

ABOUT THE AUTHOR

Aside from her family and her Savior, Robin Patchen has two loves—writing and traveling. If she could combine them, she'd spend a lot of time sitting in front of her laptop at sidewalk cafes and ski lodges and beachside burger joints. She'd visit every place in the entire world—twice, if possible—and craft stories and tell people about her Savior. Alas, time is too short and money is too scarce for Robin to traipse all over the globe, even if her husband and kids wanted to go with her. So she stays home, shares the Good News when she can, and writes to illustrate the unending grace of God through the power and magic of story.